About the Authors

Lynne Graham lives in Northern Ireland and has been a keen romance reader since her teens. Happily married, Lynne has five children. Her eldest is her only natural child. Her other children, who are every bit as dear to her heart, are adopted. The family has a variety of pets, and Lynne loves gardening, cooking, collecting allsorts and is crazy about every aspect of Christmas.

Carol Marinelli recently filled in a form asking for her job title. Thrilled to be able to put down her answer, she put writer. Then it asked what Carol did for relaxation and she put down the truth – writing. The third question asked for her hobbies. Well, not wanting to look obsessed she crossed the fingers on her hand and answered swimming but, given that the chlorine in the pool does terrible things to her highlights – I'm sure you can guess the real answer.

Chantelle Shaw enjoyed a happy childhood making up stories in her head. Always an avid reader, Chantelle discovered Mills & Boon as a teenager and during the times when her children refused to sleep, she would pace the floor with a baby in one hand and a book in the other! Twenty years later she decided to write one of her own. Writing takes up most of Chantelle's spare time, but she also enjoys gardening and walking. She doesn't find domestic chores so pleasurable!

D1322954

Greek Playboys

Greek Playboys: Hidden Heirs

LYNNE GRAHAM

CAROL MARINELLI

CHANTELLE SHAW

MILLS & BOON

First Published in Great Britain 2022
By Mills & Boon, an imprint of HarperCollins*Publishers,* Ltd
1 London Bridge Street, London, SE1 9GF

www.harpercollins.co.uk

HarperCollins*Publishers*
1st Floor, Watermarque Building,
Ringsend Road, Dublin 4, Ireland

GREEK PLAYBOYS: HIDDEN HEIRS © 2022 Harlequin Books S.A.

The Greek Claims His Shock Heir © 2019 Lynne Graham
Claiming His Hidden Heir © 2018 Carol Marinelli
Wed for His Secret Heir © 2018 Chantelle Shaw

ISBN: 978-0-263-30425-1

MIX
Paper from
responsible sources
FSC™ C007454

This book is produced from independently certified FSC™ paper to ensure responsible forest management.

For more information visit: www.harpercollins.co.uk/green

Printed and Bound in Spain using 100% Renewable electricity at CPI Black Print, Barcelona

THE GREEK CLAIMS
HIS SHOCK HEIR

LYNNE GRAHAM

PROLOGUE

Stamboulas Fotakis, known as Bull—but only behind his back, because nobody wanted to offend one of the richest men in the world—studied the new photograph on his desk. It featured his three granddaughters and his great-grandson, none of whom he had even known existed until a few weeks earlier. His competitors would have been shocked by the softness of the older man's gaze as he looked with pride and satisfaction at his only living relatives. Three beautiful girls and a handsome little boy...

At the same time—and it had to be faced—those three girls' lives and that little boy's life were in an almighty mess, Stam acknowledged with bristling annoyance. If *only* he had known they were out there, orphaned and growing up in state care, *he* would've given them a home and raised them. Sadly, he had not been given that choice and his granddaughters had suffered accordingly. But he didn't blame *them* for their chaotic lives, he blamed himself for throwing his youngest son, Cy, out of the family for defying him. Of course, twenty-odd years ago, Stam had been a very different man, he conceded wryly, an impatient, autocratic and inflexible man. Possibly, he had learned a thing or two since then. His late wife had never forgiven him for disowning Cy. In the end, all of them had paid too high a price for Stam's act of idiocy.

But that was then and this was *now*, Stam reminded himself, and it was time he sorted out his granddaughters' lives. He would begin by righting the wrongs done to his new family members. He had the power and the wealth to do that and for that reality he was grateful. He wasn't seeking revenge, he assured himself assiduously, he would only be doing what was best for his grandchildren. First he would sort out Winnie, tiny dark-eyed Winnie, who bore such a very strong resemblance to Stam's late wife, an Arabian princess called Azra.

At least Winnie already spoke a little Greek, only a handful of words admittedly, but that was a promising start. Her problems would be the most easily solved, he reasoned, although how he would hold on to his temper and deal civilly with the adulterous cheat who had made Winnie a mistress and Stam's grandson a bastard, he didn't yet know, for Eros Nevrakis was an infuriatingly powerful man in his own right.

CHAPTER ONE

'MR FOTAKIS WILL be free in just a few minutes,' the PA informed Eros Nevrakis as he stood at the window overlooking the bay while she regarded him with far more appreciation than the magnificent view could ever have roused in her. He was a tall, broad-shouldered man in his early thirties, and his legendary good looks had not been exaggerated, the young woman conceded admiringly. He had a shock of black glossy curls and brilliant green eyes that more than one appreciative woman had been heard to compare to emeralds.

The view from the small island of Trilis would not be half as impressive as that from Bull Fotakis's private estate, Eros was thinking with rueful amusement. On this particular morning Eros was in the very best of moods. After all, he had made several offers through intermediaries to buy back Trilis from Stam Fotakis and those offers had been royally ignored. That he had finally been awarded a meeting with the reclusive old curmudgeon was a very healthy hint that Bull was finally willing to sell the island back to Eros.

Trilis, however, was greener and rather less developed than the extensive estate that Fotakis owned outside Athens and maintained as his headquarters, complete with office blocks and employees on-site. Of course, Fotakis had always been a famous workaholic. When Eros's father had gone bust in the nineties and had been forced into selling his family home, everyone had assumed that Fotakis was planning to build a new base on the private island, only that hadn't happened. Should he ever contrive to regain ownership of the island, Eros planned to open an upmarket resort on the coast that would generate jobs and rejuvenate the local economy. The old man, however, had done nothing with Trilis but hadn't seemed interested in selling it either.

So, what had changed? Eros ruminated, irritated that he was unable to answer that question. He preferred to know what motivated his competitors and opponents because ignorance of such revealing details was always risky. Going in blind wasn't smart, especially when Fotakis was too rich to be tempted by money. Eros turned the question around, considering it shrewdly from another angle. What did *he* currently *have* that Fotakis *wanted*? Eros asked himself then, reckoning that that was likely to be a far more accurate reading of the situation. Bull Fotakis was notoriously crafty and devious.

At the same time, Eros was uncomfortably aware that he would pay just about any price to regain the island of Trilis because it was the sole possession his father had truly regretted losing.

'It is our *family* place and if you lose family, you lose everything. I learned that the hard way,' his father had rasped painfully on his deathbed. 'Promise me that if you do well in the future, you'll do everything you can to buy Trilis back. It's the Nevrakis home and your ancestors and mine are buried there.'

Eros compressed his sensual mouth, shying away from such sentimental recollections from the past. He had learned from his father's mistakes. A man had to be *hard* in business and in his private life, not soft, not easily led or seduced. And a man forced to deal with a Greek icon of achievement like Bull Fotakis had to be even tougher.

'Mr Fotakis will see you now...'

Stam's gaze was hard when it zeroed in on Eros Nevrakis. A good-looking louse, he conceded grudgingly, exactly the type calculated to turn a young and naive woman's head. Nevrakis hadn't *told* Winnie that he was married. Stam had drilled every relevant fact out of his reluctant granddaughter. He had recognised her shame, gasping in relief that, despite his initial troubling assumptions about her character, her morals *were* in the right place. Winnie would *never* have knowingly slept with another woman's husband. Nevrakis had lied to her, conning her into a demeaning living arrangement before hanging her out to dry without a single regret.

Eros saw a small stocky bearded man with eyes as sharp as tacks set in a weathered face. His hair and his neat little beard were white as snow but there was no suggestion of Santa Claus about him. Eros took a seat and refused refreshment, keen to get down to business once the usual pleasantries had been aired.

'You want Trilis back,' Stam remarked, startling Eros with that candid opening and the complete lack of any social chit-chat. 'But *I* want something else.'

Eros leant back in his chair, long powerful legs

carefully relaxed in pose. 'I assumed as much,' he quipped.

'I believe that you're divorced now.'

So random did that remark seem that Eros was disconcerted. He blinked, lashes longer than a girl's, Stam noted in disgust, while wondering simultaneously how he was going to tolerate the lying rat as a grandson-in-law. Unfortunately, little Teddy couldn't get his father's name without his mother also getting a wedding ring, so choice didn't come into it. Stam refused to stand back and allow his sole great-grandchild to remain illegitimate. He knew that was an old-fashioned outlook, but he didn't care because he hadn't got to the top of the ladder by bending his principles to suit other people's and he had no plans to change.

'I can't imagine why you would remark on that fact,' Eros drawled softly. 'But it is true. I was divorced last year.'

Stam gritted his teeth. 'Was that because you were thinking of marrying your mistress?'

'I have no idea where this strange conversation is heading,' Eros retorted crisply, lifting his strong chin in a challenging move of quiet strength. 'However, I can tell you that I've never had a mistress, but if I *did* have one, I seriously doubt that I would marry her.'

Stam went rigid with offence until he reminded himself that Nevrakis had no idea that he *could* be causing offence because he was not aware that Winnie was Stam's granddaughter and would undoubtedly never have dared to lay a single finger on her had he known that salient fact. He then chose to entertain himself by approaching his goal in a roundabout manner.

'My granddaughter is a single parent who needs a husband. That is my price for the island of Trilis. If you agree to marry her, no cash need change hands.'

Stunned by that bald assurance, Eros straightened in his seat. 'You want me to *marry* your granddaughter?' he exclaimed, so taken aback by the idea that he could not even hide his consternation. 'I didn't know you had one. I'm sure I read somewhere that you had no relatives left alive…'

'Until recently, I thought that too,' Stam admitted equably. 'But then, surprises are the joy of life, don't you think?'

Still in the dark as to why Bull Fotakis should offer him such a staggering proposition, Eros could only think that he had always hated surprises. Surprises had, after all, marked some of the worst moments of his life since childhood, starting with the one when his father had killed Christmas by dropping in with his youthful girlfriend on his arm to announce that he was divorcing Eros's mother for making *him* feel old. Eros might have been only eight years of age at the time, but he had been old enough to feel every ounce of his mother's agonised pain and humiliation that the man she loved had fallen out of love with her. That experience had given him an inbuilt hatred of broken marriages and divorce, most especially because he could date the origins of his father's financial downfall from that same moment.

'I'm not sure I agree,' Eros sidestepped quietly. 'I'm certain you could offer your granddaughter to any one of a dozen wealthy, successful men and create an enthusiastic stampede… Why me?'

'You're not a fool,' Stam conceded, his weathered

face grim at that grudging acknowledgement because he wasn't sure he *wanted* a grandson-in-law strong enough to stand up to him.

'I hope not,' Eros said in a calmer tone, but his brain was working at supersonic speed in an effort to work out the mystery of Fotakis's interest in him as a potential grandson-in-law. 'A single parent, you said...' he added, playing for time.

'*Ne*... Yes, a handsome little boy, *my* great-grandson.' Stam could not hide the possessive note in his voice or the pride because both his sons were dead and the sight of that little boy had softened his tough old heart. 'He needs a father figure, for who can tell how many years I have left?'

'You seem hale and hearty to me,' Eros murmured drily. 'But you still haven't explained why you have chosen me for this role.'

'And you still haven't explained how much you're willing to sacrifice to regain that island,' Stam countered smoothly. 'But I can assure you that if you fail to marry my granddaughter, I will ensure that you *never* reclaim Trilis.'

'Then we would appear to have reached the end of our meeting,' Eros retorted levelly, vaulting upright with the fluid grace of an athlete. 'I have no desire to remarry, and while I would *like* to reclaim Trilis, the loss of my freedom would be too high a price to pay.'

Stam loosed a sardonic laugh. 'Even if my great-grandson is also...*your son*?'

Those two words halted Eros in his tracks. His handsome dark head turned back, an expression of sheer incredulity etched in his lean bronzed features. 'Impossible!' he grated. 'I have no children!'

Stam surveyed him with loathing, as yet unconvinced that Eros was entirely unaware that Winnie had been pregnant when she had left his country house. 'Two more words: Winnie Mardas... Of course, you may not remember her?'

'Winnie?' Eros Nevrakis echoed in raw disbelief. 'She's *your* granddaughter?'

'Surprise...surprise,' Stam said meanly.

Eros hovered, his big powerful physique screaming with tension and scantily leashed energy. 'And you say...she has had *my* child? *My* son?'

'I do,' Stam confirmed. 'Of course, you're fully able to carry out your own DNA testing if you so wish. That's your business. All I care about is that you marry her without telling her that I interfered. Is that clear?'

Nothing was clear to Eros in that moment. He was in a severe state of shock laced with outrage. Two years back when he had last seen her, Winnie hadn't told him that she was pregnant, hadn't even hinted at such a possibility. She had just walked out of his life and never got back in touch. He was instantaneously enraged and equally appalled. A man had a *right* to know that he was a father, didn't he? The days when a man was routinely left in ignorance of paternity were long gone. These days a man's importance in the parenting stakes was supposed to be valued and acknowledged. Eros knew that the first person he would be consulting would be a lawyer.

'Eros...' Stam prompted. 'Did you hear what I said?'

'Is she *here*? Is she in Greece?' Eros demanded wrathfully.

'Sadly not, she's still in London living with her sisters. I can give you the address.'

'Please do.' Eros's clipped tone denoted savage impatience.

'You are not to tell her that *I* gave you the address,' Stam warned him as he tossed him a piece of paper already prepared with the relevant details. 'You do not tell her that you have met me and discussed her personal affairs.'

'You like to be the ringmaster without the applause?' Eros said derisively. 'Not sure I can deliver that.'

For all his seventy-odd years, Stam reared out of his chair like a coiled spring bouncing back into shape. 'If you let out one *word* of my role in this mess, I will destroy you!' he raked back at the younger man in threat. 'And you *know* I can do it!'

'But you don't know *me*,' Eros tossed back with perfect indifference to how Stam Fotakis felt about anything he did. He reckoned that Bull Fotakis could do many things to make business more challenging, but Eros was a billionaire in his own right with equally powerful friends and he was confident that the older man could *not* destroy him.

Stam dealt him a crushing appraisal in retribution for his disrespect. 'A married man taking one of his domestic staff to bed? I understand you perfectly. You picked her because she was poor and powerless and unlikely to be indiscreet for fear of dismissal. You made her your mistress and shifted her down to your country house for sleazy weekends. Be assured that I know exactly what kind of a man you are! A cheating, manipulative bastard!'

Eros flung back his handsome head, black curls tumbling back from his brilliant green eyes. 'And yet you want me to *marry* Winnie?'

'I want my great-grandson legitimised,' Stam ground out with finality. 'You get your precious island back. I don't expect you to live with Winnie or stay with her. In fact, I don't want you to because she could do a hell of a lot better than you as a husband and that little boy will have me as a male role model! He doesn't *need* you!'

Vexed way beyond the limit of expressing his explosive emotions, Eros swung on his heel and walked out, his wide shoulders and long back rigid while he mentally rained down the hellfire of revenge on Winnie and her offensive grandfather. How dared they?

How dared they?

Talk and behave as though he were powerless? Dismiss his rights as a father as though they did not exist? Suggest he could have no value as a parent? That, indeed, he would be a negative influence on his own child? They would pay for those slurs, one way or another they would *both* pay, Eros swore with inner vehemence.

Even worse, the implication that he was the sort of man who preyed on his domestic staff like some shady creep! Winnie had never been his mistress. Eros had never had one and certainly not during his marriage to Tasha. He had been celibate for years and then Winnie had appeared and *somehow*... His teeth gritted as he thrust the memory away, along with all his other memories of Winnie Mardas. The affair had been a mistake, a very human mistake but still a mistake. He knew that very well. Temptation had led to an error and then ultimately to freedom, he reminded himself, shelving that train of thought for something much more important.

He had a child… He had a *son*, whose name he didn't even know! Engaged in frantic mathematical calculations, Eros worked out that his little boy had to be under two years of age, a mere toddler. A faint shard of relief touched him. That wasn't too late for a child to meet his father for the first time. How much worse would it have been if he had *never* found out or if the child had been much older and embittered by his father's long absence from his life?

Yeah, it could have been worse, he jeered at himself for such ruminations. But not much worse… Stam Fotakis threatening him, trying to stampede him into marriage when he had only just escaped an imprudent marriage, his first child estranged from him, the mother of his child equally estranged and her subsequent behaviour were inexcusable. Seriously, how *could* the situation have been worse?

And the whole chaotic fiasco stemmed from one mistake. Eros's own mistake, he acknowledged grudgingly. He had naively agreed to marry a young woman he didn't love and didn't desire to soothe a dying man's fears about his daughter's future. But it had never been a real marriage. He had never shared a bed with Tasha, had never even shared a home with her. Throughout their marriage they had lived entirely separate lives. He had accepted all the restrictions of marriage without receiving any of the benefits. And then Winnie had come into his life and logic, honour and restraint had gone out of the window simultaneously.

* * *

Stam Fotakis surveyed his empty office with bemused eyes. For the first time in his life, he wasn't sure how a business meeting had gone. It *had* been business, *purely* business, he told himself soothingly. But Nevrakis had gone up like a firework display, far more volatile in nature than Stam's careful research had led him to expect. He had never seen a man in such a rage, particularly not one renowned for being cooler than ice. Suppose he let that rage out in little Winnie's direction?

A new fear assailed Stam as he grabbed the phone to speak to his granddaughters' bodyguards, the security detail the girls didn't even know they had watching their every move in London. Possibly, security would have to be a little more visible in the near future, Stam reasoned worriedly. Nevrakis had left his office in violent haste…

'So,' Vivi summed up, copper hair as sleek as a swathe of silk framing her vivid face as she looked across the kitchen table at her sisters. 'Our grandfather is as crazy as a loon. Where does that leave us?'

'What we do is our choice.' Winnie threw back her head so that her mass of brunette hair tumbled down her back, enabling her to gather it up and expertly twist it into a ponytail, ready for work. 'Nobody can *force* us to do anything.'

'Agreed, but Grandad *is* our only option for the money we need,' Zoe piped up with innate practicality. 'Nobody else is willing to give us money to save John and Liz's home. We tried to get a loan and we failed.'

That unwelcome reminder fell like a brick into the tense silence.

Winnie tugged her little boy up onto her lap because he was drooping tiredly by her side. Teddy closed his eyes and relaxed, his little face drowsy below his crown of black curls. Talk was cheap and easy, but reality had just spoken in Zoe's quiet little voice, Winnie reflected ruefully. In truth, none of the three sisters had an actual choice. In the kindest way possible for a very rich tyrant, Stam Fotakis had spelt out the truth that his assistance would be given and gladly, but that financial help would come at a price they might not be prepared to pay.

And why did they need that financial help?

Their foster parents, John and Liz Brooke, whose care had transformed the sisters' lives and reunited them as a family group, were in deep financial trouble. When Winnie had learned that John and Liz were within days of having their ramshackle farmhouse repossessed and losing the foster children currently in their care, she had disregarded her long-dead father's warning and had approached her wealthy grandfather with a begging letter.

Stam Fotakis had cut off their late father, Cy, without a penny when he was barely more than a teenager. Cy had demonstrated his disdain for the family name by legally changing it to his grandmother's maiden name of Mardas, which, of course, had meant that their grandfather had had no way of tracing either his son or the family he had eventually had.

At twenty-six, Winnie was old enough to remember their parents, who had died in a car crash when she was eight, but Vivi had only the barest recollection of them, and Zoe, a mere toddler at the time, had none at all.

But all three young women were very much aware that the Brooke family had saved them when they'd needed saving, giving them the care and support they had long lacked to rise above the tragic loss of their mum and dad and the disturbing consequences that had followed because they had all had bad experiences in state care. Winnie, extracted from a physically abusive foster home, had arrived with them first, and John and Liz's caring enquiries and persistence had eventually led to the sisters being reunited within their home.

From that point on all their lives had improved beyond all recognition and gradually a happy, secure normality had enveloped the traumatised siblings. You couldn't put a price on what John and Liz had done for them, Winnie conceded ruefully, because you couldn't put a price on love. Without adopting them, John and Liz had become the girls' forever family, treating them like daughters and encouraging and supporting them every step of the way into adulthood.

'That's true.' Vivi spoke up again with a grimace at the reminder that they had failed to get a loan. 'And we can only get that money if we agree to marry men hand-picked by our crazy grandad. Obviously getting his granddaughters married off to suitable men is hugely important to him.'

'He did say they didn't have to be *real* marriages… in-name-only stuff is rather different,' Winnie muttered the reminder ruefully, because in truth she didn't want to get married either, even if it did only mean a piece of legal paper and a ring on her finger.

When she had first contacted her grandfather, she had had to provide documents to prove her identity but, barely a week later, she and her sisters and her little boy had been flown out on a private jet to Greece for several days. They had been stunned by their grandfather's wealth and his very big and opulent home and had been well on the road to liking him *until* he had mentioned his terms for giving them the money to save the roof over John's and Liz's heads.

Of the three of them, Winnie had been most shocked by those terms, particularly when it should've been obvious to a man who had bitterly lamented their unhappy childhood in foster care that *he* too owed John and Liz Brooke a moral debt for the care they had taken of his grandchildren. But evidently the concept of giving something for nothing was not one Stam Fotakis was willing to embrace. Yes, he had acknowledged he was delighted to learn of their existence and very grateful that John and Liz had given them such wonderful care…but still he had had to mention *terms*…

Winnie had immediately scolded herself for her sentimental expectations and unrealistic hopes of her grandfather. He was the same man who had thrown his younger son out of his home for refusing to study business at university and he had never looked back from that hard decision. Not necessarily a kind man, not even necessarily a *nice* man. He wanted them all married off to what he had referred to as 'men of substance' and restored to the society position he saw as their Fotakis birthright. Winnie, however, did suspect that she knew *why* Stam Fotakis had decided not to simply invite his grandchildren into his home to gift them that birthright as members of his household.

Stam Fotakis was *ashamed* of his granddaughters' current status. He had adored her son, Teddy, on sight but had been appalled that Winnie was unmarried. He had been equally shocked by the dreadful scandal in which Vivi had become innocently embroiled. In fact, Stam Fotakis didn't have a modern laid-back bone in his entire body. He believed women should be safely, decently married before they had children and that their names should only ever appear in a down-market tabloid newspaper because they were beautifully dressed VIPs.

Winnie grimaced. She had always believed that she too would be married before she had a child but a crueller fate had tripped her up and she was a little wiser now. Falling in love with the wrong man could be a disaster and that was the crux of what had happened to Winnie and her once-fine ideals. Her only consolation was that she had not once suspected that Eros was a married man, and he had most definitely concealed that reality from her. Her wake-up call had come in the shape of a visit from Eros's wife, Tasha, and she still broke out in a cold sweat just remembering that awful day. It had forced her to grow up fast though, she told herself bracingly, and she had needed that 'short sharp shock' treatment to get the strength to walk away from the man she loved.

'I have to get ready for work.' Winnie sighed, rising from her seat.

Zoe stood up, as well. 'Give me Teddy,' she urged.

'I'll put him down for a nap while I make dinner and that'll allow you to slip out without him noticing.'

Zoe was tiny like Winnie but her hair was golden blonde as their father's had been. Her grandfather had told Winnie that she bore a close resemblance to her grandmother who had apparently been an Arabian princess. Winnie shook her head over that startling recollection because nothing could have more surely pointed out that her grandfather came from a very different world. Her father, Cy, had never once mentioned his mother's exalted birth, but he had talked very lovingly about her.

Smiling at her youngest sibling, Winnie recognised how very lucky she was to have sisters who loved and cared for her son as much as she did. She could never have managed without them although the fact that, as a junior chef, she invariably worked evenings and weekends helped in the childcare department. They had also been living in a dump of a flat before they met their grandfather and Winnie had only accepted the older man's generous offer of new accommodation for her son's sake. In the space of two weeks, however, that new comfortable terraced home with its four generous bedrooms and extra space, not to mention its smart location, had changed their lives very much for the better. They weren't paying rent any more either, which meant that surviving on their low salaries was no longer a struggle.

Even so, it didn't feel safe to be depending even temporarily on the generosity of a grandfather who was very much a mixed bag of traits and tricks. Winnie was painfully aware that Stam Fotakis could decide to turn his back on them as quickly as he had laid down a welcome mat for them. Rich people, she had learned from her experience with Eros Nevrakis, could be unreliable and volatile. It didn't do to trust them or to expect them to stay the same like more ordinary folk, she recalled sickly.

'I'm sorry, I'm not in the mood tonight.' She recalled Eros murmuring in apology, as if it were perfectly normal to push her away when he was usually keen to encourage her affection. That rejection had hurt, it had hurt *so much*, acting on her like the very first frightening wake-up call to reality.

Her eyes stinging, Winnie compressed her lips and shut down the memory fast. Remembering Eros was a two-edged sword that both wounded *and* infuriated her. She had been so stupidly naive and trusting, refusing to see or suspect what her grandfather had picked up instantly…that she had not been engaged in a passionate love affair but had instead become a married man's mistress. And there was nothing remotely romantic or loving or caring about that role, she concluded as she stepped onto the Tube to travel to the restaurant that currently employed her as a pastry chef. She would've been rather higher up the career ladder had she not dropped out of her apprenticeship to become Eros Nevrakis's personal chef, she reflected resentfully. On the other hand, she would never have had Teddy without *him* and, no matter what her grandfather thought of unmarried mothers, Teddy could never ever be a source of regret.

Midevening, Vivi was just tucking the little boy into his jammies when a loud knock sounded on the front door. The knocker sounded again before she even reached the hall with Teddy clutched precariously below one arm, because you couldn't turn your back safely on Teddy for even ten seconds. 'All right…all right…try being patient,' she was muttering below her breath as she yanked open the door and gaped.

At least five men stood on the doorstep, all big, all wearing dark suits and earphones. No, the one standing closest wasn't wearing one of those communication things and he looked madder than fire.

'Are you okay, Miss Mardas?' one of the men at the back enquired.

'Who on earth are you all?' Vivi whispered, feeling unusually intimidated.

'Security, Miss Mardas. We work for your grandfather.'

'I'm not security,' Eros spelt out impatiently while trying not to squint to get a better look at the little boy anchored sideways below the redhead's arm. His brain went momentarily blank as he focused on that grinning, lively little face below the splash of black curls. His son, assuming it was his son, looked very much like him, Eros acknowledged, momentarily shocked out of the rage that had powered him all the way from Greece.

'Why would I need security?' Vivi whispered.

'I want to see Winnie,' Eros grated. 'I am Eros Nevrakis.'

Vivi froze and immediately awarded him a look of utter loathing. 'My sister is at work.'

'I will come in and wait for her, then.'

'She won't be home until after midnight, so there's no point in you waiting,' Vivi proclaimed with pursed lips.

Eros drew himself up to his full six feet four inches

and simply looked through her, unperturbed by her hostile manner. 'I will return at ten in the morning. Tell her to ensure that she is here then,' he delivered through clenched white teeth.

CHAPTER TWO

'No—NO WAY am I seeing him after all this time,' Winnie declared wearily after her shift with both her sisters treating her to an anxious appraisal. 'What on earth does he want?'

'Do you think he's found out about Teddy?' Zoe piped up worriedly.

'I don't see how.'

'Grandad knows him,' Vivi interposed thoughtfully. 'I saw the look on his face when you admitted Teddy's father was Greek and when you finally gave him the guy's name, he was really, really furious—didn't you notice?'

'No, I wasn't wanting to look at Grandad while I was being forced to tell that particular story,' Winnie admitted, her face burning at that memory.

'Well, Nevrakis can't *force* you to see him. Go to the park as usual,' Vivi advised.

'Don't you think—with him being Teddy's father—that that is a bit unwise?' Zoe murmured, as always the peacemaker.

'He's *not* Teddy's father. He's never been here for Teddy *or* Winnie when they needed him!' Vivi sharply snapped back at Zoe.

'It's just I think…well, you know…er…that fathers have rights,' Zoe said hesitantly. 'And maybe if he knows about Teddy and that's why he's here, if you don't play nice, he might start thinking about taking you to court to get permission to see him.'

'Dear heaven, I hope not!' Winnie gasped in horror but the more she thought about that risk, the more worrying the situation became. But was it really that likely that Eros would be that interested in a child?

Could Eros already know about Teddy? Could her grandfather have told him? She wouldn't have trusted Stam Fotakis as far as she could throw him. He had already told her that she should've informed Eros that she was pregnant rather than simply walking away from their relationship without an explanation. *For* walk, *substitute* run, she thought unhappily, for the discovery that Eros was a married man had devastated Winnie, and after that deception she hadn't felt she owed Eros the news that she was pregnant. She hadn't wanted anything more to do with him, hadn't ever wanted to even *see* him again…but now he had tracked her down and with Teddy around that was a game changer, wasn't it?

Clutching her hand, Teddy chattered non-stop all the way to the park. It was toddler chatter in which only one word in ten was recognisable as an actual word. They had to walk slowly too, because Teddy loved to walk. But he had short legs and if she lost patience and put him in the buggy, he would throw a tantrum. 'Not baby!' he would scream, mortally offended by such a demeaning mode of transport.

He gave a shout of excitement once he saw the

playground, tearing free of his mother's grasp to race down the path in advance of her. Winnie broke into a run because Teddy's fearless approach to life often put him at risk. By the time she caught up, he was climbing the steps to the slide. He had been as agile as a little monkey from an early age. He whooped as he went down the slide and she retreated to a concrete bench nearby, relieved to sit down because she was still tired from the night before.

Her phone buzzed in her pocket and she dug it out. It was Vivi.

'Nevrakis is coming to see you at the park,' her sibling warned her. 'I tried to put him off but he said he would stay and wait if I didn't tell him where you were.'

Near panic engulfed Winnie, her jaw dropping at the thought of being cornered by Eros in a public place. But he wasn't the type to make a scene, she reminded herself doggedly, and she couldn't avoid him for ever. It was better to be sensible, she told herself bracingly, smoothing down her warm jacket, wishing she had put on a little make-up, telling herself off furiously for even caring how she might look while her nerves rattled about inside her like jumping beans. He had to know about Teddy, had to want to see him because there was no other reason for him to seek her out now. Her mind wanted to take her back to her very first meeting with Eros Nevrakis but she wouldn't let it because memories would weaken her, tearing away the superficial calm she had learned to keep in place to make her sisters happy.

'Oh, sure, I'm over him!' she had taught herself to declare with a laugh for punctuation. 'I'm not stupid!'

Two men lodged nearby below the trees, suited and smart. Her grandfather's utterly superfluous bodyguards, whom Vivi had met the night before on the doorstep, Winnie suspected, and she ignored them. She would have to phone her grandfather about that unnecessary extravagance. Why on earth would she and her sisters need guarding when as yet nobody even knew they were related to Stam Fotakis?

In the distance she glimpsed a tall man striding down the path and her heart stuttered as though she'd received a shock, while breathing suddenly became a distinct challenge. Perspiration beaded her short upper lip, heat washing over her as she recalled what an absolute idiot she had been two years earlier...falling for her boss, *sleeping* with her boss.

Eros paused, all sleek, lithe and sexy elegance in a charcoal-grey suit and overcoat, a red silk scarf bright at his throat as he stood scanning the playground with the raw self-assurance of a highly successful tycoon. Winnie swallowed hard, her hands clenching together, nails biting into her tender palms. She had to force herself to stand upright to catch his attention because she wasn't going to hide from him and refused to behave as if she feared him.

His brilliant gaze settled on her and she went even stiffer, turning her head away to check on Teddy, standing at the top of the slide shouting for her attention, for if there was one thing Teddy loved it was an audience. He was an irredeemable little extrovert, brimming with vitality. She moved closer to the slide, ignoring Eros to the best of her ability, even as she heard his steps sound behind her.

Teddy zoomed down the slide with a whoop, clambered off at the bottom and raced round to repeat the exercise.

'Why didn't you tell me about him?' Eros breathed, soft and low and deadly.

Disconcertion turned Winnie's head in his direction and she saw him in profile because his entire attention was studiously welded to her son. That classic bronzed profile made her heart give a sick thud inside her chest and she swallowed hard, close enough to smell the rich aromatic scent of his designer cologne, close enough to be dragged down screaming into the kind of memories she always suppressed, and she took a hasty step backwards, protecting herself from getting too close.

'Why didn't you tell me that you were married?' Winnie parried quietly.

Eros gritted his even white teeth, incensed by that comeback. He turned to study her as involuntarily entranced by her tiny proportions as he had been the first time he saw her. She was a barely five-feet-tall brunette with delicate curves and a tiny waist, so small and light he could have scooped her up with one powerful hand. Of course, pregnancy could have changed her shape, he conceded, but he was challenged to picture Winnie pregnant and the loose jacket she wore concealed more than it revealed of her figure. The huge chocolate-brown eyes, sultry pink mouth and the lustrous dark mane of her hair, however, were unchanged. He tore his electrified gaze from her, angry enough to spit tacks, and concentrated his attention back on his son.

The little boy was definitely *his* son and he was of a much sturdier build than his mother. That tumble of black curls and those green eyes, the same green eyes that Eros had inherited from his late mother, unmistakeably marked Teddy out as a Nevrakis. Eros had done his homework and made his own enquiries since that meeting two days earlier with Stam Fotakis. His son was called Teddy. What sort of a name was that? His child had been named after a plush toy, he thought witheringly. But the biggest surprise of all for Eros at that moment was how looking at Teddy made him *feel*...

As though that little creature had been put on this earth purely for him to protect, he acknowledged in wonderment, watching as Teddy climbed the slide steps at speed and threw himself down it with dangerous enthusiasm and a noisy shout. Impelled by a response that bit too deep to withstand, Eros strode forward and swept the little boy upright again with careful hands. Teddy gave him a startled look and then a huge cheerful smile as Eros gently set him free again.

'Swing, Mama,' Teddy demanded, setting off in that direction.

'He's bossy like you,' Winnie said drily.

Eros ignored her. He had a great deal to say to Winnie but none of it could be safely voiced where they could be overheard.

Winnie lifted Teddy into one of the baby swings and gave him a push before standing back.

'How old is he?' Eros demanded in a driven undertone.

'Eighteen months. He's tall for his age,' Winnie muttered.

'And in all that time you didn't *once* think of contacting me?' Eros intoned through clenched teeth of restraint.

'You were married,' Winnie reminded him with a lift of her chin.

'That's irrelevant,' Eros countered with ferocious bite. 'It's not an excuse.'

'I'm not making excuses. I don't regret not telling you,' Winnie responded, outraged by his lack of guilt.

'But you will,' Eros murmured, soft as a cat padding round her on velvet paws of menace. 'You will *learn* to regret it.'

A faint chill stiffened Winnie's already rigid spine but she squared her slight shoulders, rebelling against that sense of threat. Eros couldn't push her around; he couldn't *do* anything to her. Teddy was hers and she didn't work for Eros any more or indeed depend on him in any way.

Her defiance infuriated Eros. Evidently he had underestimated Winnie when he had deemed her to be a quiet, restful sort of young woman; the type who would never cause waves in his life. He had trusted her as far as he trusted any woman, had believed he knew her inside out, had only registered how mistaken such an assumption could be after she had vanished into thin air. His wide sensual mouth compressed into a grim line.

Winnie glanced at him and her tension zoomed to a new high, her eyes lingering against her will on his lean, powerful length, her breath catching in her throat. With an effort she tore her attention away again but her senses were humming, her heart was pounding, teaching her that she had yet to attain the level of indifference she needed to be safe around him. Instead she was mesmerised by that stormy, striking male beauty of his, the honed, flawless angles of his high cheekbones, the definitive shape of his nose and the unforgettably stunning impact of those jewelled green eyes, once seen, never forgotten. She shifted her feet, fighting off her susceptibility, hating herself for noticing afresh just how gorgeous he was.

'My only regret is that I ever met you,' she declared stonily.

'A little late in the day,' Eros purred, impervious to the insult. 'I will take you to my apartment, where we will talk about where we go from here.'

'No,' Winnie argued. 'I'm going home. Teddy needs his nap.'

To Eros's mind, Teddy looked more as if he was good to go for another few hours as he gripped the swing and kicked up his legs with excitement.

'We can't talk with your sisters present,' Eros countered very drily.

'My sisters will have left for work.' Rigid with resentment that he was somehow contriving to force her into a discussion she didn't want as well as granting him access to her home, Winnie slung him a look of loathing, big brown eyes awash with annoyance.

She hated Eros Nevrakis. She had never hated anyone before but she hated him for a whole host of reasons. But she had to find out *what* he wanted, had to remember that he was Teddy's father and should for the present be handled with tact, she reminded herself quellingly. This time running away wasn't an option because she would only leave a bigger mess behind her. Her soft full lips compressed, she lifted her son out of the swing, ignoring his bitter wail of complaint.

He looked up at her with green eyes swimming with tears and her heart clenched as she set him down to walk beside her.

'We'll use my limo,' Eros informed her.

'No, Teddy and I will walk back. I'll meet you there,' Winnie told him without hesitation and she turned on her heel, needing the time alone and the peace to regroup and calm down.

Teddy dragged his heels all the way, tired now and cross, but Winnie barely noticed because all the memories she had buried were flooding her to drowning point.

Fresh from catering college and a variety of jobs in which she'd picked up experience, she had secured a sous chef position in a small family-owned Greek restaurant. When a virus had put the head chef in bed, the responsibility for providing dinner for a large party of Greek businessmen being entertained by Eros had fallen on Winnie's shoulders. At the end of the meal she had been invited to meet the client, and she could still recall getting into a panic at the prospect and dragging off her chef's hat and tidying her hair for the sort of public appearance that had never come her way before.

Eros had complimented her with flattering enthusiasm on the meal she had prepared. She had hovered there with bright red cheeks, trying not to gawp at the best-looking man she had ever met, wondering how anyone could have such extraordinarily green eyes, intense as polished tourmalines in that lean, darkly handsome face of his. He had passed her his business card, telling her that he was looking for a personal chef for his London home and that when she was free she should ring him for an interview.

She had been quite happy where she was working, but she didn't see much of her sisters because she worked such awkward hours and that more than anything had persuaded her to make that phone call. When she had been offered a salary far beyond her current earnings and accommodation in central London to boot, she had accepted, reasoning that working as a billionaire's private chef would offer her even more exciting opportunities to advance herself. With two sisters who were still students, invariably broke and in need of clothes, the ability to earn a decent wage had been very important back then.

'So, how did you get into cooking?' Eros had enquired, strolling informally into the kitchen on her first night while she'd been preparing his evening meal, his every fluid movement attracting her attention, particularly to the fabric defining his long, powerful thighs.

'My mother was a cook and she started teaching me when I was five,' Winnie had confided as she'd struggled not to look back in the same direction, perplexed by her random thoughts and embarrassing impulses in his presence. 'Both my parents were Greek, although my mother's family had been living here for years when she met my father—'

'Yet you don't speak our language,' Eros had remarked in surprise.

Winnie had tensed, her eyes shadowing. 'My parents died when I was eight and I've forgotten most of the Greek words I knew. I've always meant to go to classes but I'm too busy. Some day I'll take it up again.'

'So, what are you making me tonight?' Eros had asked with a lazy smile, his accented drawl smooth as silk in her ears.

'I put a little menu on the dining table for you.'

'Cute,' Eros had commented with lancing amusement.

'Just tell me what you want and I'll provide it,' she had urged, eager to please for he had been paying generously for her services and she'd wanted him to feel that she was worth her salary.

An ebony brow had skated up. *'Anything?'* he had pressed, laughter sparkling in his spectacular eyes, his wide sensual mouth lifting at the corners.

'Pretty much anything,' Winnie had muttered, belatedly grasping the double entendre she had accidentally made, her colour rising accordingly. 'And if I don't know how to make it, I can soon find out.'

'Is your accommodation adequate?' Eros had prompted.

'It's lovely. Your housekeeper was very helpful,' Winnie had told him cheerfully, even though it had been something of a shock to enter a household where virtually no one had spoken any English and where she'd known she would be a little lonely. There had been few staff because Eros had been the only resident and had frequently been away from home. Only the housekeeper, Karena, had lived in and she had been near retirement age, besides having only a very basic grasp of English.

Karena's entry into the kitchen that evening had concluded that conversation with Eros, for the housekeeper had usually served the meals, but a couple of nights later when Winnie had noticed how very tired the older woman had looked, she had urged her to return to her flat for the night and leave her to serve the meal. It had been a strategic error to expose herself to greater contact with Eros but at the time she had felt guilty about the fat salary she earned and the reality that she worked much shorter hours than Karena, who had been on duty from dawn to dusk and busy even when Eros had been abroad because she'd overseen the cleaning and maintenance of the house. When Karena had fallen victim to a sprained wrist, that serving arrangement had become permanent with Karena departing to her flat every evening before Eros's return.

Only a few evenings had passed before Eros had suggested she join him and, although she had demurred in surprise and discomfiture the first time, the second time he had asked she had told herself that it would be rude to refuse again and she had sat down and shared a glass of wine with him. She had asked him about his day and his foreign travels and had listened while he'd talked, sipping her wine, answering the occasional query while becoming maddeningly aware of the intensity of his beautiful eyes on her. Just sitting there she had felt all hot and tingly, flattered by his interest, his apparent desire for her company when he could've had so many more glamorous women eagerly filling the same role.

Back then Winnie had been a retiring mixture of naivety and insecurity when men were around. Keen to climb the career ladder, she hadn't dated much, and as soon as her sisters had begun looking to her as a role model, dating had become even more of a challenge. A couple of unsavoury experiences with men who had wanted much more than she'd wanted to give had kept her a virgin. Working long, unsocial hours hadn't helped, so the thrill of being in Eros's company and the sole focus of his attention had rather gone to her head. The first kiss… *No*, she didn't want to remember that which loomed large in her memory as her first major mistake. Squashing that untimely recollection, she walked past the opulent vehicle that she assumed was Eros's limousine and was unlocking the front door of the house when she heard him behind her.

'An elegant location,' he remarked, making her jump as she hurriedly crossed the threshold.

'Yes, thanks to Grandad. The house belongs to him.' Hurriedly doffing her coat, Winnie hung it up in the alcove and showed him into the lounge. 'You can wait in here while I feed Teddy and put him down for his nap…'

'Why did you choose to call him Teddy?' he queried.

'Officially it's Theodore, my father's middle name,' she proffered stiffly. 'But it was too big a name for a baby and he ended up Teddy instead.'

Uninvited, Eros followed her into the kitchen, where she strapped Teddy into his booster seat at the table and whipped between fridge and microwave, warming her son's lunch while studiously ignoring Eros's silent presence by the door.

Teddy grasped his spoon and ate, making more of a mess than usual, showing off because a stranger was present.

'I assume your sisters look after him while you're at work?' Eros prompted.

'Yes…' Winnie glanced worriedly at him. 'They're very good with him.'

'A father would have been even better.'

Breathing in deep and slow to restrain her temper, Winnie concentrated on cleaning up Teddy and the table, unstrapping him to lift him.

'Allow me…' Disconcertingly, Eros stepped right into her path and simply scooped her son out of her hold. 'Where to now?'

'Upstairs,' Winnie said thinly, reluctantly leading the way.

She pushed open the door of Teddy's room.

'This is a little girl's room,' Eros objected, only slowly lowering her son into his cot, his attention pinned to the pink cartoon mural of princesses on the wall.

'We haven't got around to redecorating yet,' Winnie retorted, sidestepping the truth that the sisters had decided not to go to that trouble and expense when they were unsure how long their grandfather would allow them to make the house their home. Stepping over to the cot, she slipped off her son's shoes and his sweatshirt and settled him down before tugging the string on the little musical mobile that had been his from birth.

Closing the curtains, she walked back to the door, watching Eros hover by the cot. 'Why's the cot in the middle of the room?' he asked.

'Because if you put it beside the furniture, Teddy will use it to climb out and I don't want the hassle of trying to persuade him to stay put in a junior bed. He's too young to understand.'

'A nanny would remove much of the burden of childcare,' Eros commented smoothly. 'It must be hard for you to work and care adequately for him at the same time.'

'Not with my sisters around,' Winnie countered steadily, refusing to rise to the suggestion that she wasn't doing the best mothering job possible.

Eros strode down the stairs only a step in her wake and she walked into the lounge. 'I suppose I should offer you coffee,' she said stiffly.

Eros sent her a winging hard glance. 'No, thanks. Let's not procrastinate.'

'If you must know, I was trying to be polite.'

Eros shrugged a broad shoulder, the edge of his jacket falling back to expose a shirt front pulling taut across his muscular torso, delineating sleek bands of abdominal muscle. As she watched, her mouth ran dry and she looked hastily away, colour warming her cheeks.

'Why bother?' Eros incised drily. 'We're neither friends nor casual acquaintances.'

'What do you want from me?' Winnie fired back at him, anxiety biting through her.

'Answers,' Eros framed silkily. 'And I'll keep on coming back at you until I get them.'

she exclaimed, vexed by that provocative assurance and, if anything, madder than ever.

'You met Tasha,' Eros acknowledged curtly. 'Eventually I did find that out and presumably that is why you chose to suddenly disappear without giving *me* any explanation.'

'Don't say that like it excuses you... *Nothing* excuses your behaviour!' Winnie slammed back at him furiously. 'And I didn't owe you anything!'

Eros studied her with intent, glittering green eyes. She still had lousy dress sense, he conceded ruefully, invariably choosing to envelop herself in drab colours and very practical clothing, but he knew her ripe body as well as he knew his own and he could see the changes in her lush figure, which even clad in leggings and an all-concealing sweatshirt was visibly fuller at breast and hip. He hardened, momentarily snatched back into hot, sweaty memories of the passion that had once threatened to consume him. His treacherous libido heated up, sending a sensual pulse through his groin and making him bite back a curse at his lack of restraint.

For a while, the sheer novelty of that passion had obsessed him and, having recognised that as a dangerous weakness, he had refused to allow himself to look for her after she vanished out of his life. He could get by fine without sex; he had got by for years and he no longer fell as easily into temptation as he had fallen with her. He was free now, he reminded himself, but that old belief that he had to always stay in control of his physical urges was still ingrained in him. Giving way to those same urges had destroyed his father's life. Winnie had made him feel dangerously out of control and that, if he was honest with himself, had unnerved him.

'At the very least, you owed me the knowledge that you were pregnant with my child,' Eros delivered in harsh condemnation.

'No, I didn't!' Winnie slammed back at him in annoyance. 'Your deception released me from any such obligation!'

His stunning eyes narrowed, black velvety lashes shading that mesmeric green. 'There was no deception on my part. For a deception to be contrived, one must deliberately engage in concealment of the truth…and I did not. I didn't tell you a single lie!'

For several unbearable seconds, Winnie searched her memory for evidence of a lie and her inability to find one merely enraged her more. He was so scheming, so specious in his arguments. 'But you also knew I hadn't the faintest suspicion that you were a married man!' she flung back at him bitterly.

Eros inclined his glossy dark head. 'Did I? Some women are content to sleep with married men without questioning their status.'

'Stop playing with words!' Winnie interrupted, rising up on her toes, pulsing with angry tension. 'That's what you're doing in defiance of the facts! You knew I wasn't *that* kind of woman… You knew I wouldn't willingly get involved with a married man!'

Again, Eros shrugged, the lean, hard angles of his sculpted features set like granite. 'None of this nonsense is pertinent now,' he claimed in a dry tone of finality. 'I will not engage in a slanging match about our past. That ship sailed a long time ago. What is germane now is that you have my son and you didn't tell me about him. Let's concentrate on that, rather than on facts we cannot change.'

Winnie tore her gaze from him with difficulty and turned her head away, momentarily at a loss. In one sense he was correct, in that there was nothing to be gained from arguing about what had happened between them two years earlier, but that also meant that he was denying her any justification for having chosen not to inform him of her pregnancy. Her slight shoulders stiffened and her head swung back, dark strands of her lush mane of hair falling across cheeks flushed by angry frustration.

'How did you become pregnant anyway?' Eros demanded without warning. 'I *always* took precautions.'

At that much-too-intimate question, Winnie practically fried in mortification inside her own burning skin and she walked stiffly over to the window, momentarily turning her back on him. 'No, there were times when you overlooked that necessity,' she told him grudgingly, forced to recall early-morning encounters when she had wakened to his hard, thrillingly aroused body pressed to hers and in warm drowsy lust and need had succumbed without either of them thinking of contraception.

'I don't remember a single occasion,' Eros informed her with a raw edge to his dark, deep, accented drawl.

'Then you must have a very short memory because I remember at least a dozen occasions when contraception was the last thing on your mind. In the shower, in the pool, early mornings when we were both half-asleep.' Winnie forced out the words like staccato bullets voiced between gritted teeth. 'In fact, you were downright careless, and I noticed but I didn't say anything. Instead, I tried to go on the pill to protect myself but by the time I saw a GP, it was too late. I had already conceived.'

'You should've drawn those oversights to my attention,' Eros delivered curtly, reflecting that if anything should've warned him that the affair was out of control, it was exactly that aberrant carelessness on his part that underlined it. He had got too comfortable with her, too *involved* to be logical and safe. It had been a high-voltage sexual affair and he hadn't been prepared for it, hadn't counted the risks or the costs, had simply waded in like a man with an unquenchable thirst and drunk so deep that even his intelligence was compromised.

Winnie twisted back to him in a sudden movement. 'Oh, really?' she carolled tartly. 'So, the fact I fell pregnant is my fault too, is it?'

'There's little point in awarding blame this late in the day,' Eros murmured curtly. 'What is done is done and we have a child…a child who is, sadly, a stranger to me. That must be remedied immediately.'

Winnie was so rigid that her very muscles ached with the strain. 'Must it?'

'Of course, it must be,' Eros declared, studying her with an incredulity that implied she would have to be witless to expect anything else. 'Teddy must learn that I am his father and I need to get to know him. I would like to spend time with him tomorrow.'

'No,' Winnie cut in without even thinking about it because Teddy had always been hers and he had never been in the care of anyone outside the family.

'Naturally, I will bring a qualified nanny with me to ensure that Teddy's basic needs are properly met while he is with me. I have a lot to learn about being a father,' Eros admitted with a candour that disconcerted her. 'But given time and experience, I will pick up what I have to know.'

'I really can't believe that you're *this* interested in Teddy!' Winnie proclaimed in consternation, watching him pace back and forth in front of her, the lithe grace of his every movement strikingly noticeable and grabbing her attention with its aching familiarity.

A hollow sensation opened inside Winnie, her breath suddenly tripping in her throat. Her nipples were peaking, suddenly tender and tight beneath her clothing. She dragged in a jagged breath as the hot melting sensation of arousal pulsed between her taut thighs. How did he do that to her? How on earth could he still do that to her when she knew he was no longer hers to crave? Never had been hers either, except in her imagination, she reminded herself guiltily, dragging her attention from him to try to focus elsewhere.

'Obviously I want to get to know my son and I expect that process to begin immediately,' Eros spelt out bluntly. 'I will not accept you putting obstacles in my path.'

'Is that a fact?' Winnie sizzled back at him, feeling as though she was under attack on every front.

'I am being frank. You have denied me my rights as a parent for quite long enough,' Eros reasoned. 'The situation must change. I will see Teddy tomorrow and take him out. He will be very well taken care of.'

'I'll come too,' Winnie broke in insistently. 'You won't need a nanny.'

'No,' Eros countered decisively, his wide sensual

lips compressing into a determined line. 'I would prefer to get to know my son away from your influence.'

'He's too young for that yet!' Winnie argued passionately. 'He's never been away from me before.'

'Then it is time you encouraged him to achieve a little independence.'

'He's only a baby!' Winnie gasped defensively.

'He will come to no harm in my care. He is my son, my family, indeed the only close family I have left alive,' Eros pointed out grittily. 'Obviously he will be looked after to the very best of my ability.'

'You *can't* simply exclude me!' Winnie said accusingly.

Eros elevated a winged ebony brow in direct challenge. 'Is that not what you have done to me?' he pressed silkily. 'I have been excluded from every aspect of his life since birth but that cannot continue and you have to accept that reality.'

'I don't have to accept anything from you!' Winnie objected vehemently, wondering how they had contrived to travel so swiftly from rehashing old issues to his shattering demand to have full unsupervised access to their son.

And that was the crux of the matter, Winnie registered belatedly. Teddy was *their* son, not only hers, not only his. It was truly the first time that she had been confronted by the unwelcome truth that she did not have total, unbreakable rights over her own child and that awareness cut through her like a knife blade, giving rise to all sorts of other worries and insecurities. Faster than the speed of light, Eros was interfering, setting down his boundaries and making unapologetic demands. Eros was not the sort of man likely to humbly sit back in the corner and wait until she decided to cede him his rights as a parent.

'You have to learn to share Teddy,' Eros intoned without hesitation. 'But try starting your judgement of me from a *fair* starting point. Why assume that I won't look after my son as well as you do?'

'I didn't make that assumption,' Winnie contradicted nervously. 'I'm just warning you now that, no matter how well you look after him, Teddy will fret away from me and that you'll find him a handful.'

'You would like me to have difficulties handling him,' Eros assumed grimly, shooting her an unimpressed glance. 'But I do not foresee a problem.'

'Have you any experience in looking after a child this young?' Winnie enquired, needled by his insuperable confidence.

'No. You must know that I am an only child and few of my friends are parents yet,' Eros admitted grudgingly. 'But with a trained childcare professional on hand to advise me, I am sure that we will manage.'

'Teddy's at an unpredictable age. He throws tantrums,' Winnie warned him ruefully. 'He can go from rage to tears in seconds.'

'Perhaps my son needs more stable and reliable care to thrive,' Eros murmured silkily, as if tantrums could only be the consequence of inadequate parenting.

In receipt of that covert criticism, Winnie reddened with furious resentment. 'As you said yourself, you have a lot to learn about children,' she responded noncommittally, however, reluctant to expose her sensitivity to any questioning of her own parenting skills. She wondered if she was a complete shrew to hope that Teddy would lose his rag with Eros and teach him the reality of dealing with a volatile toddler.

'And tomorrow evening, after I have returned Teddy to your care, we will have dinner together and discuss—like reasonable adults—where to go from here,' Eros decreed decisively.

Winnie compressed her lips. If Eros wanted access to Teddy, she supposed that they had to discuss arrangements that would be acceptable to both of them. But how would she cope with that when even the prospect of having to part with Teddy for a few hours the next day daunted her? She knew that she would spend the entire time Teddy was away from her worrying about him.

'We'll have to dine out some other time,' she told him and not without a certain satisfaction. 'I have to work tomorrow evening.'

'I'm leaving for New York the next day and I will be away for at least a week. A later date will not be convenient for me,' Eros told her levelly. 'Get a night off or plead sickness. It's up to you.'

'I won't do that, Eros. I won't let my employers down.'

'Do you know where I'm going from here?' Eros enquired grimly. 'To consult my lawyer about my legal position with regard to Teddy. You are not in a strong enough position to be difficult, Winnie. We *must* discuss provisions and soon.'

Her heart-shaped face pulled taut, her big brown eyes suddenly ducking from his as she strove to withstand the conviction that she was being deliberately intimidated and forced in a direction in which she had no desire to go. 'Are you threatening me?' she asked curtly, feeling a little like a wayward farm animal being firmly herded down a preset track.

'No. I'm being *honest*,' Eros fielded with harsh emphasis. 'I am impatient to get to know my son and I would advise you not to stand in the way of that desire. It is natural for a new father to be keen to establish a normal relationship with his child.'

'But this keen interest of yours is coming at me out of nowhere!' Winnie protested hotly.

'Your vengeful attitude ends here and now,' Eros breathed in a raw undertone.

Winnie flung her head back to look up at him, having until that moment somehow contrived to forget how very tall he was in comparison to her. He was also way too close for comfort, the faint, dangerously familiar scent of his designer cologne flaring her nostrils. 'What on earth are you talking about?' she demanded blankly. *'Vengeful?'* she questioned with incredulous emphasis on that choice of word.

'When you found out that I was married, you decided to punish me by withholding all knowledge of my child from me,' Eros extended with perceptible bitterness, his lean, darkly handsome face sardonic.

'That's nonsense!' Winnie proclaimed in shocked denial. 'I'm not that sort of person!'

'You believed that the fact I was a married man was a good enough excuse to exclude me from Teddy's life. But it wasn't. That attitude won't wash with me now. You have to adapt to a new situation.'

'And what about your situation? How is your wife going to feel about all this?' Winnie cut across his condemnatory speech to demand helplessly. 'How is *she* going to react to Teddy's existence?'

'I don't have a wife any longer. I've been divorced for some time,' Eros informed her grimly. 'All matters concerning Teddy are between you and I and nobody else.'

Winnie was shocked, having automatically assumed he was still married. From the minute she had discovered that Eros was married, she had suppressed every inappropriate urge to look him up on the Internet and learn, not only about his marriage, but about what he was doing. He belonged to another woman. He was no longer her business, should *never* have been her business. She had warned herself painfully, fearing that seeking information about him would only fuel her longing for him.

She had been too ashamed of her behaviour at having slept with another woman's husband to allow herself to give way to further temptation. Her sin had been unintentional and born out of ignorance, but the guilt of that mistake still sat very heavily on her conscience. Indeed, that wanton fling with Eros had taught her to police her every thought. She had learned not to rush into judgement of others for their mistakes. She had learned that she could be as weak and imperfect as the most foolish of women when she fell in love, all tough lessons she could've done without.

She didn't properly breathe again until Eros had left, leaving her at the mercy of insecurity and stress. Eros had always had the ability to take her by surprise and slash through her calm controlled front with ease, unearthing the much more vulnerable woman she was underneath. That acknowledgement plunged her into the steamy memory of their first kiss.

Eros had been abroad for a couple of weeks and

he had walked into the kitchen to greet her, insisting that she join him for a glass of wine again, a familiarity that her sane mind had already been questioning. There was such a thing as getting *too* friendly and informal with an employer, she had reasoned unhappily, and she had been on the brink of pulling back and making polite excuses. And then Eros had stalked into the kitchen, clearly looking for her, all bristling energy and impatience, and he had smiled at her, that breathtakingly warm smile that literally made her heart beat so fast she felt breathless.

Without further ado, he had snatched her up off her sensible feet as if she were a doll while she was still muttering naively about the special dessert she had prepared. His mouth had plunged down on hers, full of a hot demanding hunger that had set her treacherous body alight. She'd had butterflies in her tummy and had been in a daze with her entire being vibrating from that explosively sensual assault as he had slowly lowered her to the tiles again, her body brushing down against every lean, powerful inch of his. She had been viscerally aware of the hard thrust of desire that not even the most exquisitely tailored suit could conceal.

'I want you so much,' Eros had said simply. 'I missed you. I've never missed a woman like this before.'

And it had been the very simplicity of that admission that had seduced her because she had missed him too, missed those quiet, private little moments of peace and tranquillity in his company. Instead of stepping back, instead of exercising good judgement, she had joined him for the wine, even shared that wretched dessert with him, laughing when he'd teased her about her professional pride in her creations. She could've told him then that nothing had inspired her with greater pride than his evident interest in her ordinary self. When it was late, when it was past time for her to be retiring for the evening she had reluctantly stood up, and he had stood up as well and reached for her.

'Stay with me tonight,' he had urged, and he had kissed her again.

It was the first time she had gone upstairs in that house and she had gone into his palatial bedroom with him, trembling with nerves, questioning her decision every step of the way even while her body had burned with eagerness and wanton impatience to finally know what other women knew. The die had been cast at that moment. She had been a pushover, falling in love and already trustingly investing Eros with far more importance in her life than he'd been investing in her.

Looking back, she believed that Eros had merely been taking advantage of an available woman. It was even possible that the prospect of taking her virginity had turned him on because he had known she was inexperienced, had guessed, reassuring her even as she had anxiously admitted it. Nothing could have prepared her for the passionate excitement that had followed or the deep sense of closeness she'd felt afterwards with him. From that night on, she had been at the mercy of her emotions and common sense hadn't got a look-in.

Her sisters returned from work, eager to hear what had happened between her and Eros. Zoe took an optimistic view, deeming it healthy that Teddy's father and her sister were talking and a positive sign that Eros should be so interested in immediately connecting with his son.

'But what is his end game?' Vivi probed with innate suspicion.

'Presumably what he says…getting to know Teddy, spending time with him,' Winnie pointed out awkwardly as she darted about her bedroom, getting ready for work. 'What else can he get out of this?'

'He strikes me as the sort of guy who always puts himself first,' Vivi declared with a curled lip. 'What's in it for him? There must be more than what we know. All of this is very coincidental. Does he know that Stam Fotakis is our grandfather?'

'No, it was never discussed. I'll mention it tomorrow, see how he reacts,' Winnie said ruefully. 'How am I going to hand Teddy over to him and some strange nanny tomorrow?'

'With kid gloves and a brave smile,' Zoe told her wryly. 'Let's hope the nanny is experienced.'

'Mama… Mama!' Teddy wailed pathetically.

That and the shouted 'Not baby!' when they tried to persuade him into his buggy were virtually the only words Eros had heard from his son. Oh, and there was the word *no*, which Teddy was even more partial to employing. He had neither volume control nor a need for privacy when he aired his innermost feelings. Teddy didn't care how many people were around when he flung himself down on the path and screamed blue murder for his mother. And he didn't like the nanny, physically fighting her if she tried to lift him, refusing to be distracted when she tried to tempt him out of the scenes he made.

But the advantage of Teddy distrusting the unfortunate nanny was that he clung to his slightly more familiar father as if his life depended on it. More positively, Teddy had loved the monkey enclosure at the zoo, he loved chocolate and he loved playgrounds. He was a smart little boy, energetic but explosive too. He was also so attached to his mother that he was forcing his father to rethink his tentative plans to challenge, should it prove possible, his mother's full-time custody.

But now Eros could see that there was no way Teddy would be happy, even on a part-time basis, to be deprived of Winnie. Shared custody definitely wasn't the path to take. Teddy needed Winnie as he needed air to breathe. Winnie was patently the very centre of Teddy's little world and the bedrock of his security and Eros knew that he would never do anything to hurt or harm his son. When he had even briefly considered his chances of parting mother from child, had he too been guilty of vengeful thinking? Eros asked himself grimly as they headed back early from their day out to reunite Teddy with Winnie. Eros knew that he now had to change his attitude and, for the sake of his son, consider a solution he had never dreamt he would be required to contemplate.

Marriage. Bearing in mind his past experience, just the thought of marriage brought Eros out in a cold sweat. He didn't want to get married again. In fact, he had promised himself that he would *never* marry again, reasoning that that was a rational decision when he had neither a family to please nor any desire to reproduce. He hadn't cared what happened to his business empire after he was gone, had never been vain enough to hope that he might merit a footnote in history. And then he had found out about Teddy and the whole picture of his life, his expectations and goals, had changed radically overnight.

'You'll be with Mama soon,' Eros soothed Teddy as his son let loose a choked sob that warned another distressed outburst was threatening.

'He's very attached to her,' the nanny commented.

'Too young to be separated from her,' Eros agreed, wishing he had listened to Winnie instead of arrogantly assuming that she would selfishly do everything she could to come between him and his son.

'With practice at socialising he would improve. A play group and the company of other children would be good for him,' the nanny opined.

'We'll see.'

Eros was forcing himself to think over Stam Fotakis's outrageous proposition from a different angle. He could live without owning the island of Trilis, however he could not live without his son being a regular part of his life. At the same time, if he was to be forced to marry Winnie anyway to gain consistent access to Teddy, why shouldn't he reclaim Trilis as part of the deal?

Even so, he refused to marry Winnie on the kind of terms that her grandfather had suggested, as a mere prelude to *another* divorce. If he married her, it would have to be a *real* marriage and both his wife and his child would naturally live with him. How would Winnie feel about that option?

Did that matter? Did he even care? Eros liked to

win and he had no intention of meekly meeting the old man's unreasonable demands and surrendering his son. By all accounts, Stam Fotakis had been a pretty poor father to his own two sons and Eros did not want him taking charge of Teddy. If there was something in the marriage for Eros, however, sufficient to compensate him for the loss of his freedom, now that was a different matter, he mused thoughtfully. Teddy *and* Winnie, not to mention the family island in the package, now that was a deal worthy of consideration by any hot-blooded man. He wondered, though, just how much pressure he would have to put on Winnie to achieve that package and then shelved the thought, broodingly reminding himself that she deserved whatever she got for denying him his son…

CHAPTER FOUR

'How do I look?' Winnie asked her siblings.

'Scared,' Vivi declared bluntly.

Winnie smoothed damp palms down over her ample hips and looked nervously in the mirror. The dress was wine red, purchased for their trip to Greece to meet their grandfather, the stretchy fabric hugging her curves to define every ounce of excess weight. And there *was* excess, she thought ruefully, because she had yet to lose all the extra pounds she had gained during pregnancy. Her long hours, the high-powered pressure of working in a busy kitchen and the irregular, often snatched meals had all played havoc with her intention to get back down to her original weight. 'I look fat,' she said curtly.

'It's not a date,' Vivi pointed out drily.

'You are *not* fat,' Zoe protested. 'You're just small and curvy and obviously he likes that.'

'Doesn't matter what *he* likes!' Vivi interrupted. 'If he tries to lay a finger on you, scream the place down, Winnie!'

'Vivi,' Winnie said gently, her sister's drama ironically calming her. 'Eros and I can barely speak to each other politely. He's hardly likely to make a pass at me. That's not what this is about.'

'Well, be careful about what you agree to,' the redhead warned her. 'We don't want to lose Teddy every weekend just because you're usually working.'

'I won't agree to anything tonight. I'll ask for time to think over any suggestion he makes.'

'Don't be late. You have to get up early tomorrow,' Zoe reminded her.

The sisters were catching the train down to John and Liz's home for their regular monthly catch-up with their former foster parents. Their grandfather had bought out the couple's mortgage to ensure that the house wasn't repossessed but he had refused to sign the property over to John and Liz until his granddaughters had met his terms and married. Winnie suppressed a troubled sigh as she slid her feet into vertiginous sparkly heels borrowed from Zoe and never worn. Zoe loved glitter and sparkle but had to be dragged at gunpoint into social situations.

Winnie thought ruefully about the financial difficulties that had plunged the Brookes into crisis. After John had suffered a stroke, money had been in short supply for years afterwards. John's plumbing business had failed, leaving the kindly couple deep in debt. Although he had eventually made an excellent physical recovery, they had been unable to meet their mortgage payments and they had fallen behind until eventually they had been facing the loss of their home.

Reminding herself soothingly that that worry was currently at bay, thanks to their grandfather, Winnie left the house and climbed into the taxi waiting outside for her. Eros had phoned her to tell her she would be picked up, his dark, deep voice cool and very much to the point. Why did that make her recall Eros practically purring down the phone as he'd chatted to her when he'd been far from home? In all, she had only known him for a few months. It had been a meaningless fling for him, she told herself impatiently, refusing to idealise what they had once shared. Their affair, as such, had stretched over two months and had encompassed long weekends spent together but Eros had often had to travel abroad.

The taxi dropped her off at a contemporary apartment block and she travelled up in the lift to the penthouse, her mouth dry as a bone as she contemplated seeing Eros again. He was Teddy's sperm donor, she instructed herself sourly, nothing more.

A manservant ushered her into a large open-plan space tiled in limestone, sparsely furnished and showcasing several modern artworks. Her coat and scarf were taken while she curiously scanned her surroundings, surprised to find Eros occupying such a contemporary setting. His country house had been late Georgian and, like his spacious city town house, traditional in decor. Of course, he was divorced and single again, she reminded herself resolutely, and it was perfectly possible that the historic properties had been more his wife's style than his.

Yet where had his wife been all those many months while she was working for Eros? In Greece, only seeing him on special occasions? Winnie ground her teeth together, angrily stamping out her curiosity while scolding herself for her lack of discipline in allowing her mind to wander. She could not afford to be woolly-minded, or sentimentally slipping back into the past around a man as shrewd and quick to take advantage as Eros Nevrakis.

'Would you like a drink before dinner?' Eros enquired from behind her, forcing her to spin round in surprise, and in doing so she almost overbalanced in the very high heels she had worn in an effort to look taller...and therefore slimmer.

Eros reached out an arm as strong as steel and clamped it to her side to steady her, long fingers biting into the curve of her hip. Of course, he was noticing that there was more value to every pound of her than there had been two years earlier, she mocked herself, knocked off balance by his proximity. Bigger was bigger and couldn't be concealed.

'Thanks... Er... I don't mind if I do,' she muttered uneasily, stepping back from him in haste.

Eros, already entranced by her back view, was practically mesmerised by the front view. The thin fabric outlined her superb violin curves, enclosing lush full breasts, a still-tiny waist and a glorious rounded bottom. *Ne*... Yes, there was more of her but it was a voluptuously *sexy* more that sent lust rocketing through him.

Hugely self-conscious beneath that keen green-eyed appraisal, Winnie pushed her hair back from her brow.

'You've grown your hair,' Eros remarked.

'Too busy to go to the hairdresser,' she parried awkwardly, studying him nervously from below her lashes, afraid to be caught in the act of staring.

For, my goodness, Eros deserved to be stared at. Clad in designer jeans that cupped his lean hips and faithfully outlined every sleek line of his long muscular legs, and a silver-grey shirt that defined the width of his shoulders and the breadth of his powerful torso, he was dazzlingly male. Winnie clutched the glass of wine he gave her, grateful to have something to occupy her hands.

'Teddy's a terrific little boy,' he commented, surprising her with that compliment.

Winnie nodded, managing a smile. 'I think so too,' she said inanely and then winced for herself.

'Obviously we both want what's best for him and we want to make him happy,' Eros intoned.

'The road to hell is paved with good intentions,' Winnie muttered ruefully. 'Please don't overwhelm Teddy. Let him get to know you in his own good time. He's like most young kids—he doesn't adapt well to sudden changes in his routine.'

'That's a tall order. I spend most of my time in Greece,' Eros volunteered, glancing at the manservant now lodged in the doorway. 'I believe our meal is ready.'

'You used to spend most of your time in London,' Winnie remarked, settling down at the polished, beautifully set table to look at her exquisitely presented starter without appetite. But then nerves always squashed her hunger, she reflected, even if nerves had never squashed her hunger for him.

It was not an acknowledgement she was keen to make but there it was, the elephant in the room that couldn't be ignored. Colliding with those black-fringed green eyes of his, she experienced what could only be likened to a sugar rush of excitement. It made her feel like a feckless teenager and a flush of chagrin coloured her face as she firmly focused her attention on her food.

'My base is in Greece now,' Eros informed her smoothly. 'I wouldn't be able to spend much time with my son here.'

Winnie stiffened, since there was nothing she could do about that problem. 'That's unfortunate,' she said awkwardly.

'But not an insuperable problem,' Eros murmured silkily.

'Good,' she said hastily, tension lancing through her more sharply than ever as if there was some invisible threat nearby that she had to watch out for.

The threat was Eros, of course it was, all male, all powerful, arrogant Eros, who liked to order his world exactly as he liked it and who would very much dislike anything or anyone who got in his way. 'Who's cooking for you now?' she asked brightly, keen to dial down the intensity of the dialogue with a man who could somehow make the simplest statements sound ominous, making gooseflesh prickle at the back of her neck.

'I had food sent in tonight from one of my favourite restaurants. I'm not here often enough now to maintain a permanent chef,' he admitted as the second course arrived and the manservant topped up their wine glasses.

And there it was, she thought melodramatically, Eros exerting control again. He had smoothly brought the thorny topic of his rare visits to London right back to where they had started and placed it before her again like a reproach, cutting through her attempt to sidetrack him.

'You may know my paternal grandfather,' Winnie remarked abruptly, determined not to fall into the trap of shouldering blame for *his* unavailability to act as a regular father. 'Stamboulas Fotakis. My sisters and I only met him recently.'

Eros's scrutiny was level and cool and uniquely un-informative. 'Who hasn't heard of Bull Fotakis? He's a legend in his own lifetime. Why didn't you mention that connection two years ago?'

Winnie laid down her knife and fork and grasped her glass. 'To be honest, mentioning it never even crossed my mind. At that point I hadn't met him or, indeed, had any contact with him. My father parted with him on bad terms but we don't have any other relatives. My sisters were too young when my parents died to appreciate that we did have a grandparent still living. When I told them about him, they were curious and keen to get to know him,' she said truthfully. 'We are very grateful for the house he allows us to live in.'

The lean, strong lineaments of his darkly handsome face had pulled taut. 'It's my job to be keeping you and my child, *not* your grandfather's,' he declared bluntly.

He would make a terrific poker player, she thought wryly, for he had betrayed no strong reaction to her admission of her grandfather's identity, indeed had merely turned the spotlight straight back to himself.

'That's a rather old-fashioned outlook, if you don't mind me saying,' Winnie dared, pausing to sip her wine and refresh her dry mouth.

'I *do* mind you saying it,' Eros countered, green eyes glittering like shards of sea glass between lush black lashes. 'My son and the mother of my child are solely my responsibility. There's nothing old-fashioned about that conviction. Even the law would back me up. *I* should be maintaining both of you.'

Winnie paled, her appetite dwindling even more beneath the sheer weight of his gaze. He was *so* intense and Teddy emanated that same intensity in whatever he did, suggesting that it was a family trait. 'Let's not argue,' she muttered uneasily, gathering that he was planning to persuade her to accept financial help from him.

'Undoubtedly, we will find much to argue about,' Eros told her, dismaying her with his insouciance at that prospect because Winnie was no fan of conflict, particularly around Teddy. 'Eat up,' he urged lightly.

'Why is it so important for you to be a big part of Teddy's life?' Winnie pressed more boldly.

'My father divorced my mother when I was eight and I barely saw him after that,' Eros admitted, disconcerting her with that admission. 'He remarried and my stepmother had no interest in kids. That marriage broke down, as well. My father lived a chaotic life after he left my mother and he didn't have the time or the energy to continue being a parent. By the time I was eighteen and he was dying, he was a stranger.'

Winnie winced. 'I'm sorry. I had no idea.'

'But perhaps you will now understand why I see my role in Teddy's life as being a role of crucial importance for his benefit as well as mine,' he murmured sibilantly, his eyes veiled, his expression grave.

'Yes,' she conceded reluctantly. 'Yes, I can see that an absent father would leave an impression on you.'

'Fortunately for me, when I was setting up my first business, I met an older man who acted as my mentor and steered me away from more imprudent investments,' he admitted wryly. 'Without Filipe's backing, my first venture would have run aground. He was the father my own father was too busy and selfish to be. I don't ever want my son to view me in that light.'

'Naturally not,' Winnie agreed, pushing her plate away.

Involuntarily, she was entranced by the informative glimpse he was giving her of his younger years because Eros had always been very tight-lipped about his background. He had backed away or ignored intrusive questions and if she persisted, he had shut her down with brooding silence. He had stubbornly resisted her once-overwhelming desire to know everything there was to know about him, but then possibly he had been afraid that he might stumble if he talked too freely and accidentally reveal that he was married. Nothing would ever persuade her that he had kept that dark secret unintentionally.

She watched him eat his dessert with eyes that brimmed with growing amusement and memories. Eros had a very sweet tooth. He only ever indulged it at mealtimes and she knew he worked hard in the gym to stay lean and fit. He ushered her back into the comfortable living area, carrying her wine for her.

Winnie grew apprehensive again, sensing that Eros was about to state his demands with regard to their son. He strolled over to the windows and opened the doors onto the balcony, allowing the sounds of the world outside to intrude. She followed him out onto the roof garden, clutching her glass like a lifeline and settling down in a padded seat while he leant up against the balustrade, unperturbed by the light breeze tousling his black curls.

'I've reached the conclusion that we should get married,' Eros murmured silkily and without the smallest effort to prepare her for that startling announcement. 'It would settle every problem and then we could both support Teddy.'

Winnie froze in shock and stared at him, huge brown eyes welded to his lean dark features and the brilliance of his intense green eyes. Memories unravelled inside her head, tossing her back in time, momentarily burying her in intimate recollections. Eros always looked most alert in the grip of passion and she sensed that for some reason the idea of marrying her fell into that same category of being something he wanted a great deal. Why, she had no idea, but she was convinced that it was truly important to him. Certainly not for sex or for her own self, she gathered, since he had let her walk out of his life two years earlier and made no attempt to see her again. Finding her when she had only moved back in with her sisters wouldn't have been that much of a challenge for Eros. But at best on his terms, she had only been a fling and at worst, a casual mistress, not a woman he either needed or really cared about and he hadn't looked for her.

'Why do you think that we should marry?' she almost croaked, her throat dry with stress and confusion.

'Teddy.' Eros shrugged a shoulder. 'There's no other way to give him everything he needs.'

'That's nonsensical!' Winnie objected boldly. 'Loads of couples live separate lives and share their children perfectly happily.'

'And how are we going to share Teddy when I'm based in Greece?' Eros derided.

'That's not my problem,' Winnie told him thinly. 'Maybe you could start spending more time here?'

'I asked you to marry me,' Eros reminded her very drily. 'Don't you think you should be a little more gracious?'

An angry flush of chagrin mantled Winnie's cheekbones. Suspicion infiltrated her, swiftly followed by comprehension. Hadn't she just told him that one of the richest men in the world was her grandfather? In Eros's eyes, she had evidently become an eligible bride because she was no longer a penniless cook. 'No, I don't,' she snapped back resentfully. 'You certainly wouldn't have asked me to marry you two years ago!'

'Not unless I wished to be tried as a bigamist,' he fielded with sardonic bite. 'I wasn't free to marry then and Teddy didn't exist. But now we have Teddy to consider and I would like my son to carry my name.'

'He's perfectly happy with *my* name!' Winnie parried with spirit. 'You know very well that you don't *really* want to marry me, Eros. I'm just a woman you slept with who became inconveniently pregnant.'

Eros ignored that statement. 'I want my son in my home and I can't have him *without* his mother.'

Winnie lost her angry colour and dropped her gaze, the pain of rejection slicing through her. 'Oh, thank you very much,' she framed curtly.

'*Thee mou...*' Eros growled in sudden seething frustration. 'Of course I want you too!'

Winnie rose from her seat and set her glass down with a sharp little snap. 'Well, maybe...just maybe, Mr Ego, I don't want you!' she slung back.

'It would take me only five minutes to prove otherwise,' Eros bit out in unhesitating challenge. 'Let me list all the many reasons why we should marry.'

'Oh, spare me the lecture, please,' Winnie muttered witheringly. 'Or why not start with the fact that the idea would never have occurred to you if I hadn't told you that I was related to Stam Fotakis?'

Eros stared back at her in shock, noticeably turning pale beneath his bronzed skin, the angles of his high cheekbones starkly prominent and taut. 'You actually think I want you for the money you may one day inherit?' he breathed in incredulous rage.

No, definitely not a gold-digger, Winnie decided, reckoning that no man could fake that amount of disbelief and outrage. It was time for her to bow smartly out of their civil little dinner date before they came to physical blows. 'I think I should go home now.'

A hand closed round hers and jerked her back around before she could walk indoors again. Shimmering sea-glass eyes locked to her flushed face like lasers. 'This has *nothing* to do with you being a member of the Fotakis family. This is between us.'

'Well, no, actually it's not,' Winnie argued, drymouthed with tension. 'This is about you wanting Teddy and having to take me too and apparently make the best of a bad bargain.'

'*Thee mou*... Where are your wits?' Eros growled down at her with lancing impatience. 'I want you.'

'You didn't want me so much that you came looking for me two years ago!' Winnie flared back at him in an outburst that, despite her best efforts, emerged as accusing in tone.

'I was married. Our relationship was wrong. That

is why I didn't seek you out again,' Eros breathed in a fierce undertone. 'I didn't want to be tempted back into our affair.'

'A pity you didn't feel like that when you first met me!' Winnie tossed back at him accusingly. 'We'd all have been a lot happier if you'd done the right thing from the start!'

'But we wouldn't have had Teddy,' Eros pointed out unarguably. 'And now that I have met him, I wouldn't change the past even if I could.'

Alarmingly conscious of the hand closed round her narrow wrist, the fingers lazily stroking her arm as if to soothe her, Winnie dropped her head, knowing that in spite of the unhappiness Eros had caused her, she would never wish that Teddy had not been born because he had brought so much love, light and comfort into the world with him. Eros had broken her heart but Teddy had healed her, giving her the focus and the strength to rebuild her life.

'I *do* want you,' Eros grated, pushing up her chin, green eyes blazing bright as crystal in sunlight, crushing her soft full mouth under his, tasting her with a ravenous hunger that electrified her where she stood.

Her lips parted and something tightened deep down inside her pelvis as his tongue plunged into the sensitive interior of her mouth. A faint tremor racked her, her tongue tangling with his, her body instinctively straining towards him. Her breasts were full and tender and the burst of heat between her thighs compelled her headlong into his lean, muscular length, craving the contact that that overwhelming hunger had unleashed. The hard thrust of his arousal against her stomach was unmistakeable.

The sure, deft exploration of his hands over the swell of her bottom and then up over her tender breasts, cupping, squeezing, partially soothed the raw need traversing her and yet simultaneously drove it even higher. A whimper of choked sound was wrenched from her throat. She was utterly lost in the powerful sensations coursing through her, urging her on and destroying her every defence because what she was feeling was utterly mindless.

'Look at me…' Eros urged, his dark, deep, insistent drawl sending a tingling sensation down her taut spine. 'I want you. You want me. It's very simple.'

With a mighty mental exertion, Winnie forced her body back from the lure of his and stepped back a further pace for good measure. Her cheeks were burning with mortification and inside herself she was beating herself up for revelling in that kiss. 'No, it's not simple.'

'But it could be if we both act like reasonable people,' Eros intoned. 'I don't want to be forced into a custody battle with you.'

Winnie froze. 'C-custody?' she stammered in horror. 'Battle? Why would you do that?'

'Because if you say no to marriage, I have no other option,' Eros replied without hesitation. 'I want Teddy in my life, Winnie, and I won't settle for anything less.'

Winnie was pale and still in retreat from him. 'Obviously I'm willing to agree arrangements for you to see Teddy,' she reminded him. 'I wouldn't have come tonight if I hadn't been willing.'

His lean dark features were shuttered and hard.

'Occasional meetings here in London? That's not enough. I want more.'

Winnie steeled her backbone to stay upright and she stared back at him, struggling to conceal her horror at the pressure he was putting on her. 'You can't have more,' she told him flatly. 'You can see Teddy whenever you're able but I won't agree to anything beyond that.'

His extraordinary eyes narrowed to glittering shards of green. 'Then we go to court and, be warned, I will arm myself with every piece of ammunition that I can lay my hands on to strengthen my own case...'

'You're threatening me,' she whispered shakily, a chill spreading through her body from deep down inside her, surprise and fear assailing her in a sickening wave.

'You're leaving my child in the care of a woman who was accused of working in a brothel, her name and her face plastered all over the gutter press!' Eros condemned.

Winnie, literally, felt faint with shock that he should already be aware of that embarrassing truth. He was talking about her sister Vivi, poor Vivi, whose first job had inadvertently led to her reputation being ruined. Vivi had believed she was working for a modelling agency but in fact it had also been an escort agency, which was raided by the police and closed down for operating illegally as a brothel. Being both photogenic and naive, Vivi had been branded as a prostitute by the tabloids as she was seen fleeing the premises that same day.

'And your other sister, who rarely goes out in public and suffers from panic attacks. How safe is Teddy with *her*?' Eros enquired lethally. 'What if she has one of those attacks when she's supposed to be looking after my son?'

'I hate you!' Winnie ground out rawly, anger splintering through her like a lightning bolt, for there was nothing she would not do to protect her younger sisters. 'How did you find out such confidential details about my family?'

'Such details are available to anyone with the cash to have you investigated,' Eros told her levelly.

'You're hateful,' Winnie told him with a scornful, dismissive jerk of her slight shoulders. 'I wouldn't marry you if you were the last man alive after an apocalypse! I have no respect for a man prepared to sink low enough to threaten my family while he tries to steal my son, and I wouldn't trust a word you said—'

'Teddy is my son and my family too,' Eros reasoned, lifting his strong chin. 'It is right that I do everything within my power—no matter how dirty I have to get—to do what I believe to be best for my son.'

Winnie had already retreated all the way back into the apartment. 'Well, just you keep on telling yourself that if it makes you feel better but, unlike you, I have standards and rules I wouldn't break… No—no matter what the temptation was!'

'You can't expect me to play nice in a situation where you expect me to accept that my own child will be perpetually out of my reach,' Eros argued fiercely, green eyes snapping with intensity.

'When the dust settles,' Winnie responded curtly, 'just remember that *you* are the one who wanted to make this a battle and fight dirty. *I* was the one prepared to be reasonable and fair.'

'Really?' Eros slanted a scornful brow. 'Were you fair when you concealed the birth of my child from me? Were you fair when you denied Teddy his right to have a father? Were you being fair when you suggested that I could *maybe* arrange to be in London more often to see my son?'

Her heart-shaped face tight and pale with angry tension, Winnie screened her eyes and remained silent, reluctant to engage in further argument with him because it wasn't getting her anywhere. No, none of that was fair. But it had not been any fairer on her when Eros had concealed the reality that he was a married man. It was, however, even more unjust when he threatened to expose her sisters in court as unsuitable carers for Teddy because of past experiences that neither young woman could have avoided or controlled.

Zoe had been bullied and abused in foster care. Vivi had been left to take the fall for a wayward young heiress from a powerful family. In short, life *wasn't* fair, Winnie conceded unhappily. She had first learned that when her loving, hardworking parents had died at the hands of a drunk driver and she had learned it afresh when she had trustingly given her heart to a man who had broken it.

But Eros wasn't going to get his hands on Teddy too, she swore vehemently to herself. She would fight back by appealing to her grandfather for help. The older man wanted her to marry some man of *his* choosing, so he would hardly support the idea of her marrying Eros, nor would he want Eros to have more power over his grandson than he had.

Indeed, so worked up was Winnie that she could not even wait until she got home to speak to Stam Fotakis. She phoned her grandfather on the way home and told him that Eros had demanded that she marry him.

'It's past time,' Stam commented, sending her reeling with that unforeseen response. 'But better late than never. He's the boy's father and when you marry him, my grandson gets his name and his birthright. Nevrakis isn't from an old family but he has good social standing and pots of money and at least he's not a spendthrift, womanising idiot like his late father…'

Winnie was gobsmacked by that reply enumerating Eros's advantages and it momentarily silenced her.

'Of course, you'll marry him. Why wouldn't you? He owes you a wedding ring,' her grandfather informed her sternly. 'It'll put *right* everything that was done wrong. Tell me the date and I'll even put in an appearance on the day.'

'I was planning to ask you to get me a good lawyer to fight him,' Winnie almost whispered, already reckoning that that was a hope doomed to failure.

'No, you'll have the benefit of my legal team when you're *divorcing* him,' Stam assured her with calm emphasis.

'But if I don't marry him, he's threatening to fight me for custody of Teddy.'

'But why wouldn't you want to marry him and put everything right?' the older man demanded in what sounded like honest disbelief. 'You said you would marry to please me.'

'Yes…anyone *but* Eros,' Winnie mumbled shakily.

'Nevrakis is my choice but don't worry, you and the little boy will be coming home with me after the wedding,' Stam informed her with immense satisfaction.

No way was he prepared to entrust Nevrakis with his granddaughter and great-grandson's future happiness, Stam reflected grimly. He would care for Winnie and Teddy, and give them the support and security that they needed to flourish. How could he possibly trust Nevrakis to do that for him? Neither respect nor care had featured in Nevrakis's behaviour during his affair with Winnie and Stam had never believed that a leopard could change his spots. Winnie and Teddy would be safer with him. It was his job to ensure that no further harm came to his family, so naturally they would have to leave Nevrakis and come home with Stam after the wedding. That was the only way that he could fully protect the pair of them from further harm.

It occurred to Winnie, even in her shell-shocked state of betrayal, that Eros wouldn't like getting married and then finding that his wife and child had flown, and she tottered into the house, only to be engulfed by her sisters and their frantic questions. For the first time ever, she found herself being less than honest with her siblings. How could she tell them that Eros had threatened to expose their secrets and frailties in an open courtroom? It would seriously distress and frighten them.

My goodness, had her grandfather engineered Eros's sudden reappearance in her life? What else was she to believe? Stam Fotakis was a control freak. He liked to pull strings, enjoyed manipulating people into doing his bidding. Was it her grandfather who had told

Eros about Teddy? She should have worked out that reality from the minute Eros had appeared without warning, she censured herself severely. Where had her wits been when she'd accepted that that was only a coincidence? Combined with her grandfather's admission that he *wanted* her to marry Eros and Eros's sudden proposal, she felt as though she had been dangled like bait on a fish hook. What else didn't she know? What else had either man not told her? It infuriated her to be left in ignorance.

'Why the hell would you want to marry him?' Vivi demanded furiously.

Zoe cleared her throat. 'He's gorgeous, he's rich and she used to love him *and* he's Teddy's father. I disagree but I can understand where Grandad's coming from. Those inducements do provide quite a strong argument.'

'He's a rat!' Vivi objected.

'We also have John and Liz and Grandad's proposition to consider,' Winnie reminded her sisters quietly. 'He wants me to marry Eros and if I don't *have* to live with him, I think, I think I'll do it and that'll be that, *my* duty done.'

'But you *can't*,' Vivi argued emotively, her eyes full of compassion. 'Let's face it, you really don't want to be forced to have anything to do with Eros Nevrakis.'

'No, but beggars don't have choices,' Winnie breathed starkly. 'This is the price for my having made the mistake of having an affair with him. I'll do it for Teddy and for John and Liz.'

But she lay in bed that night thinking about that kiss she had succumbed to, and hating herself like poison for still being that weak and vulnerable with a man who had almost destroyed her two years earlier. She had spent weeks locked in her bedroom before she had found employment, listening to songs of heartbreak on endless replay until the reality that she was pregnant and *had* to make plans for the future had finally pierced her shell of self-pity and made her pick herself up and shake herself down again.

A marriage that was only a marriage on paper to satisfy her grandfather would suit her to perfection. Eros wouldn't be able to threaten her or her sisters with her grandfather behind her as support, she told herself urgently. All she had to do was play along, let the arrangements take their course and wait for Eros to get stung in the tail by Stam Fotakis just as she and her sisters had been. Eros would not get her as a wife and he would not get Teddy either and, bearing in mind the way he had threatened her and Vivi *and* Zoe, that was exactly what he deserved… *Wasn't it?*

She had to look after Vivi and Zoe. Hadn't that always been her role as big sister? Yet her sisters had been separated from her as children and she had not been able to prevent them from suffering through unhappy and challenging experiences in foster care. That sad failure still on her conscience, Winnie knew that there was nothing she wouldn't do to protect her sisters' well-being now that they were adults.

And naturally she wanted nothing more to do with Eros, naturally she didn't want to live with the man! After all, he had pulled the wool over her eyes before and hurt her terribly. Obviously, she didn't want to give him another opportunity! Eros was her fatal flaw, her weakness. It was a shameful truth but there it was. She had no common sense around him and her defences were paper-thin. If she didn't guard herself, she would get hurt again and spending too much time exposed to Eros was an inexorable way of putting herself in jeopardy. She would just be an accident waiting to happen, she thought with a shiver of foreboding.

CHAPTER FIVE

WINNIE WOULD HAVE been surprised to appreciate that her future husband on paper only was well aware of the size and calibre of the odds stacked up against him. Eros was shrewd and he already knew that his future grandfather-in-law loathed him for the sin of turning *his* granddaughter into an unmarried mother. Forewarned was forearmed as far as Eros was concerned and no sooner had Eros received a cool little phone call from Winnie informing him that she had thought the situation over and that she *would* marry him than he began putting in place the kind of security he had never dreamt he would have to hire.

Nevertheless, Stamboulas Fotakis was devious, and Eros had no intention of letting the older man control or manipulate him. Stam would have to be satisfied with having shocked Eros with the news that he was a father at their first meeting, for it was the only winning move he would get to make in the game unfolding. Eros would not allow either his wife or his child to be damaged by the conflict between himself and Teddy's great-grandfather. Stam would have to wise up and accept the status quo, Eros reflected grimly, determined to protect his future family from every malign influence, including that of an old man who was bitter and unforgiving.

While Eros was plotting with the same dexterity that his future grandfather-in-law excelled at, Winnie was shyly admitting that she was about to marry Teddy's father to John and Liz Brooke and receiving their entirely innocent approval and congratulations, for she had never told them that Eros had been a married man at the time of her son's conception. Vivi rolled her eyes in sympathy for that concealment of the unlovely truth and sat chatting to one of the teenage foster kids at the kitchen table while Zoe, as usual, busied herself round the kitchen as a background girl, hoping to deflect any interest anyone might have in her.

'I know it may seem old-fashioned for you young parents to get married these days but I'm very pleased,' Liz confided, squeezing Winnie's small hand, her plump face wreathed in a bright smile of pleasure. 'Marriage seems more secure to my generation. I wasn't criticising.'

'No, I know you weren't.' Winnie gave the older woman a hug while John, a quiet man at the best of times, beamed approval and mentioned that it would do Teddy good to have a father around.

The very first pang of guilt pierced Winnie at that moment because she knew she would be leaving Eros straight after the wedding to return to her grandfather's house. Teddy *wasn't* going to have a father around. Instead he would only enjoy occasional visits from him. Unfortunately for her, it went against her inherently honest nature to deceive anyone, *even* Eros. She knew that Eros was expecting her to stay with him, to act as a wife and a mother by his side, and the awareness of that lowering fact prevented her from experiencing even an ounce of satisfaction over the reality that she would be spiking Eros's big guns and threats with superior power.

Now, however, Winnie was finally looking beneath those superficial reactions and admitting a less welcome truth to herself. Frankly, she was terrified of the mere prospect of having to live with Eros, she admitted guiltily. In such a position she would end up letting her guard slip and she would let him hurt her all over again. In reality she was being a total coward about Eros because she was struggling to keep everyone else happy. She wanted to please her grandfather, save John and Liz and protect her siblings, and she could see no way other than marrying Eros to achieve those goals. What other option did she have?

So, of course, she was going to have to leave Eros after the wedding. That would make her grandfather and her sisters happy and it would also ensure that she didn't need to risk herself in Eros's radius again. It wouldn't make Eros happy, she acknowledged ruefully, but since she couldn't credit that he really wanted to marry her, she was convinced that he would soon see the benefits of almost immediately regaining his freedom.

Her grandfather phoned her when she returned home, telling her with positive good cheer that he had deposited sufficient funds in her bank account to cover what he called 'wedding fripperies.' 'All you have to do is buy your and your sisters' dresses. I will take care of everything else.'

In that assumption, however, Stamboulas Fotakis discovered himself to be sadly mistaken because Winnie's future husband informed him that the ceremony of marriage *had* to take place on the island of Trilis because it had been where his ancestors had married. Stam had never viewed Nevrakis as a sentimental man but on that one point the younger man was stubbornly immovable, and Stam knew that he could hardly refuse his future grandson-in-law the right to use the island and the house he had already promised him because it would be a sign of bad faith. Exasperated, Winnie's grandfather found himself having to adjust his plans to fit someone else's and it had been a very long time since Stam had suffered through that experience and bitten his tongue.

Perfectly conscious that he was creating waves, Eros flew out to Greece and organised a helicopter to take him out to the private island where no Nevrakis of his acquaintance had set foot in over thirty years. Even when his parents had still been together they had not visited the island because his father had very much preferred city life. The house had been renovated in the eighties, presumably sometime after Winnie's grandfather had acquired ownership, and since then it had been maintained in pristine condition, so, on that score, Eros had no complaints. The property was fully fit for occupation and for wedding catering.

Eros stood on the cliff gazing out to sea, enjoying the sunlight slowly tapering into a peach-coloured sunset while he thought with satisfaction about showing that same view to his son and to his wife. He was certain that Winnie had absolutely no idea of her grandfather's intention of stealing her and Teddy back on their wedding day. Unfortunately for Fotakis, the minute he had gone into a rant at their first meeting, insisting that neither Winnie nor Teddy actually *needed* Eros in their lives, Eros had smelled a rat and acted accordingly.

Where Winnie was concerned, however, he was convinced that she did not have a single sly, cheating bone in her little curvy body. That was, after all, what had first attracted him to her, he freely acknowledged.

He could read her expressive face like a picture book. She scored low in the feminine guile and calculation stakes and she didn't play power games like her grandfather or like many of the women Eros had met in his thirty years. No, what you saw was what you got with Winnie, unlike her grandfather, prepared to pressure a bridegroom into a wedding that he had no intention of allowing to become a marriage. Stam, however, was known for having done something similar with his eldest son, refusing to accept the wife his son had chosen and eventually becoming estranged from his own flesh and blood over his choice of partner. It was a track record that telegraphed a loud warning to Eros that he was dealing with a man who only ever paid heed to his own feelings and beliefs. He had displayed sufficient antipathy for Eros to recognise that the older man would not willingly accept him as a member of his family circle.

Winnie and her sisters went shopping. Neither Vivi nor Zoe paid the smallest heed to Winnie's plea to keep expenses to the minimum. In fact even Zoe laughed at that suggestion, reminding Winnie that it was to be a society wedding and the last thing Stam Fotakis would want was his grandchild dressed like a bargain-basement bride. Even Winnie, nonetheless,

was overwhelmed by the whole bridal-salon experience and the kind of feminine extras that there had
never before been room for in her budget.

Eros phoned her around noon and Zoe answered
Winnie's phone because Winnie was being eased into
a foaming mass of lace by two assistants.

'It's Eros…' she said, extending the phone once
Winnie had emerged again.

'Lunch?' Eros enquired.

'Er…' Tumbled and flushed, Winnie stared at herself in the full-length mirror and knew she still hadn't
found the right dress because it was too fussy and
frilly for her taste. 'I'm trying on wedding stuff,' she
muttered. 'Today's not good.'

'Dinner tonight, then,' Eros decided arrogantly.

'No, I—' Winnie began, keen to avoid him as much
as was humanly possible.

'I haven't seen you since you agreed to marry me,'
Eros reminded her darkly. 'Is there a reason for that?'

Something like panic infiltrated Winnie and she
dragged in a stark breath, reminding herself that she
had to play along and that avoiding him altogether
wasn't an option. 'No, tonight will do fine. What
time?'

Zoe dropped the phone back into Winnie's bag and
looked at her expectantly.

'Dinner tonight,' she muttered in explanation.

'Put on your acting shoes,' Vivi advised. 'Of
course, he's going to expect to see you and discuss
arrangements and the like.'

'I suppose,' Winnie mumbled grudgingly.

'Not that dress. Makes you look like a dumpy version of a ballerina doll,' Vivi whispered, making her older sister loose an involuntary giggle.

Even so, Winnie found it a challenge to regain her former light-hearted mood and reminded herself that it scarcely mattered what she wore to a fake wedding. But she chose a gown she liked, a sleek elegant dress that did wonders for her small curvy figure, reasoning that she needed to look her best with so many guests being invited by her grandfather and Eros.

She borrowed a dress and shoes from Zoe to wear that evening. Her own wardrobe was small and contained few smart outfits. The dress was black and unremarkable in every way, which suited her attitude to dining out with Eros.

'It's a funeral dress,' Vivi scolded. 'It's long and it's shapeless—'

'And it will do fine,' Winnie cut in impatiently.

'Don't mind me,' Vivi said drily. 'But you're supposed to be playing the happy bride-to-be.'

'I'm not happy about any of this,' Winnie admitted ruefully.

'That man is about to get exactly what he deserves!' Vivi proclaimed vengefully.

'Two wrongs don't make a right,' Zoe reasoned with a wince, squeezing Winnie's hand in sympathy. 'Maybe you'll decide to give him another chance... Who knows?'

'Get a life, Zoe!' Vivi exclaimed. 'Eros wants his son, *not* Winnie.'

Winnie's slight shoulders hunched and colour faded from her cheeks. That even her sisters saw that so clearly mortified her.

'I'm sorry,' Vivi muttered ruefully to her older sister. 'But what else are we supposed to think? He's divorced but he didn't come looking for you even when he was free, *did he*?'

'No,' Winnie conceded, sucking in a steadying breath when faced with that truth again, hating herself for squirming at the reminder. What did it matter with only a fake wedding ahead of her? What did *any* of it matter now? She had loved him but *he* hadn't loved her, the oldest story of heartbreak in the world and one of the most common, she told herself impatiently.

'Maybe he felt guilty too,' Zoe muttered. 'Maybe he didn't feel entitled to be happy after his divorce.'

'Oh…*you*!' Vivi scolded her optimistic kid sister. 'You'd find a bright side to any catastrophe!'

None of those somewhat distressing conversations put Winnie in the mood to see Eros again. She reckoned she was oversensitive to the pain that Eros had caused her and equally thin-skinned when it came to that past being discussed because he had been a subject her siblings had staunchly avoided during the period when she was nursing a broken heart. Fortunately, she had moved on, got over him, *completely* got over him, she reminded herself doggedly.

It didn't help to walk out to the limousine that was there to collect her and see Eros standing beside the open passenger door in dialogue with a man who was unmistakeably one of her grandfather's security team. One glance at that classic bronzed profile and the sheer height and elegance of him in a formal dinner jacket and narrow black trousers and she was challenged to even swallow.

Her heart started thumping very fast inside her, a memory stirring of Eros arriving late at the country house one Friday evening, having attended a banking dinner he couldn't avoid. Heat washed up over her dismayed face and she ducked past Eros and darted straight into the limo, only unfortunately nothing could drown out her recollection of having had mad passionate sex on the sofa in the drawing room with him that night. She had been shocked by how desperate he had seemed for her and then foolishly pleased, deeming it a sign of deeper attachment. She hated looking back with hindsight, seeing how stupid she had been, continually mistaking sex for love.

'What's wrong?' Eros asked, studying her rigidity.

'Nothing's wrong!' Winnie proclaimed, dry-mouthed with tension, thinking wildly of an excuse to explain her discomfiture. 'It's all the wedding stuff… such a fuss. I can't think straight.'

'I thought all women enjoyed that sort of thing,' Eros admitted.

'Me…not so much,' she said truthfully, even knowing that once, had it been a real, *proper* wedding backed by love and need, she would have been overjoyed to be marrying him. That time was past, gone, she recalled, furious with herself for even *thinking* along those lines.

'It won't last long,' Eros said soothingly, trying not to remember the planning insanity of his first wedding. 'We're getting married the middle of next week on Trilis.'

'Trilis? Where's that?'

'A private island in Greece where the Nevrakis family started out as olive farmers and also ran a small hotel.'

'I assumed I'd be getting married at Grandad's house.'

'My family always get married on the island,' Eros countered smoothly.

Winnie swallowed hard on the objections brimming on her lips, wondering how much harder it would be to leave an island after the public wedding show was over. She had no doubt that her grandfather had already factored in that added difficulty to his plans because he was not a man to leave anything undone. But guilt gnawed at Winnie's conscience because Eros was taking the wedding as seriously as though he were a real bridegroom…

My family always get married on the island.

She wondered if he had married his first wife there and then punished herself for that inappropriate piece of curiosity by reminding herself of how he had threatened to harm her entirely innocent sisters. Eros Nevrakis did not deserve her guilt, she told herself urgently. He was as ruthless as a killing machine in shark form, taking what he wanted without care for what it might cost someone else.

Stam Fotakis had already helped her and her sisters a great deal and she owed the older man not just gratitude but loyalty, she reminded herself firmly. She had to choose sides, there was no other option and every instinct warned her to choose her family and put them first. Perhaps then she could pursue her dream of establishing a closer relationship with her grandad.

Eros took her, not to his apartment, which relieved her, but to an exclusive club where they were seated in a very private velvet-lined booth that was screened-off from the crowd. She had noticed the attention he received on arrival, the subtle straightening, turning of heads that all signalled the arrival of an envied, highly attractive and very wealthy alpha male. Female heads turned even faster and lingered on Eros, glancing at her, brows lifting because she didn't look glamorous enough to fit the expected mould. People were probably wondering if she was a niece or the daughter of a friend or even an employee.

After what had felt like a very public entrance, the booth felt *too* cosy and *he* felt too close, her spine tingling at the dark timbre of his accented drawl, gooseflesh rippling across her skin when he carelessly brushed her hand with his as he passed her the menu. Iridescent sea-glass eyes enhanced by lush black lashes surveyed her levelly from across the table, his lean, dark, classically handsome features so strikingly flawless that, for a split second, she couldn't rip her attention from his spectacular bone structure.

His obvious relaxation taunted her simmering tension. Winnie could feel every breath she drew along with the wanton tightening of her nipples and the lick of pulsing heat curling between her thighs. It was unnerving that he could still awaken those responses in her treacherous body and it made her hate him more than ever for destroying the idealistic, romantic innocence that had been hers before she met him.

'You're incredibly quiet tonight,' Eros remarked lazily. 'I used to like that about you.'

'But a quiet woman is less of a challenge.'

'By the time I met you I had had enough of being challenged,' Eros admitted, lashes dipping, evading her scrutiny as if he already feared that he had revealed too much.

Challenged by his wife? Possibly Tasha had discovered his infidelity, although she had not appeared remotely suspicious of Winnie when she'd arrived at the country house and Winnie had behaved like an employee for Tasha's benefit for the first time in weeks. She had made a meal for his wife and it had hurt her pride to play the servant, driving home the lesson of how very foolish she had been to get into bed with a man whom she knew next to nothing about. It hadn't helped either to see a wife very much more beautiful than she was herself. Tasha was a sleek, shapely blonde with lively blue eyes and a pronounced air of energy, chattering into her phone constantly to rap out instructions to an employee and answer queries in a variety of languages. Beautiful, accomplished and confident, everything Winnie was not.

Winnie had packed and left that house and her job that same day, filled with shame and regret. Memories could be so cruel, she registered abruptly, realising that she had carried that demeaning sense of being less and second best ever since that humiliating day.

'We will make this marriage work,' Eros told her arrogantly over the first course of the meal. 'It *has* to work for Teddy.'

Chilled inside by that insistent statement, Winnie toyed with her food, thinking about Teddy, who was perfectly happy with his mother and his aunts. *But for how long will that phase of his childhood last?* a little voice prompted her for the first time. Children grew up fast and developed more complex needs.

Eros would still have visiting rights though, and Teddy would learn to value his father and divide his loyalties as all children of parents who lived apart had to do. He would be fine, absolutely fine, she told herself bracingly.

'This is very important to me,' Eros intoned in the smouldering silence. 'Why do I get the impression that you're not even listening?'

Winnie faked a yawn with her hand. 'I'm sorry. I'm very tired.'

It would be the first time a woman had fallen asleep on him, Eros reflected grimly, exasperated by her silence, her seeming refusal to make the smallest effort. What was the matter with her? This was *not* Winnie as he recalled her, but then she had walked out on him, become a mother alone, struggled to survive and the experience was bound to have changed her. Yet if they were to stay together, they had to find a bridge between the past and the present. Sex? He knew he couldn't wait to have her under him again, over him, in front of him…just about any way he could have her.

No, *that* hadn't changed, he acknowledged reluctantly, that raw driving hunger to possess that she incited and which he had never understood or accepted. It had hurt his pride, it had exasperated him with *her*, with *himself* because he distrusted anything he couldn't control and he *hadn't* been able to control the fierce need she provoked. Yet he had repeatedly tried to explain it to himself, talk himself out of those urges, constantly challenging himself with self-denial while he fought to get his discipline back.

Unarguably, however, the truth remained that Win-

nie sat there in an ugly cloaking black dress that revealed nothing of her very sensual curves and with
only the smallest encouragement he would *still* have
spread her across the table and fallen on her like a
sex-starved animal.

CHAPTER SIX

'YOU LOOK AMAZING!' Vivi sighed as Winnie performed a twirl in front of the built-in cheval mirror on the wall of the luxury cabin.

It was a beautiful dress, fashioned of Venice lace and organza, cut to fit Winnie's shapely figure like a glove. An enticing row of pearl buttons ran down her spine to her hip. The sweetheart neckline emphasised her sister's curves while the mermaid style flared out from her knees with very real elegance and not with the kind of fullness of fabric that would have accentuated Winnie's diminutive height.

'We all do but, like all brides, Winnie takes the crown,' Zoe murmured fondly. 'I feel like pinching myself to see if this is real. Here we are on a fabulous yacht, cruising to our sister's wedding on a private island… It's like a dream or like suddenly being plunged into a movie.'

'I wonder if you'll feel quite so chirpy when it's *your* wedding day,' Vivi remarked with an edge of warning.

'But we don't have to worry about that. Grandad is going to whisk us all away again before we need to worry about consequences.' Zoe's bright confidence in Stamboulas Fotakis's ability to work miracles was unconcealed. 'Eros wanted to transport all of us to the island because he made the island a no-fly zone to keep the paparazzi from buzzing the wedding from above,' she reminded her siblings. 'And Grandad got around that change of plan by borrowing a pal's massive yacht for the occasion.'

'Yes, Grandad's pretty wily,' Winnie agreed, still studying her reflection, her heart beating so fast with nerves it felt as though it were thumping through her entire body like a ticking time bomb on countdown.

'Pittee,' Teddy told her, yanking on her gown for attention.

'*Pretty?* That's a new word. Wonder where he picked up that one,' Vivi commented, snatching her nephew up into a hug. 'No, you're not allowed to touch Mama's dress with those little hands, but I'm wearing black, so you can do all the grabbing you want round Aunt Zoe and me!'

Teddy giggled with delight as Vivi turned him upside down, swung him round and dumped him on the massive bed for a spot of tickling and the sort of rough play he adored. Winnie paced anxiously. Eros had visited them in London twice to see Teddy but Winnie hadn't seen him since that tense and disturbing evening meal they had shared. She had been at work, for, although her grandfather and Eros had both scoffed at the idea of such dutiful behaviour, Winnie had worked out her notice, giving the restaurant owner time to find and engage her replacement.

The yacht was slowing down radically to enter the harbour and dock. When they disembarked they were heading straight to the church before moving up to the

Nevrakis house on the hill for the reception. When it came to making the return trip to Athens, both Winnie and her sisters already had their instructions. All they had to do was slip away and walk back down to the little harbour, where the yacht would await their arrival. Teddy would be brought there in a separate manoeuvre. 'Why not leave straight after the church ceremony?' she had asked her grandfather. 'Surely that would be easier.'

His answer had disturbed her.

'I want my guests and his to see Nevrakis dance to my tune and then become the abandoned bridegroom on his wedding day,' Stamboulas Fotakis had assured her with satisfaction.

Winnie had paled and instantly felt queasy because, strange as it might seem, that aspect of her grandfather's plans hadn't occurred to her. Worrying about how she and her son might get away again had consumed her and she had never paused to stop and think about what her unexpected vanishing act would actually mean to Eros or how it would affect him, beyond angering him, of course. And somehow, she didn't know why, the concept of humiliating Eros in front of a crowd made her feel quite sick and ashamed. That kind of revenge wasn't her style even if it was her aggressive grandad's. She didn't want to *hurt* Eros because he was her son's father and insulting and injuring him could only damage an already strained relationship. Why hadn't she thought of that issue sooner? Now it was too late, she conceded unhappily, hurriedly reminding herself of how ruthless Eros had been when he'd threatened her vulnerable sisters. Eros could look after himself perfectly well, she reasoned feverishly.

He wouldn't walk away from Teddy but he would realise he had lost any power over her and her siblings. That was how it *had* to be. She didn't have a choice just as her sisters didn't have a choice. This was the price of saving the roof over their foster parents' heads. Goodness knew, after all the good John and Liz had done for Winnie, Vivi and Zoe and so many other troubled and unhappy teenagers, the older couple deserved the sisters' protection and the security of no longer having to fear the loss of their home. Even so, she was sad that she was getting married without the older couple's presence and knew they had been disappointed. Unfortunately, not only would it have been very hard for either John or Liz to leave their foster children for a couple of days with their busy schedule, but also she couldn't possibly tell them the truth, that it *wasn't* a real or normal wedding. Saving John and Liz had entailed a lot of fibs and half-truths that still sat on Winnie's conscience like lead weights.

'It's time.' Their grandfather lodged in the doorway, ultrasmart in his tailored morning suit and cravat. 'You look delightful, Winnie. Nevrakis will be disappointed when he realises that he doesn't get to keep you or my great-grandson.'

Oxygen rattled in Winnie's tight throat. 'Eros is tough. He'll get over it,' she said flatly, thinking of the man who had moved on untouched by their broken relationship and the hurt inflicted on her. 'He's one of life's survivors.'

'As are you,' Vivi reminded her as they walked out onto the deck and began the delicate operation of getting the bride off the yacht without brushing her gown against anything that could mark its pristine ivory threaded with gold folds.

Two classic cars bedecked with flowers awaited them at the harbour and a sizeable crowd provided an audience. Winnie accompanied her grandfather into the first, her sisters and her son entered the second. Her chest tight as a drum with tension, she struggled to smile like a bride when her grandfather urged her. Every floral tribute she saw, every well-wisher reminded her that she was taking part in an unsavoury plan. The cars ferried them only a couple of hundred yards to a picturesque little stone church overlooking the sea with a little village full of white-painted houses climbing the hill behind it.

'There won't be many witnesses to the ceremony in a place this small,' Stam Fotakis lamented at her side, but his granddaughter was relieved by the same fact.

John and Liz took their foster kids to church but pressured no one who preferred not to go. Winnie discovered a new fear bubbling up in her chest, the fear that she was enacting a heavenly punishable offence in undergoing a wedding ceremony without the intent of following through. A civil ceremony would have been preferable, she brooded uncomfortably. A squad of people waited outside the church to witness the bride's arrival, calling out greetings and good wishes. With her sisters beside her, however, she felt stronger and less oversensitive.

Inside the dim old church with its candles, painted murals of the saints and beautiful white floral displays, her focus leapt straight to the man at the foot of the aisle. Eros turned round, his classic bronzed profile alert to her arrival. Beneath her gown, she could feel her entire body heat and flush with awareness. His brilliant green eyes were gilded in the candlelit interior and her mouth ran dry. Even the morning suit that made her grandad look a little rotund and small could only embellish Eros's all-male beauty, showcasing every lithe athletic inch of his broad-shouldered, lean-hipped, long-legged length.

'Gorgeous dress,' he muttered half under his breath as they both turned to face the Greek Orthodox priest.

Finding her breath in the ritual that followed, bearing up to the crushing solemnity of the occasion in which she understood only sporadic words were a challenge for her. Eros slid the ring, an elaborate engraved platinum circle, onto her finger and she breathed again because it was done. She was the wife of the man she had once loved to the edge of insanity and her eyes stung with a sudden rush of moisture because the wounding memories seemed very close to the surface at that moment and she welcomed those thoughts, needing the armour of her hatred for him to defend her from other feelings and sensations.

'Papa!' Teddy shook free of Zoe's hand and pounced on Eros as they moved down the aisle again.

That word, that very designation, being openly awarded to Eros shook Winnie up. When had *that* started? Why had nobody warned her? Of course, it was reality, she reminded herself soothingly, and not all the wishing in the world could change it. Even before the wedding she had been tied for life by her son to a man she despised. An unscrupulous guy without principles, who took what he wanted when he wanted without regard for the consequences to anyone else.

For all she knew, she brooded, his wife had divorced him for his infidelity and if he hadn't been faithful to Tasha, he wouldn't be planning to be any more faithful to his second wife, for cheaters were known to repeat their habits.

Those grim ruminations rebuilt her defences and bolstered her strength to face the walkout she had to stage. Eros might be Teddy's *papa* but he was *not* a nice guy, not a man in need of her sympathy or guilty conscience, she told herself urgently.

While unaware of his bride's dark thoughts, Eros, nonetheless, read her tension and assumed it was caused by her shy dislike of being the centre of attention. That was so very different from his first wedding that there was no comparison to be made and he was relieved by that acknowledgement. He had never seen the point of bestowing blame on either himself or Tasha for a marriage breakdown that had seemed inevitable to him from the very first day of their convenient arrangement.

He had done his best to uphold their paper marriage. He had done his duty for years, struggling not to be selfish, struggling to be fair and honourable even when it had become an almighty challenge and their marriage had been in name only. That he had finally failed was something he no longer held against himself as he had once done. Nobody was perfect, neither him nor anyone else. All that troubled him in the present was that Winnie had somehow ended up paying the ultimate cost for his failure. For that same reason he could tolerate Stam Fotakis's loathing with calm control because, in the old man's shoes, he knew that he might well have felt the same.

Winnie settled back into the classic car while Teddy, who complained hugely, was strapped into a car seat. 'You thought of everything,' she remarked in surprise at the presence of the seat.

'Obviously we would want Teddy with us,' Eros parried.

As the car climbed the steep driveway that wound up past the little village, Winnie craned her neck, curious to see the Nevrakis home. 'For how long have your family lived here?'

Eros saw no reason to tell Winnie that he had only reclaimed the island by marrying her. What would be the point? It would only make her more suspicious than ever about his motives, he reasoned impatiently. In time she would learn that fact and he would deal with it then.

'The first house was a farmhouse owned by my great-grandfather, the olive farmer, who turned it into a small hotel. My grandfather razed that building to the ground and rebuilt and in due course, when he died, my father did the same even though he had no intention of ever making this his permanent home.'

Winnie's brows lifted in bewilderment. 'No intention? Then why on earth would he—'

'I think a weird mixture of family pride and his innate streak of extravagance persuaded him into wasting his inheritance here even though he found island life boring. Although Trilis is quite a reasonable size, it couldn't possibly offer him the social life he enjoyed in Athens.'

'So, you didn't grow up here on the island?' Winnie asked, determined to satisfy her curiosity now that Eros was finally answering her questions.

'No, I grew up in an Athens apartment, almost exclusively with my mother. She's gone now too,' Eros confided flatly. 'So are my grandparents on both sides. There is only me and Teddy and now you in the Nevrakis family. There are a few distant cousins attending the reception but no close relations. I'm surprised you didn't invite your foster parents.'

Winnie went pink and trotted out her excuses about how difficult it was for either John or Liz to leave home even for a short time. 'As foster carers they have constant meetings with social workers, schools, birth parents.'

An ebony brow slanted up. 'Still, you were very fond of them as I recall and I'm sure they would've made a special effort.'

'I didn't want to put them under that pressure,' Winnie muttered in desperation. 'John's health can be dicey.'

It was a relief to step out into the sunlight again and see her sisters emerging from the car behind. They all stared at the house, which she thought was stupendously large for a property in which Eros's father had apparently not planned to live. Extravagant, Eros had labelled his father, and Winnie was inclined to agree as they entered a grand marble-floored hall to be greeted by staff offering drinks on silver trays.

Her grandfather strolled to her side. 'It is done,' he pronounced with satisfaction. 'The ring you deserve is on your finger now.'

Winnie looked down at her finger uncomfortably just as Eros stretched out a hand to her, obviously keen to introduce her to some of the guests arriving. The next hour and more passed in a whirl of introductions and harmless chatter, by which time Teddy was flagging, hungry and overtired.

'I took the liberty of bringing in a nanny for the day,' Eros murmured, disconcerting his bride. 'Teddy can have an early lunch and a nap to recoup his energies while the adults celebrate.'

Winnie could not argue with such a sensible suggestion and the warm, friendly woman who approached with a ready smile was very different from the coldly efficient carer Eros had hired in London for the zoo trip. Agathe swiftly gained her son's trust and, with his aunt Zoe's comforting presence secured as well, Teddy had no objection to being carried off upstairs.

In the doorway of a vast pillared ballroom full of tables and chairs for the reception, Winnie paused and swallowed her surprise. 'I expected a canvas marquee in the garden,' she admitted.

'No, my father covered even the most remote possibilities when he built this place,' Eros confided with rueful amusement. 'And perhaps you can also see why he eventually ended up bankrupt.'

As they were escorted to the top table, Winnie scanned the fabulous view of the sea and the island from the house's splendid clifftop location. A wall of glass ran down one side of the ballroom, multiple doors opening out onto a furnished terrace. Her curious gaze lingered on the borrowed yacht dominating the little harbour and she paled, losing her focus again. Soon, *soon*, she reminded herself, she would be sailing away with Teddy and her sisters and this nightmare wedding would simply be like something from a bad dream that she would never have to think about again.

Long brown fingers feathered down her rigid spine and her entire body tingled, locked into sudden instinctive craving. She glanced up at Eros from beneath her feathery lashes and, with a husky growl deep in his throat, he reached for her, taking her so much by surprise that she simply froze, locked into place like a statue.

His firm, yet soft lips forced hers apart and his tongue delved and she shook and shivered as a gathering storm of sensation bombarded her. In all her life she had never wanted anything as much as she wanted Eros at that moment. A piercing dart of feverish longing shot from low in her body, rousing sweet tingling heat, clenching the muscles in her pelvis so tight she gasped, even more painfully aware of the response between her thighs.

'*Thee mou*... I want you,' Eros muttered roughly into her hair as he jerked his mouth off hers again as though he had been burned.

And in a way, they had *both* been burned, Winnie acknowledged feverishly, conscious of the tiny tremors racking the lean, powerful body melded to hers and the thrusting proof of his arousal. She still wanted him; it made her hate herself but Winnie had never been the sort to deny an obvious truth. The same passionate attraction that had blindsided them the first time around hadn't died and hadn't been conquered by common sense or pride or even guilt. She was ashamed of it, ashamed of the shake in her hand as she used the table to steady herself on locked knees that still trembled. It was a moment when she was almost grateful for the reminder of how much power Eros could still have over her and how very dangerous he could be to her peace of mind. *Been there, done that, got Teddy... Never again*, she told herself with finality.

'Your nerves are showing,' Vivi whispered under cover of releasing her sister's gown from where it had caught on her high-heeled sandal.

Winnie compressed her lips. 'I'm no good at faking it,' she admitted.

'Good news on my wedding night,' Eros murmured sibilantly, lean hands splaying possessively across her hips from behind, the combination of both voice and touch very nearly inducing a panic attack in Winnie as her triangular face flared hotter than hellfire.

Winnie barely touched the meal set in front of her. She nudged stuff round the plate, trying to conceal her lack of appetite. She listened to the world-famous harpist playing atmospheric Greek folk songs, tapped her foot with determination when livelier music followed and only tensed when her grandfather caught her eye with a faint tilt of his chin. Almost as quickly her sisters were approaching her, talking about needing to straighten her hair and, without hesitation, she slid out of her seat and followed them out of the reception to the palatial cloakroom.

'There's a car waiting at the back entrance. All you have to do is walk out across the courtyard garden,' Vivi began tautly.

'I can't leave without Teddy!' Winnie gasped in consternation.

'Grandad's men are fetching Teddy,' Zoe told her soothingly. 'We only have to get down to the harbour.'

Winnie didn't feel comfortable walking out of a house where her son slept upstairs, unaware of his family's departure but her sisters were as nervous as she was, and nerves made the two younger women assertive, thrusting her through the French windows into the fresh air, both of them catching onto her wrists, urging her in the right direction, giving her no chance to change her mind.

'This doesn't feel right,' she protested in the courtyard garden, a sunny tranquil space that mocked the drama being enacted.

'We need to get out of here...*fast*!' Vivi exclaimed impatiently, pushing her sister through the gate into the rear lane where an SUV idled its engine in readiness.

Having been alerted by the security team he had engaged, Eros observed their departure from the same rear hallway. A kind of white-hot rage unlike anything he had ever felt before surged through him when he saw Winnie pass through the last barrier in the direction of the waiting car.

His wife walking out on him.

Nothing could've prepared him for that view. Nothing until that instant could've persuaded him that Winnie would do anything so dishonest as to enter a church with him, speak marital vows and then take off like a bat out of hell afterwards. But there she was, the living proof of his delusional belief that she was *different* from the other women he had known. And the truth was that she wasn't one bit different from her predecessors, who had convinced him that women were in no way the more delicate, honest and reliable sex, he derided grimly. In fact, she was one of the worst deceivers and the biggest fraud.

Winnie was shaking like a leaf by the time she

finally boarded the yacht, perspiration marking her brow, eyes wide with apprehension, her heart pounding fit to burst. Her grandfather's cheerful greeting made her turn angrily away. 'Teddy?' she began anxiously.

'Teddy will be here in approximately thirty seconds,' Stamboulas Fotakis assured her confidently.

But the car that drove down to the harbour was not the one the older man was apparently expecting. It was a sports car, with a child seat fitted, driven by Eros. He climbed out, whisked his sobbing son from the seat into his arms and lounged back against the bonnet of the sports car cradling the little boy with supreme cool.

'Oh, dear heaven…' Winnie whispered, dry-mouthed. 'Eros *knows*.'

Her grandfather said something very rude in Greek about Eros's ancestors.

'I can't leave,' Winnie breathed shakily. 'There's no way I can leave Teddy here.'

'Don't be ridiculous. We'll come back for him. Nevrakis can't guard him 24/7,' Stam Fotakis growled. 'Nor can he keep him from his mother.'

But Winnie was unconvinced. She studied Eros, the man she had married mere hours earlier. She didn't need to speak to him to understand exactly what he was telling her. His message was etched in the slumberous relaxation of his lean, powerful physique as he leant back against the car and in the steady direction of his gaze. He had Teddy, and in their son he held *all* the cards that could possibly be played.

'Winnie…' Her grandfather rested a heavy hand on her rigid shoulder. 'Listen to me.'

'No,' she said curtly. 'Listening to you is where I went wrong. If I don't go back, Eros will fight tooth and nail to keep Teddy and I will *not* risk losing my son.'

'I won't let him do that.'

'He's already outwitted you and you hate him. I can't trust your promises when it comes to the well-being of the most important person in my life,' Winnie muttered shakily, stepping back from her siblings' attempts to offer her sympathy. 'I'm going back.'

'But you *can't*!' Vivi exclaimed. 'You didn't sign up for that!'

'Winnie *has* to go back for Teddy. What else can she do now?' Zoe groaned.

Winnie watched Eros straighten as she climbed back down into the tender that would whisk her back to shore. She watched him smile with satisfaction, the fierce gratified smile of a man who knew he had won the most important game he would ever play. It was a game very much centred on family.

She had played the same game and lost, alongside her grandfather, she acknowledged between gritted teeth, ready to spontaneously combust with anger, resentment and anxiety about the kind of welcome that awaited her on shore.

CHAPTER SEVEN

ANOTHER CAR DREW up at the harbour and Winnie waited while the car seat was installed, freezing into stillness as Eros approached her and extended Teddy, who was sleepily snuffling and tear-stained. Her husband's silence unnerved her as much as the chill in the emerald-green eyes welded to her flushed and discomfited face. Eros turned the sports car and drove off ahead of them, her transport whisking her at a more sedate pace back up to the house on the hill and the reception she had vacated in such a panic. Still half-asleep, Teddy clung to her.

Emerging from the vehicle, Winnie stilled and bit at the soft underside of her lower lip. 'What now?' she whispered unevenly as Eros stalked up to her.

Eros's brilliant gaze flashed like a storm warning between lush black lashes. '*Now* we entertain our guests until their departure. Luckily for us, your grandfather is not known for his company manners. That he left early with your sisters will not surprise anyone. You went down to the harbour merely to say goodbye to your family.'

His icy intonation had scoured every scrap of colour from Winnie's cheeks. 'We have to talk.'

'*After* the wedding,' Eros traded with sardonic emphasis. 'I refuse to parade my mistakes in front of an audience.'

Her teeth clenched so tightly at his ready admission that marrying her had been a mistake that she hurt her gums. Even so, she swallowed hard on an acid retort because, whether she liked it or not, discretion made better sense, particularly when it would protect Teddy from witnessing the conflict between his parents.

What remained of the afternoon and early evening felt unbearably long and was an unimaginable strain for Winnie. Her jaw ached from smiling and with the amount of effort required to keep Teddy entertained and in a good mood. It felt like a relief to pop her son into a bath after a quick supper and then hand him over to the hovering nanny until it occurred to her that she still had to face Eros.

For a bridegroom, Eros had contrived to give her a very wide berth since their return to the reception and when one of the guests had expressed surprise at the newly married couple's failure to take to the dance floor, Eros had smoothly concocted the excuse that his bride was suffering from a recently sprained ankle that was still tender.

Yes, Winnie was learning all sorts of unwelcome facts about the man she had married, facts that were distinctly unsettling. Eros was outrageously nimble and versatile in a tight corner and a far better dissembler than her grandfather, who had struggled to conceal his hostility throughout the wedding. With Machiavellian cunning, Eros had masked his suspicions yet still contrived to coolly outmanoeuvre the older man. Eros had played them all, she recognised angrily, let her make an absolute fool of herself traipsing down to the harbour while knowing from the outset that as long as he retained physical possession of their son, *she* was unlikely to leave. Eros had won by using Teddy as a weapon and that infuriated her.

As she hovered in the doorway of the fully furnished nursery, listening to Teddy's drowsy little snuffles as he drifted off to sleep, Eros materialised by her side. She hadn't heard his approach and she flinched back a step.

'Let's go downstairs,' he suggested, his tone perfectly pleasant and in no way threatening.

But Winnie wasn't hoodwinked because she gazed up into that lean, darkly handsome face and collided with green sea-glass eyes as cool and cutting as ice shards and her tummy turned over sickly as if she were falling from a great height.

'I've dismissed the staff for the night,' Eros volunteered. 'They'll clean up tomorrow. The nanny, Agathe, will be staying, however, for Teddy's benefit.'

'I am capable of looking after my son on my own,' Winnie framed curtly.

'Are you?' Eros sounded dubious on that score.

Determined to retain her temper, Winnie compressed her generous mouth as she traversed the stairs ahead of him.

'After all,' Eros continued, refined as a polished steel rapier in her wake, 'you were ready to sacrifice my relationship with Teddy, regardless of how losing his father would affect him.'

'No, I wasn't. You would still have had access to him whenever you wanted!' Winnie argued vehemently as she whirled round in the echoing hall, which was far too grand in size and space for comfort.

His beautiful shapely mouth curled in disagreement. 'Not if your grandfather had anything to do with it. I think we both know that Stam had every intention of writing me back *out* of Teddy's life!'

'That may be true but *I'm* Teddy's parent and I wouldn't have allowed that to happen,' Winnie claimed with spirit, too overwrought to stand still and walking restively through the huge reception room ahead, which was still littered with glasses. Indeed with all the debris from the wedding reception, it made her think of a ghost ship abandoned by its crew.

'Thankfully you are no longer Teddy's *sole* parent,' Eros ground out with grim emphasis, watching her cross the ballroom at speed to head through the nearest doors onto the terrace outside. For Eros it was like being brought back to the scene of the crime...an unwelcome reminder of the wedding that hadn't really been a wedding and the blushing bride, who had never intended to be a bride. His temper was as raw-edged as the sharpest knife. 'Now you have to share that responsibility with me.'

'I don't intend to share anything with you!' Winnie flung back at him over her shoulder as she reached the fresh air and drank it in deep, struggling to control the nerves flashing through her and the confused emotions bombarding her. She would not allow Eros to make her feel ashamed of what she had done, she swore to herself. Sometimes life enforced unpleasant choices and she had done the best she could with poor prospects.

'But you're stuck here now,' Eros pointed out softly,

even while his dark deep drawl vibrated in the smouldering silence. 'And you will *not* leave this island or take Teddy from it until I am satisfied that I can *trust* you.'

So shocked was Winnie by that provocative threat that she spun round to face him again, brown eyes huge with disbelief in her expressive face, her chest heaving.

For an instant, Eros found his concentration slipping. Even in a rage, he was still a man and the heave of Winnie's luscious lace-covered breasts was as eye-catching as it was arousing. It also brought to mind the lowering awareness that this was not how he had expected to spend his wedding night. But then how would he know what was normal on a wedding night? he asked himself sardonically. He had never had a normal marriage and now it looked as if history was set on cruel repeat, a possibility he absolutely refused to accept a second time around.

Either he was married or he wasn't. There would be no halfway deal, no unreasonable conditions set between him and Winnie. Yet at the same time he refused to contemplate another divorce. They had to put Teddy first and, as far as he was concerned, putting Teddy first entailed giving their son *both* parents beneath the same roof.

'You can't be serious!' Winnie exclaimed, challenging that outrageous announcement that he would not allow her to leave the island.

'You haven't given me a choice,' Eros parried with harsh conviction. 'Do you think I don't appreciate that your grandfather will be standing by waiting for the opportunity to steal you and Teddy back from me?'

Her lashes flickered up on startled eyes and she turned her head away again, the muscles in her slight shoulders rigid with strain. Something else she hadn't thought about, she scolded herself in exasperation: Stam Fotakis would not take defeat lying down. Her grandfather would remain determined to get his own way and he would not be fussy about his methods. But it galled her to see herself and her child at the centre of a tug of war between two powerful men.

'If you somehow contrive to escape and return to Stam, that will be your choice,' Eros delineated in a driven undertone. 'But you will *not* sacrifice *my* son to his care.'

'Oh, drop the drama!' Winnie scoffed. 'My grandfather would not harm a hair on Teddy's head and nothing you can say would convince me otherwise!'

'I only have to look at your family's history to know that Stam has very poor parenting skills and I won't subject my son to that experience.'

'I don't know what you're talking about,' Winnie argued in frustration. 'Grandad cares about Teddy.'

'I *assume* he cared for his own sons at one time, as well,' Eros countered very drily. 'But he still flung your father out to sink or swim for defying him when he was only a teenager. As for your uncle, Nicos, he made the mistake of marrying a woman your grandfather disapproved of. She was a divorcee and Stam refused to even meet her. When your uncle died, your grandfather and he were estranged.'

Winnie dropped her head, her eyes troubled, because she hadn't known that salient fact. Stam had told her only that his elder son had died in an accident, not that father and son had been at daggers drawn at the time of his passing. And rightly or wrongly, it did make her question her innate faith in the older man because evidently her grandfather had made an almighty mess of keeping his own family together.

'And don't kid yourself that Stam would give Teddy any easier a ride if he failed his expectations,' Eros completed grimly.

'Point taken,' Winnie conceded stiffly, wanting the subject dropped because it was patently obvious that Eros knew more about her grandfather than she did.

'And Stam will never accept me. He's too much of a snob,' Eros added grimly. 'In his eyes, I'm nouveau riche…and there're no princess grandmothers in my family tree!'

'That sort of thing isn't important to me,' Winnie muttered uncomfortably.

'Pedigree is *very* important to your grandfather. Don't ever forget that. He wanted a ring on your finger to gloss over the reality that you were an unmarried mother and that's where my role was supposed to end. I was good enough for you to marry but not good enough to be accepted into the Fotakis family.'

'Scarcely matters now,' she mumbled helplessly.

But Eros wasn't listening. He stalked indoors, his long lithe legs powering him towards the bar in the corner of the ballroom. Momentarily released from tension, Winnie allowed herself to breathe again. She congratulated herself on not losing her temper and leant back against the iron balustrade, letting the strain slowly trickle out of her muscles.

Eros strode back, his entire focus locked to Winnie's slight figure. With her luxuriant mane of dark hair shifting in the light breeze below the sparkling diamond tiara and her caramel eyes bright in her heart-shaped face, she looked tiny and gorgeous and that reluctant acknowledgement only unleashed a stronger tide of aggression within him. She had betrayed his trust and she wasn't a fitting mother for a vulnerable child. How *could* she be? In marrying him and as quickly walking out on him again she had demonstrated that she had very few principles, least of all when it came to reliability and honesty.

Winnie didn't really want a drink but she accepted the glass of wine Eros extended because she was thirsty and if he was offering a polite olive branch, she was more than willing to grasp it. Taut as a bowstring, she sipped nervously at the wine.

'When I asked you to marry me, it was the real deal,' Eros intoned with level diction, his lean, darkly handsome features sombre. 'There was no deception involved and no lies. I intended to be a husband to you and a father to my son and I planned to fulfil both roles to the very best of my ability.'

Winnie breathed in so deep she felt dizzy when the cool salty air flooded her lungs. She flung her slim shoulders back, brown eyes bright with anger. 'Don't you dare try to talk down to me when you threatened to harm my sisters by exposing their secrets!'

'That doesn't excuse you for entering that church and speaking vows you had no intention of following through on!' Eros ground out wrathfully. 'That was *wrong*!'

'Your threats were equally wrong.' Winnie fought back with a flush rising in her cheeks. 'I couldn't risk allowing you to humiliate my sisters any more than I could risk losing my son, so don't you *dare* tell me that you were offering me "the real deal" because you didn't give me any options!'

'I chose to do what was best for all three of us and I put Teddy first. You've *never* put him first,' Eros condemned grimly. 'If you had, you wouldn't have kept us apart.'

'Wouldn't I have?' Winnie gasped, so furious that she could hardly breathe for the tightness of the corseting built into her grown and squeezing her ribs. 'You were such a great role model for an innocent little boy, weren't you? A married man having an affair with an employee behind his wife's back? Do you really think you were the kind of father I wanted or needed for my son?'

'Perhaps not but I *was* his father and I had rights,' Eros reminded her without remorse. 'Rights and responsibilities you were happy to ignore and deny.'

Clutching her wine glass, Winnie gave way to her impatience and moved forward to push past him and return indoors. 'We've already been through this argument. There's no point going there again!' she proclaimed.

'I married you in good faith. I didn't even demand a signature on a prenup. *Why?* I was fool enough to trust you.'

Breathless and troubled with her cheeks on fire with mortification, Winnie snatched up the bottle of wine on the bar and refilled her glass. 'More fool you, then!' she shot back at him defiantly, reasoning that as he had already won the most important battle she had little more to lose from aggravating him.

Eros was outraged. Quiet, trusting, naive little Winnie, it seemed, had only ever existed in his own imagination, a romantic fiction more than a reality. 'A fool no more,' he reminded her with dark satisfaction. 'I have my wife and my child in my home where I wanted them to be.'

'And much good may it do you!' Winnie hurled back as she moistened her dry mouth with more wine. 'I am *not* your wife in any way that counts.'

Eros dealt her a sizzling all-male smile of one-upmanship, recalling how his bride had melted in his arms a bare hour before she'd walked out on him. Some things Winnie could fake but not that burning chemistry and in retrospect he recalled the signs of disquiet he had noticed in her and misinterpreted as shyness. To a certain degree she had changed. She had toughened up, learned to challenge him and she refused to hang her head and admit regret. But at heart and in the only field that really mattered, he told himself, she was still *his* Winnie, as red hot for him as he was for her.

That flashing smile made Winnie feel dizzy where she stood and she blinked, her throat convulsing as she acknowledged the strain of trying to defend herself when her own heart and logic also screamed that she had done wrong. Two wrongs would never make a right. Her grandfather's machinations and desire for revenge had tied her up in knots. But she *had* put Teddy first when she'd readily agreed to her son having a proper relationship with his father.

Marriage, however, had been a step too far for her, a much too personal and humiliating step that had cost her the independence and pride she had worked so hard to re-establish since Teddy's birth. Between them, her grandfather and Eros had torn her life apart.

Even worse, Eros had hurt her badly once and she wasn't prepared to risk that happening again. Naturally she could be civil to her son's father, but she couldn't treat him as a husband or trust him, not when she was degradingly conscious that he had only married her for Teddy's benefit.

'You married me intending to cheat me of both a marriage and a son,' Eros grated in a tone of raw frustration. 'What is your answer to that?'

Winnie drained her wine and set the empty glass down with a sharp little snap on the bar before turning on her heel and simply walking away from him.

'Winnie!' Eros ground out wrathfully.

Winnie paused. 'You know, I always hated my name. My parents shortened it from Winifred to Winnie and now I don't like Winnie either,' she muttered almost conversationally. 'It makes me think of a horse—'

'Thee mou...' Eros bit out, his strong jaw clenched hard as she turned in a reluctant half circle to look at him again. 'What nonsense are you speaking?'

'I've got nothing more to say to you.' With extreme unwillingness, Winnie focused on him again. Eros Nevrakis, her husband, and he was as gorgeous as a lustrous jungle cat, full of energy and predatory drive. He was judging her as she had once judged him because she had lied by omission in agreeing to marry him when she'd had no intention of staying married to him or even of living with him. He had found her out when he'd caught her in the act of leaving him and there was no coming back from a sin that barefaced.

'I have plenty to say to you.'

Halfway up the sweeping staircase, Winnie stilled

and turned back. 'Really? That must feel very much out of character. A little more than two years ago when it mattered, you had nothing to say to me.'

His stunning bone structure snapped taut, stormy green eyes narrowing with wariness. 'You vanished. You didn't give me the chance to say anything.'

'Be honest for once,' Winnie challenged. 'You had nothing of any value to say to me back then. I was just a fling for you.'

Eros gritted his even white teeth. 'We've got enough trouble in the present without digging back into the past!' he derided without hesitation.

'But that past formed the present and my opinion of you and, no matter how hard I try to be civilised and gracious and consider Teddy, I can't get over the fact that I hate you more than any man alive!' Winnie flung truthfully.

As Winnie raced on up the stairs, Eros froze where he stood, colour ebbing from below his bronzed complexion. She didn't *hate* him, she told herself fiercely; she refused to accept that. Why the hell had she brought up the past? That past was better left buried and untouched. He couldn't go back and change anything about it. He had been married...*fact*. He had let her down when she had most needed him...*fact*.

As Winnie pushed through door after door in vain search of her luggage, she finally arrived in front of the double doors at the end of the corridor and thrust the doors wide. Her single suitcase filled with old garments she had been content to leave behind sat still packed by the wall.

Eros leant back against the doors to send them slamming shut. He watched her twist to try to reach the buttons at the back of the gown, the same buttons he had planned to undo one by one as he stripped her bare. His mouth ran dry, the throb at his groin a provocative reminder of his susceptibility to a woman he could not trust. The reaction infuriated him.

'You lied to me,' he condemned.

Winnie spun round, her face aflame. 'I didn't lie. I went through with the wedding.'

'You think that's enough to excuse you?' he derided.

'No, but it's the best you're going to hear.'

'You don't hate me,' he told her, stalking with fluid, boneless grace across the wooden floor that separated them. 'A woman doesn't kiss a man the way you kiss me when she hates him.'

Winnie tossed her head, lustrous strands of mahogany hair tumbling round her hot face. 'That's just sex,' she told him dismissively. 'It doesn't have anything to do with emotions. I believe *you* taught me that.'

Taut with arousal, Eros surveyed her in frustration and reached for her. 'Let me undo those buttons for you.'

'They're hooks underneath, not buttons,' she muttered breathlessly, as if she was making a very important point. Eros turned her round, long, lean fingers gentle but firm on her slight shoulders. With just that single touch her treacherous body ran from zero to fifty in awareness and she stiffened, disturbingly conscious of the hooks giving way at her spine and the smooth brush of his fingers across sensitive skin.

'I can't be that way again with you… I just can't!' she exclaimed in sheer desperation, all too conscious of the melting heat blossoming low in her pelvis, the licking temptation ready and willing to drag her down into sensual oblivion. She supposed that was natural. Eros had taught her to crave him and she had suppressed that side of her nature ever since, refusing to acknowledge it, afraid of falling victim to that weakness again.

Lean hands heavy on her shoulders, Eros nudged her hair out of his path and pressed his mouth passionately to the soft skin at her nape, sending a darting tingle of shivering lust down her taut spinal cord. 'I haven't been with any woman since I was last with you,' he admitted in a charged undertone.

Still quivering from the wickedly provocative assault of his hungry mouth on her skin, Winnie went rigid at those words and then suddenly tore herself free to spin round and look up at him in frank disbelief. 'I don't believe you,' she told him boldly.

Stormy green eyes pierced hers in unashamed challenge. 'Whether you accept it or not, it happens to be the truth.'

Oxygen bubbled in the back of her throat, scrambling her breathing as she gazed up at him in bewilderment. 'But *why*? I mean, you were divorced... Why wouldn't you have found someone else?'

His proud bone structure pulled taut, his exotic cheekbones prominent, the shadowy hollows beneath adding stark definition. 'I've never been into casual encounters and I didn't want to rush into anything either. I won't let sex control me or push me in the wrong direction again.'

Her lashes fluttered, bemusement claiming her. She was barely breathing as she listened because he had never told her that much before and, ironically, he both gave to her and then took away again with those words. First, he implied that what he had shared with her had *not* been casual and then he suggested that sexual desire had once got him involved with the wrong woman. Did he mean her or his ex-wife? Or some other woman from his past?

What did strike her almost dumb was that Eros, for all his gorgeous vital masculinity and electrifying sexuality, had almost as many quirks, inhibitions and fears as she had. Nothing had ever shaken her as much as that revelation because it simply transformed her view of him, turning him from the ruthless, dishonest sexual predator she had believed him to be into a much more human male with his own secrets and vulnerabilities.

Winnie stared up at him, her heart-shaped face solemn. 'You're telling me the truth, aren't you?'

An ebony brow quirked. 'Why would I lie about something like that? What man boasts about celibacy in this day and age?'

Winnie closed her eyes because of the scratchy sting prickling at the backs of them, fighting off the threat of tears. Her feathery lashes drifted down onto her cheeks to conceal her expression. With a husky groan, he hauled her into his arms. Passionate urgency sprang from every line and angle of the lean, fit body pressed hard against hers. His hungry mouth crushed hers, his tongue sliding between her lips to delve deep until a shudder racked her slight frame.

'I don't want to rip the dress,' Eros muttered roughly, spinning her round in front of him and addressing his attention to the many buttons still to be undone.

'Why not? I'll never wear it again,' Winnie murmured, already wondering what lay ahead for them now because they were racing fast into unknown territory and, although she knew she ought to step back and demand her own space and resist the intimacy he wanted, she was as still as a statue, her pupils dilated, her body all of a quiver in anticipation of what he would do to her and how that would make her feel.

Eros ran through hook after hook, impatience gripping him in waves, and he too was fighting off second thoughts. He was picturing her as she'd walked down the aisle towards him, reminding himself that that had all been showmanship designed to fool him and lull him into a false sense of security. She had *never* intended to be his wife, *never* intended to share his bed and his fury at that reality that was still dug down deep inside him. What was he playing at? Getting entangled with Winnie again was like playing with fire and it would be all the more dangerous because of her connection to Stam Fotakis, who would destroy him if he could.

He stared down at the subtle line of her smooth back and the violin curve of her shapely hips slowly being exposed, and ferocious need broke through the defensive barriers his brain was trying to resurrect. Suddenly nothing mattered beyond *having* her again. He pushed the parted edges of the bodice apart and watched the wedding dress fall down to her feet in a silky pool of lace. Underneath she wore white lace panties and pale thigh-high stockings and he took his time appreciating that view of feminine perfection.

Slowly he turned her back to face him and then he dropped to his knees in front of her to smooth lean

brown hands very slowly up over her beautiful legs
until he reached the delicate skin above the lace stocking tops. Winnie went rigid beneath the caress, staring down at him with almost dazed eyes as he gently
nudged her slender thighs apart. She could feel every
brush of his fingertips across her inner thighs and
it set up a chain reaction in her pelvis, awakening a
surge of heat that made her squirm.

'There's so much I want to do that I don't know
where to begin,' Eros said softly as his hands curled
into the edges of her panties and slowly peeled them
down.

Winnie literally stopped breathing, fierce colour
sweeping up her throat to engulf her face. She had
never been more conscious of being bare.

'Am I *still* the only guy to see you like this?' Eros
growled as he tugged the undergarment free by dint
of delicately lifting each stiletto-heeled foot in turn.

Winnie toyed with the idea of lying out of pride
but then her innate practicality squashed that idea.
'When would I have had the time?' she muttered ruefully. 'First I was pregnant and then I had Teddy and
then I was struggling to look after him and work unsocial hours.'

Smiling with unashamed satisfaction, Eros leant
forward and planted a kiss on her lower belly. 'I'm
grateful,' he confided quietly.

Her tummy muscles tensed. Alarmingly conscious
of the stretch marks that were slowly fading into sil-
very lines there, Winnie swallowed hard, wondering if
he had noticed, reckoning he was too smooth to comment on her flaws. And, of course, there were flaws,
she scolded herself, because a body that had carried

a baby changed and there was nothing to do but live with those changes.

Impervious to her insecurities, Eros vaulted upright and scooped her up to settle her down on the wide bed. As he stood over her, he threw off his jacket, jerked loose his grey silk spotted tie and unbuttoned his crisp white dress shirt. All male purpose blazed in the smouldering green eyes welded to her.

'I have never wanted anything so much as I want you at this moment,' he told her rawly, and she recognised the faint hint of anxiety that accompanied that admission as if that level of desire spooked him.

Yet he had always made *her* feel like that, she acknowledged, as though she was especially sexy and necessary to him, as though he truly *needed* her on some deep fundamental level. It was hardly surprising that she had fallen in love with him. But all Eros had ever needed from her was sex, she reminded herself ruefully. Quickly, she shrugged the thought away again, possessed as she was by a powerful need of her own to live in the moment and look neither forward to a dim future nor back to a past that still wounded her.

Eros pulled off his shirt, exposing a bronzed torso straight out of her most feverish feminine fantasy, lean muscle rippling with his every movement to define powerful pectorals and a stomach that was a taut flat study of hard, corrugated sinew. She stared, her hands falling back from the curves she had been trying to cover, the foolishness of such reticence with her child's father sending a tide of self-conscious red up into her cheeks. It was a little late in the day for modesty, she told herself impatiently, particularly when there was nothing modest about what Eros made her feel.

Excitement was already licking up through her like a storm warning, her mouth dry, her heart beating so fast it felt as if it was pounding through her entire body. Eros had always had the ability to make her feel like a very different woman from her quiet and sensible self. He only had to look at her a certain way, touch her a certain way and she was transformed into a wanton creature that wanted, *craved*, needed…

'I have no patience, *moraki mou*,' Eros breathed as he stripped off his trousers, revealing black boxers that he skimmed off with a similar lack of ceremony.

'You never had,' Winnie whispered shakily, striving not to stare at his body, a hot flush surging at the heart of her and a wave of desire she could not suppress.

Eros laughed, assailed by memories he hadn't examined in years, and acknowledged that when it came to her patience had never been his strong suit. Desire had ridden him hard, frustrating his attempt to keep their affair cool and within bounds, demanding more from him than he had ever wanted to give. He shook off the disturbing memories to concentrate on the pale voluptuous vision of loveliness that was Winnie lying across the bed, her wondrous curves exposed for his appreciation.

He came down to her in one lithe movement, all controlled grace and masculine heat, claiming her mouth with demanding, shattering force and for several long moments Winnie was in heaven because nobody could kiss like Eros. Big hands cupped her full breasts, pushing them together to enable him to hungrily tease her straining nipples to lush promi-nence. Darting arrows of erotic need raced to her core. He worked his sensual path down over her writhing length. He made her hot as hell, her hips rising invol-untarily as he ground down on her, letting her feel the full force of his arousal against the most tender spot on her entire body.

'*Thee mou...* You drive me insane,' Eros husked, his hands lifting to pinch at her already swollen and sensitive nipples, wrenching a long, sobbing breath from her parted lips as her back arched in helpless response.

He forced her still before tugging her thighs apart and burying his mouth there to feast on her sensitive flesh with a passionate carnality that made her jerk and moan. Long fingers traced her tender folds and glided between, probing her honeyed depths with pre-cision while his thumb delicately strummed against her, and then he employed his tongue. She shook and gasped as the slow tormenting rise of an explosive climax ached unbearably in her pelvis.

Eros watched her rise beneath him with a breath-less little scream at the intensity of the pleasure flood-ing her, and then fall back, limp and drained against the tumbled pillows. The look of bliss on her face sent a zinging throb of lust straight to his groin, leaving him hard as steel.

'Let me touch you,' she mumbled breathlessly as he lifted back from her and she sat up, taking him by surprise as she tugged him back down onto the bed beside her. 'I have my own agenda.'

'You...*do*?' Eros prompted, taken aback by her sudden boldness for she had always been a shy lover, content to let him take charge.

Winnie nodded feverishly, her heart-shaped face a curious study of self-consciousness and determination. Her small hands spread across his pectoral muscles and then slowly traced down over his tautly muscled stomach, feeling him flex and tense beneath her ministrations even while she recognised his surprise in some dismay.

In the past with Eros, she had been passive, far too afraid of making a clumsy wrong move and either making him laugh or turning him off. But the news that there had not been another woman in his bed since he had last been with her had thrilled Winnie as much as it had startled her and now all the fantasies she had once suppressed, all the desires she had been afraid to express, were powering her. A little voice in the back of her head was also reminding her that Eros could hardly keep his hands off her and that it was past time that she was woman enough to explore her own hunger for him.

She lowered her head, mahogany hair trailing softly across his stomach as she traced the little furrow of dark hair usually visible above his waistband with the tip of her tongue. As she simultaneously stroked his long, thick, urgent length with her hand, his hips lifted and she heard his breathing hitch in surprise. He was so smooth and hard and warm and, as she soon learned, incredibly responsive to her smallest touch. His hand dug into her thick hair and he arched up to her with an uninhibited moan of pleasure as she laved him with her tongue. For the first time ever with Eros, Winnie felt truly powerful and sexy.

He withstood her attentions for only a few moments before he dragged her back up to him with a kind of wildness that excited her and rasped, 'I can't take any more of that. I want to come inside you...'

Flushed and breathless, Winnie grinned at him. 'To be continued, then,' she mumbled.

With a wildly impatient hand, Eros grabbed protection from beside the bed and yanked her slight body under him with decisive force. Delighted giggles at his unashamed urgency tumbled from Winnie's lips. Crushing her reddened mouth beneath his, he extracted a hungry kiss of retribution.

'Silence, *mikri magissa mou*,' Eros urged roughly as he pushed back her thighs with hard hands.

Mikri magissa mou... My little witch. Winnie savoured the label with pleasure, satisfied that her more daring approach had passed muster.

Almost at the same moment, Eros plunged with a savage growl of satisfaction between her thighs and the ability to think clearly was stolen from her. Her body lurched and shivered with the sweet piercing delight of giving way to his, sensations that she had forced herself to forget racking her with waves of delirious pleasure. Every stroke set her on fire, her excitement climbing with every slick move of his hips as he picked up speed, and then there was nothing but the breathless surging exhilaration of his dominance pushing her to the summit again. Heart racing, body writhing, she burned up in the fiery blaze of release that consumed her from the inside out. Electrifying ripples of excitement convulsed her and held her suspended until she tumbled back in a daze to the real world again.

Eros freed her from his weight and then pulled her into his arms, which startled her because once Eros had been chary of touching her after sex, his innate reserve kicking in immediately afterwards, making her drown in discomfiture at a moment when she had craved something less ephemeral than physical satisfaction. Now he took the time to stroke her damp hair back from her brow, gazing down at her with glittering emerald-green eyes while he traced the voluptuous line of her lower lip with a thoughtful fingertip.

'I'd like to ditch the protection and have another child,' he admitted huskily, disconcerting her even more with that confession. 'I missed out on all that the first time around and I'd enjoy the chance to experience it with you.'

'Are you insane?' Winnie was startled enough to demand before she could even consider the meaning of such an unexpected proposition. 'Teddy is only eighteen months old. We don't even know if we *have* a future together.'

'I might trust you a little more if I could see you *commit* to that future with me by conceiving another child,' Eros confessed with measured cool. 'The future is there for us to grab and we've got nothing to lose by going for it straight away and ignoring your grandfather's feelings about us staying married. Of course, if you *prefer* to keep your options open...'

'I'm not ready to have another child yet,' Winnie muttered flatly, still struggling to master her shock at such a suggestion from him. 'Particularly not with a man who once chose not to tell me that he was married and who broke my heart. You may not trust me but *I* don't trust you either! Only couples who are happy and secure together should bring babies into the world.'

At that unhesitating rejection, dark colour sprang up in a feverish line across his high cheekbones, accentuating his shimmering sea-glass eyes. 'We *could* be happy.'

'Could!' Winnie scorned as she snaked free of him and wriggled off the edge of the bed to head into the bathroom, needing space and privacy from him. 'That's not enough!'

His sheer high-voltage sexuality sent her brain careening into the realms of fantasy. But way before that acknowledgement, she had been knocked emotionally sideways by his insistence that he had not slept with another woman since he had last been with her two years earlier. And that had shocked her, but what had shocked her even more was that she had believed him and, rightly or wrongly, it had brought her barriers crashing down, making her vulnerable. It had also encouraged her to do what she had sworn never to do again and that was sleep with Eros. But at the same time, she was currently married to Eros Nevrakis, which *had* to change her outlook.

Or did it? she reasoned frantically. Did being married to the man she had once loved change anything? According to him, she would be a virtual prisoner on Trilis until he felt that he could trust her again. And when was that likely to be? Particularly when she was not prepared to risk having another child with him. And yet with that suggestion he had ignited the strangest secret yearning inside her. Why? Second time round with Eros, pregnancy would be a very different experience for her because she wouldn't be going it alone as she had been forced to do while carrying Teddy. And wouldn't it be wonderful to have that support and to feel valued while bringing a much-wanted second child into the world?

As soon as she recognised that dangerous thought, she stood on it hard and loathed herself for being so weak, so susceptible to Eros's smallest suggestion. He was asking her to *prove* her commitment to their marriage but *was* she committed? Or simply playing for time while she decided what to do next? And how was he planning to demonstrate *his* commitment? Did he really think that suggesting that she have another child with him was sufficient?

As she vanished into the bathroom, Eros lay there for long minutes, seething with angry exasperation and an unfamiliar sense of rejection. Winnie could be such a plodder, proceeding directly and without deviation from one milestone to the next, no cutting corners, no shortcuts, no risks that could be avoided taken. Their affair had probably been the most dangerous impulse she had ever given way to and it would be a very long time, if ever, before she forgave him for not telling her that he was on paper, at least, a married man. Perhaps it was past time he explained exactly why he had never mentioned it, perhaps she would then begin to accept that the future was what they alone could make or break.

The bathroom door stood ajar and he pressed it back. Fresh from the shower, Winnie was already towelling herself dry, a glorious vision of tumbled dark hair and damp pink sensuality, chocolate-brown eyes anxious as they zeroed in on him.

'Er...*what*?' she muttered awkwardly.

'*Entaxei*... Okay, you win,' Eros breathed tautly, his bone structure rigid. 'I'll tell you about my marriage.'

CHAPTER EIGHT

CLUTCHING HER TOWEL to her full breasts, Winnie froze in astonishment and stared back at Eros. 'But you don't *want* to talk about it…'

Eros shrugged a bare bronzed shoulder. 'I owe you,' he said flatly, striding back into the bedroom to rifle through the drawers in the dressing room.

Having followed him on stiff legs, Winnie sank down uneasily on the foot of the bed, watching while he dragged out a pair of jeans and began to pull them on, lean muscles flexing with his every graceful movement. Colour burned her cheeks and she couldn't think straight for several moments because Eros was knocking her off balance on too many different levels at once.

'You seem shocked that I'm willing to talk about my first marriage,' Eros commented in surprise.

'Even quite recently, you weren't willing to do that,' Winnie pointed out tightly, struggling to get her flailing emotions under control.

Eros sent her a steady look from his stunning green eyes. 'I was too angry then but you're my wife now. You have a right to know certain facts.'

Winnie nodded dumbly, fearful of what was coming next, wanting to know about that marriage and yet in the strangest way reluctant to know, because she was convinced that he was certain to tell her things that would hurt.

'A property developer called Filipe Mantalos gave me my first business loan when the banks wouldn't touch me,' Eros told her, disconcerting her yet again with that opening. 'I believe I mentioned Filipe to you before?'

'Yes, I remember. He helped you out when you were starting up,' she recalled vaguely.

Eros compressed his wide sensual mouth. 'Without Filipe's support and backing I would never have got that first business venture off the ground and into profit. At the time, Felipe was a widower with a daughter he adored called Tasha.'

Unprepared for the sound of that familiar name, Winnie flinched, wondering what else he was about to tell her. Had his first wife, Tasha, also been his mentor's daughter? When he had first mentioned Filipe, Eros had been quite clear about Filipe's role in his life when he was a younger man. For all intents and purposes, Filipe had been the father Eros's own father had been too selfish to be and clearly the relationship had meant a lot to Eros.

'Eight years ago, Filipe developed a brain tumour. He had surgery but the tumour returned and was eventually deemed inoperable,' Eros told her gravely. 'Filipe was always a very practical man. He immediately began sorting out his affairs and working out how best to protect Tasha, who was still a student. He was a wealthy man and he asked me to look after his daughter's inheritance until she was old enough to handle the money herself but, because she was young and vulnerable and very much in love with me, he asked me if I would consider marrying her.'

'Consider...*marrying her*?' Winnie erupted into sudden speech with wide incredulous eyes. 'What age was she, for goodness' sake? Very much in love with you? You were already involved with her?'

'No, prior to our marriage, I had no dealings with Tasha beyond sharing a dinner table with her occasionally in her father's company. She was only seventeen and I haven't dated a teenager since I was one myself,' Eros countered drily. 'I was simply a regular visitor to her home and a close friend of her father's. Without any encouragement from me, Tasha decided that she had fallen in love with me and she convinced Filipe that it was a lasting love while I believed it was only a teenage infatuation. Her father, however, wanted her to be happy and he trusted me to look after her.'

'Naturally, but—'

'He knew I wasn't in love with Tasha but neither was I in love with anyone else. He asked me to marry her and give the relationship a chance,' Eros volunteered grimly. 'He was dying. I couldn't say no to him. Because I wanted him to leave this world in peace, I agreed and a wedding was arranged before Filipe's condition deteriorated.'

'You should've said no if you didn't have feelings for her!' Winnie argued helplessly. 'It was emotional blackmail.'

Eros tensed even more. 'It wasn't like that. I believed that I knew what I was doing. I didn't love Tasha but I *did* care what happened to her. She was a very emotional teenager and I didn't want her to be alone and unprotected as I had once been myself. There are a lot of sharks in the world, particularly if you have money. And Filipe left Tasha *very* well provided for.'

'If she was only seventeen, what age were you?' Winnie pressed.

'Twenty-five.' Eros paced restively across to the windows, his discomfort at the subject he was talking about painfully apparent to her. 'But it was a huge gap. She was a very young seventeen year old because her father had spoiled her and shielded her from real life. I was a very serious twenty five year old because my childhood had been less than idyllic and I knew how hard I would have to work to overcome my father's bad reputation in business. Tasha and I had very little in common.'

Winnie released her pent-up breath in a slow hiss. 'I think you were crazy to marry her. She would've been far too immature for you at that age and if she thought she loved you, marrying her was only encouraging her expectations.'

'I didn't encourage her.' Eros's proud dark head reared up and back and he sent her a reproving glance from glittering green eyes. 'I didn't take her to bed either. In fact, we never had sex.'

Brown eyes locked hard to his lean, darkly handsome features, Winnie stared back at him. *'Never?'* she stressed in wonderment.

'Never,' Eros confirmed. 'Tasha wanted us to have a normal marriage from the start but I disagreed. She wasn't ready for an adult relationship and she deserved a husband who loved her. She also needed to have the freedom her father had denied her to enjoy all the usual youthful experiences. I hurt her pride a lot when I turned her down but I didn't think there was an alternative.'

'So, what happened after that?' Winnie pressed, hanging on his every word, her mind buzzing with conjecture and shock and bewilderment. Whatever she had believed of Eros's marriage, she had always assumed that it was a normal marriage between two people who had, at least, started out loving each other.

'We made an agreement. Tasha wanted to study design and set up her own interiors business. She transferred to a student course in London and I told her that she was free to date anyone she wanted, which she duly did. Unfortunately, however, she couldn't bring herself to extend the same freedom to me. She was too jealous, too possessive to accept the idea of me being with another woman,' he admitted tautly. 'And I *did* promise her that if she still felt the same way about me after she had graduated, I would give our marriage a try.'

'Why on earth would you make a promise like that when you didn't want her in the first place?'

Eros vented a groan. 'Because she was heartbroken that I wouldn't agree to have a normal relationship with her. Although I was convinced that she'd grow out of her infatuation, she refused to accept it. I was trying to let her down gently and allow her to save face. *Thee mou*... I assumed she'd grow out of thinking she loved me!'

'It was still a promise too far. It left your life in limbo,' Winnie pointed out, reckoning that it had been very short-sighted of him to agree to such unequal terms.

A grim look tautened Eros's strong face. 'You have no idea how guilty I felt because I couldn't return her feelings,' he admitted ruefully. 'At one stage, she was crying and threatening to harm herself. I would have said anything, promised almost *anything* to calm her down.'

'Oh…' Winnie swallowed hard, picturing Eros struggling to calm and control a teenage drama queen and wincing in sympathy.

'But you're right. It was the wrong thing to promise because, naturally, both of us were likely to change. But for several years, our unconventional arrangement did work,' Eros told her wryly. 'Just as her father had hoped I was able to watch over her, control her finances and ensure that nobody took advantage of her. We would see each other occasionally for dinner but we never occupied the same house and we lived entirely separate lives. Tasha moved from luxury student accommodation into her own apartment above her first design studio.'

'No wonder you seemed to be single when I met you,' Winnie muttered. 'No wonder there was no sign of a woman in your life. Why didn't you tell me that you were trapped in a marriage that you never wanted?'

'It wouldn't have been fair to Tasha to admit that I felt trapped. She was my wife and I did try to be loyal to her. In fact, I kept my promise to her until I met you because there were no other women before you,' Eros admitted with a twist of his sensual mouth. 'And then with you around suddenly, life became very, very complicated in all sorts of ways. I was married but in my own mind I was still single...and then there was that stupid promise I'd made to her.'

'But presumably she took advantage of the freedom you offered *her*?'

'Of course, she did. In fact at the time I was involved with you, she was actually living with one of her boyfriends. And then *that* broke up very messily and she came running back to me for support, convinced that it was the perfect time for us to try having a normal marriage. That was when you met her, when she turned up at the country house without warning,' he revealed impatiently. 'But by that stage, I knew that I wanted out and that I needed my freedom back. Ultimately she agreed to the divorce.'

'She *is* very beautiful,' Winnie remarked uneasily, an image of Tasha's Scandinavian fairness and endless legs still haunting her. 'Why didn't you want to give her that final chance?'

'Because I felt more like her big brother and when I finally admitted that to her, she realised that that was unlikely to change,' he confessed wryly. 'I didn't tell her about you though. I didn't want to hurt her.'

A dawning awareness of certain unwelcome facts was keeping Winnie quiet and unresponsive. Right from the outset Eros had put Tasha's needs before her own, she concluded unhappily. He had sent Winnie down to his country house, where Tasha was less likely to see her or learn about her existence. He had continually protected Tasha's feelings and had tried to remain loyal to her in mind, if not in body. When he had finally gone for a divorce, Winnie had already disappeared from his life and even after he had regained his freedom, he hadn't come looking for her. Those truths *hurt*. He might not have loved his wife but she had received a level of caring and loyalty from him that Winnie had never commanded. In short, Winnie had only ever been runner-up on Eros's scale of who was most important to him, at least until he had discovered that she had given birth to his son.

As the silence stretched to an uneasy length, Eros breathed in deep. 'I should have told you the truth when we first met. I regret keeping quiet but while I was with you, I was an emotional mess. Our affair was so intense it unnerved me and the more I thought about it, the more wrong it felt but I couldn't make myself walk away.'

'Then it's probably a good thing that I did the walking away for you,' Winnie pronounced in a tone of finality.

'Winnie?' Eros prompted with a frown of incomprehension.

Stiff with discomfiture at the wounding thoughts flaying her like knives, Winnie stood up, too hurt and proud to do anything other than conceal her true feelings. 'Well, I'm glad you've finally told me the whole story,' she muttered hastily as she frantically thought about how best to quickly escape an even more awkward conversation. 'But, you know, all I can think about right now is food.'

'*Food?*' Eros repeated in astonishment, for he had been bracing himself for questions, comments and further condemnation of the choices he had made.

Winnie forced an apologetic smile to her lips. 'Yes. I'm afraid I didn't eat much today and now I'm starving, so I think I need to raid the kitchen.'

Without further ado, she crossed the room to her suitcase and began to open it in search of something to wear.

Eros frowned at her, perplexed by her mood. He wasn't stupid. He could see that she was annoyed with him and trying to deflect attention from that reality. But did he really want to drag any more of the past into the present? It was their wedding night and it had been preceded by a very long and upsetting day. Maybe, in seeking to avoid further divisive debates and concentrate on practicalities, Winnie had the right idea, he acknowledged uncertainly.

He watched as she dragged a faded silky robe out of the tumbled contents of the case and, dropping the towel, donned the robe in a series of jerky movements. Her heart-shaped face was taut, brown eyes dark and evasive as she walked to the door.

'I bought you a new wardrobe of clothes,' Eros admitted abruptly.

Winnie whirled back round to look at him in surprise. 'Why would you do that?'

'It's a gift,' Eros hastened to assure her.

'How very generous of you,' Winnie responded in a tone that hinted that she thought it rather weird that he should interest himself in what she wore.

But Eros, who found her appealing even in a faded robe that had seen better days, always noticed what she wore because he rarely took his attention off her when she was in his vicinity.

'I don't feel comfortable with you wearing clothes bought by your grandfather,' Eros admitted in blunt addition.

Winnie tensed. 'You're not in competition with Grandad—'

'Of course not, you're my wife,' Eros countered with a possessive edge to his intonation as he studied her.

'All Grandad paid for was my wedding dress. The majority of my own clothes are still in London,' Winnie confided carelessly. 'I don't have summer stuff though, so I can certainly use anything in that line.'

She was *not* going to argue with him, not going to argue with him about *anything*, Winnie told herself urgently. She would get upset, she would be out of control, leaking emotion that would give away too much of what she was truly feeling. And she didn't even know *what* she was feeling, did she?

Hurt. Why did Eros *always* hurt her? Why was she always looking for more from him? What was the point? She had to adjust to the new status quo, and *fast*. She was stuck being married and stuck on an island with a man who neither loved nor trusted her. She still had her son and Eros was terrific in bed. *Count positives,* not *negatives*, she instructed herself fiercely. That was what her sister Zoe would tell her to do...

CHAPTER NINE

'I WANTED TO eat chocolate round the clock,' Winnie admitted ruefully, wondering how Eros could possibly be interested in what her pregnancy had been like but, for all that, he kept on pressing for more information. 'Now, why couldn't I have craved something healthy like salmon or salad while I was pregnant? No, I had to crave chocolate. I put on a good bit of weight.'

'I bet it suited you,' Eros murmured, wishing he had been there for her when it would really have mattered to her and counted in his favour. As she lay in his arms, he ran an appreciative hand over the lush fullness of her breasts cradled in a bikini top. He dipped his fingertips into the cups, skimming the fabric out of his path to expose her breasts and expertly tease the sensitive peaks. 'I *adore* your curves.'

Her mind went blank and she forgot what she was about to say as her spine arched helplessly into the hard, muscular heat of the lean, powerful body holding hers. The tingling rise of heat between her thighs controlled her utterly. 'Someone might see us!' she framed in sudden breathless panic.

'Nobody can see us down here,' Eros replied, turning her across his lap to lower his mouth to the pouting nipples he had bared. 'It's a private beach and we're shielded by the cliffs,' he reminded her thickly while he played with the swollen pink crests until she was gasping and squirming and weak with liquid arousal.

He raked a finger across the taut crotch of her bikini pants. The breath sobbed in her throat as the tender flesh beneath throbbed with pulsing need. How Eros could smash her control that fast when they had made love only a few hours earlier, she had no idea. She only knew that as he began to wrench the bikini pants down and off, she was as impatient as he was. He dipped a finger into her overheated core and she vented a shameless moan, digging her hips into his hard thighs, her whole body ablaze with excitement.

'You're so ready,' Eros growled appreciatively, twisting her round to face him and pushing his shorts down as he lifted her over him and brought her down.

Protection in place, Eros lowered her over him, watching her chocolate eyes widen and the pupils dilate as he entered her hard and fast. And then there wasn't time or space for anything but the wild excitement engulfing them both. He cupped her hips, controlling the pace, rocking up into her when she didn't move fast enough and suddenly all the sensations he induced were tumbling in a feverish, overwhelming surge of power over Winnie and she got lost in them, gasping, moaning, struggling to vocalise the extraordinary strength of the eagerness gripping her. She was straining, climbing, reaching for that ultimate climax and he forced her through the barriers, her body shattering like glass from the inside out, leaving her drained and limp.

Eros responded by lifting her up and flipping her

under him instead, continuing the pace in a pagan rhythm. Her heart thundering, her breath catching in her tight throat, she pushed up to him, her body catching fire again as he ground down into her hard and that hint of erotic force convulsed her in fresh spasms of blissful pleasure. His magnificent body shuddered over hers until he finally groaned with uninhibited satisfaction.

But even in that moment, his shrewd brain was working at full tilt. He couldn't keep his wife a semi-prisoner for ever, he couldn't *force* her to remain his wife either, but when it came to any reference to the future or that thorny word, commitment, Winnie was maddeningly elusive. He gritted his teeth, wondering if he was destined to live for ever with Stam Fotakis peering critically over his shoulder, ready to whisk Winnie away the instant there was a shaky moment in their marriage.

Both his arms wrapped round her slim, trembling body with innate possessiveness, Eros suppressed a sigh. All marriages had shaky moments, he reckoned ruefully, but he couldn't afford to put a foot wrong. He had to tell Winnie that the island had only become his on their wedding day. He also needed to tell her about her grandfather's threats. But unfortunately, Winnie was already sufficiently wary without him giving her added encouragement to distrust him. And who did he blame for that reality? Eros swallowed a groan, his every past sin and mistake threatening to pile up on top of him all at once.

Winnie held Eros close, her slender length quaking with the aftershocks still pulsing inside her. Her fin-

gers stroked through his damp black curls and brushed
against a stubbled jawline on her way to tracing the
fullness of his sensual lower lip. As she revelled in
that physical closeness a helpless tenderness flashed
up through her. For a startling instant, his brilliant
sea-glass eyes held hers fast and in that instant everything became so clear to her. She wanted to hold him
for ever, she never wanted to let him go again because
she loved him, had, it seemed, never *stopped* loving
him. She had no idea how she had contrived to deny
that fact over the past month. Of course, she hadn't
wanted to admit that distinctly humiliating truth even
to herself and she couldn't picture ever telling him.
That was her secret, not something for sharing even
with her sisters.

But, how could she not tell the truth to Vivi and
Zoe? She was accustomed to telling them everything
and was still on the phone to them most days. She had
told them that she was happy but had sensed that they
were not convinced. Unfortunately, her sisters had
returned to London straight after the wedding. Eros
had suggested that she invite them out for a visit but
neither Vivi nor Zoe had sufficient annual leave to
take another break from their jobs so soon after the
wedding.

After all, only four weeks had passed since she'd
married Eros, planning to leave him. Since then she
had been living on the island with Eros and her son,
waking up and falling asleep to the timeless sound
of the waves beating the shore below the house. Eros
hadn't kept her a prisoner as he had threatened but
he hadn't allowed her to go anywhere alone either,
citing his concern that her grandfather would try to

steal her back by some nefarious means, ignoring her protest that she would not allow the older man to do anything of that nature.

For the first couple of weeks, Eros had taken her and Teddy and their nanny, Agathe, sailing round the Greek islands. Although the yacht had been rather more compact than the giant one her grandfather had borrowed to transport them to Trilis, it had still carried a full crew and its opulent furnishings and spacious cabins had ensured they'd enjoyed perfect privacy. The cruise had been a very relaxing experience, blowing away the tension of the wedding day that had gone wrong. And she now owned two fabulous rings. The first, a magnificent solitaire. *Not* an engagement ring, Eros had insisted even though he had put it on *that* finger. And the second? An eternity ring, a hoop of sparkling sapphires to mark the birth of their son.

In Mykonos, they had gone to clubs and danced into the early hours, and Winnie had been surprised by how much she had enjoyed her first experience of being part of a couple that went out in public. At the country house, they had had quiet dinners, nights in rather than nights out. But this time around, she thought happily, everything was different and Eros treated her differently, as well. He was consistently affectionate, both in and out of bed, tender in private moments and always, always interested in her and very focused on her comfort and enjoyment. There had been swimming picnics in wild, secluded coves where Teddy could run about naked, long lazy lunches in little tavernas off the beaten track and more than once she had fallen into bed tipsy and giggling, having enjoyed herself so much that she'd felt positively guilty about it. They had dodged paparazzi cameras on the beach at Paros and had then been skilfully intercepted by them when they were shopping on Corfu.

When she looked at that tabloid photograph she barely recognised herself because, with her feet pushed into casual leather flip-flops and clothed in a bright red sundress from the wardrobe Eros had bought her, she seemed to have somehow metamorphosed into a more extrovert and less inhibited version of herself. She had a deep tan now and her hair was a tumbling mass of natural waves streaked lighter in places by the sun. She had stopped watching what she ate and was waiting ruefully on the pounds piling back on although the constant activity in and out of the bedroom had to be holding the weight at bay.

Eros was very active, very physical. He had taken her windsurfing and paddleboarding. She swam like a fish and she swam every day. Eros was teaching Teddy to swim and he had hauled them both up every hill on the island to appreciate the views, Teddy sitting on his shoulders or waving his arms in excitement from the confines of a baby backpack. Eros was a great father and he had a hands-on approach to his son that had very much impressed Winnie. Watching Eros with Teddy had convinced her that their son would lose a great deal if he was deprived of his father's daily attention. Teddy was already throwing fewer tantrums. It could be that he was growing out of that phase, but Winnie was also able to see that her son thrived on winning his father's approval and quickly shied away from the kind of behaviour that made Eros frown.

With her, Eros was still the same entertaining and sexy man he had always been, but he was much more considerate and caring with her and ready to talk about anything she wanted to talk about, which was the biggest change she had noticed in him. Indeed, being with Eros and Teddy *made* her happy. And one night a week the staff went home early and Winnie cooked up a storm and they ate on the terrace beneath the stars, which brought back memories of how they had first got to know each other.

But her own contentment and Teddy's didn't mean that Winnie could close her eyes to the necessity of seeing her grandfather and having a straight talk with him. She couldn't just leave matters as they had been when she had decided to return to Eros on her wedding day. Unfortunately, she was very much aware that Eros would not be keen on her going anywhere near the older man.

'I need a shower.' Winnie sighed. She slid off the lounger and pulled on a cover-up before stooping to cram her discarded bikini and other possessions into a beach bag. 'And then it'll be time for lunch and Teddy will be awake.'

'What do you want to do this afternoon?' Eros enquired lazily before adding, 'I could do with getting on with some work—'

'That's fine. I'll have Teddy.' Winnie breathed in deep. 'But I'd like to go and see Grandad tomorrow.'

Eros stopped dead in the middle of the long steep path that led back up to the house. *'No,'* he said with emphasis.

'I wasn't asking for permission,' Winnie warned him. 'Nor am I planning to take our son with me. It would be nice if you could invite Grandad *here* to see Teddy.'

Eros studied her with incredulous green eyes. 'In your dreams!' he grated.

'No, it'll happen. I can't say when because I haven't got a crystal ball but it *will* happen,' Winnie assured him evenly, sliding past him to continue on up the path. 'I'm not going to allow my grandfather or indeed anyone else in my family to be at odds with my husband. I'm going to sort it *all* out.'

'I won't allow it,' Eros growled.

'Not listening…not listening, Eros!' Winnie carolled as she walked steadily on even though she was out of breath from the climb and her cover-up was sticking uncomfortably to her perspiring skin. 'Families shouldn't be divided.'

'And what bush did your mother find you under after the stork delivered you?' Eros asked cuttingly. 'Families are often divided. My own, for a start.'

'That was a divorce, rather a different situation,' Winnie reasoned. 'But I know it hit you hard as a child when your parents parted.'

'No, what hit me hard was my mother's heartbreak,' Eros sliced in grimly. 'She never got over my father and she couldn't move on. A marriage should mean *more* than a legal obligation.'

'I think it does to most people,' Winnie contended evenly. 'From what you've told me I suspect your father succumbed to a midlife crisis and that sent his life off the rails.'

'I used to see marriage as a sort of sacred trust,' Eros ground out rawly. 'That's why I didn't want to marry Tasha and why I stayed married longer than I should've. I kept hoping the differences between us would magically melt away but I'm not that naive now and I'd be a fool to let you spend time with a man who hates me and wants to destroy our marriage.'

'Well, you see, the point is I'm not *asking* you to "let me" do anything,' Winnie responded with spirit. 'I'm going to Athens even if it means climbing on the ferry and spending hours getting there.'

'And how the hell do I know that you're planning to come back to me?' Eros demanded with suppressed savagery.

'Aside from the fact that Teddy is staying here?' Refusing to react to the brooding darkness in his lean, strong face, Winnie rolled her eyes. 'Maybe it's time you tried trusting me.'

'Not going to happen,' Eros intoned grimly. 'Last time I trusted you, you said your vows in church and then scuttled off onto that yacht to leave me!'

Winnie went pink with mortification and then suddenly she lifted her head high and tilted her chin in defiance. 'Last time I trusted you, you turned out to be a married man,' she reminded him thinly. 'People in glass houses shouldn't throw stones. We've both made mistakes—'

'This marriage is *not* a mistake,' Eros sliced in, his intonation raw-edged.

'Only time will tell us that,' Winnie parried quietly.

A lean hand enclosed her arm to hold her back as she started up the stairs. 'Then give us that time,' he urged. 'Running off to see Stam Fotakis this soon is like inviting the fox into the chicken coop. He'll cause trouble for us if he can.'

'Grandad only wants what he thinks is best for me,

what he thinks is best for all of us. I'm going to tell him about your first marriage,' Winnie told him as she tugged her arm free of his hold and went upstairs.

'You're going to do...*what*?' Eros demanded in shaken disbelief.

'You heard me. I want Grandad to understand that you were in a very unusual situation.'

'What I told you was private,' Eros grated.

'*Please,*' Winnie pressed. 'At the very least he needs to know that your marriage wasn't a regular marriage.'

In an impatient gesture, Eros flung back his dark head, seduced against his will by the softness of those caramel eyes. 'Oh...as you wish!'

'Thanks. Grandad may be stubborn and difficult but I won't cut him out of my life.'

'He cut your father out of his,' Eros reminded her unkindly.

It was a low blow and, from the landing, she flung him an unimpressed look. 'He admitted that that was a mistake but once he'd taken a stance he was too proud to climb down. People change, Eros.'

'You haven't changed in the essentials. You still want to believe the best of everyone,' Eros condemned as he drew level with her. 'It doesn't work. Believe it or not, there are bad people in the world who get a kick out of doing you down and hurting you.'

Winnie thrust wide their bedroom door with angry force. 'You think I don't know that after my experiences in foster care?' she flung back at him in disbelief.

'I don't know. You *won't* talk about those experiences,' he pointed out.

Winnie went very still and then crossed her arms defensively in front of herself. 'In the very first home I went to, my trainers were stolen and I was accused of selling them and lying about it. Vivi was badly bullied by the other girls. In the second I was repeatedly punched by an older boy because I wouldn't give him money. That I didn't *have* any money didn't seem to occur to him because he said I talked too nicely to be poor. The third place, I no longer had my sisters because we'd been separated. The foster father was a wife beater and one night I got in the way of his fists,' she recited emotionlessly, her hands clenching in on themselves. 'After that I was in a state home for a while and by the time I moved back into foster care, I was developing breasts, which was really bad news.'

As she'd talked, Eros had paled. 'Why did you never share all this with me before?'

Winnie compressed her lips. 'People don't want to know about that sort of stuff.'

'But I want to know everything because I care about you,' Eros said levelly. 'So keep talking.'

'If it wasn't men leering at me on the home front, it was adolescent boys. I had several scary experiences as a teenager but I managed to keep myself safe. By the time I got to John and Liz's home, I was viewed as antisocial and difficult. They changed all that. They changed *everything*,' she admitted chokily, tears rolling down her cheeks. 'But do you know why I'm telling you all this? Because I want you to know that family means everything to me and I don't expect perfection. Family can encompass a whole pile of different people. It can be your friends, people like John and Liz, even misguided people like my grandfather, who don't know when to mind their own business.'

Eros crossed the distance between them and hauled her into his arms, desperate to comfort her. He was appalled at what she had gone through without proper support. 'I'm sorry.'

'No, you're not,' she whispered helplessly. 'You're like Grandad. Of course, you don't like each other. You're just sorry you're not getting your own way.'

'Partially,' Eros admitted gruffly, brushing her hair back from her tear-stained face. 'But it's important to me to protect you. I don't want you to get hurt and I'm afraid I don't trust your grandfather not to hurt you.'

'You can't keep me locked up here for ever.'

'Like a princess in a tower?' His charismatic smile curved his sensual lips. 'No...but I'd like to.'

'I know...' Acting on impulse, mesmerised by the stunning jewelled eyes welded to her, Winnie stretched up and covered his mouth with hers. 'But you can't.'

'That doesn't mean I'm giving up.' Eros claimed her parted lips with fiery hunger and drank deep of her response, holding her so close that she could feel every stark line of his big powerful body, including his blatant arousal.

'You can't be...again?' she mumbled weakly. *Really?*

'Really,' Eros husked, long fingers lifting the hem of her dress, gliding up to the junction of her thighs to pry them apart and explore, his body already aching for the silken oblivion of hers.

He pushed her back against the wall and hoisted her up against him, the carnal play of his fingers ensuring her readiness. A moment later, he plunged into her and buried himself deep, his breathing raw and ragged in her ears as his hips hammered against hers. It was fast and hard and very erotic, and she shot to a climax so swiftly that she saw stars behind her eyes. Only when her legs slid limply down his hard thighs in the aftermath and they were both panting did she register that he hadn't used a condom.

'You didn't use protection!' she gasped.

Eros blinked, green eyes still dark and sultry with sexual satisfaction. He groaned out loud, raking his tousled black hair from his brow with frustrated fingers. 'I'm sorry.'

'No…no, it's okay… At least, it should be,' Winnie muttered, feverishly calculating dates. 'We should be fine. It's not the right time. I should see a doctor, see about taking the pill.'

'No discussion?' Eros lifted a judgemental black brow.

'Not on that topic…maybe in a year or two if we're still together,' Winnie suggested with characteristic practicality.

'I'm not pushing it. Whatever you decide is okay with me…' he conceded, surprising her. 'And, Winnie? We *will* still be together.'

As Winnie walked into the bathroom, Eros appeared in the doorway. 'I'll head into my Athens office tomorrow and drop you off at your grandfather's estate on the way. But I won't be able to pick you up coming home because I have a meeting in Piraeus and I don't know how long it will run. When you're ready to leave, your security team will arrange it.'

Winnie turned slowly from her beach-flushed reflection in the mirror and gave him a huge smile. 'Thank you,' she said warmly, appreciating the reality that he had listened to her and respected her right to do as she wished even if it went against his own instincts.

'Four security guards to look after me is overkill!' Winnie hissed in disbelief as she saw the men getting out of the car behind to supervise her visit to her grandfather's home. 'Grandad's not about to kidnap me, for goodness' sake. Don't you think that you're taking this security stuff too far?'

'Better safe than sorry,' Eros told her, impervious to reason. 'If they see anything remotely suspicious, they will immediately contact me.'

'And if they contact you, what are you planning to do?' Winnie demanded incredulously. 'Storm the house to extract me in a military assault?'

Eros studied her with a ferocious glitter of emerald fire lighting his stunning eyes. 'I will do whatever it takes to protect my wife and my marriage.'

Winnie groaned out loud. 'This is one of those masculine things, isn't it? A show of strength?'

Eros gave her a flashing, utterly beguiling boyish grin that lit up his lean, dark features. 'It'll annoy the hell out of Stam. I'm warning him politely that I will not tolerate further interference in our marriage. He'll tell you, of course, that I'm paranoid.'

'I don't care,' Winnie whispered softly before she reached for the car door. 'Paranoid or not, you're mine...'

The assurance fell into a sudden silence as she immediately regretted those revealing words and Eros stilled in surprise. 'Am I?'

Far more hers than he had ever been before, Winnie adjusted painfully, her heart-shaped face suffused with mortified colour. She loved him but that didn't mean she had to wave that fact like a big banner in his face. In fact, coolness would be far more effective with Eros. Weren't men supposed to always want what they thought they couldn't have? What came easy was always deemed less valuable.

'I'll see you later,' Winnie framed, climbing hastily out of the car and walking towards the grand front door of her grandfather's home. She had given the older man a brief call the night before to tell him that she was coming to visit. She was hopeful that the month she had been on the island would have given him the chance to calm down and develop a more accepting attitude towards her marriage.

Stam Fotakis was in his office but he immediately rose from behind his desk and ordered his PA to serve coffee.

'I thought you might have taken the morning off,' Winnie remarked wryly as he instructed his PA to hold his calls.

'I *never* take a day off,' Stam informed her with pride, studying her over the top of his reading glasses. 'Unless I'm celebrating, of course, and the fact you've arrived without luggage suggests that I have nothing to celebrate...*yet*.'

Winnie quickly caught his drift and almost winced before deciding to be equally direct. 'I'm not planning to leave Eros. We've decided to stay together,' Winnie admitted, watching the older man's craggy face tighten and darken at that unwelcome news. 'I'm here to ask you to back off and accept our marriage.'

'*Thee mou...*' Stam Fotakis breathed with a sudden frown of condemnation as he studied her strained and anxious face. 'You're still in love with the bastard!'

His perception made Winnie pale but she stood her ground. 'You have to recognise that Eros and I are a couple and that it is absolutely in Teddy's best interests that we make a go of our marriage.'

'You'd walk through fire for Nevrakis, wouldn't you?' her grandfather breathed in a tone of incredulity as he sprang upright again. 'When will you learn that he is simply *using* you?'

'*How* is Eros using me?' Winnie pressed levelly. 'I know the best of him and I know the worst of him. Let me tell you about his first marriage.'

Her grandfather raised his hand in an immediate silencing motion. 'I don't want to hear some sob story.'

'It's not a sob story—it's an explanation,' Winnie argued and, as quickly and as simply as she could, she told her grandad about Eros's first marriage.

'Am I supposed to be impressed that I've married you off to a sentimental idiot with silly romantic notions about honour and loyalty?' Stam Fotakis demanded, frowning at her in concern. 'You're making excuses for him, Winnie. He was a married man and he turned you into his mistress!'

'It wasn't like that between us.' Winnie lifted her chin, although it took courage to fly in the face of such opinions. 'And I respect stuff like sentiment and honour and loyalty. I *like* that he didn't blame Tasha or anyone else for the mess he involved us all in. I *like* that I wasn't one of many lovers he took. I *like* that he knows he made mistakes but that he's trying to make up for it now.'

'You do realise that he's not in the same class as a Fotakis?' her grandfather said, frowning with disapproval. 'That in getting to marry you he was punching above his weight? That the very fact that he is now known to be *my* grandson-in-law is likely to make him even richer? And that for an ambitious man, he's done very, very well for himself?'

'Eros is more interested in being a good father to Teddy than in profiting from any association with you,' Winnie told the older man proudly. 'And I'm not a snob. I don't care that he doesn't come from some aristocratic family that have ties stretching back to ancient Greece.'

'But surely it *is* important to you that Nevrakis is honest with you?' Stam prompted, subjecting her to a troubled appraisal and pausing before continuing wryly, 'Well, I'm sorry to disappoint you and damage your faith in Nevrakis, but he *hasn't* been honest with you.'

Stam watched as Winnie turned white before his eyes. He was being cruel to be kind, he told himself soothingly. She had to know the truth, had to accept it. He would keep no more secrets where Winnie was concerned.

As Winnie sipped the coffee she held cradled in one hand, her grip on the saucer had tightened and the cup rattled betrayingly. With great difficulty she held herself still as she stared back at the older man. 'I presume you can prove what you're saying...?' she asked shakily.

Stam breathed in deep. 'Nevrakis agreed to marry you to get his family island back. I scooped Trilis up for a song over thirty years ago when his father went bust and Eros naturally wanted to reclaim it. In recent years he's tried to buy it back on several occasions but I wasn't interested. On the day of your wedding, however, the island of Trilis became his. A little sweetener to the deal, as it were. It cost him nothing,' Stam completed heavily, watching anxiously as her expressive face telegraphed her shock. 'Didn't he mention that bribe? It *was* a bribe. Didn't he admit that he had never in his life before set foot on that island until I agreed to him flying over there to check the place out for the wedding?'

'No…he didn't mention any of that,' Winnie almost whispered, leaning forward to set down the cup and saucer on his desk before she embarrassed herself by dropping it.

'If I hadn't bribed him to marry you, he wouldn't even have considered giving up his freedom,' her grandfather emphasised. 'And *this* is the man you're willing to sacrifice a splendid future for?'

'What splendid future?' she questioned blankly half under her breath.

'Without Nevrakis, you and Teddy could live here with me and eventually you would meet a man more worthy of your attention.'

'A man you chose, who meets your approval,' Winnie guessed sickly. 'A man who doesn't fight back, a man who allows you to call all the shots.'

'Am I *that* arrogant?' Stam dealt her a reproachful look.

'I don't think you can tolerate or like anyone who defies you,' Winnie muttered ruefully, struggling desperately not to think about what he had just told her about Eros.

She felt as though she had been dropped from a height and had landed on her head, because it was aching and full of chaotic, unhappy thoughts. Eros had married her to regain a stupid island? How did that make sense? Trilis was, admittedly, a beautiful island and Eros had ties there that went back over a hundred years: the little graveyard on the headland contained worn headstones etched with the Nevrakis name. His family had helped to build the church and the little primary school on the steep cobbled street running up out of the village. She had dreamt of Teddy starting school there one day... In a daze, she shook her thumping head in a vain effort to clear it.

'I like you,' the older man reproved her gently. 'And yet you are in your quiet little way every bit as defiant as your father was. I don't want Nevrakis to hurt you again. That is why I told you about the island.'

'I'm afraid I've nothing more to say to you right now,' Winnie said tightly as she rose from her seat, striving not to recall Eros's forecast that her grandfather would hurt her.

Or had it been more of a case of Eros fearing what the older man might choose to *tell* her? A faint shudder of distress and revulsion racked Winnie's slight frame, her eyes prickling a tearful warning and forcing her to blink rapidly. Eros had got an island out of marrying her, a sort of marital buy one, get one free offer. How was she supposed to feel about that? *Of course he hadn't told her.* He wasn't a fool. He was bright enough to know how any woman would feel if she knew a man had had to be bribed into marrying her. Oh, she perfectly understood his silence on the subject, just as she understood the anguished regret flooding her.

Once again, she had walked, blindfolded by love, into a disaster. To make that mistake once with a man was unpleasant, but to make it twice was unforgivable...

'You've only just arrived. You can't leave now,' Stam protested in dismay.

'But you've said what you wanted to say to me. You pushed me into marrying him and now you're trying to push me into leaving him, and I won't be pushed again,' Winnie told him flatly. 'What happens next is my business.'

Only she didn't *know* what would happen next, didn't know what she intended to do with the information she had been given. Beyond confronting Eros, she could see no further, but she paused at the door of the office to look back at her grandfather. 'Whatever happens between Eros and I, I still hope to see you visiting your great-grandson on Trilis some day soon because he shouldn't be affected by adult squabbles.'

'*Squabbles?*' Stam echoed in disbelief at that insulting term for what he deemed to be a perfectly natural hostility towards the man who had dared to wrong his granddaughter. 'I'll never visit you or Teddy there!'

'That's sad,' Winnie murmured ruefully. 'Family should come first, even if you can't always approve of what they're doing with their lives.'

Winnie walked stiffly back out to the foyer, where her bodyguards awaited her. She was in a daze. Eros had married her to get the island back. Eros had forced her to marry him to *ensure* that he got that island back.

Evidently, her grandfather had employed the perfect carrot to tempt. On her own, she hadn't been tempting enough for a man who had already been through one unsatisfactory marriage and would naturally have been chary of locking himself into a second marriage with a woman he might lust after but didn't love.

And that was her situation in a nutshell, she decided sickly while her security team engaged in a series of frantic phone calls to organise a departure that had come much sooner than anyone had expected. Pale as death, she stared at the wall, willing herself to be strong and make decisions. Eros had never loved her and that was unlikely to change. Even for Teddy's sake she couldn't stay in a marriage in which his essential indifference would chip away at her self-esteem every day until she had nothing left.

She was strong, independent, she reminded herself resolutely. She would confront him and deal with the situation without getting overemotional or crying or shouting. Shouting would be pathetic. Shouting would reveal that she had been hurt. She would be cool, *dignified*. As she worked that out, her shoulders eased back, her head lifted higher…and at the same time she would somehow make Eros Nevrakis very, very sorry that he had ever been born…

CHAPTER TEN

EROS SPRANG OUT of the helicopter and took a shortcut across the grass to the house. His lean, darkly handsome features were tense. Winnie had stayed barely half an hour with her grandfather, and after leaving she had ignored his phone calls and his texts. That wasn't like her. Winnie was never petty or moody and it took a lot to rile her. But nothing could silence Eros's conviction that something had gone badly wrong.

Even so, there was no way that he could have persuaded her *not* to visit Stam Fotakis. Winnie might be petite but she could fight like a heavyweight if anyone tried to drive her in a direction she didn't want. That was why he had let her fly free. He was determined not to make her grandfather a source of contention between them. After all, he wanted Winnie to be happy.

And she *had* been happy before she'd left him earlier that day even if she had been nervous about confronting her grandfather, a man known the world over for his stubborn intransigence. Had the wretched man threatened her in some way? Rage gripped Eros at that suspicion, rage as volatile and blinding as a lightning storm on a dark night. Had he made a major mistake when he'd stood back and allowed her to see Stam again so soon after the debacle of their wedding day? Disappointed by Winnie's decision to stay with her husband and child, the older man must be gnashing his teeth in frustration. Had he taken that dissatisfaction out on Winnie?

Eros strode into the hall, which was curiously empty of staff, and frowned, slowly turning in a half circle.

'You're home…' Winnie commented in an odd, flat voice as she walked out of the spacious lounge. 'Sooner than expected.'

He wheeled round. Winnie was wearing an elegant black knee-length dress, her slim legs and delicate ankles on display. He breathed in deep because she looked superb, the outfit clinging just enough to hint at her spectacular curves. He wouldn't tell her how fantastic she looked because she tended to argue with him when he tried to pay her compliments. But no other word could have better described the tumbling mass of lustrous dark hair bouncing on her slim shoulders and the bright brown eyes sparkling with vivacity above her soft pink mouth.

'I cut short my meetings once I realised you would be back early.'

'Now, why would you have done that?' she questioned suspiciously, although he could not for the life of him imagine anything she had to be suspicious of.

'You stayed a very short time with your grandfather and I was worried that the visit had somehow upset you,' he admitted pointedly.

'It didn't take long for Grandad and I to say all that we had to say to each other,' Winnie told him ominously, staring at him.

It offended her sense of justice that even after a very busy day, Eros still looked spectacular, his charcoal-grey suit smooth and unwrinkled, exquisitely tailored to his lean, powerful body, his shirt white and immaculate, his green silk tie still straight and, yes, that shade exactly picked up the hue of his stunning eyes. Only the breeze outside that had tousled his luxuriant black curls and the dark encroaching shadow of stubble accentuating his beautifully shaped mouth suggested that hours had passed since their last meeting.

Eros quirked a winged ebony brow. 'Anything I should know about?'

'Now, why would you ask me that question?' Winnie asked sweetly. 'Is your conscience bothering you?'

'You're acting very oddly,' Eros remarked drily, and glanced around in the humming silence. 'Where are the staff? Where's Teddy?'

'I gave the staff the night off and Agathe took Teddy down to the village to have tea with her parents. They asked to meet him,' she told him grudgingly.

'Are you cooking tonight, then?' Eros enquired lazily.

'You'd better hope not. I might be tempted to poison you if I had to feed you,' Winnie told him roundly.

'So, Stam told tales,' Eros gathered without skipping a beat, his intonation as cool as an icicle.

Inflamed by that controlled coolness, Winnie shifted several feet and lifted an opulent gilded china vase from a table.

'Very ugly, isn't it?' Eros commented.

'Not as ugly as the truth of what you did to me,'

Winnie countered, studying him with a blazing anger she could no longer hide.

'What did I do?' Eros asked sibilantly, thinking that there was no way that she would throw the vase because she was not the scene-throwing, violent type.

A split second later, Eros learned his mistake as his wife pitched the vase at him with all the force of a shot-putter throwing for a world record. He ducked and she missed, the vase shattering harmlessly against the wall behind him.

'You let my grandfather *bribe* you into marrying me!' Winnie condemned in wrathful disgust.

'No, I didn't,' Eros fielded succinctly.

'He gave you an *island* to marry me!' Winnie flung back at him in shrill disagreement.

'I took the island because he was offering it but that's *not* why I married you,' Eros told her emphatically.

'You accepted this island as a bribe,' Winnie repeated, refusing to listen.

'It would've been foolish not to accept it when I was planning to marry you anyway,' Eros declared, stalking forward as she coiled her hands into fists and made a desperate slashing movement with one of them, frustrated by his self-assurance in the face of her accusation.

A big hand engulfed one of hers in his to hold her fast in front of him and his brilliant green eyes clashed with angry brown. 'The only *truly* important thing that happened the day I first met your grandfather was his revelation that I was the father of a son. Yes, he offered me this island and my family once had a great attachment to this place, but that offer would not have driven me all the way to London to see you, nor would it have made me marry you. It was Teddy who initially motivated me.'

'I don't believe you. You didn't tell me the truth about the island or anything!' Winnie threw back at him tempestuously.

'Of course I didn't,' Eros took the wind out of her sails by replying. 'I was very angry before I married you. I was furious that you had kept my son from me,' he reminded her, retaining his grip on her hand when she tried to snatch it away again. 'But I got over that anger and I didn't want you to distrust me any more than you already did. Telling you about the island within weeks of marrying you would have damaged our relationship and I wasn't prepared to risk that. We had enough difficult ground to cover without borrowing trouble.'

'I refuse to listen to your excuses,' Winnie told him between angrily gritted teeth.

'They're not excuses—they're the reasons why I remained silent. Why shouldn't I have accepted the island when he offered it? My father did ask me to try to reclaim Trilis if I could ever afford to do so. But because I didn't grow up here and wasn't familiar with it, this place didn't mean as much to me as perhaps it should've. Once I saw it for the first time, I felt differently,' he conceded ruefully. 'I felt a connection, although not, admittedly, with this grandiose house.'

Winnie shook her head in a kind of blind panic, terrified of being persuaded out of her belief that she had to leave him to find the happiness she craved. 'I'm going to move out and find somewhere to stay in Athens…so you'll still be able to see plenty of Teddy.'

'I would need to see plenty of you as well for that arrangement to work,' Eros fielded forcefully. 'We can't live in separate houses. I need *both* of you to survive.'

'You have *never* needed me!' Winnie exclaimed, wrenching her hand angrily free of his.

'All that's changed,' Eros countered ruefully, 'is that I no longer fight that need. Two years ago, when you walked out on me, my life suddenly lost all focus.'

'Nonsense, you didn't even miss me!' Winnie argued vehemently.

Eros rested level green eyes on her. 'Of course, I missed you. By the time you left you had contrived to become the centre of my world.'

Winnie frowned at that startling statement. 'I don't believe you.'

'It wasn't supposed to turn out like that. It was supposed to be a casual affair but it was never casual between us,' Eros reasoned with a wry curl to his sculpted mouth. 'I was working eighteen-hour days just so that I could rush down to the country to spend long weekends with you. I was phoning you every day, sometimes more than once. I was behaving like a teenage boy in love for the first time. Often, I walked through the door and within minutes we were in each other's arms. That's *not* a fling. That's *not* a casual relationship. But I was in denial about that because I was still married and I didn't have the courage or the experience to recognise how important a part of my life you had become.'

'I remember you pushing me away.'

'Because sometimes I felt out of control with you and it unnerved me because I wanted you too much for my peace of mind. I tried to tell myself that being with you wasn't harming anyone even though I knew that I was lying to myself. Nevertheless, I still couldn't make myself break off our relationship either,' he admitted in a driven undertone, his beautiful green eyes disturbingly unguarded in their anxious intensity as he studied her. 'The fact that I felt everything for you that Tasha wanted me to feel for *her* only made me feel worse.'

Involuntarily, Winnie was listening. 'Did it?'

'After the divorce when I was still thinking about how I had failed I decided that I was no better than my womanising father,' he said gruffly. 'I had made you unhappy and I had made Tasha unhappy. She was my wife and she loved me and yet I couldn't love her back. I watched my mother go through that with my father when he fell for another woman and I couldn't stand to do that to anyone else. With that on my conscience I didn't feel that I had the right to pursue any personal happiness.'

Winnie stared back at him, disconcerted by the amount of guilt he still bore from the past. 'You should never have agreed to marry her and her father should never have put pressure on you to marry her.'

'And if I did marry her, I should have gone for a divorce the minute she began having relationships with other men,' he added heavily. 'But I'd agreed to that and it wasn't fair to change the rules because they no longer suited me. I tried to keep my promise to her and when I turned to you, I failed, so I didn't make you *any* promises.'

'You didn't,' she agreed ruefully.

'I couldn't admit to myself that I'd fallen for you,

I couldn't let myself chase after you when you left either because that would have been admitting that the divorce was all about you. And I couldn't admit that to myself back then,' Eros confided starkly. 'Because that's what my father did to my mother—fell for another woman and went for a divorce. And even though my marriage to Tasha was never a proper marriage, I still couldn't accept that I could have anything in common with a man who was that weak and cruel.'

Winnie was bemused. 'Fallen for me?' she repeated shakily.

'I think I fell for you the first time I met you. You were shy and you smiled at me and my heart felt full and I couldn't take my eyes off you,' Eros confessed gruffly. 'And it was always like that. I couldn't wait to see you when I got home. I couldn't wait to *be* with you.'

Winnie was listening to that avalanche of words tumbling from him with wide, confused eyes. 'You're trying to say you fell in love with me two years ago?' she prompted with a frown.

'Winnie…' Eros gripped both her hands fiercely in his. 'A man who is only interested in clandestine sex doesn't spend hours simply talking to a woman or hanging about the kitchen while she cooks, and he doesn't have to phone her every day so that he knows every little thing she does in her life.'

'Maybe it was a sort of love,' she reasoned reluctantly. 'But it still wasn't enough to overcome your guilt and persuade you to come after me once you were free.'

'I'd have come after you if I'd known you were pregnant. Nothing would have kept me from you!' he swore with fierce intensity. 'But you didn't tell me and I didn't know if you loved me either.'

'Were you blind?' Winnie asked helplessly.

'Winnie, you don't cling or flatter or act like I'm the most important person in your world. You never did. If I'd known you loved me, it would've made a difference because then I would've known that staying away from you was hurting you. But not knowing that, I believed I'd made a big enough mess of your life and that I should leave you in peace.'

'You are so stupid,' Winnie whispered in wonderment. 'And that possibility never crossed my mind… that you could be so stupid and blind about emotional connections. I never wanted perfect. I never expected a perfect man.'

'Just as well. I'm not perfect, never will be,' Eros muttered gruffly. 'But I do love you more than anything else in the world. I was too bitter to recognise that when I married you and then you got to me again.'

'I *got* to you?' Winnie queried.

'Yes, you have a way of doing that. I'm not a naturally cheerful or optimistic person,' Eros volunteered ruefully. 'But being with you makes me happy and of course I appreciated that. The thought of losing you again *terrifies* me, so now you tell me what I have to do to put this right. I can give the island back to your grandfather.'

'You'd *do* that?' She gasped.

'Sooner than lose you? Of course I would,' he admitted bluntly. 'It's a geographical location, it's not my heart, it's not the centre of my life. *But you are.*'

Winnie was beginning to rather enjoy the conversation. She stared up into those troubled emerald eyes of his, reading his sincerity, and slowly she smiled, the tension round her mouth falling away. 'You love me, not just Teddy.'

'Of course, I don't only love Teddy. *Thee mou...* You *gave* me Teddy!' Eros reminded her in reproach. 'Is that what you've been thinking?'

'Yes, I did think that when I married you,' she confessed unevenly. 'I thought you were only marrying me to gain access to our son. I assumed that's why you were willing to blackmail me into agreeing to marry you.'

'Once I got over that initial anger at having been kept from Teddy, I wanted both of you and I didn't care how I went about achieving that. That's not forgivable, I know,' he conceded tautly. 'But I had a voracious need to get back what we'd had together two years ago and *lost*...and I was determined to let nothing stop me reaching for that.'

Her lashes lifted on reflective eyes. 'What we had then *was* special...wasn't it?' she almost whispered, scared to hope, scared to believe. 'That wasn't just my imagination.'

'Something I never saw or felt with any other woman,' Eros admitted starkly. 'And I wanted it back...you and Teddy both. I've been trying to show you that since our wedding day...that we can be together and happy and building a wonderful future. But not one sign would you give me that you saw our marriage as anything other than a patched-up job likely to fall apart.'

Winnie went pink. 'Another baby was a fairly big ask,' she began.

'And I dropped that,' he reminded her wryly. 'So,

what do you want to do about the island now? Shall I give it back?'

'Keep it. It's your family place and we like it here,' Winnie reasoned with immense practicality. 'It's not as though Grandad wants it back. In fact, he would probably be offended if you tried to return it. I think all we need to do is learn to trust each other again. And we mustn't allow Grandad to influence us.'

'He tried to threaten me into agreeing to marry you. Did he admit that?' Eros demanded in a rueful undertone.

'Threaten you? In what way?' she pressed in consternation.

'He threatened to destroy me in the business world. He could certainly have made doing business more of a challenge by interfering with my suppliers and competing on contracts, but he has enough enemies of his own that I would always have found allies,' Eros declared with assurance. 'His threats were not a serious concern.'

Winnie was shaken at that confession. Stam had been far more ruthless in his methods of achieving his goal than she could ever have guessed. Wanting her to marry Eros, he had attempted to force both of them into doing his bidding and at that moment she recognised that it was time she too disclosed the pressure her grandfather had put on her and her siblings to marry the men of his choice.

'I have something to tell you,' she said awkwardly.

'You can tell me anything,' Eros said encouragingly, settling her down on a comfortable sofa while still gripping her hand, almost as though he was afraid to let go of her even temporarily.

Winnie told him about her foster parents' predicament with their mortgage, which her grandfather now owned. Eros dropped her hand and shot upright, incredulous green eyes glittering. 'He's blackmailing you and your sisters? That's *why* you married me?' he demanded. 'Why the hell didn't you tell me this sooner? I could've stopped him in his tracks and protected all of you by buying John and Liz another house!'

Winnie dealt him a shaken appraisal. 'Well, that wouldn't have worked, not without us coming clean with John and Liz about what we were trying to do on their behalf. And they wouldn't have accepted your generosity *or* ours! John and Liz are much too proud and independent to allow anyone else to settle their financial problems. That's why what we were trying to do to help them had to be behind the scenes and kept secret,' she told him ruefully. 'And that property has been in Liz's family for generations, so moving them to another house wouldn't be the same either.'

'You married me to save the roof over their heads. You married me for a stay of execution on a mortgage that cost your wily old grandfather a ridiculously *small* amount of money!' Eros objected in raw wonderment. 'I don't know whether to compliment you for a selfless act of sacrifice or shout at you for being so naive.'

'No shouting, please,' Winnie muttered heavily. 'My sisters and I had to do *something*. We couldn't just stand by and watch John and Liz lose everything they valued.'

'And it didn't once occur to you that you were marrying a very wealthy man who could have stepped in to offer other options to protect *all* of you from Stam's blackmail?' Eros derided in disbelief.

'No… I would never have been willing to ask you for money,' Winnie asserted ruefully.

'You can ask me for anything,' Eros murmured thickly, settling down beside her again and reaching for her hand. 'No restrictions either. Anything you want is yours.'

Winnie tilted her head back, lustrous mahogany hair tumbling back from her heart-shaped face and her caramel gaze locked to him with all-encompassing warmth. 'All I want out of all this is you.'

'I'm already yours, heart and soul,' Eros asserted hoarsely. 'I have been for a very long time. I'm crazy in love with you. Even the news that you married me to save your foster parents' home doesn't put a dent in my enthusiasm,' he confessed, his mouth quirking at that rueful acknowledgement. 'But then if the sight of you walking out on me on our wedding day didn't cure me of loving you, it looks as though nothing ever will…'

'Amen to that,' Winnie muttered, leaning closer, her heartbeat quickening as the achingly familiar scent of him drenched her.

'I have just two small requests,' Eros breathed thickly, leaning down to brush his sensual lips softly across hers, awareness surging through her body like a rocket to awaken every nerve ending into a sweet ache of anticipation.

'And what are they?' she mumbled in a dizzy haze.

'We admit we love each other every day.'

'Easy… I can do that,' she sighed dreamily. *'And?'*

'We go through another wedding ceremony, one in

which you mean every word you say,' Eros instructed, toying with her bottom lip in the most erotic way.

Winnie trembled. 'We can do that too. In fact, it would mean a lot to me,' she confided. 'But if you don't kiss me soon, I might change my mind.'

Eros flicked his tongue between her parted lips. 'I want much more than a kiss, *kardoula mou*,' he husked.

Winnie's slender fingers sank into his black curls to tip him closer. 'And you think I don't?' she teased, buoyant with happiness, every fear laid to rest.

'I don't want to be surprised half-naked by our nanny,' Eros confided, pulling back from her with a groan at the necessity to bend down and scoop her up into his arms. 'We're going to bed.'

They didn't make it up the stairs all in one go. Eros paused to kiss her and things got a little hot and heavy on the first landing and then they heard their nanny Agathe's measured voice outside and they fled to their bedroom. Later they would get up and be good parents and bathe Teddy and play with him awhile before putting him to bed, but just at that moment, they were both punch-drunk on a wave of love and lust, made all the keener by the knowledge that they could so easily have held on to their pride and lost each other. And in renewing their love, they found fresh confidence and exulted in that intimacy.

Six months later, Winnie smoothed her maternity frock down over the slight bump of her pregnancy. Yes, ultimately Eros had got his way. At least, she had agreed to *try* for another child but she certainly hadn't expected to conceive the very first month and indeed had assumed that it might take the better part of a year. Eros had confessed, however, that he was very motivated to delivering the required result and she had to admit that from the moment she had conceived, no newly expectant mother could possibly have been more spoiled and supported than she had been.

It had been a very busy few months. Eros had bought a house more suited to a toddler's needs in London and they were spending more time there so that Winnie could see her sisters on a regular basis. As they were slowly transforming the house on Trilis into a comfortable and less imposing family home and their main base, it also made sense to have somewhere else to go when the building work on the home front reached crucial stages. Winnie found the island more relaxing and she was forging friendships there. She loved the fact that her son could run wild in their extensive grounds and that the property was large enough for her sisters to join her there whenever they had time off. Eros was travelling less and he had set up a working office in the house.

Two months after they had admitted their love for each other, they had had a wedding blessing ceremony in the little church by the harbour and that had strengthened them as a couple. Saying those vows and meaning them, not to mention her steadily improving grasp of the Greek language, had been a crucial acceptance of their new future together. Eros had insisted that he had only suggested it to benefit from a second wedding night and the apparently unbeatable lure of all those buttons, which were actually hooks. But Winnie, who had been disconcerted by the many little romantic touches her husband had thought up to embellish the occasion—not least the surprise presence of her foster parents, John and Liz—wasn't fooled. He had made that day as special as he made her feel and she could not have been happier.

That very evening they were holding a party in honour of her grandfather's seventy-fifth birthday and he was bringing her sisters with him. Winnie smiled cheerfully. It had taken months for Stam Fotakis to recognise the wisdom of putting away the big guns and making the best of his eldest granddaughter's marriage and family. Eros had had to visit the older man to personally invite him to visit them on the island while Winnie had done her bit in insisting on throwing the birthday party for him. Offered a virtual red carpet, Stam had grasped the opportunity with alacrity and any loss of face involved by that climbdown had been wonderfully soothed by his great-grandson, Teddy, running across the lawn to greet with him with a delighted shout of excitement.

'Your sisters are looking very well,' her grandfather remarked, scanning Vivi in her fuchsia-pink dress, a daring colour for a redhead, but frowning at Zoe, who was practically welded to a seat with its back to the wall. 'Zoe's going to have to get over that shyness.'

'It's not shyness. She just doesn't like crowds,' Winnie said defensively.

'I offered that husband of yours a business deal and he turned me down,' Stam informed her grimly. 'He doesn't trust me. Said it would put me in the driver's seat if he lost his shirt. He's shrewd. I'm beginning to like that about him. I wouldn't like to see you married to a fool.'

Winnie grinned at that grudging admission but

tactfully made no comment. Across the room, Vivi was rifling frantically through a magazine and then passing it to Zoe to read. Curious, Winnie walked over just as Eros appeared and fell into step beside her, Teddy clutching his hand.

'What are you looking at?' she asked Vivi.

'Don't ask,' Vivi advised, white with suppressed anger.

Zoe grimaced. 'The Duke of Mancini has taken over another bank. He must be minted.'

'Let me see…' Winnie grasped the business magazine, ignoring the photo of the very good-looking Italian banker who had destroyed her sister's reputation. 'Have you ever come across him in business?' she asked Eros.

'No, he's rather too rich for my blood.' Eros curled an arm round his wife's back and didn't even raise a brow when Vivi vented a very rude word. 'A member of the Italian elite.'

'Pig!' Vivi pronounced with fierce loathing. 'He's a *pig*!'

'Don't read the article,' Winnie advised softly.

'That's the guy who labelled her a prostitute in the tabloids, isn't it?' Eros prompted in an undertone as they moved on. 'I remember the name from the investigation I had done.'

'Yes, that's him and, like a rose in a dung heap, he is still flourishing against all the odds!' Winnie muttered bitterly.

'I wouldn't take any bets on that continuing,' Eros murmured as his son wriggled deftly free of his hold. 'Not with Stam gunning for him. I could almost, but not quite, feel sorry for the guy.'

'Grandad has never once mentioned his name,' Winnie protested.

'Stam likes to play his cards close to his chest,' Eros breathed, striding across the floor of the ballroom to stop his son from clambering up on a chair to reach the precious birthday cake. He ignored the screams of protest that followed with the cool of a practised parent and, surprisingly quickly, Teddy ditched his fake sobs and started chattering to his father instead.

Man and child looked so alike with their matching green eyes and black curls that it always lifted Winnie's heart to see them together. When Agathe appeared to reclaim the little boy, Winnie relaxed more because Teddy was too lively to be anything other than an accident waiting to happen at an adult party. Some outside exercise and supper would better suit his needs.

Eros brought her a soft drink while she was out on the terrace. 'Remember the massive row we had out here on our wedding day?' he prompted.

'I don't want to remember that,' she said truthfully. 'I was feeling so miserably unhappy and angry.'

'You have to go through the bad stuff to get to the good stuff,' Eros told her philosophically. 'My ego was squashed beyond recovery when my bride walked out on me.'

Winnie gazed up into his darkly handsome face, fingers tingling at the prospect of brushing back that silky black hair from his brow, eyes lost in the mesmeric enticement of his, her body slowly humming to life like an engine being switched on. 'If it was, you made a very fast recovery.'

'But then I had you to recover with,' Eros husked, easing her back against the railings to hungrily claim a kiss, groaning as she strained against him. 'You are a witch, *agape mou*. Now I have to stay out here until I'm fit to be seen in company again.'

'I think we can manage that,' Winnie whispered with a wanton little shift of her hips that made his lean, powerful length shudder in response against hers. 'I love you so much, Eros.'

'And for some reason I love you even when you're teasing the hell out of me,' he admitted raggedly.

* * * * *

CLAIMING HIS
HIDDEN HEIR

CAROL MARINELLI

For my great friend Frances Housden.

An inspiring woman and wonderful writer.

Love always,

Carol xxx

PROLOGUE

HE WOULD NOT be hiring Cecelia Andrews.

Property magnate Luka Kargas had already decided that Candidate Number Two would be his new personal assistant.

'Ms Andrews is here for her interview,' Hannah, his current PA, informed him.

'There's no need for me to meet her,' Luka responded. 'I've decided to go with Candidate Two.'

'Luka!' Hannah reproached, a little braver now that she was leaving. 'At least have the decency to see her. She's been through two extensive interviews with me, and as well as that it's pouring outside. She had to come across London in the middle of a storm.'

'Not interested,' Luka said, because he didn't buy into sob stories. 'It's a waste of my time.'

And a slice of Luka's time was precious indeed.

But then Luka suddenly remembered that Ms Andrews had been personally recommended by Justin, a contact he wanted to keep onside.

'Fine, send her in,' Luka said, deciding to see her briefly but then to get rid of her as soon as he could.

Impatient fingers drummed the desk as he waited, and then Candidate Three was shown in.

'Ms Andrews.' Luka stood and shook her right hand, noticing that on her left she wore an engagement ring.

Nothing would induce him to hire her, for she would have to have the most patient fiancé in the world to tolerate the ridiculous hours she would have to devote to him.

And *everyone* knew his reputation.

He just had to give her a few minutes of his time so he could tell Justin that he had interviewed her but gone with another candidate.

'Please,' he said. 'Take a seat.'

Cecelia knew that although he had called her Ms Andrews he was awaiting correction and an invitation to call her by her first name.

There would be no such invitation to do so.

Ms Andrews would do just fine, Cecelia had decided.

She had read about him, thoroughly researched him, and even been told by his current PA during two prolonged interviews about his bad-boy ways.

'You would have to deal with his girlfriends, or rather his exes,' Hannah had explained. 'It can be quite a juggling act at times. Luka works hard all week and then works just as hard breaking hearts at the weekend.'

Cecelia had seen it all before, and not just through her work. She abhorred the rich, debauched kind of lifestyle he led and with good reason—her mother, Harriet, had lived and died the same way.

Still, Luka Kargas's morals were his own concern, not hers. Cecelia had her sights set on working for royalty and he was a step in the right direction, that was all.

'He has a yacht, currently moored in Xanero,' Hannah had said.

'That's where he's from?' Cecelia checked, although she had found that out in her research.

'Yes, though you won't be expected to travel there with him and you won't be involved with the family business there. Luka keeps that strictly separate.'

She would not be falling for him, Cecelia had reassured both his incumbent PA and herself. The only thing the career-minded Cecelia wanted from Luka Kargas was his name on her résumé and the glowing reference that, after a year's hard work, he would surely provide.

But now she had finally met him, and as his long olive fingers had closed around hers, the very sensible Cecelia's conviction that she would not be attracted to him in the least had wavered somewhat.

'Hannah said you got caught in the storm,' Luka frowned.

The skies had darkened just over an hour ago.

Luka, from his vantage point of the fortieth floor, had watched the black clouds gather and roll over London.

Candidate Two had arrived drenched and had asked Hannah for a ten-minute delay before proceeding with the interview.

Usually that would have been enough to ensure a black mark against her name but, having watched the storm himself, Luka had accepted the excuse and the rather bedraggled candidate.

Cecelia Andrews was far from bedraggled, though.

She wore a dark grey suit that was immaculate, her blonde hair, worn up, was sleek and smooth, while her make-up was both discreet and in place.

Hannah had insinuated that a drowned rat sat in the entrance yet the woman who sat before him was far from that.

'I got caught up in the storm,' Cecelia said, 'but I wasn't caught out—I heeded the warnings.'

And she might want to start heeding them now, she thought, for the impact of him on her senses was like nothing she had ever known.

He wore a dark suit and tie and his crisp white shirt accentuated his olive skin; he hadn't shaved that morning.

The air in the room had changed, as if the charge that had lit the sky for the past hour had joined them.

Luka Kargas was everything her aunt had warned her about, and though she had told herself she could handle it, and that there was no way she could ever be attracted to someone like him, Cecelia hadn't allowed for the impact of Luka close up.

They skipped through the formalities, both determined to get this over and done with and move on with the day.

'Hannah will have explained that the hours are long,' Luka said.

'She did.'

'Sixteen-hour days at times.'

'Yes.' Cecelia nodded.

'And there's an awful lot of travel,' Luka said. 'Though for all that the working week is hell, you do get every weekend off.'

She smiled a tight, slightly disbelieving smile.

'You do,' Luka said, as he read those full lips. 'Come Friday night, the entire weekend is yours.'

'Though I'm guessing I wouldn't be out of here by five p.m.?'

'No,' he said. 'Usually around ten.'

So not really the entire weekend to herself, Cecelia thought as his black eyes scanned through her paperwork. 'Why are you finishing up with Justin?'

'Because I didn't want to live in Dubai.'

'I go there a lot,' Luka said, 'which would mean, by default, so would you.'

'That's fine. I just don't want to live there,' Cecelia said, and she knew, she just knew, he was alluding to the fact she had a fiancé whose needs would have impacted on her decision.

He was right.

Gordon wouldn't consider it.

'Do you speak Greek?' he asked.

'No,' Cecelia said, suddenly hoping it was a prerequisite for the role and that this torture would therefore come to an end. It was torture because her stomach seemed to be folding in on itself and she all of a sudden could feel the weight of her breasts. She had never had such a violent reaction to another person, though of course it was one-sided.

Luka Kargas looked thoroughly bored.

'Do you speak any other languages?' he asked.

'Some French,' Cecelia said, even though she spoke it very well and had both lived and worked in France for a year.

Anyway, he didn't want her French, whether a little or a lot of it, for he screwed up his nose.

Good, because Cecelia had now decided that she did not want this job.

She liked safe, and for very good reasons.

Cecelia liked her world ordered, and ten minutes alone with Luka Kargas had just rocked hers.

His black eyes were mesmerising and his brusque indifference had her re-crossing her legs.

Until this moment, sex had been a perfectly pleasant experience, if sometimes a bit of a chore.

Now, though, she sat across from a man who made her think of it.

Actually sit and think about torrid, impromptu sex at two p.m. on a Monday afternoon, and that could never do.

'Ms Andrews…'

'Cecelia,' she corrected, but only because she didn't want to sound like some uptight spinster.

And she wasn't.

She was engaged to be married, and right now she found herself desperately trying to hold onto that thought.

Oh, this really would never do!

'Cecelia.' He nodded. 'I see that you don't have any real experience in the hospitality industry.'

'No, I don't,' Cecelia said. 'Not a jot.'

'A jot?' His black eyes looked up and met her green ones and she saw that his were not actually black but the deepest of browns.

'I don't have any experience in the hospitality industry, none at all.'

'And I note that you wear an engagement ring.'

'Excuse me…' Cecelia frowned '…but you can't comment on that.'

He waved his hand dismissively.

Luka read her emergency contact and saw that it wasn't her fiancé but, in fact, her aunt.

And she intrigued him a touch. '*Are* you engaged?'

'Yes.' Cecelia bristled. 'Not that it's any of your business.'

'Cecelia, if you are considering working for me, then you might as well know from the outset that I am not known for my political correctness. I'll tell it to you straight—I don't want a PA who is in the throes of planning a big wedding, neither I don't want someone who is going to have to dash off at six because her fiancé is sulking.'

Cecelia's jaw tightened because at times Gordon did just that.

'Mr Kargas, my personal life is not your concern and, let me assure you, it never will be.'

Never, because she was not taking the job!

He heard the double meaning behind her words and almost smiled but then checked himself.

'Come over here,' he said, and stood up and headed to the floor-to-ceiling windows.

It was like no interview she had ever experienced before, Cecelia thought as she stood and walked over to join him.

Gosh, he was tall.

And he smelt as if he had bathed in bergamot with a testosterone undertone.

'See the view,' Luka said.

'It's amazing.' Cecelia nodded, looking out across a gleaming, wet and shiny London. The grey skies were starting to clear and black clouds were lined with silver but there was no rainbow that she could see.

'It's all yours,' Luka said, and Cecelia frowned. 'When you finish on a Friday, right up to Monday morning the world out there is your oyster.' Then he looked over at her. 'But when you're here…'

He expected devotion. Cecelia got his meaning.

'When can you start?' Luka asked.

Before she declined, Cecelia took a deep breath and thought of the perks of this job—a salary that was almost twice her current one, endless travel and the Kargas name on her résumé for ever.

And then she thought of the pitfalls.

Sixty-hour weeks spent beside this stunning man.

Her attraction to him was as unexpected as it was unsettling.

She actually didn't know what to do.

'I'd like some time to think about it,' Cecelia said in response to his offer.

'Well, I'm looking for someone who trusts their own instincts and can make prompt decisions.'

Luka now wanted her working for him.

She had impressed him when he had not expected to be impressed, yet something told him that if she walked out of the door Cecelia Andrews would not be coming back.

He could *feel* her hesitation.

And because he was Luka Kargas he knew when to push, and how. 'So, I'll ask again, when can you start, Cecelia?'

Never! Her instincts screamed.

Yet she had so badly wanted this job and the challenge it would bring and, though he was undoubtedly attractive, Cecelia knew herself well enough to be certain she would never get involved with anyone at work.

'Now,' Cecelia said, shocked at her own decision. 'I can start now.'

'Then welcome aboard.'

And as he shook her hand, Cecelia told herself she could handle it.

CHAPTER ONE

LUKA, AFTER CAREFUL consideration I've decided…

Waking just before her alarm went off, Cecelia lay listening to the hiss of bus doors opening on the street outside her London flat and working out how best to resign.

And when to do it?

Did she get it over and done with in the morning? Or wait until the end of the day to tell him that she would not be renewing her contract?

Most people would say she was mad to quit.

The pay was amazing, the travel wonderful, if exhausting, but in the eleven months she had worked for Luka, Cecelia had hit the limit on her primness radar.

He was a playboy in the extreme.

And that wasn't some vague, unsourced opinion.

It was fact.

Cecelia ran his diary after all!

Quite simply, she couldn't do it any more and so on Friday, as Luka had headed to the rooftop to swan off in his chopper for a debauched weekend in France, Cecelia had reached for her phone and accepted a six-month contract as personal assistant to an esteemed and elderly foreign diplomat.

While the money and perks would be worse in her

new job, the peace of mind it would bring was, to Cecelia, worth its weight in gold.

Only as she reached for her phone to check the time did Cecelia see the date and remember that it was her birthday.

There was never much fuss made of it and she had long since told herself to get over that fact. Her aunt and uncle, who had raised her since the age of eight, simply didn't bother with such things and before she had died, neither had her mother.

She saw that a message had come in overnight from Luka.

Shan't be in today, Cece. Cancel my meetings and I'll call you later.

Cecelia ground her teeth at the annoying shortening of her name that she had repeatedly asked him to stop using. But then she frowned, because in the eleven months that she had worked for Luka he had never taken a day off. Luka had a phenomenal workload yet never missed a beat. But now, on the one day she really needed to speak to him, he wasn't going to be there.

Cecelia wanted her resignation handed in and sorted, and for her time with Luka to be over. As well as that he had an important meeting with Mr Garcia and his entourage in NYC later today. Although it was an online meeting, it had been incredibly hard to set up and it was going to be extremely messy to cancel.

Despite the absence of her boss—in fact, *because* of the absence of her boss—today was shaping up to be an exceptionally busy one, and so Cecelia forced herself up and out of bed.

She showered quickly and began to get ready.

Her routines were set in stone and, despite the extensive travel and odd hours required by her job, there were certain things that never changed. She could be in Florence, New York, or home in London but these things remained—her clothes were set out the night before, as was her breakfast, which she ate before tackling her hair.

Routines were vital to Cecelia's sense of well-being, for during the first eight years of her life, when she had lived with her mother, chaos had been the only certainty.

The reddish fire to Cecelia's strawberry blonde mane had, courtesy of foils, been dimmed to a neutral blonde. She smoothed and sleeked out her long curls and then tied them back into a neat, low ponytail.

Next, Cecelia applied her make-up.

She didn't wear much, but as Luka's PA it was expected that she was always well turned out.

It wasn't always the case. A famous actress she had once worked for had insisted that Cecelia wear no make-up whatsoever as well as extremely plain clothing. With another employer, for practical reasons, her wardrobe had mainly consisted of boots and jeans.

Cecelia's skin was pale and needed just a dash of blusher to liven it up. She added a coat of mascara to her lashes, which enhanced her deep green eyes, but, as she did so, a rather bitchy voice coming from the radio caught her attention.

'What on earth did she expect, getting mixed up with Luka Kargas?'

Cecelia stabbed herself in the eye with the mascara wand at the sound of her boss's name.

It wasn't so much that it was a surprise to hear Luka mentioned, more an annoyance that even at seven a.m.

and alone in her bedroom *still* there was no escape from him.

Luka was extremely prominent and, although his name often graced the finance reports, his antics and bad-boy ways were regularly discussed in the tabloids and on the news.

They were having a field day discussing him now!

It would seem that he had used every last second of the weekend to create his own particular brand of havoc. A wild party had taken place aboard his yacht, currently moored off the coast of Nice, on Friday.

Cecelia sat at her dressing table, lips pursed as she heard that the raucous celebrations had continued on to Paris, where Luka and selected guests had hit the casinos. Now it was a case of tears *after* bedtime for some supermodel who had hoped that things might be different between herself and Luka.

Well, more fool her, then, Cecelia thought.

Everyone knew Luka's track record with women.

But they didn't really know Luka—there was a private side to him that no one, and certainly not his PA, had access to.

From what Cecelia could glean, Luka had led a very privileged life. His father owned a luxurious resort in Xanero. The famed Kargas restaurant there was now the flagship venue of its own very exclusive brand in several countries. Luka, though, focused more on expanding the hotel side of things and lived life very much in the fast lane. He dated at whim and discarded with ease and all too often it was Cecelia mopping up the tears or fielding calls from scorned lovers.

Yes, he was a playboy in the extreme.

And he unsettled her so.

Cecelia had once glimpsed that life.

Her mother Harriet's death had been intensely embarrassing for her well-to-do family for she had died as she'd lived and had gone out on a high—knickers down and with the proverbial silver spoon up her nose.

Harriet had left behind a daughter with whom no one had quite known what to do. Her father's name did not appear on the birth certificate and Cecelia had glimpsed him just once in her life.

And she never wanted to see him again.

Cecelia's staid aunt and uncle, who had always sniffed in disapproval at Harriet's rather bohemian existence, had, on her death, taken in the child. With tangled curls and sparkling green eyes, little Cecelia had been a mini replica of her mother, but in looks only.

The little girl had craved routine.

In fact, it had been a very young Cecelia who had kept any semblance of order in her mother's life.

She had put out her own school uniform and taken money from her mother's purse to ensure there was food, and she'd always got herself up in the morning and made her own way to school.

After an unconventional start, Cecelia now lived a very conventional life and was efficient and ordered. Even though she travelled the globe with her work, she was generally in bed by ten on weekdays and eleven at weekends.

She had perfectly nice friends, though none close enough to remember her birthday, and this time last year she had been engaged.

Gordon and the break-up had been the only problem she had caused for her aunt and uncle, who could not fathom why she might end things with such a perfectly decent man.

It hadn't been Gordon's fault, and she had told him so when she'd ended it.

It was bloody Luka's!

Though of course Cecelia hadn't told Gordon that.

Still, there wasn't time to dwell on it this morning.

She pulled on her flesh-coloured underwear and then glanced out of the window where the sun split a very blue sky, and found she simply could not face putting on the navy linen suit that she had laid out last night.

To hell with it!

Given that Luka wouldn't be in the office today, and that she wouldn't now be sitting in on meetings, Cecelia made an unplanned diversion to her wardrobe.

She wasn't exactly blinded by colour. But there was the dress she had bought to wear to a friend's wedding she had recently attended.

It had been a rare impulse purchase.

It was a pale cream halter neck, which Cecelia had decided as soon as she'd left the boutique was too close to white and might offend the bride.

She loved it, though, and, maybe because it was her birthday, she decided to wear it.

While it showed rather too much of her back and arms, she took care of that with the pale lemon, sheer, bolero-style cardigan she had bought on the same day.

The dress was mid-calf-length so she didn't bother with stockings, and then she tied on some espadrilles.

Yes, perhaps because Cecelia knew she would soon be leaving Kargas Holdings she was finally starting to relax.

As she closed the front door to her flat, Cecelia decided that despite Luka's absence she would still be giving in her notice today. It would be far easier to do it over the phone or online.

'You're looking very summery,' Mrs Dawson, her very nosy neighbour, said as she passed her in the hall. 'Off to work?'

'I am.'

The pale lemon bolero didn't even make it past the escalators to the underground. It was hot and oppressive and as she stood, holding a rail, she saw that Luka's weekend escapades had made headlines on the newspaper a commuter held.

She looked at the photo beneath the headline. It was of Luka on the deck of his yacht moving in on a sophisticated, dark-skinned beauty. His naked chest and thick black hair were dripping water over the woman and though their bodies did not touch it was an incredibly intimate shot.

Cecelia tore her eyes from the picture and stared fixedly ahead but that image of him seemed to dance on the blacked-out windows of the Tube.

Having left the underground, Cecelia walked towards the prominent high-rise building that housed Kargas Holdings. She smiled at the doorman and then entered the foyer and took the elevator. She had a special pass that allowed her to access the fortieth floor, which was Luka's in its entirety.

There weren't just offices and meeting rooms, there was also a gym and pool, though Cecelia couldn't recall him using them—they were more a perk for the staff.

And there was a suite that was every bit as luxurious and as serviced as any five-star hotel. When in London, Luka often slept there when he chose to work through the night or had a particularly early morning flight.

Yes, it was his world that she entered, but knowing that he wasn't there meant Cecelia breathed more easily today.

It was just before eight and it would seem that she had beaten Bridgette, the receptionist, to work. There were a couple of cleaners polishing windows and vacuuming and the florists had arrived, as they did each morning to tend the floral displays.

Cecelia made a coffee from the espresso machine before heading to her desk that was housed in a large area outside Luka's vast office.

The gatekeeper, Luka called her at times, though she felt rather more like a security guard at others.

As well as greeting his clients and guests, Cecelia was the final hurdle for his scorned lovers to negotiate if they somehow made it past the security in place downstairs.

Occasionally it happened, though generally Cecelia fielded them by phone.

And there it was again, springing to mind—the sudden image of him, wet from the ocean and dripping water, and Cecelia shook her head as if to clear it.

She hung her little cardigan on a stand and was just about to take a seat when his voice caught her completely unawares.

'Is that coffee for me, Cece?'

Cecelia swung around and there, strolling out of his office, was Luka. Apart from being unshaven there was little evidence of his wild weekend on display. He wore black pants and a white fitted shirt that showed off his toned body and his thick black hair, which, though perhaps a little tousled, still fell into perfect shape.

And he was not supposed to be here.

'I thought you weren't coming in today,' Cecelia said.

'Why would you think that?'

'Because you texted me in the middle of the night and told me you weren't.'

'So I did.'

He looked at the usually poised and formal Cece caught unawares. To many it might seem no big deal— she was simply holding a coffee and wearing a summer dress. Usually she was buttoned to the neck in navy or black, but it wasn't just her clothing that was different today.

'Thanks,' he said, and took from her hand the coffee she had made.

'It's got sugar in it,' she warned as she took a seat at her desk, 'and, please, it's Cecelia, not Cece.'

'Habit,' he said.

'Well, it's a very annoying one.'

Good, Luka thought.

Her cool demeanour incensed him.

His choice of name for her was deliberate, for he loved to provoke a reaction, even if it was only mild.

'How was your weekend?' she asked politely, pretending of course that she had heard nothing whatsoever about it.

'Much the same as the last,' he answered, and then came over behind Cecelia's desk and, to her intense annoyance, he lowered himself so that his bottom was beside her computer. 'Do you ever get bored?' he asked.

'Not really,' Cecelia lied, for she had realised she had been bored with Gordon.

He had also worked in the City and they had fallen into a pattern of meeting for drinks on Wednesday, allowing time to catch up with friends on a Friday. It had generally just been the two of them on a Saturday, followed by a vague hint of an orgasm that night and generally a boring drive on Sunday with a pub lunch somewhere.

And then perhaps another anti-climactic tryst that night.

It hadn't been Gordon's fault.

Cecelia held back in sex just as she held back in life.

In fact, the fault lay with the man now lounging against her desk, for he had opened her eyes to sensations that should surely remain unexplored.

Oh, she should never have taken the job, Cecelia thought as Luka persisted with a conversation she would rather draw to a close.

'But don't you ever get tired of doing the same old thing?' he asked.

'I like the same old things,' Cecelia answered.

He glanced at her neat, ordered desk and knew that the inside of her drawers would look exactly the same.

And then, just to annoy her, just to provoke *some* reaction, he picked up her little pottery jar that held her pens and things and moved it to the other side of her desk. 'Live a little.'

'No, thank you.' She smiled grimly and moved the jar back where it belonged. As she did so he got the scent of freshly washed hair.

That was it.

Cecelia didn't wear perfume; there were no undertones that he could note, and not just in her scent.

She was impossible to read, unlike any woman Luka had ever met. He had long ago given up flirting with her—the disapproval in her eyes kind of ruined the fun.

And as reckless as he was, Luka only ever played with the willing.

'You look nice,' he told her, and he felt the scold of her slight frown for daring to comment on something personal. Cecelia kept things very strictly business, yet she responded politely.

'Thank you.'

But Luka did not leave it there. 'You're wearing a dress.'

'That's very observant of you, Luka.'

'I'm just mentioning it because you don't usually.'

'Well, it's been a long, warm weekend. I couldn't face wearing a suit.'

'No, but—'

'Luka,' Cecelia interrupted him, 'if you have an issue with me dressing more casually than normal, then please just say so and it won't happen again.'

'I have no issue with you wearing a dress.'

'Then there's nothing to discuss.'

'Are you sure about that?' Luka said. He hadn't intended to address this today but clearly the moment was upon them.

'What I wear—' Cecelia started to say, but then Luka cut in.

'Do you have another *dental appointment* today, Cecelia?' His voice had changed and he delivered his words with a threatening edge by using her correct name. 'A final interview perhaps?'

He was rather certain that she was leaving, and more certain now because to her pale cheeks there came a very rare flush.

PAs came and went.

Luka was very used to that.

He was an exceptionally demanding boss and was aware that few could keep up with his impossible schedule for very long.

Usually all he required was for the incumbent PA to train the next one to standard before she left and ensure that the handover was seamless.

That Cecelia might be about to leave, though, brought a sense of disquiet like nothing he had known.

He liked her in his life, Luka realised, and he didn't want her to be gone. But three prolonged dental appointments in recent weeks had served as ominous signs, and he'd been certain of it when she had avoided discussing the renewal of her contract.

'Is there something you've been meaning to tell me?' he asked.

'Actually, yes.' She took a breath and then glanced over at the sound of the elevator door opening and saw that Bridgette had arrived.

Cecelia did not want an audience for this.

'Would it be possible to have a word in private?'

'Of course,' Luka said. 'You know my door is always closed.' When she didn't smile at his little joke he stood from the desk. 'Come on through.'

Luka decided he would have to talk her out of it.

And he knew just how to do it.

CHAPTER TWO

IT FELT LIKE a very long walk to his office.

Luka led the way and Cecelia actually felt a little sick because she still wasn't certain that it was the right thing to do.

Cecelia was very career minded and knew that by resigning she was throwing an amazing role away—Luka's empire was rapidly expanding, with hotels in New York City and Singapore on the cards, and to be a part of it would be amazing on her résumé.

But as he held open the door and she walked in, Cecelia knew she had little choice but to leave.

She could feel his eyes on her back.

On her skin.

They most certainly were.

Cecelia had the drabbest wardrobe he had ever seen.

Granted, she was always groomed and elegant, but Luka had long ago decided that she could make a modest outfit out of a handkerchief.

Not so today.

On the day she would tell him that she was leaving, he got the first glimpse of her spine.

Her back was incredibly pale, and he wondered if she should check her Vitamin D levels because he was sure that body rarely, if ever, saw the sun.

Luka had run into her out of work once and she'd been dressed in much the same monotonous, drab tones.

It had been at a museum exhibition a couple of weeks after she had started working for him, and not *quite* by accident. Luka had heard her discussing going with her fiancé and he'd wanted to see what made Cecelia tick, sexually speaking.

Pale English men, with skinny legs apparently.

They hadn't even been holding hands and had stood as politely as two strangers while admiring an incredibly erotic work of art.

She'd jumped when she'd seen him, though! And blushed just a touch as she'd introduced Gordon to him.

And all the more Luka had wanted to know her in bed.

'Please,' he said now. 'Take a seat.'

Luka gestured to a chair and then went around his desk while Cecelia took her seat.

And then she faced him.

He really was a very beautiful man.

Aside from fancying him rotten and everything, Luka Kargas really was exquisite to look at.

Those velvet eyes awaited hers but she could not quite meet them and she took in the high cheekbones and full plump mouth.

Cecelia liked mouths.

Gordon's had been a bit small and pinched but she had only really thought that after she had seen Luka's.

No, she should never have taken the job in the first place.

The very second she'd entered his luxurious office and he had stood to greet her, Cecelia had known she should turn and run.

Until that point, she and Gordon had seemingly ticked

every box, yet that had changed the moment she'd shaken hands with Luka.

She had known that she *had* to end her engagement the night she had come back from the museum and while being intimate with Gordon had found herself imagining Luka instead.

It had been the best orgasm of her life!

Luka was everything that her aunt had warned her about.

Despite somehow knowing it could only end badly, and that she should leave now, instead she had taken the job.

And now she was here.

About to resign.

'There is something you wish to discuss?' Luka said, and she nodded.

It was all very formal and deliberately so, for Luka was not about to make this easy on her.

Quite simply he had never known a better PA and he did not want that to change.

He wanted Cecelia to stay and Luka *always* got what he wanted.

'So?' he invited. 'What is it that you have to say?'

It wasn't the first time she had handed in her notice and Cecelia was about to deliver her well-rehearsed lines yet she just sat there in strained silence. For when he held her gaze, as he did now, there felt like a limit on the oxygen in the vast room and superfluous words were rather hard to find.

'I'm leaving.'

'Pardon?' Luka checked, and cocked his head a little, as if he hadn't heard. He would make her say it again, and more explicitly this time.

'I shan't be renewing my contract.' After such an appalling start the words now came tumbling out. 'I've given it considerable thought and though it's been an amazing year I've decided that it's time to move on.'

'But for all your *considerable thought*, you haven't discussed it with me.'

'I don't need your permission to resign, Luka.'

Oh, this wasn't going well, Cecelia thought as she heard the snap in her voice.

Yet she was almost at breaking point and that was verified when Bridgette buzzed.

'There's a woman called Katiya down in Reception, asking to see you, Luka...'

He rolled his eyes. 'I'm busy.'

'She's very insistent. Apparently you'll know why.'

'Tell Security that whoever lets her up will be fired.'

He looked over at Cecelia. 'Why can't women take no for an answer?'

'Why can't my boss?'

'Touché,' he conceded and then decided to play the sympathy card, 'Cecelia, *one* of the reasons I changed my mind about taking the day off was that I have just found out my mother is very unwell.'

'I'm sorry to hear that.' Cecelia said. 'If there's any...' She stopped and then she closed her mouth rather than continue.

'You were saying?' Luka checked, and when she didn't respond he spoke for her. 'Because actually there is something you can do for me. Cece, I am going to be away a lot in the coming months. My mother has cancer and will be undergoing extensive treatments...'

She felt her own rapid blink.

Luka never spoke of his family.

Ever!

'I am going to have to spend a lot of time in Xanero.

You're an amazing PA and I hope you know how much I appreciate you.' He saw the swallow in her throat and went in for the kill. 'At this difficult time, I don't want to deal with someone new.'

'Luka, I am sorry to hear that your mother is unwell but it doesn't sway my decision.'

She really was as cold as ice, and yet, and yet…as he looked across the desk he could see tension in her features and that those gorgeous green eyes could not meet his.

'Can I ask you to stay on for another six months? Naturally you'll be reimbursed…'

'Not everything is about money, Luka.'

He saw her green eyes flash and knew full well she thought him nothing more than a rich playboy.

She knew nothing about his start in life and Luka certainly wasn't about to enlighten her.

No one knew the truth.

Even his own parents seemed to believe the lie that had long been perpetuated—that the resort on Xanero Island and the original famous Kargas restaurant housed within it had given Luka his start in life.

Well, it hadn't.

Sex had.

Affluent holidaymakers looking for a thrill had first helped Luka to pave his way from near poverty to the golden lifestyle he had now.

The more sanitised PR version was that the first Kargas restaurant had given Luka his start.

Lies, all lies.

Not that he had any reason to tell Cecelia that.

Luka did not have to explain himself to his PA.

'What if I offered more annual leave?'

'I've already accepted another role.'

And so, when being nice and accommodating didn't work, Luka grew surly. 'With whom?'

'I don't need to answer that.'

'Actually, Cece—'

'Don't call me that!' she reared. 'Luka, on the one hand you tell me how much you appreciate the work I do and yet you can't even be bothered to get my name right.'

Finally he had his reaction.

'So you're leaving because I don't call you by your correct name?'

'No.'

'Then why?'

'I don't have to answer that.'

'Actually Ce-cel-i-a—' he drawled every syllable of her name '—if you look at your contract you cannot work for any of my rivals for a period of a year and you cannot—'

'Don't.' She halted him. 'Luka, I am allowed to leave.'

She was.

'Of course you are.' He just didn't like that fact.

'I've got four weeks left on my contract and naturally I'll start looking for my replacement straight away. Unless you have anyone particular in mind?'

'I'll leave all of that to you.'

'Sure.'

He flicked his hand in dismissal and Cecelia read the cue and headed out, though she did not return to her desk.

Once alone in the quiet of the bathrooms she leant against one of the cool marble walls.

She'd done it.

Possibly it was the worst career move she would ever make, but soon sanity would be restored to her mind.

No longer would she stand on a busy Tube in rush hour, wishing that somehow she was the woman lying beneath that depraved, beautiful face as he leaned in for a kiss…

No more would she have to breathe through her mouth when he was close just to avoid a hit of the heady scent of him.

Finally, the clenching low in her stomach at his lazy smile would dissipate.

Order would be restored to the chaos he had made of her heart.

Not yet, though.

It really was an awful day.

Flowers were delivered for Luka that Cecelia signed for, and then stupidly she read the card.

Oh, the offer from Katiya was very explicit.

And if he would just give her the elevator code then Katiya could come right up now, it would seem, and get straight on her knees.

Cecelia returned the card to the envelope and took them in to him.

'A delivery for you.'

'From?'

'I have no idea.'

He opened the card and then tossed it.

'Have them if you want,' he said, gesturing to the flowers.

'No, thank you.'

'Then put them somewhere that I can't see them.'

In case you get tempted? Cecelia wanted to ask.

But of course she didn't.

And then the downstairs receptionists messed up and a call was put through to Luka, but thankfully she

was in his office at the time and it was Cecelia who
answered it.

'I just need to speak to him...' a woman, presumably Katiya, sobbed.

'I'm sorry, Mr Kargas isn't taking any unscheduled
calls,' Cecelia duly said.

Luka didn't even look up from his computer.

'What time do you have to finish today?' he asked
when she ended the call.

'Any time,' Cecelia said, surprised by the unusual
question, because Luka never usually bothered to ask.
'Why?'

'I want you to move the meeting with Garcia to the
close of business there.'

'I'll see what I can do.'

'And I need you to sort out my flight tomorrow to
Xanero. I'll be away for a couple of weeks.'

'A couple of weeks?' Cecelia checked, because for
him to be away for that length of time was unheard
of. Luka used his jet the way most people used public transport.

'I already told you,' Luka said and his voice was curt.
'My mother is ill.'

With his flight arranged, Luka rang Sophie Kargas and told her that her only child would be back tomorrow.

'One thing,' Luka said. 'I shan't be there to hold your
hand and watch you give in. You're going to fight this.'

'Luka, I'm tired, I don't want any fuss. I just want
you to come home.'

He could hear the defeat in her voice and he knew
only too well the reason. The treatment would mean
regular trips to Athens and Theo Kargas liked his wife
to be at home.

Yes, it was a very long and difficult day spent avoiding each other as best they could but the tension hung heavy in the air at the office.

'I have your mother on the phone,' Cecelia said as afternoon gave way to evening.

'Tell her I'm in a meeting.'

'Of course.'

He really was a bastard, Cecelia decided as she relayed the message to the feeble-sounding woman.

'But I just need to speak with him for a moment.'

'I'm so sorry,' Cecelia said. 'Luka can't take any calls right now. I know he's busy trying to clear up as much of his schedule as he can today.'

Luka sat with his hands behind his head and his feet on the desk.

He could not face speaking to his mother again today and hearing how she had as good as given up on life.

Well, he would deal with all that tomorrow, for what Luka had to say would be better said face to face.

Leave him.

It wouldn't be the first time he had said it to his mother, but he hoped it would be the last.

Always he had hoped that his father would die first, if only to afford his mother some peace.

He glanced at the time and saw that it was approaching seven.

The meeting with Garcia was now scheduled for ten.

Luka got up and put on his jacket and then headed out of the office.

Cecelia didn't look up; instead she carried on tapping away on her computer, pretending she hadn't noticed him.

'Truce,' Luka said, and he saw her shoulders drop a little as her tense lips relaxed in a small smile.

'Truce,' Cecelia said, and she looked up at him.

'Let's go and get dinner.'

Her heart dropped.

Not that she showed it.

Cecelia wanted this day to be over.

More than anything she loathed going to dinner with him.

Or rather she loved going to dinner with him.

Luka was incredibly good company.

But that only made it all so much worse.

CHAPTER THREE

'I'LL JUST GO and freshen up,' Cecelia said and reached for her bag.

'Sure.'

He was lounging on her desk again and she had to step over his long legs to get past.

In the luxurious bathrooms of Kargas Holdings, Cecelia stared in the mirror and told herself that in four weeks this slow torture would be over.

She retied her hair and topped up her lipstick and, unable to help herself, checked her phone to see if her aunt—or anyone—had messaged her for her birthday.

No.

As disappointing as it was about her aunt and uncle, the real truth was that Cecelia could think of nothing nicer than going out for dinner with Luka on her birthday.

Except this wasn't a date—she was going out with her boss for a work dinner and Cecelia knew she would have to spend the next couple of hours constantly reminding herself of that fact.

When she came out, Luka was standing, waiting, and she felt his eyes on her as she retrieved her little bolero and put it on.

God, but he loathed it.

It was the colour of mustard and he'd far prefer to see her pale flesh. He would love to tell her just that, but with Cecelia he was constantly on his best behaviour.

'Ready?' he checked, and she nodded.

'Ready.'

His driver delivered them to a gorgeous Greek restaurant on the river that had recently opened.

'Time to check out the competition,' Luka said as they were led to a beautifully set table, but Luka refused it.

'We'll eat outside,' he said.

They were soon seated at a beautiful spot overlooking the river.

'The music would drive me crazy in there,' Luka told her, though the real reason was that they had the air-conditioning cranked up and he wanted her to be rid of that cardigan.

What the hell was wrong with him, Luka thought, that he would sit outside just for the thrill of seeing her upper arms.

Her arms!

'Here's perfect,' Cecelia said as she took her seat. 'There's a lovely breeze from the river.'

'Of course there is,' Luka said, but she didn't understand his wry smile.

It certainly wasn't the first time they had eaten together, although it wasn't often that they did. When they travelled, Cecelia had taken to having her breakfast sent to her hotel room as she could not bear to see him breakfasting with whomever he was seeing at the time.

Often, when away, she and Luka had lunch together but generally there were guests or clients involved.

As for dinner?

She had no idea, neither did she want to know what

Luka did by night and so, when away, and the working day had ended, she generally opted for room service.

Now she looked through the menu but could not concentrate for she was certain he would again try to dissuade her from leaving.

He didn't, though, and instead he selected the wine.

'What would you like?'

'Not for me.' Cecelia said.

'Of course not.' He rolled his eyes. Heaven forbid she relax in his company, but he asked for sparkling water.

She gave her order to the waiter, which, despite its fancy wording, was basically a tomato salad.

Luka ordered *bourdeto*.

She had seen it on the menu and read that it was made with scorpion.

Apt, for there would be a sting in his tail and she could feel it.

Oh, the surroundings were beautiful and the conversation polite but she could feel her own tension as she awaited attack. For Luka did not give in easily, that much she knew.

Life was a chessboard to him and every move was planned.

Now that his mother was ill, he had very good reasons to want an efficient PA, one capable of steering the helm while he was away.

Yes, she was braced, if not for attack then for the silk of his persuasion. But she must not relent, not now that she had finally had the courage to hand in her notice.

'A taste of home,' he said as their dishes were served.

'Will it be nice to be there?' Cecelia asked. 'Aside from the difficult news, I mean.'

Luka just shrugged.

'Will you be staying with your family?' she asked.

She wasn't probing, she told herself, for there were arrangements to be made that would undoubtedly fall
to her.

'The resort is huge. They have a villa there but on
the other side to mine.'

'What's it like in Xanero?'

'The island is stunning.'

'It's still a family business?' Cecelia checked.

'Yes.' It wasn't an outright lie but there was so much
he left unsaid.

'Your father's still the chef there?'

Luka didn't answer straight away.

The truth was, his father had never been the chef
there. Well, once, for the briefest of times.

It was all part of an elaborate charade that Luka went
along with, only so that his mother could hold her head
up in town.

'He's semi-retired,' Luka said, and that wasn't really
a lie—Theo Kargas had spent his adult life semi-retired.
Still, rather than talk about home he moved the subject
to the upcoming weeks. Not everything had been cancelled. Luka would be working online and there was a
trip to Athens he would keep. It was doable yet it was
complex as Luka was booked out weeks and months
ahead of time, so there was never much room for manoeuvre.

'I'll tell Garcia that the trip to New York will have
to wait.'

'He won't like it.'

'Good,' Luka said. 'You know what they say about
treating them mean to keep them keen. He needs me
far more than I need him, yet he has started to forget
that! Still, perhaps we can go when I return.'

'Of course.' Cecelia nodded. 'When you know more

how things are at home I'll schedule it again. Hopefully by then your new PA will be on board and he or she can go along too.'

He didn't like the sound of that.

Luka looked over to where she sat, sipping on sparking water with that mustard-coloured cardigan covering cream shoulders, and *still* he wondered what made her tick.

Cecelia intrigued him.

She was as cold as ice and so buttoned up and formal that, even though he knew she'd been engaged, he privately wondered if she was a virgin, for he simply could not imagine her in bed.

But on occasion he found himself imagining it anyway!

'What happened to Gordon?' Luka suddenly asked.

Her silence was a pointed one.

'Come on,' he said, 'you're leaving—I can ask now.'

'I like to keep my private life private,' Cecelia said, stabbing an olive with her fork.

'I know you do,' Luka said. 'Come on, what happened?'

Cecelia hesitated.

Certainly she would not be telling Luka that at inappropriate times images of him had kept popping into her head! And neither would she tell him that she had thought herself content until he'd appeared in her life.

Instead, she told him a far safer version. 'I decided that my aunt and uncle's version of the perfect man for me didn't fit mine.'

'Your aunt and uncle?' he checked, recalling that Cecelia's aunt was her next of kin on her résumé.

'I was raised by them after my mother died.'

'How old were you then?'

'Eight,' Cecelia said through taut lips, for she was terribly uncomfortable with the subject, but Luka seemed very intent on finding things out tonight.

'What about your father?'

She gave a slight shake of her head, which told him nothing other than the subject was out of bounds.

Not just with Luka.

She had never told anyone about the time she had come face to face with him.

He had dark hair and had worn a wedding ring.

That was all Cecelia knew. That and the fact he had shouted at her mother. When the money had run out, Harriet had called him to tell him he had a child, but it hadn't produced the result her mother had obviously hoped for.

There had been no joyful greeting. His eyes had been furious when they had met hers, and Harriet had quickly sent her daughter to her room.

A lot of shouting had ensued and Cecelia had found out that her mother had once been given a considerable sum of money for... Cecelia had frowned when she heard a word that a seven-year-old Cecelia didn't understand.

Termination.

Soon after, to her terrible distress, she found out what her father had meant.

'I don't want to talk about my father,' she said to Luka.

'Fine.' He shrugged and then gave that wicked smile. 'Tell me more about your fiancé, then.'

'Ex,' she pointed out.

'That's right.'

At the time, the only reason he had guessed her engagement was over had been the lack of a ring and the absence of his calls. There had been no tears from Cecelia or days off and no impact on her efficiency that he'd been able to see.

'Was it you who ended it?'

Cecelia gave a terse nod.

'How did he take it?'

'Luka!' she warned.

'I'm just curious. I've never been with anyone long enough to be engaged. I can't imagine getting that close to someone.' His eyes narrowed a little as he looked at her, still trying, as he had been since the day they had met, to gauge her. 'Was there someone else involved? Is that why you ended it?'

'Of course not,' she bristled.

'Did you live together?'

'I really don't want to discuss my private life,' Cecelia said. '*You* don't.'

'Yes, I do.'

'No, Luka, you don't. I might deal with your exes but I know nothing about you—'

'That's not true.'

'How long has your mother been ill?'

His jaw gritted and Cecelia gave a little smirk as she took a sip of her water.

'Fair enough.' He watched as she put down her glass and told her a truth. 'I'm going to miss *not* getting to know you, though.'

She would miss him far more than he knew.

'Is there anything I can do to dissuade you from leaving?' he asked.

She looked up at his voice for his tone had surprised her. She had expected sulky, or manipulative, or for more money to be waved in front of her.

Instead he *asked* if there was anything he could do to keep her.

'No.' Cecelia said, and then she cleared her throat, for the word had come out huskily. 'Luka, I will be here for another month and I will find the best replacement that I can. I'll train her myself. It really has been an amazing year but I'm ready for a new challenge.'

'So I'm no longer a challenge?'

'Of course you are,' Cecelia said.

He was actually a constant challenge to her senses—recklessness crept in whenever he was near, which Cecelia had to fight constantly just to keep it in check.

'How was the *bourdeto*?' Cecelia asked as his plate was removed unfinished.

Luka shrugged.

He had far more on his mind than food.

'What if I promise to stop calling you Cece?' he suggested. 'It takes twenty-one days to form a habit.'

'It actually takes sixty-six days,' Cecelia corrected. 'So there isn't time for that. But thanks for offering.' And then she smiled, something Cecelia so rarely did.

Rather, she rarely smiled *properly*, but now, as she did so, Luka watched as she checked herself midway and it dimmed.

For Luka, the fading of her smile felt like summer was ending.

It was, of course.

In a few weeks' time summer would be gone.

Of course it would come around again, but this summer, *this* one, would never return.

'Was Gordon upset when you finished with him?' Luka asked. 'And before you tell me that it's private, I know it is.'

'So why ask now?'

'Because you're the best PA I've ever had, and I didn't want to push you into leaving by getting too personal, but now that you've already resigned I don't have to behave.'

'Yes, you do,' Cecelia said, and though her voice remained even there was a flurry of nerves low in her stomach as to what her boldness today had unleashed.

So she answered the question.

'Yes, he was upset, although, to be honest, I think he was more embarrassed than upset.'

'No, I imagine he was very upset,' Luka said in his deep, low voice, and met her eyes. Suddenly the cool breeze from the river felt like a warm one.

At times, Luka would disregard her professional boundaries and flirt with her.

Like now.

That little hint of his silken charm carried from his lips and sent a slow shiver the length of Cecelia's spine.

'I'd better get back to the office,' Cecelia said, 'and set up for your meeting.'

But he would prefer to linger.

The changing world was waiting and it was nice to be here by the river.

With her.

'Garcia can wait,' Luka said.

'One day he might get tired of waiting.'

'I doubt it,' Luka said. 'Right now he wants to wrap up the purchase.'

'I thought you wanted a hotel in New York City.'

'I do,' Luka said, 'but at a price of my choosing. Anyway, we need to talk about your replacement.'

'I've informed the agency you generally use,' Cecelia said, and Luka frowned.

'You weren't referred via them?'

'No.' Cecelia shook her head.

'Ah, that's right, you were working for Justin. How did you end up with him?'

'Via the agency,' Cecelia said, and she itched to get back and away from his gaze but Luka wasn't letting her go just yet.

'How did you become a PA?'

More questions, Cecelia thought, but this wasn't such a personal one and so she was a little freer in her response. 'I never intended to be. When I finished school I had wanted to travel,' she told him, 'or go to university, but...' Cecelia hesitated. 'My uncle had a friend who needed a nanny in France. I spoke French—well, a little—and he said that way I'd get to travel and work at the same time.'

'The trust fund ran out, you mean.'

'Sorry?' Cecelia blinked.

'They would have received money to raise you, but once you turned eighteen—'

'No,' Cecelia interrupted. 'It wasn't like that at all.' She shook her head. 'They were very good to take me in.'

'Did they have children?'

'No,' Cecelia said, and she swallowed because she believed they had very much been childless by choice.

Luka's comments needled for she had always felt rather in the way with her aunt and uncle, not that she'd admit it to him. 'My uncle had a contact who needed a nanny.'

'Really, Cece! You? A nanny?'

He could not imagine the very crisp and proper Cecelia working with children and he actually smiled at the very thought, parting those gorgeous lips to show his pearly white teeth.

Gosh, he had such a nice mouth.

'I hated it,' Cecelia admitted. 'I lasted four weeks before I gave notice, but then the mother, a television producer, asked if I could work for her instead. I guess it all started from there.'

'Do you still see your aunt and uncle?'

'Of course,' Cecelia said confidently, although inside she wavered for it had always been her making the effort rather than them.

They hadn't so much as sent a text for her birthday.

Perhaps a card would have arrived in the mail when she got home.

Or there would be flowers on her doorstep.

Yet she knew there wouldn't be.

Her birthday had passed by unnoticed again and it hurt.

She would not let Luka see it, of course, but his comment about the trust-fund money drying up had perturbed her.

'Do you want dessert?' he asked, knowing the answer.

'No, thank you.'

'Tough,' Luka said. 'You're getting one.'

She went to ask what he meant but at that moment the background music wafting out of the restaurant changed to a very familiar tune and she turned as she saw a waiter with a slice of cake and atop it a candle.

The tune was 'Happy Birthday'!

And it was being played for her.

'Luka…'

Cecelia was embarrassed.

Pleased.

And utterly caught by surprise.

No one remembered her birthday.

Ever.

As a child, it had fallen in the school holidays and her mother had only liked grown-up parties, certainly not the type Cecelia had dreamed of. And after she had died, Cecelia hadn't readily made friends. In fact, at boarding school she had been endlessly teased and bullied.

At eighteen, her aunt and uncle had given up on the perfunctory birthday card and last-minute present, which had always, *always* been something she needed rather than something she might want.

This was the first time that she'd truly been spoiled on her birthday.

There were two spoons and the cake was completely delectable—vanilla sponge drizzled in thick lemon syrup that was both tart and refreshing.

And she was sharing dessert on her birthday with him.

Luka Kargas.

Cecelia was almost scared to look up for she was worried there might be tears in her eyes.

'Here,' Luka said, 'is the other reason I came into the office today.'

Now Cecelia did look up as he went into his jacket and pulled out a gorgeous parcel and slid it across the table.

It was a long box wrapped in deep red velvet and tied with ribbon that had a little gold charm attached to it.

And she frowned because Cecelia recognised the packaging.

On one overseas trip, she had enjoyed staring into the window of a lavish boutique in the foyer of a Florence hotel where they had been staying. Whenever she'd been waiting for Luka, she had indulged herself with the joy of admiring the beautiful jewellery.

She pulled back the bow, but first she had a question for she didn't quite believe what Luka had said. 'You didn't really come in just because it's my birthday?'

'Of course I did. I always try to do the right thing on my PA's birthday.'

Luka knew full well that for Cecelia he had done more than just the right thing. Usually it was flowers and perfume, or a voucher for a spa hotel, but a few weeks ago, on a business trip, he had stepped out of the elevator and Cecelia's back had been to him. He had looked to where her gaze had been focused and spied the sparkling window display of the hotel boutique.

The next morning she had been looking again.

And the next.

It had sat in his bureau at home for weeks now.

Last night, just after he had fired off the text to say that he wouldn't be in, he had remembered her birthday.

Luka had been partying hard, trying to forget the news that had come in about his mother, trying to extend the weekend into a long one, just to delay the return home.

And then he had remembered the box inside his bureau.

'Oh!' She gave a gasp of recognition when she saw the necklace. 'How on earth…?' It was thick and lavish, coiled with rubies, or glass, she wasn't sure—Cecelia hadn't even asked the price at the time, for in either case it would have been way out of her league; she had simply adored it, that was all. 'Luka, it's far too much.'

'It can double up as your leaving gift,' Luka brooded. 'Do you want to put it on?'

'No,' she said too quickly, 'I'll wait till I'm home.'

She wouldn't be able to manage the clasp and she

would burst into flames at the touch of his hands if he so much as brushed the sensitive skin of her neck.

The breeze from the river wasn't helping at all now. The tiny cardigan felt like a thick shawl around her shoulders and she simply didn't know how to react.

'How did you even know it was my birthday?' Cecelia asked, because she hadn't mentioned it and certainly she hadn't made a note of it in his diary.

'I make it my business to know.' He could see she was shaken and her reaction surprised him. He had thought she'd be more than used to a fuss being made but she actually seemed stunned, even close to tears. 'I fired a PA once, about ten years ago,' he explained as a waiter put down two small glasses, a bottle of ouzo and a carafe of iced water on the table between them.

'No, thank you,' Cecelia said as he went to pour one for her. 'You were saying.'

Luka went ahead and added iced water to the ouzo and she watched as the clear liquid turned white.

How she would love to try it, but she had to keep her guard up, for it was becomingly increasingly difficult to remember that this was work.

He did this for all his PAs, Cecelia reminded herself, and forced herself to listen rather than daydream as he told her just why he had made such a nice fuss.

'As I was firing her she started to cry.'

'Tears don't usually trouble you,' Cecelia said, thinking of the many tears women had shed over him.

'They don't,' Luka said, 'but as she was clearing out her things she said that it was her worst birthday ever. She was a terrible PA and deserved to be fired, but I didn't set out to ruin her birthday.'

'You really felt bad?' Cecelia checked, pleased that he did have a conscience after all.

'A bit,' he agreed. 'Since then I have tried to keep track. Normally I would have taken you for lunch. In fact, that was what I had planned to do but when it came to it I was sulking too much to do so...'

She smiled again and back came summer.

'I thought, given it's your birthday, that you would have plans tonight. That's why I checked what time you had to leave by.'

'No, no plans.'

It was her best birthday ever.

Luka couldn't know that, of course, but even Gordon hadn't made much of a fuss.

They'd gone for dinner.

But there had been no candles and no cake.

Gordon had bought her a cloying perfume Cecelia hadn't liked.

It wasn't so much the lavishness of the gift Luka had given her that made it the best, more the thought behind it.

How he had seen her looking at the necklace.

That he had noticed...

Yes, she was right to leave.

Because of this.

Because of those moments when he put her world to rights and she was utterly and completely crazy about him.

She had grown up with the dour warning that she did not want to end up like her mother and that men like Luka could only lead her down a dangerous path.

Yet, to her shame, it beckoned her at times.

Times like tonight.

When the easiest thing in the world would be to thank him with a kiss.

She knew where it would lead, though, for that was exactly where she wanted it to lead.

And Luka wouldn't be hard to convince!

He was easy.

That much she knew.

He was, though, at least with her, the perfect gentleman.

Well, not perfect, and not always a gentleman, but from the beginning Luka had, in the main, accepted her boundaries and there had been no overt flirting.

Occasionally he would slip, but he'd quickly rein it in. He wasn't a sleaze and played only where welcome. More than that, though, his world worked far better with Cecelia in it. He recognised talent and certainly she was brilliant at her job. Luka knew full well that he would lose the best PA he'd ever had if he chased that perpetual want.

And there was want in him.

Yet he knew his own track record, and Luka had never lasted with anyone for more than a month.

But look where behaving had got him, Luka thought.

He'd lost her anyway.

He decided now was the time to find out more about her.

'How did your mother die?' Luka asked, though he had already guessed her response—*That's personal, Luka*, or, *That's not your concern.*

She was about to deliver a response just like that, but then she remembered she was leaving.

Perfection was no longer required now that she had resigned.

And so she told him the truth, or at least the little she knew of it.

'I believe she took too much cocaine.'

CHAPTER FOUR

OH, CECELIA!

Luka hadn't expected to find out much at all, let alone that her mother had died from a cocaine overdose.

He thought of her, so prim and controlled, and had assumed her upbringing had caused that. Well, he concluded, it *had*, but not in the way he had imagined.

Still, he said nothing, because he didn't want to say the wrong thing, and he desperately wanted to hear more.

Cecelia liked his patient silence. There wasn't so much as a flicker of reaction that she could read in his expression as she revealed the dark truth, and Cecelia inwardly thanked him for that. 'She was at a party, I've been told.'

'Was it a one-off—?' he started to ask, but Cecelia cut in.

'No, it was a regular occurrence. My mother loved to party, she lived a very debauched life.'

'And you lived with her?'

'I did.' Cecelia nodded.

'What was that like?'

She wanted warm memories of her early childhood.

Cecelia wanted to say that in spite of everything there had been so many amazing times and that despite her mother's ways she'd been loved.

Yet she could not, and so she described what it had been like to live with her mother. 'Unsafe.'

Yes, he understood her a little better now.

He thought of her neat desk and tidy drawers and her utter reluctance to unbend and have fun, but now he watched as she reached for her purse and stood.

'We had better get back,' Cecelia told him, deciding that she had said far too much.

'No, sit,' Luka said, but she shook her head.

'I don't have time to sit by the river and reminisce,' Cecelia said. 'And neither do you. You have a meeting with Garcia at ten.'

'I've already said he can wait.'

Well, she wouldn't.

Cecelia walked off swiftly, embarrassed and unsure why she had told him about her mother when usually she did all she could to conceal that side of her past.

Usually she loathed people's reactions to it—their shocked expressions and the recriminations. She felt like crying as she remembered her so-called friends' reactions at boarding school when they had stumbled on the salacious news articles and the endless dissection of her mother's death.

Schooldays had certainly not been the best times of Cecelia's life.

They had read out every embarrassing detail to each other with relish as she had lain in her bed in the dorm, night after night. And then had come the endless questions.

'Was it a party or an orgy your mother was at?' Lucy, the ringleader had asked. *'And what do they mean by "compromising position"?'*

It hadn't been much better during term breaks. Cecelia's pace quickened as she thought of her aunt and uncle. They had rarely mentioned her mother and when they had they'd spoken in disapproving tones.

The deeper truth was that home had been no better, because actually her aunt and uncle had rarely spoken to her at all.

As for Gordon—well, with him, her mother had been *she who must not be named*, just a sordid part of Cecelia's past that was best forgotten.

Yet Luka had wanted to know more about it.

'Wait,' he called, and though she did not slow down he soon caught up with her. 'Why walk off when we're talking?'

'Because there's work to do, because...' *You're work*.

Constantly she had to remind herself of that fact.

Four more weeks of this felt too long, but then Cecelia reminded herself that he would be away for the next two.

She would be mad to get involved with him.

Mad.

She wasn't flattering herself to believe she could have him.

Cecelia also knew Luka well enough to know it would only be for a night, or a couple of weeks at best.

Cecelia knew, absolutely, how it would end—indifference, then avoidance—for she had seen it all too many times, and the trouble was that she did not know how she would recover.

She had never felt such *violent* emotions about someone before.

Luka Kargas was her one weakness and that would never do.

And so, after their gorgeous riverside dinner, they took the elevator back up in silence. Back in the office, she went to set up for the meeting that had been rescheduled and delayed over and over again. She made sure his notes were on his desk and she tried to ignore the rich scent of him as she chatted online with Stacey, who was Mr Garcia's PA.

'He's going to be another half-hour,' Stacey said, and Cecelia inwardly groaned for she just wanted this day to be over with. 'Are you able—?' Her voice cut off and the screen went black, and only then did Cecelia register that Luka had deliberately turned the computer off.

'What on earth are you doing?' she asked.

'I don't like to be kept waiting.'

'But you were the one who cancelled this morning's meeting.'

'So…' Luka shrugged '…tomorrow you can say that we lost the connection. I can't sit through a meeting about figures now.'

'Fine,' Cecelia snapped.

This bloody meeting had been moved and delayed so many times that she wondered how anyone did business with him.

Yet she knew the answer.

Luka was brilliant.

And they would wait.

'I want to talk to you,' Luka said.

'Is it about work?' Cecelia asked.

'No.'

'Then there's nothing to discuss. I'll go and pack for you,' Cecelia said. 'And then I'll be off.'

She headed to his suite.

Usually it took five minutes to pack for him as she had it down pat, but he wasn't going away for business and his wardrobe here consisted mainly of suits, shirts and ties.

She stood in his suite looking at his wardrobe for a moment as if more choices might appear, and then headed out.

He was sitting on her desk, as he had been this morning, only she chose not to sit down this time.

'I don't know what to pack,' she admitted. 'Are you staying here tonight?'

Luka nodded.

'Then I can go to your apartment and select a more casual wardrobe. I'll bring your luggage in with me in the morning.'

'Sure.'

She picked up her bag and gave him a tight smile. 'Thank you for dinner and cake and my gorgeous present.'

'You're most welcome.'

His dark eyes met hers and she wondered if she should give him a kiss on the cheek to thank him, just as she would anyone else who had given her such a nice night and gift.

Only he was not anyone.

But tonight of all nights, her hard-won control slipped and she leant in and gave him a light kiss on the cheek.

She merely brushed the skin of his cheek with her lips, and she even held her breath to lessen the impact the gesture would have on her senses. She would taste him later; in the elevator she would run her tongue over her lips and recall the warmth of his skin on her mouth.

And she would recall too the ache in her breast at the mere graze against his shirt.

She pulled back and her bag bit into her shoulder as she ached to drop it to the floor and give in to her craving for this man.

Luka did not want to get this wrong.

He read women with ease, and his kiss was so rarely refused—yet with her he could not be certain.

She had chastised him with her eyes on so many occasions, he could almost feel the sting of the slap she would deliver if he put so much as a finger wrong.

It would be worth it, Luka decided.

'I'll see you tomorrow,' Cecelia said, her voice a touch high as she willed her legs to move and take her from danger.

Yet, and yet… 'But if you need anything before that…'

She had said the same words a hundred times before— or was it a thousand times?—but they sounded different tonight.

His response was different tonight too. 'I need to be with you.'

No slap was delivered, she just stared back. And right when she thought she might finally know his kiss, instead his hands came to her arms.

'Aren't you going to try it on?'

She thought again of those slender dark fingers in her hair and his mouth near her cheek as he did the clasp, only this time, instead of refusing, she nodded.

'Let me help,' Luka said. He took her bag from her shoulder and retrieved the present and then dropped the bag to the floor.

He slowly prised open the box and as she watched his long finger run over the stones and she felt as if he was stroking her on the inside.

Luka could hear the trip in her breathing and felt the charge in the air; he breathed in the scent of seduction. For that was what she did, Luka concluded—without so much as a word or a move, she seduced.

'Turn around,' Luka said, and he moved from lounging against her desk.

Cecelia did so.

At his simple command she turned and faced the wall.

She had known how this evening would end, how this year would end.

And they ended tonight, she was suddenly rather certain of that.

But it didn't matter now.

She was leaving.

Cecelia went to lift the long ponytail she had retied many times today, but he pushed her hand down. 'I've got this,' Luka said.

She could barely breathe as she felt his hands come around her throat and the brush of his fingers against the pulse in her neck. He was tall and, she was certain, hard behind her, and she ached to lean back into him.

She felt the coolness of the necklace fall between her breasts as he put it on and the brush of his fingers as he did up the clasp. But then, instead of turning her around to admire the necklace, his fingers moved to the tiny bolero. She both heard and felt his voice. 'I hate this,' he said, and his words reverberated deep within her as he pushed the fabric down over her shoulders.

Luka would not rush this, for he had waited a long time and so first he removed the little bolero that he had loathed on sight.

One arm was freed, and then the other, and as the garment fell silently to the floor, she felt it dust her calf.

She shivered as he ran fingers along the bare flesh of her arms, something he had wanted to do all night.

'Luka...' His name from her lips was so loaded with lust that he did not take it as a reproach. Instead, he lifted her hair and the spine that had teased him this morning was now his to explore.

She felt his lips on the back of her neck as soft as the kiss she had delivered to his cheek and the message was the same, for it felt like a promise.

Every notch to her spine that was exposed by her dress was rewarded with a graze of his mouth, and then there was the ache of no contact for a moment.

Followed by delicious relief.

'I want to see this necklace on you as it should be seen,' he said. She felt his hands on her neck as he undid the tie of her halter neck and she bit her lip as he undid her flesh-coloured strapless bra.

Her breasts felt heavy and there was a yearning for his touch there, but instead he freed her hair and arranged it over her shoulders. For a second, just a second, his fingers grazed her breasts.

He felt her hard nipples, and now it was his breathing that was jagged for the longing to see her was intense. But their first kiss would be a naked one, Luka decided.

Cecelia could barely stand. She heard a noise and glanced to the side, seeing Luka toss his jacket over a chair. She turned back to face the wall, not sure whether she could bear to watch him undress.

And then she heard him strip off his shirt and she almost folded over at the thought of his naked chest behind her.

Her thighs were trembling and she would have no choice but to ask to sit soon, but then came his hands on her shoulders and another command. 'Turn around.'

Now she faced him and he looked at her usually pale face all flushed as if she'd already come. But instead of reproach in her green eyes there was the beckoning of an aurora as they glittered with the promise of what was to come.

'It's looks beautiful.'

The necklace fell between her breasts yet, as fine as it was, it garnered only a glance because he had found perfection elsewhere. He experienced a fierce desire to taste her there and to explore with his fingers, though they had not yet so much as kissed.

His lips were warm as they brushed over hers. Her breasts got the tease of his naked skin as their bodies came together, then his arms pulled her in as she moaned at the contact. He tasted of anise and all things forbidden and delicious.

And then he kissed her hard and she kissed him back hungrily, for she had craved him for close to a year. Her hands slipped through the arms that held her and came up behind his head to pull him closer.

He had expected reticence, that her tongue would require his coaxing, yet instead together they fuelled urgent desire. The woman who rarely blushed, who was always so cool and distant now burnt at his touch. He had imagined a slow seduction perhaps, and then he laughed in his head that he had thought her a virgin for the woman in his arms was wanton and wild.

He pressed against her hips and her grip tightened in his hair.

Tiny nips and wet, hot kisses were shared as Luka pressed her to the wall. She was grateful for the support it gave as her legs were trembling.

Luka pressed into her and moved her hands from his head and down past his flat stomach to the hard heat that was pressed into her.

He pulled back and their foreheads met as they watched her free him.

And, because it was Luka, of course he had protection to hand. But before he was lost to latex, Cecelia held him for a moment, as she had so long wanted to—stroking his thick, hard length as beads of silver moistened her palm.

She licked her lips and he moaned a low curse, for he wanted to carry her now to his suite. Luka wanted the rest of Cecelia's clothes to be gone, but his want was more immediate now. He pushed her hand away and sheathed himself with rapid, practised ease and then got back to her mouth.

He was so tall that even with Cecelia in high espadrilles she was no match for him.

Their teeth clashed and suddenly too much was not enough. He pushed up the dress and his hands roughly roamed her inner thighs and felt her hot and wet as he tore at her knickers and then crouched enough to sear into her.

He was rougher than she had ever known yet there was liquid silk to ease his path.

Cecelia had never been more frantic and as he lifted her legs she wrapped them around him. He was strong enough with his grip to allow her to hold his face and kiss him back hard.

It was the roughest and most delicious coupling.

For they matched.

His hands held her buttocks and his fingers dug in so deep that they would surely leave a bruise, yet she ground onto him. And far from reticence, it was Cecelia coaxing him to come. 'Luka!' She could not focus on kissing, and she tore her mouth away. He could feel the tease of intimate muscles and he thrust in hard and then swelled to the tight grip of her orgasm and her sensual sob called him to deliver deep.

Luka did, shuddering his release deep into her to the last twitches of hers.

And that part had her dizzy. The moan of him carried

without breath to her ears, and the sensual slide of their hot, damp bodies as they slowly brought themselves back from the far reaches of the divine space they had been in together. Kissing again, with languorous relish as the world faded in.

He lowered her down and she could feel the thump, thump of his heart against the flutter of hers. Cecelia rested her head on his shoulder and she was herself for the first time.

And herself was more reckless than she had ever dared to be.

'Come on.' He was tidying up, picking up discarded clothes, ready to be headed for his suite and to bed, to resume proceedings, this time at a more leisurely pace.

But she would not be waking up there, Cecelia decided.

One taste of heaven was more than enough and she had always sworn to leave before he dictated terms.

'I need to get home.'

She picked up her bra, but since it would be almost impossible to do it up she pushed it into her bag.

'Cece…' he said, and she didn't correct him, but she did pick up her shredded knickers and added them to her bag, and then with rather unsteady hands did up her halter neck.

'I really do need to get home, Luka.'

'You're not just running off.'

'I'm not running,' she corrected. 'I just want to go home.'

Her voice was incredibly composed. He looked at the necklace, heavy between gently curving breasts and the gorgeous flush of her climax.

But aside from throwing her over his shoulder, or

dragging her, it would seem that he couldn't stop her from leaving. She had made up her mind.

Usually it would be perfect.

A good orgasm, and then the absence of conversation—except there was more to her that he wanted to explore, and he was rather sure that there was more to come for *them*.

But she was checking herself in a small mirror compact, as she often did before she headed out.

'Thanks for an amazing night,' Cecelia said, and then, just as she had done previously, she leant forward and gave him a kiss on the cheek, as if the past half an hour had not taken place.

'Don't go home yet,' Luka said.

'I want to, though.'

And he couldn't really argue with that.

He watched as she walked to the elevator and pressed the button.

Cecelia stepped in and pressed for the lobby, unable to stop herself leaning against the cool mirrors, not really surprised by what had taken place.

She had wanted him so badly for months.

A man in a suit got in at the fourteenth floor and another at the seventh.

Cecelia nodded and smiled and then stared ahead as they inched down to the ground floor where she stepped out and walked across the foyer.

The cleaners had their buffers out and were polishing the marble floors.

Cecelia said goodnight to the doorman and stepped out into the night, but there was no cool breeze to greet her.

It was a sultry London night, but as she headed for the underground station she heard her name—'Ms Andrews?'

She turned around and saw that it was Luka's driver.

'Mr Kargas said you worked too late to take the underground.'

And of all the experiences of this night, this was the part she both hated and loved the most.

Loved that she was being taken care of by Luka, that he had thought to see her safely home.

Hated because by his very nature it was a mere temporary, tantalising glimpse of his world.

CHAPTER FIVE

CECELIA WAS TEMPTED to call in sick, but then that would suggest she regretted last night, which she didn't.

Instead, she regretted how she felt this morning, because rather than getting up to her alarm and facing the very early start to her day, Cecelia had brought a coffee to bed and sat in it looking at the necklace that Luka had given her.

Cecelia did not want to be one of those women who dared to hope that with her things might be different.

She just had to get through this morning and then she would have a bit of a reprieve in the next two weeks, and then hopefully by the time he came back from Xanero, normal services could be resumed.

For the first time, she hadn't put out her clothes the night before but Cecelia forgave herself that lapse.

She dressed in the navy suit that she should have worn yesterday and after checking her appearance left the flat. It was too early even for Mrs Dawson to be up and about as she left and took the Tube, not to the office but to Luka's apartment, to which she had keys.

The trouble with being a PA, especially to someone as successful as Luka, was that for the term of your contract you had access to their life in a way few did.

And, Cecelia had learned, if you happened to be crazy about the boss, it was a form of slow torture.

The doorman knew her and greeted her with a smile. She headed up in the elevator and then rang the bell and waited a moment before letting herself in.

Once, thinking he was still overseas, she had let herself in unannounced, without ringing the bell, and had found Luka in bed.

Neither alone nor sleeping.

Yes, working for Luka really was torture.

Cecelia walked in through the entrance hallway, but instead of heading to his bedroom she went through to the lounge and looked out over the view of Hyde Park, wondering how he would behave with her this morning in the office.

Would he carry on like it hadn't even happened, or would he expect her to be available to him as she served out her notice?

She gave a little shake of her head to clear such thoughts and wheeled the case she had brought with her towards the main bedroom.

Damn!

He was in bed, though thankfully this time alone.

And asleep.

It wasn't unusual to have to tiptoe around him, only this morning it was made more difficult, knowing she could have awoken next to him.

As quietly as she could, Cecelia opened up a wardrobe and, as the light inside came on, Cecelia heard him stir.

'Hey,' Luka said, his voice thick and sleepy.

'I'm just sorting out your luggage for your trip.'

And then he must have recalled what they had done the previous night because he asked, 'Why did you leave so abruptly?'

'Because I wanted to get home,' Cecelia said, and then she turned and gave him a small smile and did her best to keep it light. 'And I also wanted some sleep.'

'Yes, well, you wouldn't have got that had you stayed.' He put his hands behind his head and watched her pulling out a couple of casual shirts and adding them to the case.

'Will you be swimming when you're there?' she asked.

'What do you think, Cece?' he said.

It really had been a stupid question, given where he was headed, but it had been more to change the subject than to find out the answer.

'I think you should call me by my proper name,' she added, ignoring his question. Of course he would be swimming.

'It's not a holiday camp.' He grinned from the bed. 'The villas all have their own private pools,' Luka said as she headed into his en suite bathroom, then he let out a fond laugh of recall. 'Though there used to be just one main one. I used to work it.'

'Work it?' Cecelia laughed and called out from the en suite where she was collecting his cologne and things. 'Were you a cabana boy?'

'Yes.'

'Really?' She came to the door smiling, her hands full of toiletries. 'I was actually joking.'

'It's true, though. I used to head down there after school or during the holidays. It wasn't as luxurious then as it is now. There was a different owner then— Geo.'

'What was he like?'

'Lazy and a gambler,' Luka said, and he looked at her standing in the doorway and thought of all she had told him last night.

And all she had not.

There was a lot he hadn't told her either. He thought of her little jab yesterday about not everything being about money. She thought he'd had it all handed to him on a plate.

Everyone did.

He would have two weeks solid of it now; his father swanning around as if he had rebuilt the stunning complex from scratch, and—one thing that really annoyed Luka—complaining about the food when he feasted at the restaurant. Theo would sit there loudly stating that he made it better himself, when in truth Theo Kargas could not make his own coffee, let alone run a high-end kitchen.

Luka rather guessed that the uptight Cecelia might not be a forgiving audience for the story of his beginnings, and not the first person he would choose to share it with.

Luka wasn't used to sharing anything.

In business and in private he chose to take rather than to give.

Yet she had told him so much last night and the guilt of his past gnawed at his gut like a cancer—not that he would ever admit it.

'I would pick up the towels and get drinks and things. Then, when I finished school I got a job in Reception.'

Cecelia zipped up his toiletry bag and put it in his case and was just about to ask him about footwear when he said something that made her frown.

'Of course, I still *worked* the pool but it was in my own time and it wasn't towels that I was picking up.'

She looked up and met his eyes. 'Meaning?'

'Because I worked in Reception, I knew who the

richest women were because they had private access to the beach and the ocean view.'

'I'm not with you...'

'I think you are, Cece.'

She added a belt to his case and did not look at him but he could see two pink spots on her cheek.

In fact, she was embarrassed, wondering if it was because of the fact that sex was constantly on her mind around Luka that she was misinterpreting things.

'I made a lot of money, and I saved all of it. I made enough that when Geo lost a small fortune and was desperate for cash, I put in an offer for the restaurant and it was accepted.'

'You bought the restaurant?'

'Yes,' Luka said. 'I bought it and gave my father a share, so he might finally work in his own restaurant, as he had always said he wanted to do. Growing up, we had no money and he said there were no jobs but there *were* jobs. Pot-washing jobs but, still, it was work. He got really angry...' Luka didn't add that he'd got the worst beating of his life that night. 'My mother said he was a chef and that washing pots was beneath him. So, when I had the money, I bought him a share in a restaurant, one with the Kargas name on the door.'

'But how on earth did a pool boy get the money to buy a restaurant?'

'It wasn't the establishment it is now,' Luka pointed out.

'But even so! Are you saying you were a gigolo?'

'If you choose to call it that then, yes, I was,' Luka said, expecting her to snap his case closed and walk away.

Yet she didn't.

'But how?' Cecelia asked. 'I mean, how does it work?'

Luka shrugged. 'A smile, a nod. Often they would buy me a drink.'

'I thought it would be the other way around.'

'No.'

'And did you name a price?'

'Of course not,' Luka said. 'That would be in poor taste.'

'But how?' she asked, intensely curious. 'I mean, I just can't imagine…'

'What?' he said. 'You can't imagine naming your wants?'

'No!' Cecelia admitted. 'I can't.'

'Perhaps you should try it before you knock it!'

'No, thank you,' she said primly. 'And I can't imagine giving the cabana boy a wink and a nod.'

Luka smiled. 'The first time it happened was a surprise. I got chatting to one of the guests. She was a widow. I didn't really know her but she asked me to join her for dinner. I said no, Geo would not like me dining with the guests. She said we would dine in her suite then. And so I went up and we ate and then we…' He smiled. 'I'm sure you can guess the rest.'

'But I can't,' Cecelia said, for she wanted to know more, and in her curiosity she found herself sitting down on the bed. 'How old was she?'

'A good bit older than I was then. In her thirties, I think,' Luka said. 'She was my first.' He looked at her. 'Who was yours?'

'I don't have to answer that.'

'If you want to know more you do.'

'Gordon.'

He wrinkled his nose and Luka was surprised as something that felt like it should be called jealousy surged in his chest.

Which was ridiculous when he was telling her about his own depraved past.

'Well, my first was actually stunning—a divorcée. She was there with friends but had her own villa. I was there every night until morning and I thought I had found the keys to heaven. The morning she left she came into Reception and when Geo wasn't looking she gave me an envelope. I thought it was a letter. When I opened it there was a whole load of cash. Until that point I had thought it was a romance.'

'Were you hurt when she paid you?'

'Hell no,' he said. 'To tell the truth I was already starting to get restless.'

Cecelia suppressed an eye-roll and refrained from saying that perhaps it was an indicator of things to come, as Luka spoke on.

'I was trying to work out how to break it off but had decided to do so after her holiday. I was the naïve one back then.'

Cecelia gave a wry smile at that. 'I doubt you were ever naïve. And after she'd gone there was another?'

'Of course, although it wasn't always cash. Sometimes they would take me shopping for a watch or such like. Once a car...'

'A car?'

She started to laugh. An embarrassed laugh, but she was also very curious. 'Luka!'

'What?' He shrugged. 'I was always careful and it wasn't all sex.'

'What else?'

'Romance. Dinner. Shopping. But mainly talking.'

'You mean, saying what they wanted to hear?'

'Yep.'

'Did you care for them?'

'Some I did,' Luka said. 'Mostly it was work.' He met her eyes. 'They didn't all care for me, Cece. They paid for the full Luka Kargas treatment.'

For a few years the pool had been his playground and the pickings had always been rich.

'Anyway,' he said, 'once I had bought the restaurant I hired a decent chef and changed the décor.'

'What about your father?'

Luka didn't answer directly.

It felt disloyal to his mother to admit that his father hadn't so much as lifted a saucepan.

'The restaurant started to do well and was too busy for one chef. Though it didn't do *too* well—I made sure of that.'

'Why?'

'Because I knew it wouldn't be long until Geo blew things again and would be forced to sell. When that happened I had planned to be in a good enough position to put in an offer on the resort. With help, of course…'

'Financial help?' Cecelia checked.

'No, one of the women I was seeing helped me get my papers in order to go to the bank.' He didn't add that the woman had also warned him not to bring his father into the hotel side of things.

It was advice for which he would be grateful for ever.

'How old were you by then?'

'Twenty-two. Once the resort was safely mine I hired the best chef I could find and things really started to happen. As the guests came in I started to buy up the houses and land around it. Out of all the hotels I own, it is still the jewel in my crown. From humble beginnings it's magnificent now.'

She looked at him. He mesmerised her, he truly did.

And she was nervous too, for the more she knew him, the more she wanted him.

'Is your father still your business partner?'

'Not fully.' He shook his head. 'The hotels are mine, the restaurants belong to us both.' And then, a touch unguarded, he admitted a little more. 'I should never have gone into business with him.'

'I agree about not going into business with family,' Cecelia said, because she had seen such things go wrong in her work before. 'And, Luka, I also think it's a really bad idea getting involved with an employer.' It was Cecelia who brought it back to them. 'I'm not saying that I regret last night, but it should never have happened. I take my career very seriously.'

'I know you do, but you're leaving anyway.'

'Yes,' she agreed. 'But I still don't think it's right and I don't want Bridgette or anyone knowing that something once happened between us.'

'Once?' he checked, and he took her hand to move it to the sheet beneath which he was hardening, but she resisted and her palm came to rest on his flat stomach.

There was no solace there for his skin was warm and she could feel the silk hair that led from his navel to paradise and she ached to move her hand lower.

So much had changed since yesterday.

Not just that she was leaving.

And not just that they had slept together.

He was creeping further into her heart.

'Luka, I really think we should just draw a neat line under what happened and when you come back from Xanero we'll go back to how we were.'

She was trying so hard to hold onto her heart, while at the same time sitting on his bed and looking into his eyes.

He pulled her head towards him, and she let him, and they shared a lingering kiss. He was leaving this morning, Cecelia told herself.

Order would soon be returned.

Just not yet.

Their tongues explored each other and their mouths were hungry for sensations.

He kissed down her neck and then moved the collar of her linen jacket and kissed the shoulders that had been revealed to him only yesterday, tracing her clavicle with his tongue until her neck arched.

'Don't leave a bruise...' she said, but he ignored her, biting into her flesh and sucking as his hand pushed between her thighs, which were pressed together.

'Come to bed,' Luka said.

And without hesitation she nodded.

Cecelia stood and his eyes were on her as she undressed. He watched as the navy jacket came off and he just stared as she removed her top to reveal the purple mark on her shoulder.

She slipped off her skirt and sandals and then straightened up and removed her bra. She could see he was hard beneath the sheet, and, in response to the command from her hungry eyes, he kicked it off.

He loved that he did not have to persuade her—that he did not have to slowly remove her bra and kiss her while sliding down her knickers.

Instead, she took care of that.

For this was no accident.

Her delicately shaped curls, which he had not had time to appreciate last night, had a coppery tinge that he stared at as she removed her bra. For the first time in years he was hungry to taste a woman, and reached for her to join him in bed.

'After this morning…' she warned, but he hushed her with his mouth. 'I mean it, Luka,' Cecelia said, pulling hers away.

'Sure,' he agreed, 'so this morning we make the most of it.'

Instead of kissing her, he knelt and lowered his head to her breast.

His tongue swirled around her nipple while his mouth closed and created a delicious vacuum. He sucked hard and Cecelia felt herself clench down below.

'Luka…'

'Nice?' he asked, removing his mouth and blowing on her erect nipple. Cecelia didn't know how to answer.

It was beyond nice, it was bliss, yet his moves were so practised and sure. She closed her eyes and then his mouth moved down her stomach.

'Am I getting the full Luka Kargas treatment?' she asked.

There was a moment of arrested silence while he paused, his mouth hovering over her stomach. What she didn't know was that in Luka's world the tables had turned many years ago. He no longer went down on women.

His start had been sex and Luka had long ago perfected his routine.

But now that his wealth exceeded theirs…

Well, he paid for *their* favours.

Not directly, of course.

With jewels and exotic weekends.

Now *they* went down on *him* instead of the other way around.

But not this morning.

It had been years since…

Years since *her* pleasure had mattered.

This morning it did.

'No,' he responded to her question. 'You're getting me.'

He kissed her stomach, not lightly but as deeply and intently as if it were her mouth, and Cecelia found her breath held in her throat as his hand slid between her closed legs. 'Open them.'

She did, just a little, and she lay there, determined almost not to enjoy it. To remind herself that this was his skill.

His thumb was intent and his fingers were inside her but Cecelia's throat was tight as he teased and stroked and rubbed, for she brought up her knees in an involuntary movement.

Women had paid him for this, she told herself as his tongue set to work alongside his thumb.

There was a moan building but she held onto it, yet he read it, for he moved between her legs to increase the intensity.

Luka heard her low moan and forgot his practised moves of old for this was new.

He heard her gasps, and finally learned the scent and taste of Cecelia on his tongue.

Her thighs were shaking as he probed deeply, and her hand pressed on his head, pushing him away. He knew she resisted pleasure.

So he upped the intensity again.

'Luka…' she sobbed, because it was too intense. His tongue was penetrating and he growled—and knew the moment she felt it. She wanted to come, but knew she would come so deeply that she was terrified to let herself go.

'Come, Cece,' he said, his voice rumbling through her. It was a command, an order her body could not ignore. Her back arched and her orgasm shot through her like lightning and earthed to his mouth.

He coaxed every flicker from her so that she was flushed and near crying when her body came down.

Never had it tasted this good. This was not like the work he used to do. This was different.

He slid up her body, Cecelia pulling him those final inches. They drank from each other in a desperate kiss that was both deep and heady. Luka came up on his arms but she pulled his head back down to claim a deeper kiss.

It was nothing like either of them had known before.

He was practised to the core and she was so new to passion, yet it was fire that they made together. She did not want him to be this good.

'That *wasn't* work,' he told her. 'That was bliss.'

And so was this.

He was there at her entrance and nudging a little way in. 'Come with me,' he said to the shell of her ear. 'To Xanero…'

Luka did not want to go and now had been presented with a way to make it more bearable.

She liked the thought of fourteen nights of this. But she held back.

'No,' she said, and he pulled out. 'I mean, no to Xanero…'

But yes to this.

Her eyes were closed as he slid in deep, all the way in. If she could have examined her thoughts she feared she would rediscover her self-control, and the part of her that knew this was wrong.

And so did Luka.

But they were past caring.

The feel of him unsheathed and stretching her was sublime.

And for Luka too, for she was slippery yet tight. He drove in deep and she let out a moan that he wanted to turn into a scream.

He reached for her leg and wrapped her calf around his thigh, pushing into her again. She was more open than she had ever been.

He thrust slowly and could feel the intimate welcoming grip of her.

Her nails dug into his buttocks and she moved with him until they were lost to each other and the moment.

'Luka…' She could barely breathe, yet at her plea he took her harder and faster, making her dizzy. She could feel her climax building and this time she welcomed it.

He angled himself and took her deeper and then he tipped into rapid, rhythmic thrusts from which there was no return. It was her scream that brought him back to consciousness.

It was her first scream in bed, Luka knew as his stomach lifted and he pulsed into her, shouting his release.

Her cry came from a place she had never known, and her orgasm was so intense that for a moment she felt possessed. As if her body had been taken over by someone else, by a woman who knew how to be free.

Yet as she gloried in the sensation, his weight atop her reminded her starkly that soon she would have to dig her way out of the ashes from the fire he had brought to her heart.

CHAPTER SIX

'COME WITH ME to Xanero.'

As the mist was clearing he said it again. His weight pressed down on her even as he still rested inside her. If there was ever a weak moment this was it and Cecelia knew she was about to say yes when Luka spoke.

'Not to the resort or anything,' he added, pushing up onto his forearms. 'Or my mother would think we were serious or something. You could stay on the yacht.'

Cecelia slid out from under him and rolled to her side. He did the same.

She had almost said yes.

In a delicious weak moment she had almost succumbed, and she failed to keep the bitter edge from her tone when she responded to his invitation. 'You mean, come to Xanero as your plaything.'

'I'd work you by day...' He smiled, completely unfazed as he toyed with her breast, still throbbing from his previous attention, for this was the life he led. 'And then make up for it by night.'

'So while you're on the island I'd be cooped up—'

'Hardly cooped up. It's not a tin boat with a gas stove....'

'I have seen your yacht, Luka.'

Well, she had seen pictures of it and had seen some

of the accounts for it. It was a luxury resort in itself, and of course she knew all about the wild parties that were held there.

And now she was being invited into the playboy's bed.

Oh, the dewy mist of his lovemaking was most certainly starting to clear for suddenly Cecelia pulled herself away and sat up.

And it was then that realisation kicked in. 'Luka, we didn't use anything...'

In a life spent not making mistakes, Cecelia had just made a huge one and there was no excuse.

For either of them.

'Are you on the Pill?'

'Yes, I'm on the Pill,' she snapped as she tried to remember if she'd taken it last night, because it hadn't just been putting out her clothes for the morning that had fallen by the wayside. But surely if she went home now and took it, then she'd be fine.

But pregnancy wasn't the only thing on her mind.

'It's not just that, though.' Cecelia turned and looked over to where he lay and saw that his expression was equally grim.

He'd just told her he'd once been a gigolo—she could not believe she had been so careless.

'Cecelia, you don't have to worry about anything there,' Luka said as he moved to reassure her. 'I *always* use protection.'

'Well, clearly you don't!'

It was as much her fault as his, Cecelia knew that, and her angry tone was aimed more towards herself.

'You'll be fine,' he said, which might have sounded dismissive, but neither did he want to admit just how impossibly rare this lapse was.

She gave a terse nod and headed for the shower while Luka lay there, his hands behind his head, trying to fathom what had just taken place.

This morning he'd forgotten the rules. This morning he'd been so wrapped in the feel of her, the feel of *them*, that he'd forgotten the care he usually took.

He had complete control in the bedroom, for though he was wild he was not reckless.

Yet this morning he had been.

Not only had he invited her to come to Xanero with him—at least he had quickly reacted and told Cece that she would only be on the yacht—but for a moment he had glimpsed it. His dream, showing off the first Kargas restaurant and the now stunning resort which was by far his proudest achievement to date.

And he had told her how his ascent to the top had started.

Luka wasn't particularly close to anyone.

He kept work and family neatly separated, and certainly he had never invited an employee, albeit one who had resigned, to join him there.

The yacht was for escape, for parties and fun. It had never been used as a couples' retreat.

She came out of the shower and dressed quickly. He was relieved that she seemed as keen to leave as he now wanted her gone, for she had messed with his head.

'I'd better take your case in to the office,' Cecelia said.

'Please.' He nodded. 'I'll be in later.'

No, he wasn't a perfect gentleman, for he did not tell her to leave the case and that he would take it.

And neither would his driver magically appear.

She could take the underground.

Cecelia had said herself that she wanted to draw a neat line and get back to being his PA.

That suited him just fine.

Last night had been amazing.

So had this morning, and yet now he was left feeling deeply unsettled.

Luka chose not to get close to anyone, but this morning he had.

Xanero really was hell in paradise.

For Luka, the first week there had been a protracted nightmare—his mother seemed resigned to her fate and his father continued to lord it over the restaurant and resort.

And he had found out that his father was bullying the staff.

Bastard!

While Luka disliked how his father had rewritten history to suit the image of himself he wanted to believe, Luka could live with it if it made life easier on his mother.

But bullying would not happen in one of Luka's establishments, and for all the lies and wealth that shaped his mother's life, she was finding it no easier that he could see.

Luka had taken the yacht out over the weekend, but the pop of champagne corks and the sound of music skimming over the Mediterranean had soon grated and he had cleared everyone off except the crew as he mulled things over. Now, back on Xanero, and midway through the second week, on the Wednesday morning his decisions were made and he was ready to execute them.

He walked through the alfresco area of the restaurant where diners were enjoying the morning sun and through to the cool darkness of the main restaurant.

Theo Kargas was at the bar, speaking with the bar manager, and Luka could feel the young man's tension from across the room.

'Hey,' he said to his father. 'We need to talk.'

'About?' Theo asked, even as he crammed whitebait, crisped to perfection, into his mouth. He was utterly relaxed, for any angry words from his son always took place out of earshot of the staff.

Yes, Luka's door was always closed.

Not so today.

'I want to discuss your appalling treatment of my staff and your inexcusable conduct towards my mother.'

Theo almost choked, but then attempted a recovery. '*Your* staff? We are partners. I gave you—'

'You gave me nothing,' Luka said, and got right in his father's face. 'You actually believe your own lies. Now, as I said, we need to talk...' He gestured to a table, for he too would prefer privacy for this but the fact he had first addressed the issues in front of the bar manager had been deliberate.

Theo *would* listen, or Luka *would* act.

'I bought this restaurant,' Luka said, 'from the money I made picking up rich woman...'

'Luka,' his father warned, for a waiter was setting up the table and could hear what was being said.

'What?' Luka shrugged. 'I'm not ashamed of it.'

Well, perhaps he was a bit, but having told Cecelia the real truth about his start he felt more reconciled with it.

So he told his father a truth that had consistently been ignored. 'I gave you an opportunity to work, and you spurned it. I have put up with it for years for my mother's sake. No more. I am hiring a new manager, who shall report directly to me. One more episode of your foul temper used on my staff and I shall take you through the courts to extricate you from our agreement and the restaurant's name shall be changed to Luka Kargas.'

'It would kill your mother.'

'She's already dying,' Luka pointed out, and then he looked right at his father. 'Actually, she isn't, because I am moving her to London for her treatments and I am going to ensure that she rests and is taken care of between them.'

'You can't just swan in here and dictate—'

'Oh, but I can,' Luka said. 'I own the complex, and I have a half-share in the restaurant, and,' he added, 'I can destroy you if I so choose. You should be pleading with your wife to seek treatment, because if it wasn't for her you'd be seeing your days out in a shack on the hills and, believe me, Theo, you don't want to test me on that.'

'I'm your father!' Theo reared and stood and leant across the table and grabbed Luka's shirt.

'More's the pity,' Luka said. 'And I strongly suggest that you get your hands off me. I'm not ten years old any more, or a skinny teenager up against a brute. I could floor you and I am more than willing to do it.'

Sensibly, his father removed his hand, for it was clear Luka meant every word. But he was not finished yet. 'You have no idea the ruthless bastard I can be. I could crush you and your so-called empire in the palm of my hand,' Luka said. 'And I will say it again, just so we're clear—the *only* reason I've held back where the resort is concerned is for the sake of my mother.'

It was Luka who stood up and walked off back towards his villa.

He'd have loved to have hit his bully of a father,

but what good could come from that? So instead he stripped off and dived into the pool, pounding out several lengths before hauling himself from the water a touch breathless.

And then he messaged Cecelia.

We need to talk.

His message came up on her computer and Cecelia tensed, because though they had spoken about work both online and on the phone on many occasions, this sounded rather personal.

She replied quickly.

I'm about to call someone in for an interview.

So?

Of course he didn't mean that they needed to speak about what had taken place between them, Cecelia scolded herself for her less-than-professional reply. If Luka Kargas wanted to speak to his PA it didn't matter if she'd been about to call someone in.

'I have to speak with Mr Kargas,' Cecelia said to the interviewee. 'I'll be back when I can.'

Cecelia didn't apologise for keeping Sabine waiting, for the potential PA might as well get a glimpse of what she would be in for.

A moment later his face appeared on her screen and Cecelia got more than a glimpse.

His chest was naked and her view was of a dark mahogany nipple surrounded by a swirl of black hair. But then he angled the screen better and she saw that his hair was wet and he was squinting from the bright sun.

'What can I do for you?' Cecelia asked.

Her voice was cool, her demeanour brisk and she was determined that they were back to business.

'What are you doing?' he asked.

'Working.' She frowned. 'Marco has a few things he needs to run by you but apart from that things are ticking along.'

She was wearing a grey dress with a sheer grey silky cardigan, because perish the thought that she might show too much skin. Her hair was neat and pulled back and yet now he knew another side to her he couldn't help but see her buttoned-up appearance for what it was. A defence strategy.

'I want you to fly here,' Luka said. 'I want you here tonight.'

Cecelia stared back at him. 'For work?'

'No.'

She liked it that he was direct.

In fact, Cecelia liked it that he had basically asked her to get on a plane for sex. But what happened when he got bored? She reminded herself of all the reasons she had refused his original offer.

He would wake up one morning and instead of kisses she would sense his restlessness.

His slight disdain.

Oh, she had seen it on too many occasions not to know what was in store for her.

At least here in London she was but a taxi ride away from salvaging her pride when he told her they were through.

But in Xanero?

Did she book her own flight home?

Or would they suffer it through until she left his employ less than three weeks from now?

'If it isn't for work, then I shan't be joining you.'

'Fine,' Luka snapped. 'In that case, I need you to go and view some apartments for me.'

'Sure.'

'And I want you to interview some private nurses. Make sure they speak Greek.'

Cecelia took down the details.

It was now all very businesslike. Surly, but businesslike. Yet she ached to know more about his mother, though she resisted asking for details that were not with the remit of a professional relationship.

They had spent one night together, and she knew from his reputation that that didn't give her the keys to his private life.

'How are the interviews for your replacement going?' Luka asked.

'I'm getting there,' Cecelia said. 'I'm on the second round, so I should have a shortlist of three for you to choose from.'

'Any stand-outs?'

Cecelia hesitated.

Luka was a demanding boss but she almost had to shake the stars from potential employees' eyes to ensure they understood what the job entailed.

But one had stood out.

Sabine.

She had an incredible work history and was bright and engaging. The only trouble was that Cecelia didn't like her.

'There's one,' Cecelia said. 'Sabine. I'm just about to interview her again and give her a tour but...'

'But what?'

'I don't know,' Cecelia admitted.

'Try telling me.'

'I don't like her.' Cecelia shrugged. 'But, then, she's not for me to like. I'll see how this interview goes. She speaks Greek, which might be a help with your mother, and…'

'My mother will be coming to London for treatment, not for little get-togethers with my PA.'

He turned off the computer and closed it up.

Luka really did not want her to leave.

And yet it was perhaps for the best because despite strong words about PAs not getting involved with his family, he had told Cecelia some things he had never told anyone. And he had her interviewing nurses and looking for apartments.

He trusted her, and Luka was more comfortable trusting no one.

With that awkward conversation over, Cecelia got on with the second-round interviews.

Cecelia was self-aware enough to know that it was probably for private reasons that she couldn't take to Sabine. The young woman was gorgeous, with piercing blue eyes and straight black hair cut in a jagged, edgy style. She made Cecelia feel terribly drab.

'Luka will probably call you Sab, or Sabby…' Cecelia said in an offhand comment as she showed her around. 'It drives me crazy.'

'He can call me what he likes as long as he pays me.'

Cecelia held in a breath.

Sabine was arrogant and overly confident perhaps, but she really was the perfect match for Luka.

She could almost hear the banter between them.

'This is his suite,' Cecelia explained as she opened the door. 'It's serviced daily but I tend to check it as it sometimes needs an extra service. Not currently, though, he's still in Greece.'

'So I read!' Sabine said.

Cecelia had been doing her level best not to read about him, but once the interviews were wrapped up she found that she could not resist.

The headlines were all in the same vein: *Xanero Magnate Returns.*

It would seem that the weekend had been spent out on his yacht and she knew full well what went on on board.

She clicked on the article and there were the glossy beauties that always surrounded him and the sun hanging low in a fiery sky.

Luka didn't even wait for nightfall to get a party started.

It wasn't just the resumption of his sex life that concerned her, though—oh, but it did, *desperately* it did—but also what had happened that morning between them.

Cecelia could not believe she'd had unprotected sex. Though she kept willing herself calm, yesterday she had caved and made an appointment with her GP.

At the conclusion of the interview today Cecelia was heading there.

'Well, thank you for coming in,' Cecelia said as she walked Sabine to the elevator. 'You can expect to hear from me by the end of the week.'

'I'll look forward to it.' Sabine smiled and the women shook hands.

Cecelia really didn't like her, but it would seem she was the only one to feel so.

'She seems really nice,' Bridgette commented as Cecelia walked back from the elevator.

Yes, it was probably for rather personal reasons that

she didn't like her, Cecelia guessed, and decided that she would be putting Sabine forward.

Luka could make the final call.

'I'm going out for a couple of hours,' she told Bridgette. 'I won't have my phone on.'

'What should I say if Luka calls because he can't get hold of you?' Bridgette checked, because his PA was always supposed to be available.

'Tell him I'm…' She didn't know what to say. 'Tell him I'm taking a long lunch.'

Lunch didn't come into it.

Instead, she took the underground until she was practically home and spent the next hour sitting in the waiting room at her GP's surgery.

Cecelia was rarely there and finally, when her name was called, she rather hoped she would be in and out in a few minutes with her mind eased.

Dr Heale introduced herself and Cecelia told her the reason she was there.

'It's probably nothing,' Cecelia started. 'In fact, I'm sure I'm wasting your time…'

'Why don't you let me be the judge of that?'

Very well.

Why was discussing sex always so awkward for her? The shame came from her aunt and uncle, Cecelia knew. They spoke in whispers and were still mortified by the salacious circumstances in which her mother had died.

Cecelia did her best to push all that aside and to speak in a matter-of-fact tone. 'I had unprotected sex last week.'

'When?'

'On Monday night,' Cecelia said. 'Or rather on the Tuesday morning.'

'You're on the Pill?' Dr Heale checked, reading through her notes.

'Yes,' Cecelia said, 'though I usually take my Pill at night…'

'And you didn't?'

'No.'

'Well, you've left it too late for the morning-after pill.'

She hadn't really thought about it the morning after, but now Dr Heale was telling her that she'd had a window of a week.

That window was closed to her now.

'But it's probably fine?' Cecelia pushed, only Dr Heale wasn't exactly rushing to put her at ease; in fact, she was reading Cecelia's notes.

'Are you still with your fiancé?' she asked.

Cecelia remembered the last time she had been there, carefully going on the Pill before she and Gordon did anything.

There had certainly been no up-against-the-wall sex with him!

'Er, no.'

'Do you have a new partner?'

'Not exactly,' Cecelia croaked. 'It was a one-off, well…'

'That's fine,' Dr Heale said. 'But with a casual encounter it is, of course, more important that you're careful.'

She was right, except there was nothing casual about Cecelia's feelings for Luka.

And there was that sting of shame again—not that Dr Heale turned a hair. If anything, she was very practical.

'Perhaps, while you're here, we should run a sexual health check,' she suggested.

It looked like Cecelia would not be in and out in a

couple of minutes; in fact, she returned from lunch a full hour late.

'Luka's been calling the office,' Bridgette warned. 'And he's not best pleased that your mobile's turned off.'

He certainly had been calling, Cecelia thought when she turned it back on. She had barely sat down before he called again.

'How was the dentist?' he asked, and there was an edge to Luka's voice for he was quite sure where she had been.

'Excuse me?' Cecelia flared.

'You're the one making up excuses. Were you off visiting your new office? Or perhaps having lunch with your new boss—whoever that may be?'

'No,' Cecelia calmly responded. 'I had an appointment. Now, what can I do for you?'

You can get here, Luka wanted to answer.

He had never had to chase or pursue, and the one woman who could have made him feel better had distanced herself from him.

'How did the second-round interviews go?'

'Very well. I have a shortlist of three for you to interview.'

'Bring them in early next week.'

'So you'll be back on Monday?' Cecelia checked.

But Luka had already rung off.

CHAPTER SEVEN

CECELIA KNEW HE was back the very second she stepped out of the elevator.

That tangy citrus scent of him had never really left the place but it was stronger today.

There was a knot of tight nerves in her stomach and she had no idea how to play this. She sensed he had come out of his office as she hung up her jacket, and this was confirmed when she heard him speak.

'Hi.'

His voice was low and deep and, though expected, she still had to fight not to jump. Instead she turned around at his greeting.

He looked amazing, and even if he had gone home to deal with a difficult situation it was clear there had been time spent in the sun.

'Hi, Luka.'

'How are things?'

'Great. But Mr Garcia is insisting that you speak with him today.'

'Tell him I can fit him in tomorrow.'

'Very well,' Cecelia said as she held in a sigh. 'And you have the applicants for my replacement coming in between two and four.'

'Good.'

He'd hoped she might reconsider, given what had taken place, but deep down he knew she wouldn't have.

Cecelia was professional, and even Luka, who in the past had happily slept with his PA, knew that a line had been crossed and that it would be impossible to go back to the way they had been.

For once he did not want to talk about work.

Neither did he want to hit the computer.

After a hellish two weeks at home, quite simply he wanted to take her to bed.

Instead, there was a lot to do.

The head of his legal team was in and out of his office all morning, and Marco, head of accounting, was there too. From what she could glean, Luka was looking to sever business ties with his father.

As his mother battled cancer!

Luka's ruthlessness made her shiver.

It was approaching one o'clock when Cecelia told him that an apartment she had seen would be available for him to view this evening.

'I shan't be going ahead with that.'

'Oh.'

He had asked his mother to come to London and concentrate on surviving but the answer had been no.

She had at least agreed to have treatments in Athens, on the condition she could return home after each course.

Luka rather guessed they were his father's conditions but his efforts to persuade her otherwise had fallen on deaf ears.

At least she wasn't simply giving up now, but Luka knew that he had to do more.

He had spent the morning testing the legal waters

with his team, but it would be long and protracted to have his father forcibly removed as joint owner.

And he did not want the extra stress on his mother.

In fact, Luka, who dreaded going home, even for the occasional weekend, was starting to realise that Xanero might soon have to act as his base, at least for a while.

'You said one of the applicants spoke Greek?' Luka checked.

'Yes, Sabine.'

'And she is okay with extensive travel?'

'Yes.' Cecelia nodded. 'But, Luka, I really think Kelly, the first applicant, is more suitable.'

'Does she speak Greek?'

'No,' Cecelia said, 'but then neither do I.'

'There's a lot of things you don't do,' Luka said, and from the curl of his mouth and the charge in the air, the meaning was explicitly clear.

'Don't!' Cecelia warned. She had been wondering how they would play this and if the past would be politely ignored—well, clearly not.

And Cecelia was furious.

'I'm the best bloody PA you have ever had and don't you dare forget it. Just because I won't hop on a plane to Xanero for a shag...' Her face was on fire as he stared right back and gave her a black smile, so she upped it. 'Or get down on my knees and blow you under the desk...' She knew he was hard and she was wet too, but, hell, he had brought it to work, and she wasn't going to back down now. 'It doesn't mean I'm not brilliant at my work. Don't forget that, Luka.'

He was saved from a smart answer when her phone rang and Cecelia glanced at it to see who was calling.

'Go ahead,' Luka said, but Cecelia shook her head.

'It's fine.'

She would not be taking a call from her doctor in front of Luka, especially given the nature of the tests last week! Instead she excused herself, returned to the privacy of her desk and called the surgery.

'This is Cecelia Andrews,' she said to the reception-ist. 'A message was left, asking me to call.'

'One moment, please.'

It was closer to two moments and they were possibly the longest of her life.

'The doctor would like to see you to go over your test results.'

'I'm actually at work and it's terribly hard to get away. If I could speak with the doctor...'

'We have a policy that we don't give results over the phone. I have a vacancy next Monday at two fifteen.'

'Monday!' Cecelia yelped. There was no way she could wait.

'Actually, there's just been a cancellation for today at one thirty. If you can get here by then, it's yours.'

'I shall,' Cecelia said, and did her best to remem-ber her manners as the world imploded on her. 'And thank you.'

Luka came out then with work on his mind. 'If you could call the Athens team now...'

'It's my lunch break,' Cecelia cut in, and Luka blinked.

'Well, get something sent up and eat at your desk. I need this sorted.'

'Luka,' she said, 'I'm entitled to a lunch break, and I'm taking it.'

She was panicking now, remembering his salacious past and what that could mean for her.

She headed to the bathroom and when she returned

he saw that she had redone her hair and refreshed her make-up.

'Good luck,' he said as she walked out.

'Excuse me?' She turned around, wondering if he had guessed where she was going.

'With your new boss.' His voice was tart. 'I assume that's where you're headed.'

Cecelia said nothing.

'Just make sure you're back on time. I believe you're *entitled* to an hour.'

She hated this.

Cecelia absolutely hated this. She should never have got involved with her boss and now everything had changed.

Bristling, Cecelia took the elevator down and with no time to lose she raced for the underground and made it just in time for her appointment, where they asked her to give another urine sample.

And then she sat for the longest half-hour of her life, thumbing blindly through magazines.

Until suddenly her eye was caught by a shot of Luka, pelvis to pelvis with some beauty and dancing the night away in Barcelona. Admittedly, it was an old magazine, though it was not the type of thing she needed to see right now.

'Cecelia Andrews?'

She put down the magazine and stood up, deciding she would kill him with her bare hands if he'd given her anything.

It was the same doctor she had seen the previous week and Cecelia sat as Dr Heale went through her notes.

'I've had a look through your results and I thought it better that I see you face to face.'

Cecelia felt her heart plummet.

'All the health checks came back clear. However, I asked you to repeat the urine specimen as your BHCG came back as elevated.'

'What does that mean?' Cecelia asked, her mind swinging from one horror to another.

'It's very early days,' the doctor said, 'but the second test confirms that you are pregnant.'

'The other tests…?' Cecelia asked for she could not take it in.

'They're all clear.'

'But I'm on the Pill—' Cecelia started, but then the high horse she had been sitting on while blaming Luka for any misfortune that might come to bear on her shifted.

This predicament really was down to her.

She had missed a pill, and at the very least should have looked into the morning-after pill while there was still time for it to be effective.

A baby was the very last thing Cecelia wanted.

She would be a single mother.

Just like her mum.

And she would be single, that much she could guarantee.

'I'm only just, though…' Cecelia vainly attempted, unsure what she was even saying. 'Two weeks.'

'Four weeks,' the doctor clarified. 'Your levels are spot on. It's calculated from the first day of your last period.'

Cecelia screwed her eyes closed. A little over two weeks ago they hadn't even kissed.

Yet now she was being told that she was four weeks pregnant.

By Luka Kargas who was, by any account, the biggest rake known.

'I don't know what to do,' Cecelia admitted. 'I honestly don't know how I feel.'

'Of course you don't,' Dr Heale said. 'Why don't you make an appointment with me for next week and by then the news will have had time to sink in a bit.'

Cecelia did just that and then she made her way out of the clinic. She stood on the busy London street full of people who were carrying on with their day, oblivious to the bombshell that had dropped on her world.

She wiped her cheeks with her hand and only then did Cecelia realise she was crying.

It was as if all her emotions were in full flight, for there were tears and her heart was hammering in her chest, yet Cecelia was barely aware of them.

'Numb.'

She said it out loud just to hear her own voice and to clarify that it was how she felt.

Numb.

She could hear her phone ringing but it did not even enter her head to answer it. Instead she walked and walked through London streets, carrying her bag in her hand rather than in its usual position over her shoulder.

A baby?

It had not been in her plans—at least, not her current plans.

Even when she and Gordon had spoken about one day having children it had been a sort of dim and distant thing in the far-away future, and even then she hadn't really been able to picture it.

Her career was the most important thing in her life. It was the only thing she really had, but how the hell was she going to be able to carry on with it with a baby?

Luka would carry on.

A baby wouldn't affect *his* career.

The numbness was fading and the sting of sensation was coming back as she briefly envisaged Luka's reaction if she told him the news.

And the aftermath.

She had worked with him for almost a year and knew the bastard he could be. As recently as this morning he'd had his legal and accounting teams working out how to screw over his own father.

She could not stand to think of the meeting that would take place about her if he found out about the baby!

Cecelia walked into a bar and ordered a glass of water. She sat on a stool but the world would not stop spinning.

She started a new job in a couple of weeks' time.

It was only a six-month contract, though.

Which would take her up to seven months pregnant.

Really, she could not have planned it better, except she had not planned on being pregnant at all.

Her phone was ringing again and, unthinking, she answered it.

'Where the hell are you?' Luka demanded. 'Bridgette's gone home with a migraine and I'm playing receptionist to my potential PAs!'

'You'll have to manage without me,' Cecelia said, for there was no way she could go back to work this afternoon and face him. Even keeping her voice remotely normal was taking a supreme effort.

He heard the chink of glasses and a burst of laughter in the background and the effort behind her words. He could picture her with her new boss, all cosy on some sofa in a club. 'You still have two weeks left to serve your notice, Cecelia. I suggest that you get back here now.'

'And I just told you that I can't.'

She was not being defiant, there was just absolutely no way she could make it into work.

He rang off and Cecelia sat watching a woman wheeling in her baby in a pram, wrestling with the glass doors.

It was not her world.

Meanwhile, Luka sat and stared at his phone.

It was not a world he was used to either and, as Luka quickly found out, rejection was certainly not his forte.

He did not kill her with kindness.

Cecelia arrived at work the following morning and nodded to the doorman.

She made her way up in the elevator and again saw that she had beaten Bridgette to it.

Yet she was not the first here.

Or the second.

Her desk had been moved. And it was not arranged the way she usually left it.

There was a laptop on it that wasn't hers and when she went behind it there was a bag on the floor that felt like finding the wrong shoes by the bed.

She had spent the night fighting not just whether or not to tell him but, if she did, how.

He had, she realised, removed the opportunity to do so.

'Cecelia.'

She turned to the low, familiar sound of his voice and the clipped tones at Luka's unfamiliar correct usage of her name.

'I have hired your replacement.'

'So I see.'

'There is no need for you to stay on.'

'What about…?' Her mind darted to the million and one things she needed to pass on. 'There's the Athens—'

'Sorted,' Luka interrupted. 'Of course, you shall be paid while *not* serving your notice.'

'And this is because I didn't return from lunch?'

'No, this is because of your attitude.'

'Am I back at school?' Cecelia flared.

'Did you have an attitude problem then?' Luka smoothly responded.

No, she hadn't had an attitude problem at school.

She'd been diligent and hard-working and had toed the line, determined that her life would be different from her mother's.

And neither had she had an attitude at home, for she'd been trying so hard not to get in her aunt and uncle's way.

Her attitude only changed when she was with him.

Luka brought out both the best and the worst in her.

And he was the worst.

She knew that, and it was proved when Sabine came out.

She had the grace to offer a somewhat awkward smile in Cecelia's direction.

Her black hair was a little messy, like she had a case of bedhead… It appeared they had worked through the night.

Or otherwise.

Cecelia didn't trust Luka enough not to consider *otherwise*.

And Cecelia knew then the answer to the problem she had wrestled with since the doctor had delivered the baby bombshell to her.

No way would she tell him.

She did not want her child subjected to the life he led.

Cecelia knew from experience the damage that could cause.

And if he could snuff her out of his life overnight, if he could so calmly watch as Sabine handed her a package with all her things and escorted her out, then he could easily do the same to his child.

CHAPTER EIGHT

THE DECISION ABOUT whether to tell him was not, of course, as clear cut as that.

For the first couple of months a generous dash of anger fired Cecelia's spirit, for she certainly hadn't deserved that.

How dared he have Sabine walk her out of the office? How dared he question her attitude, when he was the most arrogant person on earth?

Her anger, combined with a healthy dose of denial as to the truth of her predicament, got Cecelia through the first trimester of her pregnancy.

Cecelia did consider a termination, but in the end could not see herself going through with it.

Her father had wanted her mother to abort her, and she was also rather certain that Luka would suggest the same.

So she hid the news from the world and worked hard in her new job.

As long as she didn't show, she could work hard and pretend that nothing had changed.

At first she enjoyed the life where sixteen or more hours of her day were not devoted to Luka's exhausting schedule, and eight hours of night time were not spent rejecting the hunger of her body for him.

Except she lied, for now she had experienced him, it was not fantasy that peppered her thoughts and dreams but intoxicating memories.

Unlike Luka, her new diplomat boss was so stunningly politically correct that he made no mention of her expanding waistline. But as Christmas approached, Cecelia formally told him that she would not be renewing her contract at the end of her term.

Cecelia had always been sensible with money and had some savings, but she was starting to glimpse how impossible it would be to combine her regular work with motherhood.

Anxiety about the future woke Cecelia up in the middle of the night, and of course there were times that she considered telling Luka.

But not like this, Cecelia thought as she nervously headed to her aunt and uncle's house to tell them the news. Not when her heart was fluttering in fear and she was constantly on the edge of tears.

On the Tube she checked her hair and make-up and could see the anxiety in her own eyes in the mirror as she tried to fathom how they would take it.

'Cecelia.' Her aunt frowned when she opened the front door to her niece. 'You didn't call to say you were dropping by.'

Should she have to? Cecelia thought, but as usual said nothing.

And neither did she remove her coat.

She sat in the drawing room as tea was served and felt as uncomfortable as she had on the day she had first arrived here.

It was a very austere house and Cecelia could remember sitting on this very seat as her grandfather had spoken with his son about boarding school for her.

'How's work?' her aunt asked.

'It's going well.' Cecelia nodded. 'The hours are much better than in my previous job. However, I've told him that I shan't be renewing my contract.'

'Have you found something else?' her aunt asked.

Cecelia took a sip of tea and then replaced the cup in the saucer and made herself say it. 'No, I shan't be working for a few months because I've found out that I'm expecting.' When her aunt said nothing, Cecelia made things a touch clearer. 'A baby.'

'I wasn't aware you'd been dating since the break-up.'

'Gordon and I finished more than a year ago,' Cecelia attempted, but she felt her face flush, because what had happened that night with Luka couldn't even be described as a date, let alone a relationship.

They weren't a couple.

Quite simply, it had been the most impulsive night of her life.

And as for the morning…

Cecelia forced herself not to dwell on that. Right now she had to get through telling her aunt.

'My contract expires a couple of months before the baby is due and I can afford to take a few months off.'

'So what does the father have to say on the matter?'

'I haven't told him,' Cecelia admitted. 'Yet.'

Deep down Cecelia knew she had to tell Luka, but for now she was trying to get used to the idea herself. Certainly she did not want to be teary and hysterical when she told him the news, which was frankly how she felt most of the time.

Not that Cecelia showed it. As always, she appeared outwardly calm.

Yes, it might be a difficult conversation to have with her aunt but Cecelia hoped that she would soon come round.

And then hope died.

She watched as her aunt added another spoon of sugar to her tea and stirred, and then placed the spoon on the saucer.

The silence had been a long one and Cecelia did not attempt to fill it. Instead, she stayed quiet to allow her aunt to process the news. When she did, her eyes met Cecelia's.

'The apple doesn't fall far from the tree, does it? Well, I raised your mother's mistake,' she said. 'You need to know Cecelia that I shan't be doing it again for you.'

Cecelia felt a shiver run the length of her spine as she met her aunt's eyes, and in that moment the past twenty years or so made a little more sense.

She had never felt welcome here and now she knew why.

A mistake.

That was what her aunt had just called her.

Deep down, Cecelia had known it, for she had done all that she could not to make any trouble for her aunt and uncle and not to live up to her mother's reputation.

It would seem in her aunt's eyes she just had.

'I should go,' Cecelia said, polite to the very end. 'Please, give my love to my uncle.'

Instead of going home, Cecelia headed for her old workplace and sat in a café nearby, looking up at the towering high-rise that housed Kargas Holdings and wondering what to do.

A mistake.

Over and over it played in her mind.

They were the same words her father had used the one time she had seen him.

She tried to fathom Luka's reaction—she pictured his beautiful features marred by anger, and she imagined them locked in a bitter row, and right there in the café Cecelia started to cry.

She simply wasn't ready to reveal the pregnancy to him, Cecelia decided, if she was breaking down just imagining it.

No, she would tell Luka about the pregnancy when she felt calmer and when she could do it without being reduced to tears.

In the end, it was an uneventful but terribly lonely pregnancy.

Her six months working for the diplomat were soon up, and of course her contract was not renewed.

She was barely speaking to her aunt and uncle, and the few friends she had were somewhat aghast that she had gone ahead with the pregnancy.

Worse, though, she missed *him*.

Luka.

Not as the father of the baby she carried.

More, Cecelia missed the many different colours he had once added to her day.

She could feel the kicks of her baby, only it wasn't just duty that had her call Luka, it was the ache to hear his voice.

His private number must have been changed, for an automated voice told her to check the number and try again.

So she called the front desk and braced herself to speak with Bridgette or Sabine and to ask to be put through to Luka.

Instead it was an unfamiliar female voice she met with.

'I'm sorry, Mr Kargas isn't taking any unscheduled calls.'

'I used to work for him,' Cecelia explained. 'I was his PA and I—'

'As I said, Mr Kargas isn't taking any unscheduled calls.'

The voice was as brusque and efficient as Cecelia herself had once been when dealing with yet another slightly desperate female on the line.

'I have to speak with him,' Cecelia said. 'Can you let him know that I called?'

'Of course,' came the terse response. 'Can you spell your first name, please…'

He did not return the call.

It really was a terribly lonely time.

And now that Cecelia did not have work to occupy her, she caved under her broken heart for the first time.

She should have walked away at the outset.

Or she should never have turned to the huskiness of his voice that night.

Yet, even heavily pregnant, just the thought of the frantic sex that had taken place hit so low in her belly that she almost sank to her knees at the memory she could never erase.

But it hadn't even been that.

No, it was the morning after she would correct if she could.

She would peel away from his kiss and reach for a condom.

She would turn from his embrace and do things more sensibly.

Yet she could not see how, for she had been lost, *they* had been lost, and so deep into each other that even with the benefit of hindsight she could not play it another way, for she wanted him even now.

Spring came, and three weeks from her due date Cecelia tried to call him one more time.

'Mr Kargas isn't taking any unscheduled calls.'

'You sound like a broken record,' Cecelia snapped, and ended the call as she realised her pride had waned. Labour kind of did that to you, and perhaps mid-contraction wasn't the best time to tell him that she was having his child.

So she called for a taxi instead.

'Good luck, my dear,' Mrs Dawson called as Cecelia headed out.

'Thank you.'

Oh, it was lonely indeed.

And painful.

Cecelia wanted her old life back.

The ordered one.

The one she'd had prior to meeting Luka Kargas.

She did not want to be a mother, and certainly not a single one, so she sobbed through the pain and rued her mistakes.

But then, at ten minutes past six on a spring morning, for the second time in her life, Cecelia fell in love.

The first time had been with Luka.

There had never been anyone else in her life she had felt that way about, no one who came close.

But second-time love was the absolute shock of her life, for as she pulled the infant from her stomach into her arms, the world, in an instant, was put to right.

She had a daughter.

A tiny daughter who was very pink with a shock of dark hair and her cry was lusty and loud.

Oh!

Cecelia had told herself during the pregnancy that even if she felt little now, love would one day grow.

Her baby would never feel as unloved as her mother had been, even if she had to fake it for a while.

Yet there was never a love less fake, for Cecelia utterly adored her baby girl on sight.

'Have you thought of names?' the midwife asked as Cecelia gazed at her child.

'I liked Emily,' Cecelia said.

That had been before she had met her, though.

That was before she had locked eyes with a tiny, dark-haired, dark-eyed girl.

Her secret.

A secret she must one day reveal, Cecelia knew that.

But not yet.

She did not want the beauty of this tiny life marred just yet, she did not want the rows and accusations that would surely follow such a revelation.

The DNA tests, the lawyers, the disdain.

Cecelia could envisage it.

And that was at best.

She had nothing in her past to predict otherwise, and so she was in no rush to reveal to the billionaire playboy that she had birthed his child.

And she knew now her daughter's name.

It was, Cecelia knew, absolutely the perfect name for her and as she first said it she kissed her baby's soft cheek.

'Pandora.'

CHAPTER NINE

S<small>UMMER HAD RETURNED.</small>

Luka had by far preferred the previous one.

But it was good to be home.

Yes, he thought of London as such.

Xanero was beautiful, and of course family was there, but it was London that was his true home.

Luka glanced up from the letter he was reading and looked out through tinted windows as his driver inched the car along the busy street.

He had been in London on occasion, but it been a hellish year on the private front, and the city had not been his base.

Amber, his ultra-efficient PA, had handed him a pile of personal correspondence and he wanted it dealt with before he turned his mind to work.

There was a pile of sympathy cards and letters that spoke of a hard-working family man that Luka did not recognise as his father.

'How was the funeral?' Amber asked.

'It went well,' Luka nodded.

Yesterday his father had been buried.

This time last year he had thought it would be his mother's funeral he would attend first, yet after months of intensive treatment and care, Sophie Kargas was doing well.

Luka had flown with her to Athens and after each treatment he would check them into the luxurious hotel he had there. Sophie had enjoyed the Princess Suite and had been treated exactly as that for the first time in her life.

'You could have this every day,' Luka had said. 'Say the word and I will take care of you and you will never have to deal with him.'

'I shall never do that, Luka,' his mother would reply.

Yet she was so much happier and lighter without him, and her decision to stay was something he would never quite understand.

And then, after each treatment, when her strength had returned they would go back to Xanero, where the new manager that Luka had hired would report directly to him.

Theo had reluctantly behaved, for he had been given no choice but to do so.

Luka had, quite literally, bought his mother a year of peace to focus on getting well.

There had been little peace for Luka, though—spending more time in Xanero had meant he'd been forced to face his demons.

No, he was not particularly proud of his start and he was tired too of the life he led.

And he regretted how he and Cece had parted.

Her decision to leave had been something he had not understood, in much the same way as his mother's decision to stay, and so he had hastened it. He had made sure she would not work out her notice and had her removed from his life in his usual style.

Yet he still thought about her each day.

And just when he had decided it was time to return to London, just when his life could get back on track and he was considering looking her up, completely out of the blue his father had died.

The funeral had been hell for Luka.

He had delivered the eulogy, and for his mother's sake he had spoken of the family man, his humble beginnings and the restaurant Theo had started. It had been a further rewriting of the past.

It was over with now.

'Is there anything—?' Amber started to ask.

But Luka cut in. 'Everything has been taken care of.'

His family life remained out of bounds to his PA.

Sabine had proved to be a nightmare.

He should have paid more attention when Cecelia had said there was something about her that she didn't like.

He had arrogantly assumed it was that Sabine was beautiful and had perhaps hoped that his hiring her would rouse a response in Cecelia.

Instead, his new PA had been the jealous one.

Sabine could not accept that he did not flirt and had no real interest in her, and when he had found her going through his private emails, he had fired her on the spot.

Amber had taken her place and, while she didn't speak Greek, he had no complaints. She was diligent and efficient and had no interest in sleeping her way to the top.

Yes, while there was nothing to complain about on the work front, he missed Cecelia.

In every way.

And never more so than this week.

He had arranged the funeral, dealt with the legalities and the only calls he had made to Amber had been regarding work.

His own mood even he could not begin to gauge.

There was a sense of relief tempered by unexpected grief.

He had no fond memories of his father, so it didn't really make sense, but there was a hollow feeling that resided within him now and an ache of sadness that he had not anticipated.

Yes, it had been a difficult year, though not on paper.

The talks with Garcia had become more productive and there was now a hotel and restaurant in Manhattan and another soon to open in Singapore. A lot of his time had been spent divided between Athens, where his mother had had her treatments, and Xanero, where she had recuperated in between.

The luxurious complex was large enough that he certainly had no need to temper his ways—after all, his family were hardly living over the fence.

He had tempered them, though.

Because he *still* wanted Cece.

Unable to face yet another sympathy card, he got back to staring out of the window.

And then Luka decided that it really had been too long, because he thought for a moment that a woman walking down the street might be her.

On too many occasions in the past year Luka had thought that he'd seen Cece.

Confidently he had once tapped a woman on the shoulder in a bar, and had then found himself staring into the wrong face.

But now, as he craned his neck for a better look, there was something about this woman's posture that held Luka's attention.

'Slow down,' he told his driver, because he no longer trusted himself to be certain when it came to her.

She looked slimmer, and the usually immaculate blonde hair that she wore tied back was more strawberry blonde and fell in untidy curls around her shoulders.

The uncertainty was short-lived, because he suddenly remembered the morning she had undressed for him and he had found out she was a redhead after all.

It really was her.

She wore a navy shift dress and flat sandals.

And it was not a designer handbag that was strapped to her shoulder.

From the way she held the sling, her burden seemed far more precious than that.

And then he saw her look down and smile and realised that she was holding a baby.

No!

He hauled himself back from the appalling assumption that the baby might be his and reminded himself that she had been a nanny once.

But she had told him how much she had hated it and had said she would never be a nanny again.

The baby was hers, Luka knew it, from the way she smiled down and caressed its head.

'No.'

He said it out loud this time and Amber looked up. 'Is everything okay?'

Luka didn't answer her, his mind was moving too fast.

It had been a year since he'd been with Cecelia.

Not quite to the day, although it would be soon.

And he remembered the very date of their parting.

Even the time.

It had been just after nine when she had left the building.

In fact, he recalled so many details.

Because life had got crazy since then, he told himself.

And life had just got a whole lot more complicated now.

'Pull over,' he instructed the driver. 'In fact, turn around.'

His driver did not point out that this busy street was not the place to execute a U-turn, and instead he complied.

Luka could feel the thump of his heart in his chest as he searched the pavement for another sight of her but she was nowhere to be seen.

His face remained impassive but his eyes scanned the crowd until he caught sight of her again and instructed his driver to pull over.

Safe from view behind tinted windows, he watched Cecelia.

She was certainly a touch slimmer than he remembered and, from what little he knew about pregnancy, if the baby was hers, shouldn't it be otherwise?

Luka took out his phone and the number he had considered calling far too many times was dialled now.

He watched as Cecelia reached for her phone.

'Hello?'

She would not know it was him, Luka realised, for after he had fired Sabine he'd had no choice but to change all his numbers.

'Cecelia.'

At the sound of his voice the world stopped.

The traffic, the noise, the shoppers on the busy street all faded to nothing at the sound of her name on his lips.

She knew instantly it was him, yet she did not reveal that. Instead, Cecelia played for time. 'Who's this?' she asked, and ran a nervous hand through her hair.

'Luka.'

'Oh.'

'Have I caught you at a bad time?'

'No, no, I'm just…' And he watched as she held the baby tighter to her, 'I'm actually on my lunch break.'

'Well, I need to speak with you. I was wondering if you could call by the office. There are a few issues we need to discuss.'

'Luka, I haven't worked for you in a year.'

'It's just a couple of accounting queries. Nothing serious but my accountant needs to verify a few things…' He wasn't even lying, because if indeed this was his baby there were certainly some things that needed to be discussed!

He was suddenly surprised that he hadn't already been fleeced.

'Can you come in?'

'I told you, I'm working.'

'After work,' Luka said. 'It won't take long. I'll have Marco stay back.'

'It's not terribly convenient.'

'Life isn't, is it?' he said, and ended the call.

She couldn't breathe.

In the middle of a packed London street she was as panicked as she had been on the day she had found out she was pregnant.

More so, for she hadn't loved her baby then.

He couldn't know about Pandora, Cecelia told herself.

No.

It must be work related.

Some document she hadn't signed or some expense that hadn't gone through.

After all, just last week she'd had to go into the diplomat's office and tie up a few loose ends.

Then, though, she had taken in Pandora.

She could hardly do the same with Luka.

Cecelia looked down at her tiny baby. The world was closing in and she knew she had to tell him.

Calmly.

She did not want Pandora to be exposed to any negative reaction, even if she was far too young to understand.

And for the very same reason, she would not be calling her aunt!

She arrived home all flustered, and of course Mrs Dawson wanted to stop for a chat.

'My daughter's just found out she's having twins!' Mrs Dawson said.

'How many grandchildren will that make?' Cecelia asked.

'Eight!' Mrs Dawson beamed. 'How's Pandora?'

'Wonderful,' Cecelia said, and watched as the old lady made Pandora smile.

'She's such a happy baby,' Mrs Dawson said. 'I never hear a peep.'

'Mrs Dawson…'

Cecelia loathed asking for help or being an imposition but she simply didn't know what else to do and Mrs Dawson had offered on several occasions.

'Could I ask you to look after Pandora for a couple of hours this afternoon?'

'I'd love to!'

'I'll pay you, of course.'

'You certainly won't. It will be my absolute pleasure.'

Why, oh, why could her aunt not have said that?

* * *

Cecelia dressed as if for an interview.

The navy suit was put on again for her visit to Kargas Holdings.

And even though she would only be gone for a couple of hours and Pandora had just been fed, she made up two bottles just in case. And her blanket and loads of nappies as well as Cecelia's phone number…

She was terribly nervous at the thought of leaving her, but Mrs Dawson was so friendly and seemed thrilled to have been asked.

'I really shan't be long,' Cecelia said. 'I just have to pop into work and I'll come straight back.'

'Pandora will be fine.'

And Pandora would be fine, Cecelia knew as she took the Tube.

But would *she* be?

Cecelia couldn't fathom what Luka's reaction might be, and she actually felt a little sick as she came out of the escalators and the building loomed up.

Cecelia could remember sitting in the café opposite and willing herself to go in and tell him.

She had no choice now.

The doorman smiled and then frowned and instead of waving her through she was told to go to Reception.

There a call was made and she stood with pink cheeks, feeling like one of his exes.

Which she was.

Sort of.

Finally, she received a visitor's pass and the code for the elevator.

Cecelia's hand was shaking as she punched in the numbers.

The air-conditioner should have been blissful, but

instead she could feel the sheen of perspiration on her face. She rubbed her palms on her skirt, just in case he decided to shake her hand.

As the elevator doors opened there was no Bridgette to greet her; instead, it was an unfamiliar woman who sat at Cecelia's old desk.

'I'll just let Luka know you're here,' she said. 'Perhaps you'd like to take a seat.'

'Actually, I think I'm seeing Marco. If you could let him know that I'm here...' She would get work out of the way and then she would speak with Luka, Cecelia decided.

'Marco?' She shook her head. 'He isn't in today.'

And then Cecelia heard Luka. 'I'll deal with this.'

For the first time in a year she felt his presence and she prickled all over at the sound of his voice.

Her head wanted to spin to face him but she resisted and instead slowly turned to him.

'Cecelia,' he greeted her.

'Luka.'

She had forgotten the absolute impact of him.

The year that had passed had dimmed him in a way she had not expected. His ruthlessness and playboy ways had been somewhat tempered by the memories of them in bed.

And he did not look in the least pleased to see her.

'Come through,' he said.

'But I thought I was seeing Marco.'

'I'm sure you soon will be,' Luka said as he led her through to his office. 'Please, take a seat.'

Cecelia was very glad to, for her legs felt as if they were made of rubber, and not just because she was nervous—yes, she had forgotten the absolute impact of him.

He looked incredible.

Gleaming was the word that came to mind.

His raven hair was worn shorter than she ever remembered it being and it accentuated his sharp features. He was tanned, and although there had never been an ounce of spare flesh on him he now looked leaner.

Meaner, Cecelia thought, and her heart kicked into a gallop, though she did her level best not to show it.

Yes, being away from him for a year had certainly tempered Luka in her mind, for now she was back she remembered her despair at his reckless ways; the constant stream of women; his wealth and the power that came with that.

And he was her baby's father.

There had never been a doubt as to that, of course, but only now, back in his world, did it truly hit home.

He had essentially fired her on the last occasion she had been here. He had had her marched out of his life over the smallest slight.

Cecelia thought of his legal team and the constant battles they waged, for he would step over anyone to get a property he wanted.

And he was Pandora's father!

Cecelia did her best to meet Luka's eyes, which seemed no longer a velvet brown but as black as night as they appraised her. There was no hint of a smile on his mouth.

'Where are you working?' Luka asked.

'At the same place that I left here for,' Cecelia answered.

'You never did say where.'

'Didn't I?'

Oh, let the games begin, Luka thought.

He was turned on and enjoying the silent fight.

He watched her pink tongue run a nervous path along her lips. He looked at her cool green eyes and he fought not to walk right around that desk and shake the news from her.

He was certain the baby was his.

Why?

Because there had been no one else since that night.

Nearly a whole damn year—and not for the lack of options or opportunity.

And if he hadn't screwed his way out of the problem, then he was certain that neither had she.

Whatever had happened that night, or rather that morning, had taken a lot to get over.

He still hadn't.

And now he knew why—this morning he had found out he was a father.

But he had only found out by chance.

'How have you been, Cecelia?' he asked.

'You mean since I was marched out of the office?'

'Please,' he dismissed, 'you exaggerate.'

'How did Sabine work out?' Cecelia asked, remembering again the humiliation of that morning.

'She didn't,' he said. 'In fact, I *did* have *her* marched out of the office and I considered taking a restraining order out against her at one point.'

'Well, if you will insist on mixing business...' Cecelia started, but then she faltered. She just could not stand the thought of him with Sabine enough to pursue her line. 'Where's Bridgette?'

'She's on annual leave.'

Well, at least that sounded nice and normal.

'So what is it that you want to see me about?' Cecelia asked.

'There were a couple of expense forms that were flagged and Marco needed—'

'Could he not have emailed?'

'I guess,' Luka said, 'but I wanted to see you myself.'

She could not tell him now, Cecelia knew, for she simply couldn't make herself say it. She could barely look him in the eye, let alone tell him news that would turn his world upside down. Or maybe it wouldn't.

She needed to think this through properly, because Luka didn't play nice, she well knew it.

Luka Kargas had an entire legal team that worked on his behalf and if he decided she was the enemy then God help her.

Cecelia knew she must leave and go and get some proper advice and then she would tell him. 'Well, if you can have Marco email me when he's next in…' She picked up her bag. 'Anything else?'

'I'm not sure,' Luka said. 'Why don't we go and get dinner and catch up?'

'I don't think so.'

'A drink perhaps?'

'No.'

'It's been almost a year,' Luka said.

'How sweet that you remembered.' She gave a tight smile. 'You must celebrate a lot of one-night-stand anniversaries.' It looked like she could not do this without it descending into a row. 'Luka…' She stood. 'I'm going to go.'

The door looked a very long way off when Cecelia turned to face it. She had no idea the game he was playing but, whatever it was, she wanted out.

No way could she watch the anger flare in his features, for already the air was thick with tension.

But a tension she could not define.

Sex, with a dash of...

Cecelia didn't know what and she would not be staying to find out.

Her hand was on the handle of the door when he called to her.

'Have you forgotten something?' Luka asked.

Foolishly, she patted her bag. 'No.'

'I meant,' he said in a voice that was like a dagger wrapped in velvet, 'did you forget to tell me about my baby?'

The caress of his voice and then the knife to her back.

Her back was to him, but if there had been any doubt Luka knew now for certain that the baby was his, for her shoulders stiffened, followed by the slight buckle of her knees before she righted herself, although she still did not turn around.

'Sit down, Cecelia,' Luka said.

She did not follow orders any more.

Instead she stood there, trying to fathom how he knew. And, given that he did, Luka's reaction was the antithesis of anything she had expected. Cecelia had been sure that when she told him, the majority of any ensuing discussions would be convincing him that Pandora was his.

She was unprepared for this. Her reactions when around Luka were always extreme for he turned her from ordered to chaotic, and so, instead of turning around and calmly facing him, Cecelia wrenched open the door.

'Don't you dare walk off,' Luka warned in an ominous voice.

Except that was exactly what Cecelia did.

The was no one at her old desk and no one at Reception as she swiftly made her way through the vast space.

There was just the gleam of furniture and the scent of flowers in the air as she headed speedily for the lift.

She desperately wanted distance between them. She pressed the button for the lift, yet no light came on to indicate that it was on its way.

Cecelia pressed it again.

No, the lifts weren't out, she quickly realised, Luka must have changed the code! Usually it was altered to stop ex-lovers making their way up to him, never to prevent them from getting out!

Well, she'd take the fire escape, Cecelia decided, and turned angrily in time to see Luka calmly walking towards her.

'Come and sit down, Cecelia, and we will talk.'

'I'll take the stairs.'

'You can try.' Luka shrugged.

Cecelia knew he'd have no scruples about going after her and hauling her straight back.

'You can't keep me here, Luka,' she shouted. 'You had me come to the office under false pretences and you have no right—'

Oh, she knew she had said the wrong thing for even Cecelia stopped in mid-sentence as he walked towards her.

'Don't you dare speak to me about *rights* when you have denied me mine,' Luka warned, and he came so close that she shrank back against the cool wall of the elevator. 'Now you are to get back to my office so we can talk.'

'Luka…' she attempted. 'I was going to tell you.'

'I don't want to hear your lies and excuses,' he said. 'I don't care what you *might* have been going to do. I want to know about my child.'

'But I have to get back to her.'

She watched his jaw grit and the angry purse of his beautiful mouth as she realised that he had only just found out that their baby was a girl.

And Cecelia knew in that instant that she would never be forgiven for keeping Pandora from him.

'Luka, I know we have to talk and I understand that you're angry but I really can't do this now.'

'When then?' he demanded. 'On her eighteenth birthday? Or perhaps when your money has run out and you want to claim your meal ticket?'

'Luka, please.'

He watched as the ordered Cecelia put her hands to her ears.

'I can't row now.'

She was muddled, caught, confused.

And it wasn't just that he already knew.

The impact of being close to him again was an utter assault to her senses.

For the best part of a year she had fought not to think of him. Now that she faced him, worst of all, she was the liar and the guilty party.

'It's my first time away from her.'

A pathetic excuse perhaps, only it was the truth and it was killing her.

'Is she with your aunt?'

'God, no!' The words shot out and then she looked up at him. 'She's with my neighbour. Luka, I know we need to talk, I accept that, but it's not going to be wrapped up in an hour.'

'You clearly don't get it, Cecelia. Whatever the location, whatever the time, I shall be meeting my daughter tonight. You have denied me my rights for long enough.'

Cecelia had seen him like this before, though it had been in the workplace, and she knew Luka well enough to know that arguing would be futile. But aside from that, he was completely right—she had denied him his rights long enough.

'We can go to your home,' Luka said, 'or we can speak here or at mine, and then you take me to meet her or have her brought to me. But before you decide, know this, Cecelia. If you refuse to take me to my daughter, then the next contact we have shall be via a lawyer. I don't currently employ an expert in family law, but my team is already looking into it. Mess up again and the best shall be retained.' He saw her already pale skin go even paler but he felt no guilt. None at all. And he told her why. 'You started this, Cecelia.'

'Do you blame me?'

'Yes,' Luka swiftly answered. 'I blame you completely.'

CHAPTER TEN

CECELIA CHOSE HOME.

The drive to her flat had been a silent one. She had tried to speak once, to tell him his daughter's name, but he had told her to save it.

'If I want to know anything, I will ask.'

Right now, Luka had enough to process. He had a child. A girl.

He had been a father for three months and not known.

He could not deal with even one more piece of information that had been kept from him or he might just lose it.

Things would be at his pace from this point on and if Cecelia could take her time then so could he!

'I thought you said we needed to talk,' Cecelia pushed, wanting as much as possible out of the way before they got home.

'Well, I've changed my mind,' Luka said. 'It's too late for all that.'

Luka actually felt ill at the thought that anything could have happened to his daughter and he wouldn't have known.

He looked over at Cecelia, who sat opposite him, and he thought of the secret she had kept from him and that only by chance had he found out.

White hot was the rage that seared through Luka and he was doing his level best to contain it.

'We're here,' Cecelia said as his driver pulled up close to the main door to her flat. But as the driver came round and opened the door, Luka didn't immediately get out.

Luka, who could face anything, was for the first time nervous at the prospect of what lay ahead, for in a moment he would meet his daughter for the first time.

'Aren't you coming in?' Cecelia asked.

'Of course I am.' Luka shot Cecelia a look of contempt. 'I'm hardly going to meet her in the street.'

She could feel his loathing as he entered her small flat. She hadn't noticed how messy it was when she had headed out.

Cecelia noticed now.

The ordered world she had once inhabited, one where she put out her clothes for the next morning the night before, had long since gone. The tiny bundle that she had birthed meant that she lurched from one feed to the next and grabbed a quick shower and a scrape of her comb through her hair in the short bursts when Pandora slept.

Cecelia did not attempt a rapid tidy.

Instead, she glanced at the magazines on the coffee table to distract her anxious thoughts. There were some colic drops too and a couple of mugs, and some baby blankets strewn across the sofa—the aftermath of a difficult night.

It had been a difficult, yet wonderful three months.

She was permanently exhausted and lonely too. She was barely speaking with her aunt and uncle and she was not exactly inundated with friends. The few Cecelia had were either single or child-free by choice. There had been cards, flowers and visits when Pandora had first been born, but, understandably they did not want their Sunday brunches pierced by a baby's cries and Cecelia didn't have space in her brain for decent conversation.

She was a mother.

A new one.

Yet she had a three-month head start on Luka.

'Would you like…?' Cecelia started but Luka wasn't here for a chat and neither would he be taking a seat.

'Could you fetch my daughter, please?'

'Of course.'

Mrs Dawson was nosy enough that she would have seen the expensive car pull up and know that Cecelia had a guest, and so she didn't invite her in for a chat.

'She was as good as gold,' Mrs Dawson said, as she handed Pandora over. 'Fell asleep in my arms.'

'Thank you so much.'

'And she's just been fed,' Mrs Dawson said as she collected up her things.

Pandora was wrapped in a soft lilac blanket and Cecelia held her close and inhaled the delicious baby scent. Oh, yes, her tiny world was changing and Cecelia did not want to let her go. Having thanked Mrs Dawson, she headed across the hall but Pandora picked up on her tension and started to cry.

Good, Cecelia thought, even as she moved to hush her. *Let him see how it really is. Tell me off, write your cheque and be gone.* For she could not deal with the thought of handing Pandora over to him. And, no, she did not want her daughter spending weekends and holidays with a father who partied just as hard as he worked.

As she stepped into the lounge he was there waiting, so tailored and exquisite and with angry black eyes. She could not believe that Luka was really in her home.

He did not belong here.

Luka belonged in his office castle or creating merry hell aboard his yacht.

The expensive scent, the stunning suit all felt like too much to process right now.

Her child's father was a reckless playboy, and in her arms she held the consequence of their one night together.

She soothed Pandora as Luka stood watching but he made no move to come over. 'I really was going to tell you,' she told him.

'Then why didn't you when I called you earlier today?'

'I was standing in the street!'

He heard the urgent sincerity in her voice and for the first time today he knew she was telling the truth. Cecelia did not know he had been watching her when she had taken the call.

Still, the grain of honesty from her barely appeased him for it accounted only for a few seconds of the past year.

'Why didn't you say anything back in the office?' he asked as he gazed at the bundle she held in her arms. Really he could see only the blanket and he was playing for time, nervous now to meet her.

'I couldn't do it face to face.' Another truth, not that he believed her, Cecelia could see. 'I tried to call you a couple of times during the pregnancy. I couldn't get through.'

'You didn't try very hard.'

'No,' she admitted.

'Why?'

That she couldn't really answer but she tried. 'I was scared of your reaction. I thought you'd tell me to get rid of her, or say that I'd tried to trap you by getting pregnant...'

'I was there that morning, Cecelia. I do know how babies are made and that it takes two.'

It was the closest she had come to a smile since facing him again, but Luka did not see it. He had no interest in the past right now, for in that second the small blanket slipped a little and he saw a shock of dark hair and a pale cheek and suddenly he forgot how to breathe. There in his chest it felt as if an iron fist had sunk in.

He walked over and Cecelia felt him enter her space—only it had nothing to do with her, simply the infant she held in her arms.

She watched one, long, olive finger come and tenderly stroke the little baby's cheek. 'Can I hold her?'

'She's a bit unsettled...'

'I was only asking, to be polite,' Luka said, and now he no longer asked—he told her instead in a voice that was calm but the words hit like sleet. *'Give my baby to me.'*

She handed Pandora to him and he took her into his arms, more skilfully than she had predicted—because, of course, she had imagined how her baby would look in his arms. She watched him cradle his daughter and carefully take a seat on the couch as his eyes never left Pandora's face.

'What name did *you* choose for her?' he asked, and Cecelia heard the scold in his tone.

He would change it if he did not like it, Luka decided.

How dared she take such an important choice from him?

There were tears at the back of her nose and throat and she had to swallow before she could respond. 'Pandora.'

But he would not be changing it, for the second he heard the name Luka loved it.

It meant 'all gifts', which indeed she was, and it was Greek and…

He let out a soft, yet not quite mirthless laugh. He had decided a caustic response was his to make, yet none came, for the name was completely perfect as for the first time Pandora opened her eyes to look at him.

They were navy and surrounded by spiky black lashes and she simply stared up at her father and met his gaze.

Luka pushed back the pale blanket to reveal more dark hair and he looked at her pretty rosebud mouth. For the first time in his life he felt the threat of tears.

Luka had never held a baby, let alone thought he might father one.

Now he held a daughter he had only found out existed today. His free hand held hers, looking at the slender fingers and tiny nails. Then he traced her eyebrows and imprinted her beauty on his mind—her little mouth and the soft pink of her skin—and when she stared back at him with sleepy navy eyes Pandora gave him a smile.

Her eyelashes seemed too heavy and he watched as she closed her eyes in sleep and he simply breathed in the baby scent of her and the miracle of her existence.

And had her mother got her way, Luka would never have known she was here.

Any tenderness left his eyes as he looked up at Cecelia. 'Pandora indeed,' Luka said. 'However, your secret is out now.'

'I really was going to tell you—'

'Save it.'

'Honestly Luka, when I first found out—'

'Save it,' he said again. 'I won't have this moment marred by your lies and I won't have this discussion in front of our child.' Then he looked down at Pandora. 'Perhaps it is time to put her down.'

He stood and Cecelia nodded and held out her arms to take Pandora but Luka did not simply hand her over. 'I can take her to the nursery.'

'Nursery!' She let out a wry laugh. 'Luka, it's a one-bedroomed flat, not a penthouse apartment.'

While true, there was a small study that could be turned into a nursery in the future, but for now Pandora had been sleeping in with her. Cecelia could not bear the thought of her daughter waking up and crying in the dark alone.

Luka handed over Pandora but Cecelia would not, or could not, meet his eyes. She just held her daughter close to her and headed for the bedroom.

She knew he was furious.

Cecelia was furious with herself.

She should have told him at the very least in his office but she had panicked.

Now she had no one to blame but herself for the situation she found herself in.

Cecelia put Pandora down. Unlike last night, when she had protested every time she had been lowered to the mattress, now Pandora made not a sound.

She stared at her for a moment, aware that Luka stood in the doorway, watching them.

He wanted to know his daughter's routines and things like how to put a tiny baby to sleep. All of this was completely alien to him.

He saw that Cecelia covered her with a blanket and then kissed her fingers and placed them on the baby's head before turning to leave the bedroom.

'I don't want to argue...' Cecelia said as she walked past him.

They moved into the hallway and she awaited the interrogation, but instead it seemed he was about to leave.

'You're going?' Cecelia checked, not really believing that was it, but he was heading for the front door.

'Yes, it has been a long day,' Luka said. 'I just returned from Greece this morning.'

He had been on his way back from the airport when he had seen her.

It felt like a lifetime ago.

'I was there for my father's funeral.'

It was as if the carpet beneath her feet had turned into a flying one, for she felt the jolt of the ground and the world tip off kilter.

She had known she would never be forgiven by Luka, but what he had just revealed told her that it was a certain fact now.

His father had died without knowing he had a granddaughter.

'I'm sorry,' Cecelia attempted.

'Oh, no, you're not,' Luka said. 'How could you be when you did not know him?'

She looked into his eyes, which were not entirely unreadable for she could see the loathing there.

'When do you want to see her again?' Cecelia attempted.

'Tomorrow,' Luka responded crisply. 'A car will be here for you at nine in the morning.'

'A car?' Cecelia checked. 'Am I to bring her to you or?'

'I am taking Pandora to Xanero tomorrow. Naturally, I would like my mother to meet her granddaughter.'

'Luka, no…' She reached and caught his arm but he shook her hand off as if he could not bear the slightest touch from her. 'She's not ready to travel.'

'Why ever not?' he demanded.

'She doesn't have a passport.'

'I have a contact at the embassy and an urgent one can be arranged on our way to the airport.'

'No! She's not ready.'

'Pandora is three months old and shall be travelling on my private jet accompanied by her mother. I don't see any issue.'

'I might have plans tomorrow,' Cecelia attempted.

To no avail.

'Then cancel them.'

'Luka, I'm not trying to keep you from her. You can see Pandora tomorrow, of course you can, but you can't just walk in here and tell me that tomorrow I have to leave for Greece...'

'Are you quite sure about that?' Luka checked. 'Because the way I see it, tomorrow you can either get on a plane and head to a luxurious resort for a week...'

'A week?' Cecelia gulped.

He nodded. 'There you shall be catered for and beautifully looked after. Once there, the best nannies will be available to assist as I get to know my daughter and her grandmother meets her.' He frowned as if bemused by Cecelia. 'I thought you would jump at the chance.'

'No!'

'So you would rather spend the next few days in court? When the outcome will be the same—Pandora will be coming to Xanero, my lawyers will see to that.'

She felt sick.

It was like David and Goliath, except she wasn't the good guy here and the courts might well agree.

She would be portrayed as the bitch who had kept him from his child, up against the might of Luka Kargas.

She had lost already, Cecelia knew as she watched

him walk down the small garden path, brushing against weeds and neglected overgrown bushes because for the past months gardening had been the furthest thing from her mind.

'I'll see you tomorrow!' he called. 'Be ready.'

And even if Luka was in no mood to speak, even if she had no right to an answer, Cecelia did have a question.

'How did you know?' she called out to the dark and watched him halt. She was not asking how he had known about the baby; she was asking how he had been so certain that Pandora was his.

'How did I know?' Luka checked exactly what she was asking as he turned around. 'Are you going to try and drag things out with a DNA test to keep her from me even longer?'

'Of course not. But most men would demand one. I'm just asking why you're so certain...' Her voice trailed off as he walked back toward her, and then he came and stood closer to her than he had all evening.

So close that she could feel his breath on her cheek as he answered the question.

'I know, Cecelia, because when your legs were wrapped tight around me...' She was dizzy from lack of oxygen and she could feel his breath warm her cheek as he painted a vivid picture. 'When I screwed you slow and deep and came inside you,' he continued and her neck was rigid and her eyes screwed closed as he taunted her with the vision of them, 'you may recall that I was unsheathed.'

'Luka...' She begged with a single word that he stop. He did not.

'And given how long it took to get inside you, I doubt you went from my bed straight to someone else's. And,' he continued, 'given your abhorrence that we did not use protection, I would guess that lapse was as rare for you as it was for me.'

His voice was a taunt, both sensual and cruel as he took her back to that night. 'That is how I know,' he said, and then the thick, rich voice stopped and he pulled back and looked at her face, flushed in the porch light, confusion darting in her eyes.

He confused her, he excited her and made her want to sink to her knees and run, all at the same time.

But then he made things abundantly clear.

'We were so hot, Cecelia, and we could have been good, but you chose to walk away. You left. And then you denied me the knowledge of my child and I hate you for that.' And then, when she'd already got the dark message, he gave it a second coat and painted it black. 'I absolutely hate you.'

'No mixed messages, then?' She somehow managed a quip but there was nothing that could lighten this moment.

'Not one. Let me make things very clear. I am not taking you to Greece to get to know you better, or to see if there is any chance for us, because there isn't. I want no further part of you. The fact is, you are my daughter's mother and she is too young to be apart from you. That won't be the case in the near future.'

'How near?'

Fear licked the sides of her heart.

'I don't know.' He shrugged. 'I know nothing about babies, save what I have found out today. But I learn fast,' he said, 'and I will employ only the best so very soon, during my access times, Pandora and I will do just fine without you.'

'Luka, please...' She could not stand the thought of

being away from Pandora and she was spinning at the thought of taking her daughter to Greece, but Luka was done.

'I'm going, Cecelia,' Luka said. 'I have nothing left to say to you.'

That wasn't quite true, for he had one question.

'Did you know you were pregnant when you left?' Luka asked.

'I had an idea...'

'The truth, Cecelia.'

And she ached now for the days when he had been less on guard and had called her Cece, even though it had grated so much at the time.

And now it was time to be honest and admit she had known she was pregnant when she had left. 'Yes.'

'But,' Luka pointed out, 'given we hadn't slept together then, your resignation had nothing to do with the pregnancy.'

That was another part that stung, Luka thought as his driver opened the door to his car—she'd been leaving already.

CHAPTER ELEVEN

SILENCE WAS CRUEL.

Where once there would have been conversation…
where once he had annoyed her by shortening her
name…now that delicious voice was no longer aimed
at her.

As promised, a car arrived at nine but, rather than
Luka, it was his latest PA who got out. She introduced
herself as Amber and gave Cecelia a very efficient
smile when she raised a question and assured her that
of course there was a baby seat in the car.

The driver dealt with her bags but Luka barely
looked up when she strapped in Pandora.

He was wearing khaki linen pants and a black T-
shirt—more casually dressed than she had ever seen
him—yet he certainly cut a dash. He was wearing
shades and looked very sullen, and only when Pandora was safely strapped in did he acknowledge them.

Cecelia got a brief nod.

For Pandora, he took off his shades and she got the
benefit of his full smile, a kiss on the forehead and the
warmth of his voice.

Cecelia watched as Pandora smiled and cooed up at
him and seemed to know him already.

He looked tired, Cecelia noted.

Beautiful, but very tired and she thought of the past few days he must have had, with his father dying and finding out that he had a daughter. Yet he turned on the smiles for Pandora. She had never thought this side to Luka existed, but then again she too had fallen in love with Pandora at first sight.

As they were driven to the embassy, the incredibly efficient Amber addressed Cecelia.

'The accommodation has all been arranged but anything that you or Pandora need, please just make me aware.'

Cecelia gave a curt nod.

That used to be her world, Cecelia thought—taking care of Luka's ex-lovers and all the ensuing dramas their trysts had created.

Admittedly, she hadn't been in Amber's situation, sorting out the sudden news that her boss had a baby, but Amber was handling the situation as if it happened every day.

Oh, please let him not have slept with her, Cecelia thought as Amber carried on with her questions. 'The chef has asked if there are any food issues or allergies?'

'No.' Cecelia shook her head, then tried to soften her terse response. 'I can eat anything…'

But that wasn't what Amber had been asking—'I meant are there any allergies or issues with Pandora?'

She glanced over at Luka, who was staring out of the window. She saw the ghost of a smile on his lips as she was put in her place.

This wasn't about the mother!

'Pandora drinks formula,' Cecelia tartly responded. 'I hardly need a gourmet chef to prepare her bottles.'

'Well, I do,' Luka said, and turned to look right at

her. 'So, please answer the questions correctly. From this day forward I need to know such things.'

Cecelia briefly closed her eyes. 'No,' she answered. 'Pandora has no allergies that I know of.'

'Good,' he said, and then got back to looking out of the window.

The embassy was efficient.

The flight was, for Cecelia, an emotional hell.

There was seemingly no strained atmosphere on his part, for he simply carried on as if she were not there.

His jet was luxurious and Cecelia knew it well, though it felt very different today. Instead of joining Luka at the table for a meal and talking work, once Pandora had been fed and settled, her meal was served in an area to the rear of the lounge.

The food was no doubt sublime, but Cecelia, who had earlier said she'd eat anything, just pushed it around her plate. She felt awkward as she dined alone while Luka and Amber sat at the table and went through the sudden changes to his schedule.

That used to be me, Cecelia thought.

Her old life seemed a very long way off right now. So much was different, but how she felt about Luka remained.

All she had put on hold by leaving, all she had attempted to erase by distance, had come flooding back.

Quite simply, Luka Kargas was as devastatingly stunning to Cecelia as he had been the day they had met.

Motherhood had changed an awful lot of things, but it seemed it hadn't changed that one thing in the slightest.

With the meals cleared away, Cecelia dozed, one ear trained to listen out for Pandora.

Amber was busy on the computer and, though tired, Luka knew he was too wired to sleep.

He walked over to the bassinet and looked at the daughter he had met just yesterday.

Pandora was perfection.

Her tiny nails were trim and neat as her fingers closed around his. And she wore a little white cotton baby suit dotted with daisies.

And then he looked over at her mother and this time his face did not harden.

Cecelia wore a grey linen dress that was rather crumpled, and he noticed her once immaculate hair needed a cut. There were grey smudges beneath her eyes and even her lips were too pale.

It was as if all Cece's colour, all her energy had drained into Pandora and the anger in him dimmed a notch when he thought of all she must have been through.

And then she must have felt him watching her, for Cecelia opened her eyes and met his.

'Why don't you go and lie down?' Luka suggested. 'Pandora's due to wake soon.'

'I'll be here.'

She felt dismissed as she was shown to a cabin, though it was utter bliss to lie down after a night spent frantically packing for Xanero.

A light touch to her arm jolted Cecelia awake. She got up from the bed and headed to the main cabin for the final descent into Xanero.

Thanks to rather too many searches on the Internet as she'd attempted to put together the mystery of him, Cecelia actually recognised the island from the air. She saw white Orthodox churches with their round domes, and the sprawling whitewashed buildings that gleamed against the backdrop of an azure Mediterranean.

They landed behind the sprawling complex and were driven in air-conditioned comfort to the villa that would be her home for the next week.

Luka got out and it was he who held Pandora as he pushed open a large cobalt-blue door and stood back as Cecelia stepped in.

It was stunning, with mosaic-tiled floors, huge couches and an endless view of the ocean, but she could not take it all in with Luka there.

'I'll be fine.'

'I want to check you have everything you need for Pandora.'

There was everything she could possibly need and a whole lot more should she possibly want it. She even had her own pool, Cecelia noticed as she looked out. Then she thought of Luka and his start in life and there was both jealousy and anger combined as she thought of him chatting up women.

Of course she said nothing, just remained quiet as he showed her around, until they came to what was clearly a nursery.

There was a room with white organza fluttering in the windows and a heavy dark wooden crib made up in white bedlinen. There was a little intercom on a table, and it was a long way off from the main suite.

'Pandora sleeps in with me.'

'I have had an identical room made up in my villa,' Luka said. 'The nanny suggested that it might help for her surroundings to be familiar when Pandora is with me.'

Yes, it made perfect sense, but she felt with her heart,

not her head. 'I would like her crib moved through to my room.'

'As you wish,' Luka said.

'And she's too young to be away from me overnight.'

'You're not breastfeeding,' he pointed out.

'Another black mark…'

'Oh, grow up,' he retorted.

'Luka, I don't want her waking up in the night and me not being there.' She was starting to panic, and that was something she did not want Luka to see, but she could remember waking up and calling out for her mother in the night and she would not put Pandora through the same. 'I am not having her apart from me.'

'You worry about a night spent away from your daughter, yet your silence sentenced me to three months without her. You denied me the chance to plan for her, or see my child when she was born…so don't start complaining about one night. Cecelia, it is time to get used to the fact that I am her father and I'm not going anywhere.'

He saw her throat tighten as she swallowed and caught her rapid blink and then watched as Cecelia sat down.

'Are you okay?'

'I'm just warm…'

He frowned because it was shady and cool in here and the journey had certainly been a comfortable one.

'I was up all night, packing, trying to make sure I had everything…'

'I told you that I would take care of all that.'

'Well, I'm not very used to…'

Cecelia stopped.

She was rather too used to having to take care of everything and could not quite get her head around the fact there was now someone else.

It both unsettled her and comforted her.

The decisions regarding Pandora felt so huge at times. Even giving up the breast for a bottle had been angst-ridden.

Never had she imagined that had Luka known about Pandora she might have been able to discuss it with him.

It wasn't the heat that had unsettled her, or exhaustion.

His words had hit like shrapnel buried deep and she sat there as he poured some iced water and then handed it to her.

Yet she could not think about how his words had effected her now.

'I guessed you wouldn't have time for shopping so Amber is sorting you out a wardrobe...'

'I can dress myself, Luka.'

'Well, there's not much call for navy suits here...'

It was a dig at her staid wardrobe.

'You don't know me out of work.'

'Oh, but I can guess.'

He was right.

Cecelia had sat on her bedroom floor with her suitcase last night and known that the truth was she had nothing to pack for a holiday.

Not really.

But then he surprised her.

'I apologise,' Luka said suddenly. 'That was uncalled-for. How you dress is your concern.'

It was a rather backhanded apology and she gave a small mirthless laugh.

'I've lost weight since last year,' Cecelia said. 'And finding a capsule wardrobe so I can swan off to Greece at a moment's notice hasn't exactly been high on my list of priorities.'

'Then it's lucky that it's being taken care of,' he said, and she nodded. 'Is there anything else you need?'

'No.'

'There is a spa and a salon. You don't need an appointment. I have told them to accommodate you whenever you so choose. And there is the restaurant and a table reserved solely for you for the duration of your stay. Naturally, if you would prefer to dine here, just say.'

Cecelia nodded.

'When she wakes up, if you call the number by the phone you will be put through to the nanny, who will come and fetch Pandora.'

'How can you have arranged a nanny so quickly? Luka, I'm not just handing her over to someone you've hired in a rush…'

'There are several nannies at this resort and, given the clientele, we hire only the best. The best of the best shall be caring for my daughter. Her name is Roula and she has worked here for more than five years and was once the private nanny to royalty. You didn't check with me before you left her with a neighbour, and I did not question that choice either. I assume you want the best for her. Please afford me the same courtesy and never again suggest that I don't have my daughter's interests at heart.'

He gave the sleeping Pandora a light kiss and handed her over before striding off. Cecelia sat there, holding her daughter, his words playing over and over in her head.

'I'm not going anywhere.'

They were words she had never expected to hear, and she was scared to believe them.

Fair enough, he was angry now about being kept in

the dark, but when that anger had faded, when Pandora was teething and screaming deep in the night...

Yes, it felt like shrapnel was making its way to the surface as she recalled the fear of waking up in a house with no one there.

Pushing open her mother's bedroom door and seeing the empty bed.

Creeping downstairs, ears straining for the sound of chatter and laughter and bracing herself to be scolded for disturbing the grown-ups.

But no one had been there.

She had never known when her mother would be back, and then one day she hadn't been. Cecelia held her daughter tight and swore she would never know the same.

Cecelia jumped as the sound of a soft bell reverberated through the villa.

At the door stood Amber and two porters, along with another woman who was sultry looking and wore a sarong.

'Luka said you wouldn't have time to pack,' Amber said as she breezed in with the porters, who carried a whole lot of designer bags. 'They won't be long...'

She was mildly grateful to Luka for the excuse he had given Amber.

'And this is Roula.' Amber introduced them. 'The nanny.'

Oh, my!

When Luka had said she'd been a nanny for royalty, somehow Cecelia had imagined a crisp white dress and big black rubber shoes.

Instead, the nanny was barefoot and stunning.

'Luka suggested that I come over and meet you,' Roula said. 'You can tell me your daughter's ways and anything I need to know and hopefully meeting me will make things easier on you.'

It would be easier if she wasn't so stunning.

Pandora woke up and smiled when Roula first met her and didn't cry when she was held.

'Sophie—Luka's mother—is so excited to meet her,' Roula said. 'After such a sad loss there is sunshine again.'

There was no more putting it off, and all too soon she watched as the gorgeous Roula headed off with her daughter.

And it hurt.

Not just that they were apart, more that there was a grandmother excited to meet Pandora, a family gathering taking place from which she was excluded.

After they had gone, she opened the huge dark wooden dresser to see what clothes had been chosen for her and glimpsed an array of terribly sexy one-piece swimming suits cut high in the leg with plunging backs.

She did not belong in this world.

There was a rose-gold bikini that Cecelia held for a moment, though could never imagine putting on, and she realised that there was colour now lining her wardrobe.

There was a rose-gold silk dress too, in the same fabric as the bikini, a sensual throw-on for when you dined by the pool, Cecelia guessed.

And there were fragrances and oils by the bath.

Heaven knew, she needed them.

Her habits had long since slipped by the wayside. First to go had been her routine foils and so now her hair was back to its original strawberry blonde, with some rather long dry ends.

And she had long since stopped straightening it.

So much for looking sleek and together when she faced him and told him about Pandora.

Instead he had found out on his own.

And now, here in Xanero, she faced his wrath.

CHAPTER TWELVE

PARADISE WAS LONELY without him.

She called for lunch and ate in the villa and then, after a doze, she put on the most modest of the swimming costumes, took a book outside and read by the pool.

The book didn't pull her in, though.

All too often Cecelia found herself looking up and thinking of Luka and his misspent youth.

And so she gave in, tied on a sarong and went for a walk along Luka's private beach.

The Mediterranean shimmered like an endless sapphire and the white sand was pristine, but there was no solace there either.

For Luka's yacht was moored in the distance and she thought of the morning he had invited her to join him.

As his plaything.

They were poles apart yet eternally joined by a daughter they clearly both loved.

She had thought she'd known hell before.

Working alongside him, while loving him had been torture.

But this was worse. It did not cease at the end of the working day and there would be no annual leave.

Instead, this was her future.

He was now a permanent part of her life.

So far, he hadn't put a foot wrong, but soon she would have to deal with the glamorous beauties and his tawdry social life.

Some time soon, Cecelia was sure of it, there would be his latest long-limbed beauty lying on the sun lounger, or splashing in the water beside him with *her* daughter.

And there was no escape from that.

Pandora would talk one day and no doubt she would hear about daddy's new friends.

So Cecelia returned to the poolside to brood and that was how he found her.

She was huddled under the shade as if the sun might bite and the pool and poolside were pristine from lack of use. She startled when she looked up and saw him.

He wore only bathers and carried Pandora with a muslin cloth over her. She was asleep against his chest.

And she wore only a nappy.

'Pandora should be covered in the sun…' Cecelia chastised.

'And she is,' Luka pointed out. 'She fell asleep on the walk over here. Shall I put her down?'

Cecelia nodded and held open the door to the villa. His hair was wet and she knew he'd been in the pool.

'You didn't have Pandora by the pool, did you?' Cecelia checked.

'Of course I did, but we were always in the shade and she loved the water.'

'You took her in!' There was horror in her voice as she followed him through the villa. 'Luka, she's far too young.'

'Pandora adored it.'

She was appalled—in fact, Cecelia was furious, but she held her tongue as he tenderly lowered his daughter.

Pandora was clearly exhausted.

She barely stirred as he lightly covered her with the muslin, and as Luka walked off he tried not to glance at the large bed, or Cecelia's rumpled dress flung over the chair.

And a pile of bikinis that she'd clearly tried on and discarded.

He kept having to remind himself how furious he was, yet this woman was a constant turn-on.

Out of her bedroom, he headed to the fridge and pulled out a bottle of wine and selected two glasses.

'This is my villa,' Cecelia pointed out, not liking his bold intrusion.

'Okay, you serve, then,' he said, and handed her the bottle and glasses. 'I'll be outside.'

God, he was arrogant, Cecelia thought, and spent five minutes trying to find a corkscrew before she worked out it was a screw top.

Her temper was still bubbling, and yet it was clear he was here to talk. Well, as long as he was prepared to listen too because there was no way he was taking Pandora in the pool again.

She walked outside but it wasn't the glare of the sun that had her momentarily close her eyes.

It was his beauty.

Practically naked, except for black trunks slung low on his hips, he lay on a lounger.

He had a restless energy to him that she recognised from a year of working alongside him, and she felt a flutter of nerves low in her stomach as she approached.

She poured him a glass of wine and sparkling water for herself and then she suppressed a smile at his *You serve, then* comment.

'Here,' she said, and handed him the glass. 'Luka, we need to talk about Pandora...'

'I know we do and it's the only reason I'm here,' he said, more to remind himself, for he was on slow boil for Cece—or Cecelia as he would remember to call her now.

'How was your mother with her?'

'They got on wonderfully. She's thrilled to have a granddaughter...' He kept trying to be angry, but the truth was, it felt as if there was less and less to be angry about. 'She is concerned for you, and all that you must have been through alone.'

'Oh.'

Luka was too.

But there was something else concerning him and it was something that urgently needed to be discussed.

'I've been speaking with my PR people in the UK and it would seem that there is a lot of press interest in me at the moment.'

Cecelia felt her heart sink.

'With my father's death and the new hotels...' He didn't bother to explain it all but Cecelia got the gist.

The press would love to get their hands on the billionaire playboy now a father.

He read her concern. 'It is secure here, that I can assure you. Nobody can get a photo while you are in the complex, I took care of that long ago. The only risky place is my yacht.'

'Well, I shan't be going there!' She gave a tight smile. 'But, even so, I can't be expected to stay behind the wall...'

'Firstly, it is hardly a prison complex. There are miles of walks and you have access to my private beach. You are hardly going to be confined to four walls. You can take Pandora for a walk in the village if you feel you want to get out. I doubt a mother and baby will raise much interest.'

'I mean, if she's seen with you. Oh, God!' She stood and looked out to sea as if a thousand cameras were trained on them.

'I've already told you that the hotel and grounds are secure and I won't be joining you on any strolls.'

She felt heat flood her cheeks as again he placed distance between them and she tried to quickly change tack. 'I meant in London.'

'For now, I shall see Pandora here.' He saw the small frown form between her eyes. 'You just said you don't want any photos taken.'

'But if you're going to be in her life, how can you avoid her while in London?'

'I'm not avoiding Pandora,' Luka said, and then he put things bluntly. 'I'm going to be avoiding her mother.'

'If you want to be in her life, then that's going to prove rather difficult.'

'Amber is going through my schedule and for now, one week a month I am arranging things so that I shall be working from here.'

'But you have a home in London and you can't ask me to upend my life!'

'Hold on right there. Had you done the right thing in the first place, we would have had time to organise things better. Had you bothered to tell me I was soon to be a father I might have been able to sort my schedule better. Had you—'

'I get it,' Cecelia said, and held up her hand to halt him.

'I don't think you do,' Luka said. 'I don't believe for a moment you were going to tell me. I cannot believe I could have gone through my entire life not knowing about Pandora. She's my *daughter*...' he said. She heard the throaty rasp in his voice and she knew then how badly it was hurting him.

'Luka, I thought you would tell me to take care of things.'

'You assumed an awful lot.'

'My father asked my mother to.'

'She told you that?'

'No, the one time I met him he was shouting at her, telling her that he'd given her money for a termination. I didn't know what it meant, of course, until I looked it up.'

'I would never have asked that.'

'What would you have said then?' she flared.

'I don't know...'

'Well, neither did I!' Cecelia said, and she fought to keep herself from shouting.

'But I would have taken care of you and I would have ensured the best of care for the birth. And I would have been there when she was born and held her. And who knows what would have happened between us, but you denied us any chance of finding that out.'

Yes, he was angry.

But, yes, he understood better.

'You should have trusted me enough to tell me.'

'Trusted you! With the reckless way you live your life and your disposable attitude to women?'

'They don't have an issue with it,' Luka said. 'Well, most don't. I deliberately choose women who know what they want and are more than happy to indulge in a good time.' He could see the burn on her cheeks and he turned the knife. 'Women who don't wake up with regret...'

'Women who paid you.'

'Do you know what, Cecelia, you used to be a turn-on but I'm sick of the constant disapproval in your eyes.'

But, oh, it wasn't disapproval in her eyes, it was jealousy and it was want—not that she told him that, and so Luka spoke on.

'You're so busy being the perfect parent and before that the perfect PA you don't even know how to have fun.'

'Yes, I do.'

'You haven't even been in the pool!'

'You don't get to dictate what I do with my time,' Cecelia snapped. 'And about the pool, I don't want Pandora in the water...'

'Roula is a trained swimming instructor and, given that Pandora's going to be spending a lot of time surrounded by water, it seems prudent to teach her to swim.'

'She's three months old!'

'And she swam straight to the top.'

'Are you telling me you threw her in?'

'Roula and I were in the water with her.'

She felt ill at the thought of Pandora in the water and sick too at the thought of him and Roula, sharing that time with her baby.

'I want Pandora back home,' Cecelia said. 'This is too much. Luka, I want her back in London.'

'Tough!' Luka said. 'One week a month you are going to be here, and you can mope around and check for photographers or you can live a little.'

She incensed him, she really did.

He thought of that body of hers that never saw the sun and he did the only thing he could think of in response. He threw her up over his shoulder and carried her to the pool.

'Luka!'

Cecelia was raging and furious, not that it stopped him.

He just dropped her right into the deep end.

She flailed for a moment and then came up, and as she did, she heard another splash.

Luka.

He was there as she surfaced, spluttering and furious and swimming straight for the edge, but he caught her and held her at the waist as it was too deep to reach the bottom of the pool.

'How dare you!' she shouted.

'Have you never been thrown in the water before?'

'Of course not.'

'And do you know how to swim?'

'Of course I do.'

But it was nice, so nice to be in the water and facing him, nice to feel his hands strong on her waist and the sun beating on her shoulders.

Nice to know that her baby was doing things that she had never even dreamed of as a child and that she had a father who adored her.

And it was also scary to be under his spell again.

To know, from the ragged edge to his breathing, that he was turned on and to know from the warmth spreading through her that she was turned on too.

And to know that right now she could wrap her legs around him and be lost to Luka again.

But would it be *Bored on Monday so we might as well do it* sex for him? Cecelia pondered as she gazed into dark eyes.

Yes, she decided, because that was how he lived.

And so she disengaged from him and hauled herself from the water.

She was here as Pandora's mother.

That was all.

CHAPTER THIRTEEN

CECELIA WOKE EARLY.

Only not to the familiar cries of Pandora.

Silence really was cruel for she had been locked in a dream where Luka's kiss did not end and with an ache and heat low in her legs, and a body that throbbed for him.

She forced her eyes open and pulled herself out of bed and then went to check on Pandora.

She was asleep on her back with her little arms up above her head, as if cheering.

They had been here for almost a week and they were starting to get into a gentle routine.

The mornings were for her and Pandora alone, but around eleven Roula would come over and fetch her. Luka would take a long lunch break and spend time with her along with her *yia-yia*—her grandmother—who doted on her apparently.

Late afternoon, after her nap, Pandora would return to Cecelia.

And it was nice.

Cecelia was starting to relax into it and had, after her impromptu dip in the pool, started to swim each day and take regular walks along Luka's private beach.

It was a long stretch of cove that made for a perfect

walk, splashing through the breaking waves and breathing in the fresh sea air.

On her final full day in Xanero before she and Pandora flew home tomorrow, it wasn't by coincidence that Luka headed down to the beach to join her.

It still galled him that she had kept the news of the pregnancy from him, but he understood better why she had.

He wasn't exactly fatherhood material.

Or he hadn't been.

And he wasn't exactly a family man.

Yet he wanted to be.

He was still infatuated with Cecelia, and his desire for her had never gone, though he knew he must not rush things.

Even so, tomorrow she left for London. Three more weeks apart, and not just apart from his daughter.

He ached for Cecelia. He ached for the glimpse of the smile he sometimes prised from her reluctant lips, and for the way she sometimes made him laugh.

'Hey,' Luka said, and he saw that he had startled her.

'Where's Pandora?'

'Being spoiled,' he said. 'My mother wondered if you would like to join her for breakfast tomorrow, before we head off?'

'I've been here a week...'

'Cecelia, my mother would have had you over the first day if she'd had her own way. I have been the one keeping things separate...'

'Why?'

'Because that's what I always do,' Luka said, and then added, 'And because I was angry.'

They walked on.

'But I can't keep my worlds separate now,' Luka said.

'We have a daughter. My mother has a grandchild...' He looked at her. 'What about your aunt and uncle? Do they know about me?'

'No.' Cecelia shook her head. 'They would have had me straight over to a lawyer,' Cecelia said. 'And then they'd have gushed all over us both. You were right about them only taking me on to get to the money.'

She looked out to the cove and the glitter of his yacht but his wealth was not what beckoned her.

He saw where her gaze fell. 'Do you want to go over for lunch?' Luka asked.

'No, thank you.' It was hard enough just to walk alongside him and not break down. She wanted him so badly and was terrified she'd simply accept whatever occasional crumbs of affection he threw her way and so her response was tart. 'I thought the reason I was here was so you could spend time with your daughter.'

'Believe it or not, I actually have some work to do today—things were already piling up before my father died.'

'I'm sorry he never got to meet his granddaughter,' Cecelia said. 'I really do mean that. I feel terrible about it, in fact...'

'Don't.' Luka shook his head and then turned and looked at her 'Truth?'

'Please,' she said, and gave a pale smile. He really was a curious man, for he could so easily have held that over her. She was surprised to have her guilt so readily dismissed.

'I would not have insisted on a week of playing happy families had he been alive. I would never have exposed her to his toxic nature. Instead, I would have brought Pandora for lunch and that would have been it.'

'I thought the two of you were close.'

'That's what they wanted people to think.'

'Tell me…' Cecelia said, because she simply could not feign disinterest.

'Over dinner.' He nodded to the yacht. 'It's a nice place to talk and I'm not here by accident, Cecelia. My mother has asked if she can have Cecelia stay with her tonight.'

'Absolutely not.' Cecelia shook her head. 'I've given you as much time as you want with her but she is not spending the night away from me. There's no need for your mother to babysit.'

'But she would not be *babysitting*—she is family.' Luka closed his eyes in exasperation. 'She wants to have her granddaughter stay over and to boast to her friends. It's the Greek way.'

She could feel her panic building. It was irrational really, for she wanted Pandora to be surrounded by people who loved her, yet she could not bear the thought of her waking in the dark alone.

'Cecelia, do you really think I would leave Pandora with someone I did not absolutely trust?'

Of course not.

Cecelia knew that.

He had told her that.

And she knew that this was the future.

Time spent away from her daughter as Pandora spent time with people who loved her.

'Roula will be there too,' Luka said. 'Cecelia, I am sure most first-time mothers are anxious when they leave their baby for the first night, but that is co-parenting.'

'I know.'

She swallowed.

It sounded so odd to hear those words from him.

She had honestly thought he would have no interest in Pandora. Or, perhaps the odd visit. Cecelia had genuinely believed he would throw money at the situation.

Instead, Luka wanted to be a true parent. He wanted real time with his daughter and he wanted his family involved in her life.

He just didn't want *her*.

Only that wasn't entirely the case.

Luka turned so he was facing her and when she didn't do the same, he took her shoulders and moved her to face him.

'I want to take you to the yacht tonight because I think it's time that we speak about us.'

'Us?' An incredulous laugh shot from her lips. 'What us? You hate me, and I can't stand the way you live your life—'

'Yet we are parents together,' Luka interrupted. 'And for the record, I don't hate you, and I think you are referring to my former life.'

She assumed he meant prior to him finding out he was a parent.

For Luka, though, the anger was fading, and he was remembering how much he had missed Cecelia this past year.

And now the red mist of anger was clearing, he knew that what he felt for Cecelia had not changed.

Still, he was aware that he could be bullish and knew that to push her too fast would be wrong. She was as jumpy as a cat and a new mother too.

'Cecelia, before the world finds out we have a daughter, I think we should use that time to explore where we stand.'

'I'm not with you.'

'The desire is still there.'

He stated it as fact.

And it was.

Her nails were digging into her palms just from the effort of facing him calmly—the impact of Luka close up was as devastating now as it had been on the day they'd met.

'Perhaps, but sex isn't much to build a relationship on.'

'Why not?' Luka shrugged. 'We both enjoy it and it got us this far.'

She was about to say no but Luka would not be put off.

'Tonight we are going out on our first date.'

Second, she wanted to correct, for her birthday last year had been the most romantic night of her life.

CHAPTER FOURTEEN

THE SPA WAS gorgeous and perhaps more than a little overdue.

Instead of more foils, Cecelia had some length cut off, so that her strawberry blonde hair fell to just below her shoulders, and because it was shorter it coiled into waves.

'How about adding some more waves and wearing it down?' the hairdresser said, but Cecelia shook her head and asked for it to be straightened and put up.

There was an almost imperceptive tut from the hairdresser but she did as asked and smoothed it out and pinned it up.

Though her hair was redder than before, Cecelia felt a small sense of order returning to her world as she eyed her reflection, for she looked more like the Cecelia during her Kargas Holdings days.

Returning to the villa, she took for ever to choose what to wear—everything was too loose and to her mind too sensual.

It isn't work, though, she reminded herself as she found her hand linger upon the sheer rose-gold silk dress.

But it may well be work for Luka.

He adored Pandora, and she was terrified that he

might be merely attempting to do the right thing by his daughter. Cecelia doubted that even his best intentions could last.

She came upon the requisite little black dress and decided it was safer and closer to her usual fare. For a splash of colour she added a little sheer grey silk cardigan that she had packed herself—a throwback from her working days.

She looked at the birthday necklace and wondered if she should wear it, for it was absolutely her favourite thing.

Yet she did not want him to know that he meant everything to her. Luka had made a chance for them sound like a grim reality they ought to face.

Even as he came to her door, Cecelia was holding onto her heart.

Luka was immaculate in a suit and tie, and he had, did, and always would, take her breath away.

'You look very beautiful,' Luka duly said as she closed the door on the villa and they walked towards the speedboat that would take them out to his yacht.

Yet somehow it felt rather like heading to a formal work dinner than a romantic date. And Luka noted she was wearing another damned cardigan.

'How's Pandora?' Cecelia asked, for it felt like for ever since she had seen her. But if tonight didn't work then being apart from her daughter for prolonged stretches was something she would have to get used to.

Yes, there was an awful lot of pressure on this date.

'She is being spoiled by her *yia-yia* and also her great-aunt, my father's sister,' Luka said, and he took out his phone and showed her a photo he had taken just before he left.

If ever there was a baby who was doted on it was

Pandora. She had on a cerise dress and was a splash of gorgeousness between the two doting women dressed in black.

'My mother is so happy and relaxed. I cannot tell you the balm that our daughter is to her.'

As she boarded his stunning yacht, Cecelia couldn't help but think of all the wild debauched parties that had taken place here.

Tonight, though, there weren't the half-naked, sun-kissed and oiled bodies, or the pulse of music to dance to. And there was only one champagne cork that popped and no raucous laughter.

It wasn't so much his past that she loathed, more the certainty that he would tire of her and go back to it someday.

It was a gorgeous night, the sky as navy as Pandora's eyes and pierced with endless stars.

The deck was romantically lit and it was soft music that greeted her as they were led to a beautifully dressed table.

The waiter placed her napkin in her lap and Cecelia did her absolute best to relax.

They ate the best squid she had ever tasted—or *kalamari*, as the waiter called it—and she looked out at Xanero and saw the gorgeous buildings from her view on the water.

'It really is the most beautiful place,' Cecelia said.

'It has been both a blessing and a curse,' Luka said. 'It's a blessing now.'

'You mean now that your father's gone?' Cecelia tentatively asked, alluding to what he had said on the beach.

He nodded. 'My mother would say I should not speak ill of the dead, but there is nothing good that I can say about him. He was work-shy and a bully...'

'I thought you and he worked together in the restaurant, that he passed on all he knew.'

'He probably put in twelve hours tops in his entire lifetime,' Luka said. 'But my mother had always wanted a family business. I could have had him removed, but she pleaded with me not to. It was easier to stay away and run it from a distance.' He looked out across the water and then he told her something he could not explain, even to himself. 'And yet his death has rocked my world and I feel like I'm grieving.'

'I still grieve for my mother,' she admitted. 'Sometimes I think I miss what could have been.'

And then her eyes flicked away because, although they were talking about their parents, she was suddenly thinking of them and what *might* be, perhaps.

'I want you to love it here too,' Luka said, and she put down her fork. 'You've had a good week?' he asked.

'It's been better than I thought it would be.'

'There could be many more.'

'There's no could about it.' She looked at him and reminded herself who she was dealing with. 'Given that you've told me to be here one week a month or you'll see me in court.'

'I meant *this*, Cecelia. Us.' He saw her jaw tighten but he reached across the table and took her hand. It was as rigid as ever, her professional façade still in place. Yet as he toyed with her, she found her fingers intertwining with his and then he voiced her thoughts exactly.

'I'm going crazy, knowing you're here but not in my bed.'

He watched as her eyes screwed closed and assumed he had pushed too hard when in truth Cecelia was also fighting desire.

'We don't have to rush things,' he corrected, 'but maybe when you bring Pandora here, when there is no chance of us being seen, then away from prying eyes we can date, get to know each other, see how we work as a family…'

She felt like the only car in the showroom about to be taken on a reluctant test drive. 'And if we don't work?' she asked.

'Cecelia….'

'No, Luka, what you're basically proposing is that I be your mistress during the time Pandora and I are here in Xanero.'

'What I'm proposing is that we give us a try. I'm going to attempt to let go of the fact that you kept Pandora from me…'

'You're never going to forgive me for that, are you?'

'I don't know,' he admitted.

It killed her to hear that for it gave them such a lousy start and so she kicked back. 'Can you really blame me for not telling you?' Cecelia could no longer hold it in. 'Have you any idea the hell you put me through, dealing with all your cast-offs? I was crazy about you and you were into everyone but me!'

'And you didn't think to tell me?'

'You were my boss then!'

'Well, I'm not now.'

'No, but it's no better here, knowing what went on aboard this yacht and by the bloody pool…'

'Don't turn this around on me. You never gave me a single indication you were interested in me. In fact, you were engaged when I first hired you. I'm damned if I do and damned if I don't. You were the one in a serious relationship, remember?'

'And you were the one screwing around.' She flung

down her napkin and there was the scrape of her chair as she stood. 'I need to get back.'

'We need to speak.' Luka took her wrist.

'No, I want to get off…'

'Fine.'

He snapped his fingers to prepare the speedboat that would take them back to shore. 'Do you know something,' Luka said. 'I'm sick and tired of seeing the disproval in your eyes…'

'Well, someone has to be responsible,' she spat.

'And you elect yourself at every turn.'

'Because I'm scared that if I let go, then I might turn into my mother!' she shouted.

'Cecelia…' he was about to tell her that she was being ridiculous but then he looked at it from her side, the chaotic upbringing, the uncertainty, the abandonment. 'You will never be her. And I promise you this, the day you hit the cocaine, I shall put you over my knee…'

She almost laughed.

Almost.

But her throat was thick with tears.

'We're in this together,' Luka said. 'Did she leave you at night?'

'Many times.' Cecelia nodded. 'I would wake up and not know where she was. That's why I don't want Pandora—'

'The difference is,' Luka cut in, 'that, though it might not be her mother she wakes to, she will have family there, or a nanny who has been carefully chosen. Cecelia, there's a world of difference between having a night out and living the life your mother lived.' But Cecelia turned away and he shook his head for she would never see it from his point of view. 'We'll go and fetch her now.'

As the boat sped them to shore, Cecelia felt like an utter failure—back from a romantic night out before ten. As he helped her onto the pier she did not know how to explain it—she knew he was right, that Pandora was safe and loved, but it was about more than just that. 'Luka, you don't have to wake her. Leave her with your mother and Roula. I know she'll be fine.'

'Are you sure?'

Cecelia nodded.

'You're a wonderful mother, Cecelia.'

But as a lover she knew she had failed.

The night was over for them.

'Luka,' she tried to explain how she felt, 'I'm scared of us getting together and confusing her when we break up…'

'How about *if* we break up?' Luka asked. 'How about we don't ever break up? You're so bloody negative and contained.'

'Because the one time I lived a little, look what happened! The one time I made a mist—'

She stopped there because she didn't ever want to describe Pandora and what had happened as a mistake because she wasn't.

But Luka got there first. 'The one time you let your hair down and lived a little, to my mind, something rather beautiful happened.'

And then he looked down at her and he was angry, for she had refused on so many occasions to give them a chance.

'Cecelia, I'm not going to beg. You have to want it too.'

CHAPTER FIFTEEN

LUKA STRODE OFF.

She watched him walk angrily along the beach and she knew it was she who had messed up the night.

Yet the cheek of him!

On-call sex whenever she was here?

Or, a little voice to her heart said, could it serve as the start of being a real family?

Cecelia was terrified of loving him.

Yet she already did.

More, she was terrified of admitting to loving him and then losing him.

Of waking in the dark and it being *him* that was gone.

Or, worse, the cold pretence of normal, and pretending there was love, as her uncle and aunt had done.

Sex was all they had and when that novelty dimmed he would be back to his old life....

She walked along the white sandy beach, straying a little from the boundaries of the complex. This would be home for a while, she realised.

Not all the time, but for a year or so she would be here for a week every month.

And then not at all.

She was terrified to enjoy it and relax into it, knowing all the while that it would all soon be taken away from her.

He would always be there for Pandora, though.

She was starting to believe that things would be different for her daughter than they had been for her. That, despite her carelessness that one morning, she had chosen well for he was proving to be an amazing father—completely rearranging his world to accommodate his daughter.

'Live a little.'

She recalled his words as he had moved her little pottery jar and then she winced as she remembered her *No, thank you* response.

She remembered him throwing her into the pool and then joining her, his eyes imploring her to loosen up and be free.

He had been offering a chance for them, and rather than embrace that chance she was hiding from it. Rather than living the life she wanted to with him, she was running from it at every turn.

Yet Luka was right, the one time she had let her hair down and lived a little, something rather beautiful had happened.

She recalled his words. *'You have to want it too.'*

Oh, she did, she very much did, and she had to show him that somehow.

And so instead of heading back to the villa to spend the night feeling sorry for herself, Cecelia decided it was time to head out.

While she did head back to the villa it was only to change. She peeled off the cardigan and little black dress and instead of flesh-coloured knickers and a bra, she pulled on the rose-gold bikini.

For she might want a midnight swim!

She thought of Luka naked and wet and dripping water over her, as had been her fantasy for so long.

Over the bikini she pulled on the rose-gold dress that was so loose and flowing, and yet so sensual.

Her hair when she took it down was wavy and wild thanks to the salt spray of the ocean.

Her cheeks were flushed and her green eyes finally had their sparkle back after a week of doing nothing and actually sleeping.

Or did it have more to do with a week spent closer to him?

There could be many more weeks, if she had the courage to try....

A monthly tryst with Luka didn't sound so terrible now. They were like a little family, and being together in the pool once a month, rather than her lying lonely poolside on the other side of the complex, would be much better, wouldn't it?

Pandora would have the best mother, the best co-parents—and if Luka couldn't forgive her for not telling him about their baby that was his right.

She put on the necklace, the one he had given her and the one she would adore for ever, feeling the cold metal against her heated skin. Then Cecelia headed to the restaurant she had never so much as visited, preferring instead to hide away in the villa.

It was stunning and, yes, full of couples, but there at the bar was Luka, with his back to her.

'Your table is ready for you, Madam,' the greeter said, and she recalled it had been reserved for her all week.

The bar manager told Luka that Cecelia had arrived. He frowned, glanced over and saw that she was being seated—only it was not a Cecelia he recognised.

Well, perhaps the one he met at times in his dreams, for she looked amazing and relaxed and sexy too as she laughed at something the greeter said.

He looked over but she did not catch his eye. He was trying to work out what was going on when the bar manager spoke and placed in front of him a glass of the best champagne.

'*Gia eséna kýrie, apó tin kyría.*' For you, sir, from the lady.

And it was like in days of old, but so much better now. As he turned, Cecelia met his eyes and raised her own glass, adding a slight gesture of her head.

A gesture that invited Luka to join her.

She smiled a slow smile that was familiar from many years ago.

A flirt.

An offer.

Yes, Cecelia was a curious mix indeed, for never would he have envisaged this.

He walked over, his eyes never leaving her face. 'It's far too nice a night to drink champagne alone,' Luka said.

'I agree,' she said. 'Would you care to join me?'

'I would love to.'

He took a seat and looked over at a woman who had, from the day they had met, intrigued him. Never more so than now, and he slipped so easily back into the game. 'How long are you here for?'

'I fly back to London tomorrow,' she said. 'Although I believe it won't be the last time I'm here.'

'That's good to know,' Luka said. 'And are you here alone?'

'It's a little complicated, I don't really want to go into it.'

'That's fine.'

But this time it was not disapproval in her eyes, for it was like he was back staring into that aurora and he started to understand her some more. There was a wild side to Cecelia, one she had fought all her life to temper.

Not tonight.

She *could* be free around him.

'I have a daughter,' she said, 'but she's being taken care of tonight.'

'So you're on your own.'

'Yes,' Cecelia said. 'All night.'

'Poor you.' He gave her a smile, the one that had churned her heart since the day they'd met. 'I didn't catch your name.'

'Cece.'

He smiled that slow smile that made her stomach fold.

'I'm Luka. So, where are you staying.'

'At the Beach Side apartment.'

'Nice,' he said.

'Very.' She took a sip of champagne and then smirked. 'My ex is paying.'

'Even better,' he said, and then Luka laughed and it was the most delicious sound she had ever heard.

But then he met her eyes and his voice was serious. 'He must be a fool to have let you go.'

'Not really,' Cecelia said. 'I let him down.'

'I doubt it,' he said.

'Oh, but I did. I kept something very important from him.'

'Then he should have got over it, or perhaps he should have taken the time to work out why you did what you did.'

He saw a flash of tears and decided that there would be no tears now.

'I shouldn't really be seen drinking in the restaurant with a guest,' Luka said. He held her eyes and the tears dispersed like a chink in the mist.

'Then come back to mine.'

It was the bravest thing she had done and he was so deliciously casual in his response.

'Sure, though for the sake of discretion, you should leave first.'

She would never not want him, Cecelia knew as she stood to go, but he caught her wrist.

'Is there anything you'd like?' he asked. 'Anything at all?'

He was inviting her to name her wants.

This she did.

Cecelia bent over and whispered into his ear and then pulled back, wondering at his reaction and if he might laugh at her request, but he just nodded.

'No problem.'

She felt as if she was on a high as she arrived back at the villa.

A dizzy high and, yes, it might just be sex but she would take it if it afforded them a start.

She did not turn on the lights. Instead, she slipped off her clothes and lay on the bed. Her body felt as though it might burst into flames of desire as she lay there.

Waiting.

Not wondering as to their future, not berating herself with the impossibility of it all, just waiting for her night with him.

She heard the splash from the pool and closed her eyes as she listened to him move through the water and then she caught the slide of the villa doors.

And then, dripping wet, he leaned over her.

As per her request.

She felt the mattress indent as he knelt over her and relished the cold drops of water on her skin. 'I want you, Cece...' he told her. His mouth found hers and she closed her eyes to the bliss of his kiss. 'I've been crazy about you for so long.'

His voice was raw with want, and even if he was simply saying it for this night of fantasy, even if he simply knew how to pleasure women through years of practice, she didn't care just so long as this night he pleasured her.

His kiss tasted of salty ocean water and his body was cold and wet while hers burnt beneath him.

'There's been no one since you,' he told her. He broke the fantasy a little, yet she ached for it to be true and in response she gave in to his kiss.

His tongue was tender yet probing and she could feel his erection between her thighs. She yearned for him to enter her, yet he held back.

'I'm on the Pill,' she told him.

'That costs more, lady,' he teased. He made her laugh and he joined her, and then he stopped laughing and took her arms, which were wrapped around him, and held them above her head, so that she could not move, and could only look at him.

'I love you,' he told her, and she closed her eyes.

'Luka, don't.'

'Look at me,' he said, and she did.

'I love you.'

He was tired of holding back, tired of denying it.

'Please, please, don't just say it,' she begged. No matter how much she yearned to hear it, she could not stand that it might be a game and mere words delivered from silken lips by a man who knew what to say.

'But I do,' Luka said. He was starting to realise that Cece did need him to call the shots, and now he knew why and he went back to their conversation in the restaurant, when she had referred to him as her ex. 'Perhaps your ex should have understood that for you it's hard to believe someone might love you, when no one ever has before.'

He was so right, and so for a moment she allowed herself the bliss of believing he did as Luka took her deeply.

He moaned with relief as he slipped inside, and she gave in to bliss, to the dream that his love was hers and that the body that moved over and within her might be hers for ever.

Eyes open, she watched as he moved with her, each stroke of him inside bringing her nearer to a peak, and she gave in to his kiss and shattered to his bliss.

'Cece…' he groaned as he spilled inside her. There could be no place better than this.

In this still, dark place on a sultry night, she fell asleep in his arms and pretended this was love.

CHAPTER SIXTEEN

'I MEANT WHAT I said,' Luka told her.

She woke to his words and found he was spooned in behind her. His hand moved from her breast as he played with the stones of her necklace.

They were rubies, not glass, and way too much of a gift for a PA.

A mixed message indeed, even for him, for when it had finally arrived in his life, Luka had not recognised love either.

'Why couldn't you tell me how you felt, Cece?'

'Because so many woman have made fools of themselves over you and I didn't want to be another one of them.'

He could not argue with that.

'If it wasn't for Pandora,' Cecelia said, still facing away, 'there would be no us.'

'Had you been walking in the street that day alone, I would have called you. And,' Luka added, 'when my father died, it was you I wanted to reach out to. I told myself to wait. To get through the funeral and clear my head. I told myself I wasn't thinking straight, but I was lying because since that night with you things have never been clearer. There's been no one since you.'

She hadn't believed him when he'd told her that last

night. Cecelia had thought he was just saying the words she wanted to hear.

'I think I loved you back then but, hell, Cece, you made it hard to get close. All I can say was I loathed the thought of you being gone.'

She was starting to believe that there might be a chance for them, but her mind knew only how to doubt.

'Even if we try to make a go of it, one day you'll throw it back in my face that I kept Pandora from you...'

'Would the world end if I did?' Luka asked. He guessed that from the way life had treated her, or rather *people* had treated her, that, yes, it would seem that way to her.

He smiled that rare smile and she glimpsed a future, one where he tossed her flaw in her face and it did not end them.

'No.'

'And when—if—I do hurl it at you, perhaps you will remind me of the many women I bedded, and the flowers you ordered on my behalf, and what an ass I was...'

'Yes,' she said, torn between laughing and crying.

It was a love where perfection was not a prerequisite, one where you were allowed to mess up.

'Marry me, Cece.'

She sat up in bed and wasn't certain what she'd just heard. 'I thought we were going to take things slowly. I'll be back in a few weeks...'

'If you think I am letting you get on a plane this morning, then you don't know me at all.'

She turned and smiled.

It was the smile that felt like summer to him.

'Do you know what day it is?'

Cecelia shook her head.

'It's your birthday...'

But this year it wasn't candles and cake, or a necklace she was gifted with, but a ring.

'Were you going to ask me last night?' Cecelia gasped, as he slipped a huge diamond on her finger, faint with horror for her handling of things.

But she didn't know him completely yet, for Luka shook his head.

'No, it was always meant for this morning, because I don't want you ever to have another birthday that passed unnoticed.'

Sometimes she thought he just said the right thing, the things she wanted to hear. But this didn't feel like that. This felt real somehow.

'Come on, then!' He kicked off the sheet. 'We've a wedding to get to.'

'We can't just get married.' Cecelia laughed. 'We need approval, and what about guests and—?'

'I practically own the island,' Luka pointed out. 'I can do what I want, we can deal with the legalities later. I might just have to marry you again, but I want a wedding ring on your finger today and,' he added, 'it's never coming off.'

'But what about Pandora?'

'Where I come from, children don't generally attend their parents' wedding,' Luka said. 'Had you bothered to tell me you were pregnant we could have sorted it out and we'd have been married many months ago and Pandora wouldn't come from a broken home.'

He was throwing it all back in her face, yet she smiled.

'Luka, I don't have anything to wear.'

'Then I'll marry you in a sheet, but, Cece...' he took her arms and pinned her down, staring right into her eyes '...you have to want it too.'

'I do.'

'And you have to fight for us as well,' he said, and then halted, for she was the one who had fought for them last night. He thought of her, so shy and reserved, yet she had walked into the restaurant, and somehow forgiven his past. 'You're going to marry me now and then we're going to collect out daughter together. As a married couple, as her parents…'

Cecelia wore a silver sarong tied over one shoulder. Her hair was strawberry blonde and curly as she stood on the yacht and faced Luka.

He wore black dress pants and a fitted white shirt but no tie and he had not shaved.

It was informal, yet beautiful and impulsive too.

Yes, she might be a little more than just a visual replica of her mother, for the wanton side of her nature appeared at times. But though a sudden wedding aboard Luka Kargas's yacht might appear reckless to some, Cecelia knew that she stood before a man who was strong and who loved her.

And who would not let her fall.

The celebrant looked up at the sound of a helicopter buzzing overhead, and suggested that perhaps they move inside if they wanted to avoid being photographed.

'Sure,' Luka said, for he wanted to shield her, but as he went to take her hand and move below deck, she declined.

'It's fine.' Cecelia gave a little shake of her head. 'It will save us having to announce it.'

With him she was both brave and free.

'I love you,' he told her as he slid a wedding band on her finger. 'And if it takes the rest of my life to prove it to you, I will.'

'You already have,' Cecelia said, and then she looked into velvet brown eyes that were black when guarded. She knew him better than anyone else, and so she told him a truth. 'And I'm so proud to be your wife.'

She was.

Cecelia was proud not just of the man he was but the man he had been, for he had been strong in the face of an impossible start in life.

It meant everything to Luka to hear that.

The press got one shot—Luka Kargas on his yacht, kissing his bride, but by the time the paparazzi had got wind of the news and circled ahead, awaiting the pulse of music and wild celebrations, the happy couple had long since left.

They had somewhere else they wanted to be.

Cecelia walked up the path towards her mother-in-law's villa, feeling more than a little nervous, and saw Sophie sitting in a chair, holding Pandora. Beside them was a large silver box and a birthday and wedding breakfast awaiting.

The late-morning sun was high in the sky and there was peace in the air as they returned to their daughter... a family at last.

* * * * *

WED FOR HIS SECRET HEIR

CHANTELLE SHAW

For my gorgeous grandson Casey James

CHAPTER ONE

THE PRE-DINNER DRINKS seemed to be lasting for ever. Giannis Gekas glanced at his watch as his stomach rumbled. He had been in meetings all day and the tired-looking sandwich his PA had brought him at lunchtime had lived up to its appearance.

He sipped his Virgin Mary cocktail and considered eating the celery stalk that garnished the drink. The voices of the other guests in the banqueting hall merged into a jangle of white noise, and he edged behind a pillar to avoid having to make small talk with people he did not know and had no interest in.

It was then that he spotted a woman rearranging the place name cards on one of the circular dining tables. He supposed she might be a member of the events management team responsible for organising the charity fundraising dinner and auction. But she was wearing an evening gown, which suggested that she was a guest, and she cast a furtive glance over her shoulder as she switched the name cards.

When Giannis had taken the private lift from his penthouse suite in the exclusive London hotel, down to the foyer, he had checked the seating plan in the banqueting hall to find out where he would be sitting for the dinner. He wondered why the woman had put herself next to him.

It was not the first time such a thing had happened, he acknowledged with weary cynicism. The phenomenal success of his cruise line company had propelled him to the top of the list of Europe's richest businessmen.

He had been blessed with good looks and even before he had accrued his wealth women had pursued him, since he was a teenager taking tourists on sailing trips around the Greek islands on his family's boat. At eighteen, he had relished the attention of the countless nubile blondes who had flocked around him, but at thirty-five he was more selective.

The woman was blonde, admittedly, but she was not his type. He thought briefly of his last mistress Lise—a tall, toned Swedish swimwear model. He had dated her for a few months until she had started dropping hints about marriage. The dreaded 'm' word spelled the end of Giannis's interest, and he had ended the affair and arranged for Lise to be sent a diamond bracelet from an exclusive London jewellers, where he had an account.

Dinner would be served at seven-thirty and guests were beginning to take their places at the various tables. Giannis strolled over to where the woman was holding on tightly to the back of a chair as if she expected to be challenged for the seat. Her hair was the colour of honey and fell in silky waves to halfway down her back. As he drew closer to her, he noted that her eyes were the soft grey of rain clouds. She was attractive rather than beautiful, with defined cheekbones and a wide, pretty mouth that captured his attention. The full lips were frankly sensual, and as he watched her bite her lower lip he felt a frisson of desire to soothe the place with his tongue.

Surprised by his body's response, after he had decided that the woman did not warrant a second look, Giannis roamed his eyes over her. She was average height, with a slim waist and unfashionably curvaceous breasts and hips. Once again he felt a tightening in his groin as he allowed his gaze to linger on the creamy mounds displayed to perfection by the low-cut neckline of her black silk jersey dress.

She wore no jewellery—which was unusual at a high society event. Most of the other female guests were bedecked with gold and diamonds, and their lack of sparkling adornments focused his attention on the lustrous creaminess of her shoulders and décolleté.

He halted beside the table. 'Allow me,' he said smoothly as he drew out her chair and waited for her to sit down, before he lowered his tall frame onto the seat next to her. 'It appears that we will be companions for the evening...' he paused and glanced down at the table '... Miss Ava Sheridan.'

Wary grey eyes flew to his face. 'How do you know my name?'

'It is written on the card in front of you,' he said drily, wondering if she would explain why she had swapped the place cards.

A pink stain swept along her cheekbones but she quickly composed herself and gave him a hesitant smile. 'Oh, yes. Of course.' She caught her lower lip between her even white teeth and a flame flickered into life inside him. 'I'm pleased to meet you, Mr Gekas.'

'Giannis,' he said softly. He leaned back in his chair, turning his upper body so that he could focus his full attention on her, and smiled. With a sense of predictability, he watched her eyes darken, the pupils dilating. Charm came effortlessly to him. He had discovered when he was a youth that he had something: charisma, magnetism—whatever it was called, Giannis had it in bucketfuls. People were drawn to him. Men respected him and wanted his friendship—often only discovering after he had beaten them in a business deal that his laid-back air hid a ruthless determination to succeed. Women were fascinated by him and wanted him to take them to bed. Always.

Ava Sheridan was no different. Giannis offered her his hand and after an infinitesimal hesitation she placed her fingers in his. He lifted her hand to his mouth and she caught her breath when he brushed his lips across her knuckles.

Yes, she was attracted to him. What surprised him more was the shaft of white-hot desire that swept through him and made him uncomfortably hard. Thankfully, the lower half of his body was hidden beneath the folds of the tablecloth. He was relieved when more guests took their seats at the table and while introductions were made and waiters arrived to pour the wine and serve the first course Giannis regained control of his libido. He even felt amused by his reaction to Ava Sheridan, who was simply not in the same league as the sophisticated models and socialites he usually dated. He hadn't had sex for over a month, since he'd broken up with Lise, and celibacy did not suit him, he acknowledged wryly.

He finished his conversation with the hedge fund manager sitting on the other side of him and turned his head towards Ava, hiding a smile when she quickly jerked her gaze away. He had been aware of the numerous glances she had darted at him while he had been chatting to the other guests around the table.

As he studied the curve of her cheek and the elegant line of her neck, he realised that he had been wrong to dismiss her as merely attractive. She was beautiful, but her beauty was understated and entirely natural. Giannis suspected that she used minimal make-up to enhance her English rose complexion, and her round-as-peaches breasts did not owe their firmness to implants or a cosmetic surgeon's skill. In a room full of primped and pampered women adorned in extravagant jewellery, Ava Sheridan was like a rare and precious pearl found in the deepest depths of the ocean.

She was also as stubbornly resistant as an oyster shell, he thought, frustrated by her refusal to turn her head in his direction even though she must be aware of his scrutiny.

'Can I pour you some more wine?' He took his cue when she placed her half-empty glass down on the table. Now she could not avoid looking at him and, as their eyes met, Giannis felt the sizzle, the intangible spark of sexual attraction shoot between them.

'Just a little, thank you.' Her voice was low and melodious and made him think of cool water. A tiny frown creased her brow as she watched him top up her glass before he replaced the wine bottle in the ice bucket. 'Don't you want any wine?'

'No.' He gave her another easy smile and did not explain that he never drank alcohol.

She darted him a glance from beneath the sweep of her lashes. 'I have heard that you regularly make generous donations to charities... Giannis. And you are especially supportive of organisations which help families affected by alcohol misuse. Is there a particular reason for your interest?'

Giannis tensed and a suspicion slid into his mind as he remembered how she had contrived to sit next to him at dinner. The media were fascinated with him, and it would not be the first time that a member of the press had managed to inveigle their way onto the guest list of a social function in order to meet him. Mostly they wanted the latest gossip about his love life, but a few years ago a reporter had dug up the story from his past that he did not want to be reminded of.

Not that he could ever forget the mistake he'd made when he was nineteen, which had resulted in his father's death. The memories of that night would haunt Giannis for ever, and guilt cast a long shadow over him.

His expression hardened. 'Are you a journalist, Miss Sheridan?'

Her eyebrows rose. Either she was an accomplished actress or her surprise was genuine. 'No. Why do you think I might be?'

'You changed the seating arrangement so that we could sit together. I watched you switch the place cards.'

Colour blazed on her cheeks and if Giannis had been a different man he might have felt some sympathy for her obvious embarrassment. But he was who he was, and he felt nothing.

'I...yes, I admit I did swap the name cards,' she muttered. 'But I still don't understand why you think I am a journalist.'

'I have had experience of reporters, especially those working for the gutter press, using underhand methods to try to gain an interview with me.'

'I promise you I'm not a journalist.'

'Then why did you ensure that we would sit together?'

She bit her lip again and Giannis was irritated with himself for staring at her mouth. 'I... I was hoping to have a chance to talk to you.'

Her pretty face was flushed rose-pink but her intelligent grey eyes were honest—Giannis did not know why he was so convinced of that. The faint desperation in her unguarded expression sparked his curiosity.

'So, talk,' he said curtly.

* * *

'Not here.' Ava tore her gaze from Giannis Gekas and took a deep breath, hoping to steady the frantic thud of her pulse. She had recognised him instantly when he had walked over to the dining table where Becky, bless her, had allocated her a place. But her seat had been on the other side of the table—too far away from Giannis to be able to have a private conversation with him.

She had taken a gamble that no one would notice her swapping the name cards around. But she *had* to talk to Giannis about her brother. She'd forked out a fortune for a ticket to the charity dinner and bought an expensive evening dress that she'd probably never have the chance to wear again. The only way she could keep Sam from being sent to a young offender institution was if she could persuade Giannis Gekas to drop the charges against him.

Ava took a sip of her wine. It was important that she kept a clear head and she hadn't intended to drink any alcohol tonight, but she had not expected Giannis to be so *devastatingly* attractive. The photos she'd seen of him on the Internet when she'd researched the man dubbed Greece's most eligible bachelor had not prepared her for the way her heart had crashed into her ribs when he'd smiled. Handsome did not come close to describing his lethal good looks. His face was a work of art— the sculpted cheekbones and chiselled jaw softened by a blatantly sensual mouth that frequently curved into a lazy smile.

Dark, almost black eyes gleamed beneath heavy brows, and he constantly shoved a hand through his thick, dark brown hair that fell forwards onto his brow. But even more enticing than his model-perfect features and tall, muscle-packed body was Giannis's rampant sexuality.

He oozed charisma and he promised danger and excitement—the very things that Ava avoided. She gave herself a mental shake. It did not matter that Giannis was a bronzed Greek god. All she cared about was saving her idiot of a kid brother from prison and the very real possibility that Sam would be drawn into a life of crime like their father.

Sam wasn't bad; he had just gone off the rails because he lacked guidance. Ava knew that her mother had struggled to cope when Sam had hit puberty and he'd got in with a rough crowd of teenagers who hung around on the streets near the family home in East London. Even worse, Sam had become fascinated with their father and had even reverted to using the name McKay rather than their mother's maiden name, Sheridan. Ava had been glad to move away from the East End and all its associations with her father, but she felt guilty that she had not been around to keep her brother out of trouble.

She took another sip of wine and her eyes were drawn once more to the man sitting next to her. Sam's future rested in Giannis Gekas's hands. A waiter appeared and removed her goat's cheese salad starter that she had barely touched and replaced it with the Dover sole that she had chosen for the main course. Across the table, one of the other guests was trying to catch Giannis's attention. The chance to have a meaningful conversation with him during dinner seemed hopeless.

'I can't talk to you here.' She caught her bottom lip between her teeth and a quiver ran through her when his eyes focused on her mouth. She wondered why he suddenly seemed tense. 'Would it be possible for me to speak to you in private after dinner?'

His dark eyes trapped her gaze but his expression was unreadable. Afraid that he was about to refuse her request, she acted instinctively and placed her hand over his where it rested on the tablecloth. '*Please.*'

The warmth of his olive-gold skin beneath her fingertips sent heat racing up her arm. She attempted to snatch her hand away but Giannis captured her fingers in his.

'That depends on whether you are an entertaining dinner companion,' he murmured. He smiled at her confused expression and stroked his thumb lightly over the pulse in her wrist that was going crazy. 'Relax, *glykiá mou.* I think there is every possibility that we can have a private discussion later.'

'Thank you.' Relief flooded through her. But she could not relax as concern for her brother changed to a different kind of tension that had everything to do with the glitter in Giannis's eyes. She couldn't look away from his sensual mouth. His jaw was shadowed with black stubble and she wondered if it would feel abrasive against her cheek if he kissed her. If she kissed him back.

She took another sip of wine before she remembered that she hadn't had any lunch. Alcohol had a more potent effect on an empty stomach, she reminded herself. Her appetite had disappeared but she forced herself to eat a couple of forkfuls of Dover sole.

'So tell me, Ava—you have a beautiful name, by the way.' Giannis's husky accent felt like rough velvet stroking across Ava's skin, and the way he said her name in his lazy, sexy drawl, elongating the vowels—*Aaavaaa*—sent a quiver of reaction through her. 'You said that you are not a journalist, so what do you do for a living?'

Explaining about her work as a victim care officer might be awkward when Giannis was himself the victim of a crime which had been committed by her brother, Ava thought ruefully. Sam deeply regretted the extensive damage that he and his so-called 'friends' had caused to

Giannis's luxurious yacht. She needed to convince Giannis that her brother had made a mistake and deserved another chance.

She reached for her wine glass, but then changed her mind. Her head felt swimmy—although that might be because she had inhaled the spicy, explicitly sensual scent of Giannis's aftershave.

'Actually I'm between jobs at the moment.' She was pleased that her voice was steady, unlike her see-sawing emotions. 'I recently moved from Scotland back to London to be closer to my mother...and brother.'

Giannis ate some of his beef Wellington before he spoke. 'I have travelled widely, but Scotland is one place that I have never visited. I've heard that it is very beautiful.'

Ava thought of the deprived areas of Glasgow where she had been involved with a victim support charity, first as a volunteer, and after graduating from university she had been offered a job with the victim support team. In the past few years some of the city's grim, grey tower blocks had been knocked down and replaced with new houses, but high levels of unemployment still remained, as did the incidence of drug-taking, violence and crime.

She had felt that her job as a VCO—helping people who were victims or witnesses of crime—made amends in some small way for the terrible crimes her father had committed. But living far away in Scotland meant she had missed the signs that her brother had been drawn into the gang culture in East London. Her father's old haunts.

'Why do you care what I get up to?' Sam had demanded when she had tried to talk to him about his behaviour. 'You moved away and you don't care about me.' Ava felt a familiar stab of guilt that she hadn't been around for Sam or her mother when they had both needed her.

She dragged her thoughts back to the present and realised that Giannis was waiting for her to reply. 'The Highlands have some spectacular scenery,' she told him. 'If you are thinking of making a trip to Scotland I can recommend a few places for you to visit.'

'It would be better if you came with me and gave me a guided tour of the places you think would interest me.'

Ava's heart gave a jolt. *Was he being serious?* She stared into his dark-as-night eyes and saw amusement and something else that evoked a coiling sensation low in her belly. 'We...we don't know each other.'

'Not yet, but the night is still young and full of endless possibilities,' he murmured in his husky Mediterranean accent that made her toes curl. He gave a faint shrug of his shoulders, drawing her attention to his powerful physique beneath the elegant lines of his dinner jacket. 'I have little leisure time and it makes sense when I visit somewhere new to take a companion who has local knowledge.'

Ava was saved from having to reply when one of the event organisers arrived at the table to hand out catalogues which listed the items that were being offered in the fundraising auction.

Giannis flicked through the pages of the catalogue. 'Is there anything in the listings that you intend to bid for?'

'Unfortunately I can't afford the kind of money that a platinum watch or a luxury African safari holiday are likely to fetch in the auction,' she said drily. 'I imagine that art collectors will be keen to bid for the Mark Derring painting. His work is stunning, and art tends to be a good investment. There are also some interesting wines being auctioned. The Chateau Latour 1962 is bound to create a lot of interest.'

Giannis gave her a thoughtful look. 'So, I have already discovered that you are an expert in art and wine. I confess that I am intrigued by you, Ava.'

She gave a self-conscious laugh. 'I'm not an expert in either subject, but I went to a finishing school in Switzerland where I learned how to talk confidently about art, recognise fine wines and understand the finer points of international etiquette.'

'I did not realise that girls—I presume only girls—still went to finishing schools,' Giannis said. 'What made you decide to go to one?'

'My father thought it would be a good experience for me.' Ava felt a familiar tension in her shoulders as she thought of her father. The truth was that she tried not to think about Terry McKay. That part of her life when she had been Ava McKay was over. She had lost touch with the friends she had made at the Institut Maison Cécile in St Moritz when her father had been sent to prison. But the few months that she had spent at the exclusive finishing school, which had numbered two European princesses among its students, had given her the social skills and exquisite manners which allowed her to feel comfortable at high society events.

It was a pity that the finishing school had not given advice on how to behave when a gorgeous Greek god looked at her as if he was imagining her naked, Ava thought as her eyes locked with Giannis's smouldering gaze. Panic and an inexplicable sense of excitement pumped through her veins. She was here at the charity dinner for her brother's sake, she reminded herself. Giannis had said he would give her an opportunity to speak to him in private on the condition that she entertained him during dinner.

She did not know if he had been serious, but she could not risk losing the chance to plead with him to show leniency to Sam.

'It's not fair,' she murmured. She had to lean towards Giannis so that he could hear her above the hum of chatter in the banqueting hall, and the scent of him—spicy cologne mixed with an elusive scent of male pheromones—made her head spin. 'I have told you things about me but you haven't told me anything about yourself.'

'That's not true. I've told you that I have never visited Scotland. Although I have a feeling that I will take a trip there very soon,' he drawled. His voice was indulgent like rich cream and the gleam in his eyes was wickedly suggestive.

A sensuous shiver ran down Ava's spine. Common sense dictated that she should respond to Giannis's outrageous flirting with cool amusement and make a witty remark to put him in his place and let him know she wasn't interested in him. Except that he fascinated her, and she felt like a teenager on a first date rather than an experienced woman of twenty-seven.

She wasn't all that experienced, a little voice in her head reminded her. At university she'd dated a few guys but the relationships had fizzled out fairly quickly. It had been her fault—she'd been wary of allowing anyone too close in case they discovered that she was leading a double life. Two years ago, she had met Craig at a party given by a work colleague. She had been attracted to his open and friendly nature and when they had become lovers she'd believed that they might have a future together. A year into their relationship, she had plucked up the courage and revealed her real identity. But Craig had reacted with horror to the news that she was the daughter of the infamous London gangland boss Terry McKay.

'How could we have a family when there is a risk that our children might inherit your father's criminal genes?' Craig had said, with no trace of warmth in his voice and a look of distaste on his face that had filled Ava with shame.

'Criminality isn't an inherited condition,' she had argued. But she continued to be haunted by Craig's words. Perhaps there *was* a 'criminal gene' that could be passed down through generations and she would not be able to save Sam from a life of crime.

Ava forced her mind away from the past. She refused to believe that her kind, funny younger brother could become a violent criminal like their father. But the statistics of youths reoffending after being sent to prison were high. She needed to keep her nerve and seize the right moment to throw herself on Giannis's mercy.

In normal circumstances Ava would have found the bidding process at the charity auction fascinating. The sums of money that some of the items fetched were staggering—and far beyond anything her finances could stretch to. Giannis offered the highest bid of a six-figure sum for a luxury spa break at an exclusive resort in the Maldives for two people. Ava wondered who he planned to take with him. No doubt he had several mistresses to choose from. But if he wanted more variety, she was sure that any one of the women in the banqueting hall who she had noticed sending him covetous glances would jump at the chance to spend four days—and nights—with a gorgeous, wealthy Greek god. Giannis was reputed to have become a billionaire from his successful luxury cruise line company, The Gekas Experience.

'Congratulations on your winning bid for the spa

break. I don't blame you for deciding that a visit to the Maldives would be more enjoyable than a trip to Scotland,' she said, unable to prevent the faint waspishness in her voice as she pictured him cavorting in a tropical paradise with a supermodel.

'I bought the spa break for my mother and sister. My mother has often said that she would like to visit the Maldives, and at least my sister will be pleased.' There was an odd nuance in Giannis's tone. 'Perhaps the trip will make my mother happy, but I doubt it,' he said heavily.

Ava looked at him curiously, wanting to know more about his family. He had seemed tense when he spoke about his mother, but she was heartened to know that he had a sister and perhaps he would understand why she was so anxious to save her brother from a prison sentence.

The auction continued, but she was barely aware of what was going on around her and her senses were finely attuned to the man seated beside her. While she sipped her coffee and pretended to study the auction catalogue she tried not to stare at Giannis's strong, tanned hands as he picked up his coffee cup. But her traitorous imagination visualised his hands sliding over her naked body, cupping her breasts in his palms as he bent his head to take each of her nipples into his mouth.

Sweet heaven! What had got into her? Hot-faced, she tensed when he moved his leg beneath the table and she felt his thigh brush against hers. He turned his head towards her, amusement gleaming in his eyes when he saw the hectic flush on her cheeks.

'It is rather warm in here, isn't it?' he murmured.

She was on fire and desperate to escape to the restroom so that she could hold her wrists under the cold tap to try to bring her temperature down. Perhaps spending a few minutes away from Giannis would allow her to regain her composure. 'Please excuse me,' she muttered as she shoved her chair back and stood up abruptly.

'*Ow!*' For a few seconds she could not understand why scalding liquid was soaking into the front of her dress. The reason became clear when she saw a waiter hovering close by. He was holding a cafetière, and she guessed that he had leaned over her shoulder in order to refill her coffee cup at the same time that she had jumped up and knocked into him.

'I am so sorry, madam.'

'It's all right—it was my fault,' Ava choked, wanting to die of embarrassment. She hated being the centre of attention but everyone at the table, everyone in the banqueting room, it seemed, was looking at her. The head waiter hurried over and added his profuse apologies to those of the waiter who had spilled the coffee.

Giannis had risen from his seat. 'Were you burned by the hot coffee?' His deep voice was calm in the midst of the chaos.

'I think I'm all right. My dress took the brunt of it.' The coffee was cooling as it soaked through the material, but her dress was drenched and her attempts to blot the liquid with her napkin were ineffective. At least it was a black dress and the coffee stain might wash out, Ava thought. But she couldn't spend the rest of the evening in her wet dress and she would have to go home without having had an opportunity to speak to Giannis about her brother.

The hotel manager had been called and he arrived at the table to add his apologies and reprimand the hapless waiter. 'Really, it's my fault,' Ava tried to explain. She just wanted to get out of the banqueting hall, away from the curious stares of the other diners.

'Come with me.' Giannis slipped his hand under her elbow, and she was relieved when he escorted her out of the room. She knew she would have to call for a taxi to take her home, but while she was searching in her bag for her phone she barely noticed that they had stepped into a lift until the doors slid smoothly shut.

'We will go to my hotel suite so that you can use the bathroom to freshen up, and meanwhile I'll arrange for your dress to be laundered,' Giannis answered her unspoken question.

Ava was about to say that there was no need for him to go to all that trouble. But it occurred to her that while she waited for her dress to be cleaned she would have the perfect opportunity to ask him to drop the charges against her brother. Was it sensible to go to a hotel room with a man she had never met before? questioned her common sense. This might be her only chance to save Sam, she reminded herself.

The doors opened and she discovered that the lift had brought them directly to Giannis's suite. Ignoring the lurch of her heart, she followed him across the vast sitting room. 'The bathroom is through there,' he said, pointing towards a door. 'There is a spare robe that you can use and I'll call room service and have someone collect your dress. Would you like some more wine, or coffee?'

'I think I've had enough coffee for one night.' She gave him a rueful smile and her stomach muscles tightened when his eyes focused intently on her mouth.

She had definitely had enough wine, Ava thought as she shot into the opulent marble-tiled bathroom and locked the door, before releasing her breath on a shaky sigh. It must be her out-of-control imagination that made her think she had seen a predatory hunger in Giannis's gaze. She wondered if he looked at every woman that way, and made them feel as though they were the most beautiful, the most desirable woman he had ever met. Probably. Giannis had a reputation as a playboy and he possessed an effortless charm that was irresistible.

But not to her. She was immune to Giannis's magnetism, she assured herself. As she stripped off her coffee-soaked dress and reached for the folded towelling robe on a shelf, she caught sight of her reflection in the mirror above the vanity unit. Her face was flushed and her eyes looked huge beneath her fringe. Usually she wore her hair up in a chignon but tonight she had left it loose and it reached halfway down her back. The layers that the hairdresser had cut into it made her hair look thick and lustrous, gleaming like spun gold beneath the bright bathroom light.

Ava stared at herself in the mirror, startled by her transformation from ordinary and unexciting to a sensual Siren. She had bought a seamless black bra to wear beneath her dress and her nipples were visible through the semi-transparent cups. The matching black thong that she had worn for practical reasons—so that she would not have a visible panty-line—was the most daring piece of lingerie she had ever owned.

She ran her hands over her smooth thighs above the lacy bands of her hold-up stockings and felt a delicious ache low in her pelvis. She felt sexy and seductive for the first time since Craig had dumped her as she pictured Giannis's reaction if he saw her in her revealing underwear.

She shook her head. It must be the effects of the wine that had lowered her inhibitions and filled her mind with erotic images. Cursing her wayward thoughts, she slipped her arms into the robe and tied the belt firmly around her waist. Of course he was not going to see her underwear. She had come to his hotel suite for one purpose only— to ask him to give her brother another chance. Taking a deep breath, Ava opened the bathroom door and prepared to throw herself on Giannis Gekas's mercy.

CHAPTER TWO

HE WAS SPRAWLED on a sofa, his long legs stretched out in front of him and his arms lying along the back of the cushions. He had removed his jacket and tie and unfastened the top few shirt buttons, to reveal a vee of olive-gold skin and a sprinkling of black chest hairs. Giannis looked indolent and yet Ava sensed that beneath his civilised veneer he was a buccaneer who lived life by his rules and ruthlessly took what he wanted. Plenty of women would want to try to tame him but she was sure that none would succeed. Giannis Gekas answered to no one, and her nerve almost deserted her.

He stood up as she entered the sitting room and walked over to take her dress from her. 'I rinsed out most of the coffee and wrung out as much water as I could,' she explained as she handed him the soggy bundle of material.

'I have been assured that your dress will be laundered and returned to you as quickly as possible,' he told her as he strode across the room and opened the door of the suite to give the dress to a member of the hotel's staff who was waiting in the corridor.

Giannis closed the door and came back to Ava. 'I ordered you some English tea and some petits fours,' he said, indicating the silver tea service on the low table in front of the sofa. 'Please, sit down.'

'Thank you.' She tore her eyes from him, her attention caught by a large canvas leaning against the wall. 'That's the Mark Derring painting from the auction.'

'I followed your advice and bid for it. You were sitting next to me,' he reminded her in a sardonic voice that made her think he was remembering how she had swapped the place name cards. 'Didn't you realise that I had offered the highest bid for the painting?'

Heat spread across her face. She could hardly admit that she had been so busy trying to hide her fierce awareness of him that she hadn't taken much notice of the auction. Giannis gave one of his lazy smiles, as if he knew how fast her heart was beating, and Ava forgot to breathe as she was trapped by the gleam in his eyes. She did not remember when he had moved closer to her, but she was conscious of how much taller than her he was when she had to tilt her head to look at his face.

He was utterly gorgeous, but it was not just his impossibly handsome features that made her feel weak and oddly vulnerable. Self-assurance shimmered from him and, combined with his simmering sensuality, it was a potent mix that made her head spin.

'Congratulations on winning the painting in the auction,' she murmured, desperate to say something and shatter the spell that his fathomless dark eyes and his far too sexy smile had cast on her. She was stupidly flattered that he had taken her advice about the artwork. Her self-confidence had been knocked by Craig's attitude when she'd admitted that she was the daughter of one of the UK's most notorious criminals. Thinking of her father reminded her of her brother, and she sank down onto the sofa while she mentally prepared what she was going to say to Giannis. It did not help her thought process when he sat down next to her.

'Help yourself to a petit four,' he said, offering her the plate of irresistible sweet delicacies.

'I shouldn't,' Ava murmured ruefully as she reached for a chocolate truffle. She bit into it and gave a blissful sigh when it melted, creamy and delicious, on her tongue. 'Chocolate is my weakness, unfortunately.'

He shrugged. 'Are you one of those women who starve themselves because the fashion industry dictates that the feminine figure should be stick-thin?'

'I think it's patently obvious that I don't starve myself,' she said drily. The belt of the towelling robe had worked loose and she flushed when she glanced down and saw that the front was gaping open, revealing the upper slopes of her breasts above her bra. She quickly pulled the lapels of the robe together.

'I am glad to hear it. Women should have curves.' Giannis looked deeply into her eyes and the heat in his gaze caused her heart to skip a beat. 'Before the regrettable incident with the coffee you looked stunning in your dress, and you have an exquisite figure, Ava,' he said softly. 'I am flattered that you wanted to sit next to me at dinner.'

Clearly, Giannis believed she had swapped the name cards because she was interested in him, but her motive had been completely different. Ava swallowed. 'I need to…' She did not finish her sentence and her breath caught in her throat when he lifted his hand and lightly brushed his thumb pad across the corner of her mouth.

'You had chocolate on your lips,' he murmured, showing her the smear of chocolate on his thumb that he had removed from her mouth. Her eyes widened when he put his thumb into his own mouth.

How could such an innocuous gesture seem so erotic? She was mesmerised as she watched his tongue flick out to lick his thumb clean. Unconsciously her own tongue darted out to moisten her lips and the feral growl that Giannis gave caused her stomach muscles to clench.

Remember why you are here, Ava ordered herself. But it was impossible to think about her brother when Giannis shifted along the sofa so that he was much too close. Her heart was thumping so hard in her chest that she was surprised it wasn't audible. It felt unreal to be in a luxurious hotel room with a devastatingly gorgeous man who was looking at her as if she was his ultimate fantasy. Somewhere in a distant recess of her brain she knew she should deliver her rehearsed speech, but her sense of unreality deepened when Giannis lifted his hand and stroked her cheek before he captured her chin between his fingers.

'What are you doing?' she gasped. It was imperative that she should seize her chance to talk to him about Sam.

'I would like to kiss you, beautiful Ava.' His voice was soft like velvet caressing her senses. 'And I think that perhaps you would like me to kiss you? Am I right? Do you want me to do this...?' He brushed his mouth over hers, tantalising her with a promise of sweeter delight to follow.

On one level Ava was appalled that she was allowing a stranger to kiss her, but she did not pull away when Giannis slid his hand beneath her hair to cup her nape and drew her towards him.

Sexual chemistry had fizzed between them from the moment they had set eyes on one another, she acknowledged. Neither of them had eaten much at dinner because they had been sending each other loaded glances. She could not fight her body's instinctive response to Giannis and with a helpless sigh she parted her lips. A tremor ran through her when he kissed her again and reality disappeared.

It was as though she had been flung to the far reaches of the universe where nothing existed but Giannis's lips moving over hers, tasting her, enticing her. His warm breath filled her mouth and she felt the intoxicating heat of his body through his white shirt when she placed her hands flat on his chest.

In a minute she would end this madness and push him away, she assured herself. She had been curious to know what it would be like to be kissed by an expert. And Giannis was certainly an expert. Ava did not have much experience of men but she recognised his mastery in the bone-shaking sensuality of his caresses.

He lifted his mouth from hers and trailed his lips over her cheek and up to her ear, exploring its delicate shape with his tongue before he gently nipped her earlobe with his teeth. A quiver ran through her and she arched her neck as he kissed his way down her throat and nuzzled the dip where her collarbone joined. Her skin felt scorched by the heat of his mouth. She wanted more—she wanted to feel his lips everywhere, tasting her and tantalising her with sensual promise.

At last he lifted his head. He was breathing hard. Ava stared at him with wide, unfocused eyes. She had never felt so aroused before, except in her dreams. Perhaps this was a dream, and if so she did not want to wake up.

'Your skin is marked where that idiot waiter spilled boiling-hot coffee down you,' Giannis murmured. She followed his gaze and saw that the front of her robe had fallen open again. There was a patch of pink skin on the upper slope of one breast.

'It's nothing.' She tried to close the robe but he brushed her hand away and deftly untied the belt before he stood up and drew her to her feet. It was as if she were trapped in a strange dreamlike state where she could not speak, and she did not protest when he pushed the robe off her shoulders and it fell to the floor.

Giannis rocked back on his heels and subjected her to a slow, intense scrutiny, starting with her stiletto-heeled shoes and moving up her stockings-clad legs and the expanse of creamy skin above her lacy stocking tops. Ava could not move, could hardly breathe as his gaze lingered on her black silk thong before he finally raised his eyes to her breasts with their pointed nipples jutting provocatively beneath the semi-transparent bra cups.

'*Eísai ómorfi,*' he said hoarsely.

Even if she hadn't understood the Greek words—which translated to English meant *you are beautiful*—there was no mistaking the heat in his gaze, the hunger that made his eyes glitter like polished jet. Ava knew she wasn't really beautiful. Passably attractive was a more realistic description. But Giannis had sounded as if he genuinely thought she was beautiful. The desire blazing in his eyes restored some of her pride that had been decimated by Craig's rejection.

Soon she would end this madness, she assured herself again. But for a few moments she wanted to relish the sense of feminine power that swept through her when Giannis reached for her and she saw that his hand was shaking. Europe's most sought-after playboy was *shaking* with desire for her. It was a heady feeling. A wildness came over her, a longing to just once throw off the restraints she had imposed on herself since she was seventeen and had discovered the truth about Terry McKay.

When she was younger she had never told anyone that her father was a criminal, but the strain of keeping her shameful secret had meant that she was always on her guard. Even with Craig, she had never been able to completely relax and enjoy sex. She'd assumed she had a low

sex drive, but now the fire in her blood and the thunderous drumbeat of desire in her veins revealed a passionate, sensual woman who ached for fulfilment.

Giannis pulled her into his arms and crushed her
against his broad chest, making her aware of how strong
he was, how muscular and *male* compared to her soft
female body. But she was strong too, she realised, feeling him shudder when she arched into him so that the
hard points of her nipples pressed against his chest. He
claimed her mouth, his lips urgent, demanding her response, and with a low moan she melted into his heat
and fire. She kissed him back with a fervency that drew
a harsh groan from his throat when at last he lifted his
head and stared into her eyes.

'I want you,' he said in a rough voice that made her
tremble deep inside. 'You drive me insane, lovely Ava.
I want to see you naked in my bed. I want to touch your
body and discover all your secrets, and then I want to...'
He lowered his head and whispered in her ear in explicit
detail all that he wanted to do to her.

Ava's stomach dipped. Somewhere back in the real
world the voice of her common sense urged her to stop,
now, before she did something she might regret later. But
another voice insisted that if she let this moment, this man
slip away she would regret it for ever. She did not understand what had happened to sensible Ava Sheridan, but
shockingly she did not care. Only one thing was in her
mind, in her blood. *Desire, desire*—it pulsed through her
veins and made her forget everything but the exquisite
sensations Giannis was creating when he cupped one of
her breasts in his hand and stroked her nipple through
the gossamer-fine bra cup.

She gave a low moan as he slipped his hand inside her
bra and played with her nipple, rolling the hard peak be-

tween his fingers, causing exquisite sensation to shoot down to that other pleasure point between her legs. '*Oh*.' She would die if he did not touch her *there* where she ached to feel his hands.

His soft laughter made her blush scarlet when she realised that she had spoken the words out loud. 'Come with me.' Giannis caught hold of her hand and something—disappointment? Frustration?—tautened his features when she hesitated. 'What is it?'

She wanted to tell him that she did not have one-night stands and she had never, ever had sex with a stranger. She wasn't impetuous or daring. She was old before her time, Ava thought bleakly. Just for once she wanted to be the sexually confident woman that Giannis clearly believed she was.

He smiled, his eyes lit with a sensual warmth that made her insides melt. 'What's wrong?' he said softly, lifting his hand to brush her hair back from her face. The oddly tender gesture dispelled her doubts and the hunger in his gaze caused a sensuous heat to pool between her thighs.

'Nothing is wrong,' she assured him in a breathy voice she did not recognise as her own. She slid her hands over his shirt and undid the rest of the buttons before she pushed the material aside and skimmed her palms over his bare chest. His skin felt like silk overlaid with wiry black hairs that arrowed down to the waistband of his trousers. She heard him draw a quick breath when she stroked her fingertips along his zip.

'You're sure?'

She didn't want to step out of the fantasy and question what she was doing. The new, bold Ava tilted her head to one side and sent him a lingering look from beneath the sweep of her lashes. 'What are you waiting for?' she murmured.

He laughed—a low, husky sound that caused the tiny hairs on her skin to stand on end. Every cell of her body was acutely aware of him and the promise in his glittering dark eyes sent a shiver of excitement through her.

Without saying another word, he led her by the hand into the bedroom. Ava was vaguely aware of the sophisticated décor and the lamps dimmed so that they emitted a soft golden glow. In the centre of the room was an enormous bed. Someone—presumably the chambermaid—had earlier turned back the bedspread and Ava's heart skipped a beat when she saw black silk sheets.

The four-poster bed had been designed for seduction, for passion, and it occurred to her that Giannis would surely not have intended to spend the night alone. Perhaps he regularly picked up women for sex. The slightly unsettling thought quickly faded from her mind and anticipation prickled across her skin when he shrugged off his shirt and deftly removed his shoes and socks before he unzipped his trousers and stepped out of them.

He was magnificent—lean-hipped and with a powerfully muscular chest and impressive six-pack. In the lamplight his skin gleamed like polished bronze, his chest and thighs overlaid with black hairs. Her gaze dropped lower to his tight black boxer shorts which could not conceal his arousal, and the growl he gave as she stared at him evoked a primitive need to feel him inside her.

'Take off your bra,' he ordered.

Her stomach flipped. She would have preferred him to undress her, and on some level her brain recognised that he was giving her the opportunity to change her mind. He wasn't going to force her to do anything she did not want to do. She roamed her eyes over his gorgeous body and desire rolled through her. Slowly she reached behind her back and unclipped her bra, letting the cups fall away from her breasts.

Giannis swallowed audibly. 'Beautiful.' His voice was oddly harsh, as if he was struggling to keep himself under control. He shook his head when she put her hands on the lacy tops of her hold-up stockings and prepared to roll them down her legs. 'Leave them on,' he growled. 'And your shoes.' He closed the gap between them in one stride and pulled her into his arms so that her bare breasts pressed against his naked chest. Ava felt a shudder run through him. *'Se thélo,'* he muttered.

She knew the Greek words meant *I want you* and she was left in no doubt when he circled his hips against hers and she felt the solid ridge of his arousal straining beneath his boxers. Driven beyond reason by a hunger she had never felt before, had never believed she was capable of feeling, she slipped her hand into the waistband of his boxers and curled her hand around him.

'Witch.' He pulled off his boxer shorts and kicked them away. Ava felt a momentary doubt when she saw how hugely aroused he was. But then he scooped her up and laid her down on the bed, and the feel of his hard, male, totally naked body pressing down on her blew away the last of her inhibitions. She trapped his face between her hands and tugged his mouth down to hers, arching against him when he claimed her lips in a devastating kiss.

It was wild and hot, passion swiftly spiralling out of control and shooting her beyond the stratosphere to a place she had never been before, where there was only the sensation of his warm skin pressed against hers and his seeking hands exploring her body and finding her pleasure spots with unerring precision.

'*Oh.*' She gave a thin cry when Giannis bent his head to her breast and flicked his tongue back and forth across its distended peak.

'Do you like that?' His voice was indulgent as if he knew how much she liked what he was doing to her, but Ava was too spellbound by him to worry about his arrogance. She sighed with pleasure when he drew her nipple into his mouth and sucked hard so that she almost climaxed right then. He transferred his attention to her other breast and she dug her fingers into his buttocks, feeling the awesome length of his erection pushing between her legs. There was no thought in her head to deny him, when to do so would deny her the orgasm that she could already sense building deep in her pelvis.

Somehow he untangled their limbs and shifted across the mattress. Frantically she grabbed hold of him and he laughed softly. Ignoring her hands tugging at him, he reached for his wallet on the bedside table and took out a condom. 'You *are* eager, aren't you?' he murmured. 'Here—' he put the condom into her hand '—you put it on for me.'

Ava fumbled with the foil packet, not wanting to admit that she had never opened a condom before. Craig had always prepared himself for sex, and when they had made love it had been over quickly, leaving her dissatisfied and convinced that the problem lay with her.

Finally she managed to tear the foil with her fingernail and then unrolled the condom down his length.

'*Theos*, you're going to kill me.' His chest heaved when she finally completed her task. He pushed aside her flimsy black silk thong and stroked his fingers over her silken flesh, parting her so that he could slide one finger inside her.

It felt amazing but it wasn't enough—not nearly

enough. Ava could hear her panting breaths as she lifted her hips towards his hand, needing more, needing him... 'Please...'

'I know,' he growled. She heard a ripping sound as he tore her thong, and then he simply took her with a hard, deep thrust that expelled the breath from her lungs in a shocked gasp.

He stilled and stared down at her, his shoulder muscles bunching as he supported himself on his hands. The lamplight cast shadows over his face, emphasising the angles and planes of his chiselled features. A beautiful stranger who had claimed her body. 'Did I hurt you?' The concern in his voice touched her heart.

'No...' She clutched his shoulders as she felt him start to withdraw. The shock of his penetration was receding and her internal muscles stretched so that she could take him deeper inside her, filling her, fulfilling her most secret fantasies when he began to move.

He must have sensed that he needed to slow the pace and at first he was almost gentle as he circled his hips against hers and kissed her breasts and throat, making his way up to her mouth to push his tongue between her lips while he drove deep inside her.

She arched her hips to meet each stroke, unaware of the frantic cries she made as he established a powerful rhythm. He thrust deeper, harder, taking her higher until she clawed her nails down his back, desperate to reach a place that she had never managed to reach before, except when she pleasured herself.

He laughed softly. 'Relax, and it'll happen.'

'It won't. I can't...' Ava gave a sob of frustration. There must be something wrong with her that made it impossible for her to reach an orgasm during sex.

She felt Giannis slip his hand between their joined

bodies and then he did something magical with his fingers, while he continued his rhythmic thrusts, faster, faster...

It felt so good. The way he expertly moved his hand, as if he knew exactly how to give her the utmost pleasure. It felt unbelievably good and the pressure inside her was building, building to a crescendo. Suddenly she was there, suspended for timeless seconds on the edge of ecstasy before the wave crashed over her and swept her up in a maelstrom of intense pleasure that went on and on, pulsing, pounding through her, tearing a low cry from her throat.

Even when the ripples of her orgasm started to fade, he continued to move inside her with an urgency that took her breath away. He gripped her hips and reared over her, his head thrown back so that the cords on his neck stood out. Incredibly, Ava climaxed for a second time, swift and sharp, as Giannis gave a final thrust and emitted a savage groan as he pressed his face into her neck while great shudders racked his body.

In the afterglow, a sense of peace enfolded her and she lay quite still, not wanting him to move away, not ready to face the reality of what had just happened. Gradually the thunderous beat of his heart slowed. She loved the feel of his big, strong body lying lax on top of her and of his arms around her, holding her close. Her limbs felt heavy and the lingering ripples of her orgasm triggered delicious tingles deep in her pelvis.

So *that* was what poets wrote sonnets about, she thought, smiling to herself. There wasn't something wrong with her, as Craig had suggested. Sex with Giannis had been mind-blowing and had proved that her body was capable of experiencing the most intense passion. From Giannis's reaction he had enjoyed having sex with her. She wasn't frigid. She was a responsive, sexually confident woman.

He lifted his head at last and looked down at her, his dark eyes unfathomable, making Ava realise once again that even though they had just shared the most intimate act that two people could experience, she did not know him. Oh, she'd gleaned a few facts about him on the Internet. Mainly about his business success or which model or actress he'd dated, although there was actually very little information about him. She knew nothing about the real Giannis Gekas—his family, his interests, even mundane things such as what kind of food he liked. There was an endless list of unknowns—all the tiny snippets of information that people at the beginning of a conventional relationship would find out about each other.

All she knew was that they had been drawn together by a combustible sexual chemistry, and when she became aware of him hardening once more while he was still buried deep inside her, nothing else mattered.

'You are irresistible, *omorfiá mou*,' he murmured. 'I want you again.'

Excitement coiled through her and she wrapped her legs around his back to draw him deeper inside her. He groaned. 'You would tempt a saint. But first I need to change the condom. Don't go away.' He dropped a brief but utterly sensual kiss on her mouth—a promise of further delights to follow—before he lifted himself off her and strode into the bathroom.

Ava watched him, her gaze clinging to his broad shoulders before sliding lower to the taut curves of his buttocks, and molten heat pooled between her thighs. Everything about tonight felt unreal, as if she was in the middle of an erotic dream that she did not want to end.

CHAPTER THREE

GIANNIS STEPPED OUT of the shower cubicle and blotted the moisture from his skin before he knotted a towel around his hips and walked into the bedroom. He glanced at the bed and saw that Ava was still fast asleep. Her honey-blonde hair spilled across the black silk pillows and her hand was tucked under her cheek. She looked young and unexpectedly innocent but looks were deceptive and there had been no hint of the ingénue about her last night.

The memory of her standing in front of him in stiletto heels, sheer black stockings and a minuscule pair of knickers had a predictable effect on his body, and he was tempted to whip off his towel and wake her for morning sex. But there wasn't time, and he felt no more than a fleeting regret as he turned away from the bed, striding over to the wardrobe to select a shirt to wear with his suit. While he dressed, he thought about his schedule for the day.

He had meetings in Paris in the afternoon and a social function to attend in the evening. But first he planned to drive to his house in Hertfordshire that he had recently purchased, to inspect the renovations that had been completed and pay the workmen a bonus. It would be useful to have a permanent base in the UK, but another reason he had bought Milton Grange was because the grounds included a particularly fine garden. Giannis hoped that his mother might like to visit the house in the summer, and perhaps tending to the roses would lift her spirits, which had been low lately. Although there was nothing new about that, he thought heavily.

He had spent most of his adult life trying to make his mother happy. His conscience insisted that caring for her was a small penance and could never atone for his terrible lapse of judgement that had resulted in the death of his father. He despised himself even more because he found his mother difficult. Even his sister had suggested that their *mitera's* relentless misery was intended to make him feel guilty.

Giannis sighed as his thoughts switched from his mother to another thorn in his side. Ever since Stefanos Markou had announced that he intended to sell Markou Shipping and retire from business, Giannis had tried to persuade the old man to sell his ships to him. The Markou fleet of six small cargo ships would be an ideal addition to The Gekas Experience.

TGE already operated ten vessels offering luxurious cruises around the Mediterranean and the Caribbean. River cruising was becoming increasingly popular and Giannis wanted to expand the company and make TGE the world leader in this emerging tourist market. The Markou fleet of ships would need major refurbishments to turn them into high-end luxury river cruisers, but it was cheaper to upgrade existing ships than to commission a new fleet of vessels.

To Giannis's intense frustration, Stefanos had rejected his very generous financial offer. That was to say—Stefanos had not actually turned him down but he kept adding new conditions before he would sell. Giannis had already agreed to employ the entire Markou Shipping workforce and retrain the staff so that they could work on his cruise ships. Far more problematic was Stefanos's insistence that he wanted to sell his company to a married man.

'Markou Shipping's ethos is family first,' Stefanos had told Giannis. 'Many of the current staff are second or even third generation employees and they share the company's values of loyalty and propriety. How do you think they would feel if I sold the company to you—a notorious playboy who regards women only as pleasurable diversions? But if you were to choose a wife and settle down it would show that you believe in the high ideals which my great-grandfather, who started Markou Shipping one hundred years ago, held dear.'

Giannis had no desire to marry, but a rival potential buyer had shown interest in purchasing the Markou fleet of vessels. Norwegian businessman Anders Tromska was married and the father of two children. Stefanos approved of Tromska for being a dedicated family man who had never been involved in any kind of scandal or photographed by the paparazzi with a different blonde on his arm every week.

Giannis was prepared to increase his financial offer for the fleet of ships. But for once he had discovered that money could not solve a problem. It seemed that the only way he might persuade Stefanos to sell to him was if he magically conjured himself a wife.

He slipped his arms into his jacket and pushed the Markou problem to the back of his mind for now, turning his thoughts instead to a happier situation. His beloved *Nerissa*—a classic motor yacht which had been his father's first boat—had been repaired and restored after it had been vandalised.

Giannis had kept the boat moored at St Katharine Dock and he stayed on it whenever he visited London. He had been furious when he'd heard that a gang of youths had boarded the boat one night and held a party. A fire had somehow started in the main cabin and quickly ripped through the boat. It turned out that a cleaner who worked for the valeting company employed to maintain the boat had stolen the keys and taken his thuggish friends aboard *Nerissa*. The gang had escaped before the police arrived, apart from the cleaner, who had been arrested and charged with criminal damage.

The manager of the boat valeting company had been deeply apologetic. 'The youth who took the keys to your boat has a police record for various petty crimes. His social worker persuaded me to give him a job. To be honest he seemed like a nice lad, and his sister who accompanied him to his interview was anxious for me to give him a chance. But they say that bad blood will out in the end,' the manager had said sagely.

In Giannis's opinion, the cleaner who he held responsible for wrecking his boat deserved to be locked up in jail and the keys thrown away. *Nerissa* was special to him and he had wonderful memories of idyllic days spent on her with his father. Now that the boat had been repaired he had arranged for her to be taken back to Greece, to his home on the island of Spetses.

The sound of movement from the bed compelled Giannis to turn his head and look across the room. Ava rolled onto her back and the sheet slipped down to reveal one perfect round breast, creamy pale against the black silk sheet and adorned with a dusky pink nipple that Giannis had delighted in tormenting with his mouth the previous night.

One night with the golden-haired temptress was not enough to sate his desire for her, he acknowledged. His arousal was uncomfortably hard beneath his close-fitting trousers. He would take her phone number and call her on his next trip to London, he decided. Maybe he would instruct his PA to clear his diary for a few days so that he could fly up to Scotland with Ava. His imagination ran riot as he pictured them staying at a castle and having hot sex in front of a blazing log fire. He had heard that it often rained in the Highlands, and they would have to pass the time somehow.

But that was for the future. Right now he had a busy day ahead of him. He glanced at his watch and strode over to the bed to wake Sleeping Beauty. He had asked for his car to be brought to the front of the hotel ready for him to drive to Hertfordshire and he was keen to be on his way. But his conscience—which was frankly under-used—insisted on this occasion that he could not simply disappear and leave Ava asleep.

'Good morning.' He leaned over the bed and watched her long eyelashes flutter and settle back on her cheeks. 'It's time to get up, angel-face.' Impatience edged into his voice, and he put his hand on her shoulder to give her a gentle shake.

Long hazel-coloured lashes swept upwards. Her grey eyes were dazed with sleep before she blinked and focused on his face.

'Oh. My. God.' Her appalled expression was almost comical. 'I thought you were a dream.'

Giannis grinned. 'I aim to please. You were pretty amazing last night too.' His gaze lingered on her bare breast and she made a choked sound as she dragged the sheet up to her chin. 'But it is now morning,' he told her. 'Nine o'clock, to be precise. And incredibly tempting though you are, I have a busy schedule and you need to get dressed.'

'Oh, my God,' Ava said again. She sat up and pushed

her tangled blonde hair out of her eyes. The faint quiver of her lower lip made her seem oddly vulnerable. Giannis was surprised by the inexplicable urge that came over him to hold her in his arms and comfort her. But why did he think she needed to be comforted when he was certain she had enjoyed the passionate night they had spent together as much as he had? Just as pertinently, what qualified him to offer comfort to anyone? He destroyed things, and Ava, with her curiously innocent air, would do well to stay away from him, he reminded himself.

He was used to being instantly obeyed and he frowned when, instead of jumping out of bed, Ava slumped back against the pillows and covered her face with her hands. Giannis struggled to hide his irritation. 'You were not so shy last night,' he drawled.

'Last night was a mistake.' Her voice was muffled behind her hands. 'I must have had too much to drink.'

His jaw hardened. 'You drank a small glass of wine during dinner. Don't try to make out that you were unaware of what you were doing when you undressed in front of me, or suggest that I took advantage of you. When I asked if you were sure you wanted to have sex, you more or less begged me to take you.'

She jerked upright and dropped her hands away from her face, shaking her head so that her hair swirled around her shoulders like a curtain of gold silk. 'I did not *beg*.' There was outrage in her voice but she continued in a low tone, 'I know what I did. I was responsible for my behaviour and I'm not blaming you. But I shouldn't have slept with you. What I mean is that I should have spoken to you…asked you… Oh, this is so awkward.' Her eyes widened even more. 'Did you say that it's nine o'clock? Oh, my *God*.'

She scrambled off the bed and tugged the sheet around

her, but not before Giannis had glimpsed her naked body. At some point during the night he had removed her stockings using his teeth to tug them down her legs. He watched Ava struggle to put her bra on while she clutched the sheet to her like a security blanket. 'Don't you think it's a little late for modesty?' he said sardonically.

She picked up her torn thong from the floor and looked as though she was about to burst into tears. 'I have to go,' she said wildly. 'Sam will be going mad wondering where I am. I was supposed to have an important conversation with you last night.'

'About what?'

She bit her lip. 'It's a delicate matter.'

Giannis counted to ten beneath his breath. 'I'm in a hurry, so whatever it is you want to say—for God's sake get on with it.'

This couldn't be happening, Ava thought frantically. In a minute she would wake up from a nightmare. But in the cold light of morning she could not fool herself that having wild sex with Giannis last night had been a dream. She felt a sensation like wet cement congealing in the pit of her stomach with the knowledge that, as a result of her irresponsible behaviour, she had lost her chance to plead with Giannis to drop the charges against her brother. She felt sick with shame and guilt.

The sound of a familiar ringtone cut through the tense atmosphere and she scrabbled in her handbag to retrieve her phone. Her heart lurched when she saw that it was her brother calling.

'Sam, I've been...unavoidably delayed.' She dared not look at Giannis. 'You will have to ring for a taxi to take you to the courthouse, and I'll meet you there. You'll have to hurry—' she felt her anxiety rise '—your case is due to be heard by the magistrate in half an hour, and you mustn't be late.'

'The magistrate is ill,' Sam said when Ava paused for breath. 'I've just heard that the court cases today have been postponed.'

Ava heard relief in her brother's voice and she felt a rush of emotion. Sam hadn't said much in the weeks leading up to his court hearing, but she knew he was scared at the prospect of being sent to prison. 'Thank goodness.' She breathed out a heavy sigh. 'I don't mean it's good that the magistrate is ill, of course, but it gives us a bit more time.'

'Time to do what?' her brother said flatly. 'My case has only been delayed for a few days and it's still likely that I'll be sent to a YOI.'

Ava knew that young offender institutions tended to be grim places and she understood why Sam was scared. He might be eighteen but he would always be her kid brother. 'Not necessarily.' She tried to sound optimistic. 'I can't talk now. I'll see you at home later.'

She replaced her phone in her bag, and her eyes widened as she watched Giannis open his briefcase and throw some documents on top of a pile of bank notes. He closed the briefcase but Ava had a sudden flashback to when she had been a little girl, and had seen her father counting piles of bank notes on the kitchen table.

'Payday,' he'd told her when she had asked him about the money.

'You must be a good businessman to earn so much money, Daddy,' Ava had said trustingly. She had idolised her father.

Terry had winked at her. 'Oh, I'm an expert, honeybunch. I'm going to use this money to buy a house in Cyprus. What do you think of that?'

'Where's Cyprus?'

'It's near to Greece. The villa I'm buying is next to the beach, and it has a big swimming pool so you will be able to teach your baby brother to swim when he's older.'

'Why aren't we going to live in England any more?'

Her father had given her an odd smile. 'It's too hot for me to live here.' It had been the middle of winter at the time and Ava had felt confused by her father's reply. But years later she had learned that Terry McKay had moved his family abroad after he'd received a tip-off that he was about to be arrested on suspicion of carrying out several armed raids on jewellery shops in London.

She dragged her mind from the past as she caught sight of her reflection in the full-length mirror. She looked like a tart with her just-got-out-of-bed hair and panda eyes where her mascara had smudged. Her lips were fuller and redder than usual, and remembering how Giannis had covered her mouth with his and kissed her senseless made her feel hot all over. She could not have a serious conversation with him about her brother while she was naked and draped in a silk sheet.

As if he had read her thoughts, Giannis walked over to the wardrobe and took out her evening gown. 'Your dress has been cleaned, but I guessed you would not want to be seen leaving the hotel this morning wearing a ball gown so I ordered you something more appropriate to wear.' He handed her a bag with the name of a well-known design house emblazoned on it. 'I'll leave you to get dressed. Please hurry,' he said curtly before he strode out of the bedroom.

Ava scooted into the en suite bathroom and looked longingly at the bath, the size of a small swimming pool. She had discovered new muscles and she ached everywhere. But Giannis was no longer the charming lover of last night and he had not hidden his impatience this morning, she thought ruefully as she bundled her hair into a shower cap before taking a quick shower.

The bag he had given her contained a pair of beautifully tailored black trousers and a cream cashmere sweater. There was also an exquisite set of silk and lace underwear. Remembering her ripped thong brought a scarlet flush to her cheeks. She did not recognise the shameless temptress she had turned into last night. Giannis had revealed a side to her that she hadn't known existed.

Grimacing at the sight of her kiss-stung lips in the mirror, she brushed her hair and caught it up in a loose knot on top of her head. At least she looked respectable, although she shuddered to think how much the designer clothes must have cost. Everything fitted her perfectly, and when she slipped on the black stiletto heels she'd worn the previous evening she was pleasantly surprised by how slim and elegant she looked. Stuffing her evening gown into the bag that had held her new clothes, she walked into the sitting room.

Giannis was speaking on his phone but he finished the call when he saw her and strolled across the room. His intent appraisal caused her heart to miss a beat. 'I see that the clothes fit you.'

'How did you know my size?'

'I have had plenty of experience of the female figure,' he drawled.

Inexplicably Ava felt the acid burn of jealousy in her stomach at the idea of him making love with other women. Love had nothing to do with it, she reminded herself. Giannis was a notorious womaniser and she was simply another blonde who had shared his bed for one night. No doubt he would have forgotten her name by tomorrow.

'Obviously I'll pay for the clothes,' she said crisply. 'Can you give me your bank details so that I can transfer what I owe you, or would you prefer a cheque?'

'Forget it. I don't want any money.'

'No way will I allow you to buy me expensive designer clothes. I'll find out what they cost and send a cheque for the amount to your London office.'

His eyes narrowed. 'How do you know that I have an office in London?'

'I found out from the Internet that you own a cruise line company called The Gekas Experience. TGE UK's offices are in Bond Street.' Ava hesitated. 'I wrote to you a few weeks ago about a serious matter, but you did not reply.'

'Sheridan,' he said slowly. 'I wondered why your name on the place card at dinner last night seemed familiar.' He frowned. 'I'm afraid you will have to jog my memory.'

She took a deep breath. 'My brother, Sam McKay, used to work for a boat valeting company called Spick and Span.' Giannis's expression hardened, and she continued quickly. 'Sam had got involved with a gang of rough youths who made out that they were his friends. They coerced him into taking them aboard one of the boats that he valeted in St Katharine Dock. I don't know if the gang meant to vandalise the boat, but a fire broke out. My brother was horrified, and he stayed on board to try to put the flames out while the rest of the gang got away. He was the only one to be arrested and charged with criminal damage. But he never meant for your boat to be damaged.' Ava's voice wavered as Giannis's dark brows drew together in a slashing frown. 'It was just a silly prank that got out of hand.'

'A prank? The *Nerissa* was nearly destroyed. Do you know how many thousands of pounds of damage your brother and his friends caused?' Giannis said harshly. 'It wasn't just the financial cost of having the boat repaired. The sentimental value of everything that was lost is incalculable. My father designed every detail of *Nerissa*'s interior and he was so proud of that boat.'

'I'm sorry.' Ava was shocked by the raw emotion in Giannis's voice. She had only considered the financial implications of the fire, and it hadn't occurred to her that the boat might be special to him. It made the situation even worse. 'Sam really regrets that he allowed the gang on board. He thought that they just wanted to have a look at the boat, and he was horrified by what happened.' She bit her lip. 'My brother is scared of the gang members, which is why he refused to give their names to the police. He's young and impressionable, but honestly he's not a bad person.'

Giannis's brows rose. 'The manager of the boat valeting company told me that your brother already had a criminal record by the age of sixteen. Sam McKay clearly has a complete disregard for the law.'

He picked up his briefcase and walked over to the penthouse suite's private lift. 'I remember the letter you sent asking me to drop the charges against your brother. I did not reply because frankly I was too angry. Sam broke the law and he must face the consequences,' he said coldly.

'Wait!' Ava hurried across the room as the lift doors opened and she followed Giannis inside. She jabbed her finger on the button to keep the door open. 'Please hear me out.'

'I'm in a hurry,' he growled.

'When I read in a newspaper that you would be attending the charity fundraising dinner I decided to try to meet you. My friend works for the event's management company which organised the evening, and Becky arranged for me to sit at the same table as you. I hoped to persuade you to find it in your heart to give my brother another chance.'

'I don't have a heart.' Giannis reached out and pulled her hand away from the button and the lift doors instantly closed. 'Your methods of persuasion were impressive, I'll grant you. But it was a wasted performance, angel-face.'

Ava gave him a puzzled look. 'What do you mean?'

'Oh, come on. You obviously had sex with me because you thought I would let your brother off the hook.'

'I did *not*. I didn't plan to go to bed with you—it just… happened,' she muttered, shame coiling through her like a venomous serpent. To say that she had handled things badly would be an understatement. Last night she had behaved like the slut that Giannis clearly believed she was, but she refused to give up trying to help Sam.

The lift doors opened on the ground floor and she shot out behind Giannis when he stepped into the foyer. 'My reason for having sex with you had nothing to do with my brother,' she told him, her stiletto heels tapping out a staccato beat on the marble floor as she tried to keep pace with his long stride. Her voice seemed to echo around the vast space and she blushed when she became aware of the curious glances directed at her by other hotel guests. The terribly sophisticated receptionist standing behind the front desk arched her brows.

'Why don't you announce on national TV that we slept together?' Giannis threw her a fulminating look, his dark eyes gleaming like obsidian.

'I'm sorry.' Ava lowered her voice. 'I don't want you

to have the wrong impression of me. I don't usually sleep with men I've only just met and I don't understand why I behaved the way I did last night. I suppose it was chemistry. There was an instant attraction that neither of us could resist.'

He growled something uncomplimentary beneath his breath. 'Next you'll be telling me that we were both shot through the heart by Cupid's arrow.' Giannis halted beside a pillar. 'Last night was fun, angel-face, and maybe I'll look you up the next time I'm in town. But I'm not going to drop the charges against your hooligan brother. Even if I wanted to, I don't think it would be possible. As I understand English law, it is the Crown Prosecution who decide if the case should go to court.'

'You could instruct your lawyer to withdraw your complaint of criminal damage inflicted on your boat, and if you refuse to provide evidence to the court the case against Sam will be dropped.'

She grabbed Giannis's arm as he turned to walk away and felt his rock-hard bicep ripple beneath his jacket. 'It's true that Sam has a police record. Like I said, he was drawn into the gang culture through fear. It's not easy being a teenager in the East End,' she said huskily. 'Sam will almost certainly be given a custodial sentence and I'm scared of what will happen to him in a young offender institution. My brother is not a hardened criminal; he's just a silly kid who made a mistake.'

'Several mistakes,' Giannis said sardonically. 'Perhaps spending a few uncomfortable weeks in prison will teach him to respect the law in future.'

Giannis had not been lying when he'd stated that he did not have a heart, Ava thought bleakly. His phone rang, and she dropped her hand from his arm and moved a few steps away from him, although she was still able to overhear his conversation. A few minutes later he finished the call, and his expression was thunderous as he strode across the lobby without glancing in her direction.

She gave chase and caught up with him, positioning herself so that she was standing between him and the door of the hotel. 'I appreciate you must be annoyed that, from the sound of it, you might have lost a business deal to buy a fleet of ships. But I can't... I *won't* stand by and watch my brother be sent to prison.'

His dark brows lowered even further. 'How the hell do you know about my business deal?'

'I can speak Greek and I couldn't help but hear some of your conversation just now, concerning someone called Markou who has rejected your offer to buy his shipping company.' Ava bit her lip, and something flashed in Giannis's dark eyes that reminded her of the stark sexual hunger in his gaze when he had taken her to bed last night. 'I'm sure your business deal is important to you, but my brother is important to me,' she said huskily. 'Is there any way I can persuade you to give Sam another chance?'

He did not reply as he stepped past her and nodded to the doorman, who sprang forwards to open the door.

Ava followed Giannis out of the hotel and shivered as a gust of wind swirled around her and tugged at her chignon. Although it was early in September, autumn had already arrived with a vengeance. A thunderstorm was forecast but at the moment drizzle was falling and she could feel it soaking through her cashmere jumper. The miserable weather suited her mood of hopelessness as through a blur of tears she saw a sleek black car parked in front of the hotel.

She watched Giannis unlock the car and throw his briefcase onto the back seat. The knowledge that she had failed to save her brother from a likely prison sentence felt like a knife in Ava's heart.

'Have you never done anything in your past that you regret?' she called after him. He hesitated and swung round to face her, his dark brows snapping together.

Desperate to stop him getting into his car and driving away, Ava raced down the hotel steps but she stumbled in her high heels and gave a cry as she felt herself falling. There was nothing she could do to save herself. But then, miraculously, she felt two strong arms wrap around her as Giannis caught her and held her against his chest. In the same instant, on the periphery of her vision she saw a bright flash and wondered if it had been a lightning strike as the storm blew up.

The thought slipped away as the evocative scent of Giannis's aftershave swamped her senses. Still in a state of shock after her near fall, she rested her cheek on his shirt front and heard the erratic thud of his heart beneath her ear. She wished she could remain in his arms for ever. The crazy notion slid into her mind and refused to budge.

There was another flash of bright light. 'Who is your mystery blonde, Mr Gekas?' a voice called out.

Ava heard Giannis swear beneath his breath. 'What's happening?' she asked dazedly, lifting her head from his chest and blinking in the blinding glare of camera flashes.

When a taxi had dropped her at the hotel entrance the previous evening she had noticed the crowd of paparazzi who had gathered to take photos of the celebrity guests arriving at the party. Evidently some of them had waited all night to snap guests leaving the hotel the next morning, and they had struck gold when they had spotted Europe's most notorious playboy and a female companion.

'Hey, Mr Gekas, over here.' A photographer aimed a

long-lens camera at them. 'Can you tell us the name of your girlfriend?'

'I certainly can,' Giannis said calmly. To Ava's surprise, he did not move away from her as she had expected. Instead he kept his arm clamped firmly around her waist as he turned her to face the paparazzi. 'Gentlemen,' he drawled, 'I would like to introduce you to Miss Ava Sheridan—my fiancée.'

She couldn't have heard him correctly. Ava jerked her eyes to his face. *'What...?'* she began, but the rest of her words were obliterated as his dark head swooped down and he crushed her lips beneath his.

The kiss was a statement of pure possession. Giannis ground his mouth against hers, forcing her lips apart and demanding her response, re-igniting the flame inside her so that she was powerless to resist him.

Ava felt dizzy from a lack of oxygen when he finally lifted his head a fraction. *'What the hell?'* she choked, struggling to drag air into her lungs when he pressed her face into his shoulder.

'I need you to be my fake fiancée,' he growled, his lips hovering centimetres above hers. 'Play along with me and I'll drop all the charges against your brother.'

Her eyes widened. 'That's *blackmail.*'

His fingers bit into her upper arms as he hauled her hard up against his whipcord body. To the watching photographers they must have looked like lovers who could not keep their hands off each other. 'It's called business, baby. And you and I have just formed a partnership.'

CHAPTER FOUR

'YOU'VE GOT A damned nerve.'

Giannis flicked a glance at Ava, sitting stiffly beside him. It was the first time she had uttered a word since he had bundled her into his car and driven away from the hotel. But her simmering silence had spoken volumes.

Tendrils of honey-blonde hair had worked loose from her chignon to curl around her cheeks. She smelled of soap and lemony shampoo and he had no idea why he found her wholesome, natural beauty so incredibly sexy. He cursed beneath his breath. She was an unwelcome distraction but she might be the solution to his problem with Stefanos Markou.

He focused his attention on the traffic crawling around Marble Arch. 'It was damage limitation,' he drawled. 'Thanks to social media, pictures of us leaving the hotel will have gone viral within minutes. I couldn't risk my reputation. Anyone who saw the photographs of us together would have assumed that you are my latest mistress.'

Ava made a strangled sound. 'You couldn't risk *your* reputation? What about mine? Everyone will believe that I am engaged to the world's worst womaniser. I can't believe you told the photographers that I am your fiancée.' She ran a hand through her hair, evidently forgetting that she had secured it on top of her head. Her chignon started to unravel and she cursed as she pulled out the remaining pins and combed her fingers through her hair.

'You're right,' she muttered, scrolling through her phone. 'The news of our so-called engagement is all over social media. Thankfully my mother is at a yoga retreat in India where there is no Internet connection. She was seriously stressed about my brother and I persuaded her to go abroad and leave me to deal with the court case. But Sam is bound to see this nonsense and I can't imagine what he's going to say.'

'Presumably he will be grateful to you for helping him to avoid going to prison,' Giannis said drily. He sensed Ava turn her head to stare at him, and a brief glance in her direction revealed that her eyes were the icy grey of an Arctic sky.

'You can't really expect me to go through with the ridiculous charade of pretending to be your fiancée,' she snapped.

'Oh, but I can, *glykiá mou*.'

For some reason her furious snort made him want to smile. Usually he avoided highly emotional women but Ava's wildly passionate nature fascinated him. She was beautiful when she was angry and even more gorgeous when she was aroused, he brooded. Memories of her straddling him, her golden hair tumbling around her shoulders and her bare breasts, round and firm like ripe peaches, caused Giannis to shift uncomfortably in his seat.

He cleared his throat. 'I thought you wanted to keep your brother out of jail?'

'I do. But two minutes before we walked out of the hotel you had refused to help Sam. I don't understand why you have changed your mind, or why you need me to be your fake fiancée.'

'Like I said, the reason is business. More specifically, the only chance I have of doing a deal with Stefanos Markou is if I can prove to him that I am a reformed character. He has refused to sell Markou Shipping to me because he disapproves of my lifestyle and he thinks I am a playboy.'

'You *are* a playboy,' Ava interrupted.

'Not any more.' Giannis grinned at her. 'Not since I fell in love with you at first sight and decided to marry you and produce a tribe of children. Markou is an old-fashioned romantic and you, angel-face, are going to persuade him to sell his ships to me.'

Her expression became even more wintry. 'There's not a chance in hell that I'd marry you and even less chance I'd agree to have your children.'

Giannis's fingers tightened involuntarily on the steering wheel as a shaft of pain caught him unawares. He had thought he'd dealt with what had happened five years ago, but sometimes he felt an ache in his heart for the child he might have had. Caroline had told him she'd suffered a miscarriage, but in his darkest hours he wondered if she had decided not to allow her pregnancy to continue because she hadn't wanted to be associated with him after he'd admitted that he had spent a year in prison.

He forced his mind away from the past. 'Forgive me for sounding cynical, but I am a very wealthy man and most women I've ever met would happily marry for hard cash. However, I have no intention of marrying you. I simply want you to pretend that we are engaged and planning our wedding. I'm gambling that Stefanos would prefer to sell Markou Shipping to me rather than to a rival company because he knows I will have the ships refurbished in Greece and employ the local workforce. All we have to do is convince him that I have turned into a paragon of virtue thanks to the love of a good woman.'

'How are *we* going to do that?' Ava's tone dripped ice.

'I will make a formal announcement of our engagement and ensure that our relationship receives as much media coverage as possible. Stefanos has invited all the bidders who are interested in buying his company to meet him on his private Greek island in one month's time. With you by my side, an engagement ring on your finger, I am confident that he will sell Markou Shipping to me. The deal is as good as done,' he said with satisfaction.

She frowned. 'Are you saying that—supposing I was mad enough to agree to the pretence—I would have to be your fake fiancée for a whole month and go to Greece with you?'

'One month is less than the prison sentence your brother would be likely to receive,' Giannis reminded her. 'It will be necessary for you to live at my home in Greece because Stefanos is not stupid and he will only believe our relationship is genuine if we are seen together regularly. From now on, every time we are out in public we must act as if we are madly in love.'

'It would require better acting skills than I possess,' Ava muttered.

'On the contrary, I thought you were very convincing when you kissed me outside the hotel.'

She made a choked sound as if she had swallowed a wasp. 'I was in a state of shock after hearing you tell the photographers that I was your fiancée.' After a tense pause, she said, 'What will happen if Stefanos sells his company to you and then we end our fake engagement and you go back to your bachelor lifestyle that he disapproves of? Won't he be angry when he realises he was duped?'

Giannis shrugged. 'There will be nothing he can do once the sale is finalised.'

'Isn't that rather unfair?'

'Life is not always fair.' Irritation made his voice curt. He really did not need a lecture on morals from Ava. 'It was not fair that your brother wrecked my boat, but I am offering you a way to help Sam stay out of prison. Face it, angel-face, we both need each other.'

'I suppose so,' she muttered. 'But I can't give up a month of my life. What am I supposed to do about my job, for instance?'

'You told me you are between jobs since you moved from Scotland to London. What do you do, anyway? I noticed you avoided talking about your career.'

She grimaced. 'I am a victim care officer, and I try to help people who have been the victims of crime. I worked for a victim support charity in Glasgow and I have been offered a similar role with an organisation in London.'

'When will you start the new job?'

Ava seemed reluctant to answer him. 'The post starts in November.'

'So there is nothing to stop you posing as my fiancée now.'

'You are *so* arrogant. Do you always expect people to jump at your command? How do you know that I don't have a boyfriend?'

'If you do, I suggest you dump him because he clearly doesn't satisfy you in bed.' Giannis's lips twitched when Ava muttered something uncomplimentary. She was prickly and defensive and he had no idea why she fascinated him. Well, he had some idea, he acknowledged derisively as he pictured her sprawled on black silk sheets wearing only a pair of sheer stockings. He glanced at her and she quickly turned her head away, but not before he'd seen a flash of awareness in her eyes.

Last night they had been dynamite in bed and sex

with her had been the best he'd had in a long, long time. Was that why he had come up with the fake engagement plan? Giannis dismissed the idea. He'd been forced to take drastic action when the paparazzi had snapped him and Ava leaving the hotel, having clearly spent the night together. He could not risk that his playboy reputation might lose him the deal with Stefanos Markou.

His inconvenient desire for Ava would no doubt fade once he had secured Markou's fleet of ships. The only thing he cared about was fulfilling the promise he had made over his father's coffin, to provide for his mother and sister. Money and the trappings of wealth were all that he could give them to try to make up for what he had stolen from them. Yet sometimes his single-minded pursuit of success felt soulless, and sometimes he wondered what would happen if he ever opened the Pandora's Box of his emotions. It was safer to keep the lid closed.

'Did you choose to work with crime victims because your brother got into trouble with the police?' Giannis succumbed to his curiosity about Ava. She had made an unusual career choice for someone who had learned etiquette and social graces at a Swiss finishing school. At dinner last night he had noted how comfortable she was with the other wealthy guests, and he was confident she would act the role of his fiancée with grace and charm that would delight Stefanos Markou.

She shook her head. 'Sam was still in primary school when I went to university to study criminology.'

'Why criminology?'

For some reason she stiffened, but her voice was noncommittal. 'I found it an interesting subject. But moving away to study and work in Scotland meant I wasn't around to spot the signs that Sam was having problems, or that my mother didn't know how to cope with him when he fell in with a rough crowd.' She sighed. 'I blame myself.'

'Why do you blame yourself for your brother's behaviour? Each of us has to take responsibility for our actions.'

Every day of the past fifteen years, Giannis had regretted that he'd drunk a glass of wine when he and his father had dined together at a *taverna*. Later, on the journey back to the family home, he had driven too fast along the coastal road from Athens and misjudged a sharp bend. Nothing could excuse his fatal error of judgement. If there was any justice in the world then he would have died that night instead of his father.

Ava insisted that her brother regretted taking a gang of thugs aboard *Nerissa* and damaging the boat. She clearly loved her brother, and Giannis felt a begrudging admiration for her determination to help Sam. He remembered how scared *he* had felt at nineteen when he had stood in a courtroom and heard the judge sentence him to a year in prison.

He had deserved his punishment and prison had been nothing compared to the lifetime of self-recrimination and contempt he had sentenced himself to. The car accident had been a terrible mistake, yet not one of his relatives had supported him. His sister had been too young to understand, but his mother would never stop blaming him, Giannis thought heavily.

He looked at Ava and she blushed and quickly turned her head to the front as if she was embarrassed that he had caught her staring at him.

'What about your father?' he asked her as he slipped the car into gear and pulled away from the traffic lights. At least the traffic was flowing better as they headed towards Camden. 'Did he try to give guidance to your brother?'

'Dad…left when Sam was eight years old.'

'Did you and your brother have any contact with him after that?'

'No.'

'It is my belief that children, especially boys, benefit from having a good relationship with their father. Although I realise my views might be regarded as old-fashioned by feminists,' Giannis said drily.

'I suppose it would depend on how good the father was,' Ava muttered.

She glanced at Giannis's hard profile and wondered what he would say if she told him that it had been difficult for her and Sam to have a relationship with their father after he had been sentenced to fifteen years in prison. Her mother had refused to allow Sam to visit Terry McKay at the maximum-security jail which housed some of the UK's most dangerous criminals. Ava had visited her father once, but she had found the experience traumatic. It had been bad enough having to suffer the indignity of being searched by a warden to make sure she was not smuggling drugs or weapons into the jail.

Seeing her father in prison had been like looking at a stranger. She had found it impossible to accept that the man she had trusted and adored had, unbeknown to his family, been a violent criminal and ruthless gangland boss. The name Terry McKay was still feared by some people in the East End of London. Perhaps if Sam had seen the grim reality of life behind bars he might not hero-worship his father as a modern-day Robin Hood character, Ava thought heavily. She was prepared to do everything in her power to prevent her brother from turning to a life of crime, and keeping him out of a young offender institution was vital. Giannis had offered her a way to give Sam another chance, but could she really be his fake fiancée?

She had assumed after they had spent the night together that she would never see him again. Memories of her wildly passionate response to his lovemaking made her want to squirm with embarrassment, but she remembered too how he had groaned when he had climaxed inside her. Did he intend that they would be lovers for the duration of their fake engagement? The little shiver of anticipation that ran through her made her despair of herself. If she had an ounce of common sense she would refuse to have anything more to do with him.

But there was Sam to consider.

Desperate to stop her thoughts from going round in circles, she searched for something to say to Giannis. 'Do you have a good relationship with your father?' If she could build up a picture of him—his family and friends, his values, she might have a better understanding of him.

He was silent for so long that she thought he was not going to answer. 'I did,' he said at last in a curt voice. 'My father is dead.'

'I'm sorry.' Evidently she had touched a raw nerve, and his forbidding expression warned her to back off. She sighed. 'This isn't going to work. We are two strangers who know nothing about each other. We'll never convince anyone that we are madly in love and planning to get married.'

To her surprise, Giannis nodded. 'We will have to spend some time getting to know each other. I can't afford any slip-ups when we meet Stefanos. Let's start with some basics. Why do you and your brother have different surnames? Have you ever been married?'

'No.' Her voice was sharper than she had intended, and she flushed when he threw her a speculative look before he turned his eyes back to the road. For some reason she found herself explaining. 'There was someone who I was sure…' She bit her lip. 'But I was wrong. He didn't love me the way I'd hoped.'

'Did you love him?'

'I thought I did.' She did not want to talk about Craig. 'After my parents divorced I took my mother's maiden name.'

Ava breathed a sigh of relief when he did not pursue the subject of her brother's surname. Giannis was Greek and it was possible that he did not associate the name McKay with an East End gangster. If he knew of the crimes her father had committed she was sure he wouldn't want her to pose as his fake fiancée and he was likely to refuse to drop the charges against Sam.

Giannis slowed the car to allow a bus to pull out. 'Where did you learn Greek? I did not think the language is routinely taught in English schools.'

'My family lived in Cyprus when I was a child, although I went to boarding school in France and then spent ten months at a finishing school in Switzerland.'

'Why did your parents choose not to live in England?'

'Um…my mother hated the English weather.' It was partly the truth, but years later Ava had learned that the real reason her father had taken his family to live abroad had been the lack of an extradition agreement between the UK and Cyprus, which had meant that Terry could not be arrested and sent back to England.

Her thoughts were distracted when a cyclist suddenly swerved in front of the car. Only Giannis's lightning reaction as he slammed on the brakes saved the cyclist from being knocked off his bike.

'That was a close call.' She looked over at Giannis and was shocked to see that he was grey beneath his tan. His skin was drawn so tight across his face that his sharp cheekbones were prominent. Beads of sweat glistened on his brow and she noticed that his hand shook when he raked his fingers through his hair.

Ahead there was an empty space by the side of the road and Ava waited until he had parked the car and switched off the engine before she murmured, 'You didn't hit the cyclist. He was riding like an idiot and it was fortunate for him that you are a good driver.'

Giannis gave an odd laugh that almost sounded as though he was in pain. 'You don't know anything about me, angel-face.'

'That's the point I've been making,' she said quietly. 'We are not going to be able to carry off a fake engagement.'

'For your brother's sake you had better hope that we do.' The stark warning in Giannis's voice increased Ava's tension, and when he got out of the car and walked round to open her door she froze when she recognised an area of London that was painfully familiar to her.

'Why have we come here? I thought you were taking me home.' It occurred to her that he had not asked where she lived, and she had been so stunned after he'd told the photographers she was his fiancée that she had let him drive her away from the hotel without asking where they were going.

'Hatton Garden is the best place to buy jewellery.'

'That doesn't explain why you have brought me here.' She was aware that Hatton Garden was known worldwide as London's jewellery quarter and the centre of the UK's diamond trade. It was also the place where her father had masterminded and carried out his most auda-cious robbery.

Ava remembered when she was a little girl, before the family had moved to Cyprus, her father had often taken her for walks to Covent Garden and St Paul's Cathedral. They had always ended up in Hatton Garden and strolled past the many jewellery shops with their windows full of sparkling precious gems. She had loved those trips with her father, unaware that Terry McKay had been assessing which shops would be the easiest to break into.

'For our engagement to be believable you will need to wear an engagement ring. Preferably a diamond the size of a rock that you can flash in front of the photog-raphers,' Giannis drawled. He glanced at his watch. 'Try not to take too long choosing one.' He took his phone out of his jacket pocket. 'I need to tell my pilot to have the jet ready for us to leave earlier than I'd originally planned.'

Ava stared at him. 'You own a *jet*?'

'It's the quickest way to get around. We should be in Paris by lunchtime. I'm going to be busy this afternoon but I'll arrange for a personal shopper to help you choose some suitable clothes. This evening we will be attending a high-profile function at the Louvre that is bound to at-tract a lot of media interest. By tomorrow morning half the world will believe that we are in love.'

'Wait…' She stiffened when he slid his hand beneath her elbow and tried to lead her towards a jewellery store. Her heart plummeted when she saw the name above the shop front.

Ten years ago her father had carried out an armed rob-bery at the prestigious Engerfield's jewellers and stolen jewellery with a value of several million pounds. But Terry McKay's luck had finally run out and he had been caught trying to flee back to Cyprus on his boat. In court,

CCTV footage had shown him threatening a young female shop assistant with a shotgun.

Ava had been devastated to discover that her father was a ruthless gangster. Even worse, several national newspapers had published a photo of her and her mother with the suggestion that they must have been aware of Terry's criminal activities. If Julie McKay *had* harboured suspicions about her husband, she had not told her daughter. But Ava knew that her mother had worshipped Terry and been blind to his faults.

She stared at the jewellery shop. 'I can't go in there.'

Giannis frowned. 'Why not? Engerfield's is arguably the best jewellers in London.'

'What I mean is that I can't wear an engagement ring or go to Paris with you until I've seen my brother and explained that our relationship is fake.'

'You cannot tell anyone the truth in case someone leaks information to the press. I mean it,' Giannis said harshly as Ava opened her mouth to argue. 'No one must have any idea that our engagement is not real.'

'But what am I going to say to Sam?'

He shrugged. 'You'll have to invent a story that we met a few weeks ago, and after a whirlwind romance I asked you to marry me. That will explain why I dropped the charges against Sam because I did not want to prosecute my future brother-in-law.'

'I don't want to lie to my brother,' she choked. 'I hate deception.'

'Do you really want to have to admit to him that you slept with me the night we met? *That* is the truth, Ava, and I will have no qualms about telling Sam how we got into this situation.'

'*You* told the paparazzi that I am your fiancée. The situation is all your fault.' She winced when Giannis tightened his grip on her arm and escorted her through the door of the jewellers.

'Smile,' he instructed her in a low tone when a silver-haired man walked over to meet them.

Somehow Ava managed to force her lips to curve upwards, but inside she was quaking as she recognised Nigel Engerfield. Ten years ago he had been commended for his bravery after he had tried to protect his staff from the gang of armed thieves led by her father. At the time of her father's trial Ava remembered seeing the shop manager's photograph in the newspapers. Would he remember *her* from the photo of Terry McKay's family that had appeared in the press a decade ago? She was sure she did not imagine that the manager gave her a close look, but to her relief he turned his gaze from her and smiled at Giannis.

'Mr Gekas, what a pleasure to see you again. How can I help you?'

'We would like to choose an engagement ring. Wouldn't we, darling?' Giannis slid his arm around Ava's waist and his dark eyes glittered as he met her startled glance. 'This is my fiancée…'

'Miss Sheridan,' Ava said quickly, holding out her hand to Nigel Engerfield. She was scared he might remember that Terry McKay had a daughter called Ava.

'Please accept my congratulations, Mr Gekas and… Miss Sheridan.' The manager's gaze lingered on Ava. 'If you would like to follow me, I will take you to one of our private sitting rooms so that you can be comfortable while you take your time to peruse our collection of engagement rings. Is there a particular style or gemstone that you are interested in?'

'What woman doesn't love diamonds?' Giannis drawled.

Nigel Engerfield nodded and left the room, returning a

few minutes later carrying several trays of rings, and accompanied by an assistant bearing a bottle of champagne and two glasses. The champagne cork popped and the assistant handed Ava a flute of the sparkling drink. She took a cautious sip, aware that she had not eaten breakfast. Maybe Giannis had the same thought because he set his glass down on the table without drinking from it.

'Please sit down and take as much time as you like choosing your perfect ring,' the manager invited Ava, placing the trays of rings on the table in front of her.

She looked down at the glittering, sparkling rings and felt sick as she remembered how, when she was a little girl, she had loved trying on her mother's jewellery. After her father had been arrested, the police had confiscated all the jewels that Terry had stolen—including her mother's wedding ring. Everything from Ava's privileged childhood—the luxury villa in Cyprus, the exotic holidays and expensive private education—had been paid for with the proceeds of her father's criminal activities. There was nothing she could do to erase her sense of guilt, but working as a VCO was at least some sort of reparation for what her father had done.

'Do you see anything you like, darling?' Giannis's voice jolted her from the past. She looked over to where he was standing by the window. Sunlight streamed through the glass, and his dark hair gleamed like raw silk when he ran a careless hand through it. His face was all angles and planes, as beautiful as a sculpted work of art. But he was not made from cold marble. Last night his skin had felt warm beneath her fingertips when she had explored his magnificent body.

Ava could recall every detail of his honed musculature that was now hidden beneath his superbly tailored suit. Oh, yes, she saw something she liked, she silently answered his question. His eyes captured hers, and her heart missed a beat when she glimpsed a predatory gleam in his gaze.

Hastily she looked down at the glittering rings displayed against black velvet cushions. Even though the shop manager had suggested she should take her time to choose a ring, she knew that Giannis wanted her to hurry up.

Inexplicably a wave of sadness swept over her. Choosing an engagement ring was supposed to be a special occasion for couples who were in love. The young assistant who had poured the champagne had looked enviously at Giannis and clearly believed that their romance was genuine. But Ava knew she was an imposter. The web of deceit they were spinning would grow and spread as they sought to convince Stefanos Markou that Giannis had given up his womanising ways because he had fallen in love with her. But of course he never would love her. He needed her so that he could win a business deal and she needed him to save her brother from prison.

What they were doing was wrong, Ava thought miserably. How could she even trust that Giannis would keep his side of their arrangement? He was playing the role of attentive lover faultlessly, but it was just an act—although that did not stop a stupid, idiotic part of her from wishing that his tender smile was real.

'Sweetheart?' Giannis walked over to the sofa and sat down beside her. 'If you don't like any of the rings, I am sure Mr Engerfield has others that you can look at.'

She swallowed. 'I can't do this…'

The rest of her words were smothered by Giannis's mouth as he swiftly lowered his head and kissed her. 'I think you are a little overwhelmed by the occasion,' he murmured, smiling softly at her stunned expression. He looked over at the shop manager. 'Would you mind leaving us alone?'

As soon as Nigel Engerfield and his assistant had stepped out of the room, Giannis did not try to hide his impatience. 'What is the matter?' he growled to Ava. 'All you have to do is choose a diamond ring, but anyone would think you are about to undergo root canal treatment.'

'I never wear jewellery and I hate diamonds,' she muttered.

He swore. 'I thought we had an agreement, but if you've changed your mind I will find another way to persuade Stefanos Markou to sell his ships to me—and your brother will go to prison.'

Ava bit her lip. 'How do I know that you will drop the charges against my brother?'

'You have my word.'

'Your word means nothing.' She ignored the flash of anger in his eyes. 'Phone your lawyer now and instruct that you no longer want to press charges against Sam.'

Giannis glared at her. 'How do I know you won't immediately go to the press and deny that you are my fiancée?'

'You'll have to trust me.' Ava glared back at him and refused to be cowed by his black stare. In the tense silence that stretched between them she could hear the loud thud of her heart in her ears. Giannis was a man used to being in control, but if he thought she was a pushover he had a nasty surprise coming to him.

Finally he took out his phone and made a call. 'It's done,' he told her moments later. 'You heard me inform my lawyer that I have decided not to press a charge of criminal damage against Sam McKay. Now it is your turn to keep to your side of the bargain.'

Ava felt light-headed with relief that Sam would not face prosecution and prison. 'I won't let you down,' she assured Giannis huskily. She glanced at the trays and selected an ostentatious diamond solitaire ring. 'Does this have enough bling to impress the paparazzi?'

He frowned at her choice and studied the other rings. 'This one is better,' he said as he picked out a ring and slid it onto her finger.

She stared down at her hand, and her throat felt oddly constricted. 'Really?' she tried to ignore the emotions swirling inside her as she said sarcastically, 'Don't you think a pink heart is romantic overload?'

'It's a pink sapphire. You said you dislike diamonds, although there are a few small diamonds surrounding the heart. But the ring is pretty and elegant and it suits your small hand.'

The ring was a perfect fit on her finger and, despite Ava's insistence that she did not like jewellery, she instantly fell in love with the pink sapphire's simplicity and delicate beauty. Once again she felt a tug on her heart. Didn't every woman secretly yearn for love and marriage, for the man of her dreams to place a beautiful ring on her finger and tell her that he loved her?

Giannis was hardly her fairy tale prince, she reminded herself. If they had not been spotted by the paparazzi leaving the hotel together, she would have been just another of his one-night stands. She stood up abruptly and moved away from him. 'I don't care which ring I have. It's simply to fool people into thinking that we are engaged and I'll only have to wear it for a month.'

He followed her over to the door but, before she could open it, he caught hold of her shoulder and spun her round to face him. His brows lowered when he saw her mutinous expression. 'For the next month I will expect you to behave like you are my adoring fiancée, not a stroppy adolescent, which is your current attitude,' he said tersely.

'Let go of me.' Her eyes darkened with temper when he backed her up against the door. He was too close, and her senses leapt as she breathed in his exotic aftershave. 'What are you doing?'

'Giving you some acting lessons,' he growled and, before she had time to react, he covered her mouth with his and kissed the fight out of her.

He kissed her until she was breathless, until she melted against him and slid her arms up the front of his shirt. The scrape of his rough jaw against her skin sent a shudder of longing through Ava. It shamed her to admit it, but Giannis only had to touch her and he decimated her power of logical thought. She pressed herself closer to his big, hard body, a low moan rising in her throat when he flicked his tongue inside her mouth.

And then it was over as, with humiliating ease, he broke the kiss and lifted his hands to unwind her arms from around his neck. Only the slight unsteadiness of his breath indicated that he was not as unaffected by the kiss as he wanted her to think.

His voice was coolly amused as he drawled, 'You are an A-star student, *glykiá mou*. You almost had *me* convinced that you are in love with me.'

'Hell,' Ava told him succinctly, 'will freeze over first.'

CHAPTER FIVE

PARIS IN EARLY autumn was made for lovers. The September sky was a crisp, bright blue and the leaves on the trees were beginning to change colour and drifted to the ground like red and gold confetti.

Staring out of the window of a chauffeur-driven limousine on his way back to his hotel from a business meeting, Giannis watched couples holding hands or strolling arm in arm next to the Seine. What it was to be in love, he thought cynically. Five years ago he had fallen hard for Caroline when he'd met her during a business trip to her home state of California. *Theos*, he had believed that she loved him. But the truth was she had loved his money and had hoped he would pay for her father's political campaign to become the next US President.

Caroline's pregnancy had been a mistake but, as long as they were married, a baby, especially if it was a boy, might help her father's campaign, she'd told Giannis. Images of widower Brice Herbert cuddling his grandchild would appeal to the electorate.

However, having a son-in-law who had served a prison sentence would have been a disaster for Brice Herbert's political ambition. Caroline had reacted with horror when Giannis had revealed the dark secret of his past. He'd sensed that she had been relieved when she'd lost the baby. Motherhood had not been on her agenda when there was a chance she could be America's First Lady. It was probably a blessing in disguise, she'd said, and it meant that there was no reason for them to marry. But he could never believe that the loss of his child was a blessing. It had felt as if his heart had been ripped out, and confirmed his belief that he did not deserve to be happy.

The limousine swept past the Arc de Triomphe while Giannis adeptly blocked out thoughts of his past and focused on the present. Specifically on the woman who was going to help him prove to Stefanos Markou that he had given up his playboy lifestyle. He should have predicted that Ava would argue when he had given her his credit card and sent her shopping, he brooded.

'I packed some things when you drove me home to collect my passport. There is nothing wrong with my clothes,' she'd told him in a stiff voice that made him want to shake her.

'I am a wealthy man and when we are out together in public, people will expect my fiancée to be dressed in haute couture,' he had explained patiently. 'Fleur Laurent is a personal shopper and she will take you to the designer boutiques on the Champs-élysées.'

Most women in Giannis's experience would have been delighted at the chance to spend his money, but not Ava. She was irritating, incomprehensible and—he searched for another suitable adjective that best summed up his feelings for her. *Ungrateful*. She did not seem to appreciate that he was doing her a huge favour by dropping the criminal damage charge against her brother.

Giannis frowned as he remembered meeting Sam McKay briefly when he'd driven Ava home before they had flown to Paris. He had been surprised when she'd directed him to pull up outside a shabby terraced house. It was odd that her family had moved from Cyprus to a run-down area of East London. Perhaps there had been a change in her parents' financial circumstances, he'd mused.

He had insisted on accompanying Ava into the house to maintain the pretence of their romance. He wasn't going to risk her brother selling a story to the press that their engagement was fake. But, instead of a swaggering teenager, he'd discovered that Sam was a lanky, nervous-looking youth who had stammered his thanks to Giannis for dropping the criminal charges against him. Sam had admitted that he'd been stupid and regretted the mistakes he had made.

Giannis understood what it was like to regret past actions and, to his surprise, he'd found himself feeling glad that he had given Ava's brother a chance to turn his life around. While Ava had gone upstairs to look for her passport, Sam had shyly congratulated him on becoming engaged to his sister and had voiced his opinion that Ava deserved to be happy after her previous boyfriend had broken her heart.

The limousine drew up outside the hotel and Giannis glanced at his watch. His meeting had overrun but there was just enough time for him to shower and change before the evening's function at the Louvre started. He hoped Ava would be ready on time. *Theos*, he hoped she hadn't run out on him.

He was aware of a sinking sensation in his stomach as the possibility occurred to him. He acknowledged that he had struggled to concentrate during his business meeting because he had been anticipating spending the evening with Ava. If he hadn't known himself better he might have been concerned by his fascination with her.

But experience had taught him that desire was a transitory emotion.

'I wouldn't have thought that you would be interested in a fashion show,' she had remarked when he'd told her about the evening's event.

'The show is for new designers to demonstrate their talent. I sponsor a young Greek designer called Kris Antoniadis. You may not have heard of him, but I predict that in a few years he will be highly regarded in the fashion world. At least I certainly hope so because I am Kris's main financial sponsor and I have invested a lot of money in him.'

'Is money the only thing you are interested in?' she'd asked him in a snippy tone which gave the impression she thought that making money was immoral.

He had looked her up and down and allowed his eyes linger on the firm swell of her breasts beneath her cashmere sweater. 'It's not the *only* thing that interests me,' he'd murmured, and she'd blushed.

There was no sign of her in their hotel suite, but Giannis heard the sound of a hairdryer from the en suite bathroom. Stripping off his jacket and tie as he went, he strode into the separate shower room and then headed to the dressing room to change into a tuxedo.

He returned to the sitting room just as Ava emerged from the bedroom, and Giannis felt a sudden tightness in his chest. His brain acknowledged that the personal shopper had fulfilled the brief he'd given her to find an evening gown that was both elegant and sexy. But as he stared at Ava he was conscious of the way another area of his anatomy reacted as his blood rushed to his groin.

'You look stunning,' he told her, and to his own ears his voice sounded huskier than usual as his customary sangfroid deserted him.

'Thank you. So do you.' Soft colour stained her cheeks. Giannis was surprised by how easily she blushed. It gave her an air of vulnerability that he chose to ignore.

'The personal shopper said I should wear a statement dress tonight—whatever a statement dress is. But I don't think you will approve when I tell you how many noughts were on the price tag,' she said ruefully.

'Whatever it cost it was worth it.' Giannis could not tear his eyes off her. The dress was made of midnight-blue velvet, strapless and fitting tightly to her hips before the skirt flared out in a mermaid style down to the floor. Around her neck she wore a matching blue velvet choker with a diamanté decoration. Her hair was caught up at the sides with silver clasps and rippled down her back in silky waves.

He had a mental image of her lying on the bed wearing only the velvet choker, her creamy skin and luscious curves displayed for his delectation. Desire ran hot and urgent through his veins and he was tempted to turn his vision into reality.

Perhaps Ava could read his mind. 'I don't know why you booked a hotel suite with only one bedroom. The deal was for me to be your *fake* fiancée.' She walked past him and picked up the phone. 'I'm going to call reception and ask for a room of my own.'

Giannis crossed the room in two strides and snatched the receiver out of her hand. 'If you do that, how long do you think it will take for a member of the hotel's staff to reveal on social media that we don't share a bed? We are supposed to be madly in love,' he reminded her.

'Did you assume I would be your convenient mistress for the next month? You've got a damned nerve,' she snapped.

He considered proving to her that it had been a reasonable assumption to make. Sexual chemistry simmered between them and all it would take was one kiss, one touch, to cause a nuclear explosion. He watched her tongue dart out to moisten her lower lip and the beast inside him roared.

Somehow Giannis brought his raging hormones under control. What was important was that their 'romance' gained as much public exposure as possible so that Stefanos Markou believed he was a reformed character preparing to devote himself to marriage and family—the ideals that Stefanos believed in.

Throughout the day Giannis had asked himself why he was going to the lengths of pretending to be engaged, simply to tip a business opportunity in his favour. But the truth was that he needed Markou Shipping's fleet of ships to enable him to expand his cruise line company into the river-cruising market. The ships could be refitted during the winter and be ready to take passengers early next summer, which would put TGE ahead of its main competitors.

'We can sort out sleeping arrangements later,' he told Ava. 'The car is waiting to take us to the Louvre. Are you ready for our first performance, *agápi mou*?'

'I am not your love.'

'You are when we are out in public.' He took hold of her arm and frowned when she flinched away from him. 'You'll have to do better than that if we are going to convince anyone that our relationship is genuine.' Impatience flared in him at her mutinous expression. 'We made a deal and I have carried out my side of it,' he reminded her. 'You told me that I would have to trust you, and I did. But perhaps I was a fool to believe your word?'

'I am completely trustworthy,' she said in a fierce voice. 'I will pretend to be your fiancée. But why would

anyone believe that you—a handsome billionaire playboy who has dated some of the world's most beautiful
women—have fallen in love with an ordinary, nothing
special woman like me?' She worried her bottom lip with
her teeth. 'What are we going to say if anyone asks how
we met?'

He shrugged. 'We'll tell them the truth. We met at a
dinner party and there was an immediate attraction between us. And, by the way, there is nothing ordinary
about the way you look in that dress,' he growled, his
eyes fixed on her pert derrière encased in tight blue velvet when she turned around to check her appearance in
the mirror.

'Sexual attraction is not the same thing as falling in
love,' she muttered.

She was nervous, Giannis realised with a jolt of surprise. If he had been asked to describe Ava he would have
said that she was determined and strong—he guessed
she'd have to be in her job working with crime victims.
But the faint tremor of her mouth revealed an unexpected
vulnerability that he could not simply dismiss. For their
fake engagement to be successful, he realised that he
would have to win her confidence and earn her trust.

He lifted his hand to brush a stray tendril of hair off
her face. 'But mutual attraction is how all relationships
begin, isn't it?' he said softly. 'You meet someone and
wham. At first there is a purely physical response, an
alchemy which sparks desire. From those roots love
might begin to grow and flourish.' His jaw hardened as
he thought of Caroline. 'But it is just as likely to wither
and die.'

'Are you speaking from experience?' Ava's gentle tone
pulled Giannis's mind from the past and he stiffened
when he saw something that looked worryingly like com-

passion in her grey eyes. If she knew the truth about him he was sure that her sympathy would fade as quickly as Caroline had fallen out of love with him.

For a fraction of a second he felt a crazy impulse to admit to Ava that sometimes when he saw a child of about four years old he felt an ache in his heart for the child he might have had. If Caroline hadn't... *No.* He would not think of what she might have done. There was no point in torturing himself with the idea that Caroline had ended her inconvenient pregnancy after he had told her he'd been to prison. The possibility that his crass irresponsibility when he was nineteen had ultimately resulted in the loss of two lives was unbearable.

Ignoring Ava's question, he walked across the room and opened the door. 'We need to go,' he told her curtly, and to his relief she preceded him out of the suite without saying another word.

Ava applauded the models as they sashayed down the runway in the magnificent Sculpture Hall of the Musée du Louvre. The venue of the fashion show was breathtaking, and the clothes worn by the impossibly slender models ranged from exquisite to frankly extraordinary. The collection by the Greek designer Kris Antoniadis brought delighted murmurs from the audience, and the fashion journalist sitting in the front row next to Ava endorsed Giannis's prediction that Kris, as he was simply known, was the next big thing in the fashion world.

'Of course Kris could not have got this far in his career without a wealthy sponsor,' Diane Duberry, fashion editor of a women's magazine, explained to Ava. 'Giannis Gekas is regarded as a great philanthropist for his support of the Greek people during the country's recent problems. He set up a charity which awards bursaries to young entrepreneurs trying to establish businesses in Greece. But I don't know why I am telling you about Giannis when you must know everything about him.'

Diane looked at Giannis's hand resting possessively on Ava's knee, and then at the pink sapphire ring on Ava's finger, and speculation gleamed in her eyes. 'You succeeded where legions of other women have failed and tamed the tiger. Where did the two of you meet?'

'Um…we were seated next to each other at a dinner party.' Ava felt herself flush guiltily even though technically it was the truth.

'Lucky you.' Diane winked at her. 'Who needs a dessert from the sweet trolley when a gorgeous Greek hunk is on the menu?'

Ava was saved from having to think of a reply when the compère of the fashion show came onto the stage and announced that the Young Designer award had been won by the Greek designer, Kris Antoniadis. Kris then appeared on the runway accompanied by models wearing dresses from his bridal collection.

Giannis stood up and drew Ava to her feet. 'Showtime,' he murmured in her ear. 'Just smile and follow my lead.'

Without giving her a chance to protest, he slid his arm around her waist and whisked her up the steps and onto the runway, just as Kris was explaining to the audience how grateful he was to Giannis Gekas for supporting his career. There was more applause and brilliant flashes of light from camera flashes when Giannis stepped forwards, tugging Ava with him.

'I cannot think of a better place to announce my engagement to my beautiful fiancée than in Paris, the world's most romantic city,' he told the audience. With a flourish he lifted Ava's hand up to his mouth and pressed his lips to the pink sapphire heart on her finger.

He was a brilliant actor, she thought caustically. Her skin burned where his lips had brushed and she wanted to snatch her hand back and denounce their engagement as a lie. The idea of deceiving people went against her personal moral code of honesty and integrity. But she must abide by her promise to be Giannis's fake fiancée because he had honoured his word and halted criminal proceedings against her brother.

And so she obediently showed her engagement ring to the press photographers and looked adoringly into Giannis's eyes for the cameras.

At the after-show party she remained by his side, smiling up at him as if she was besotted with him. For his part he kept his arm around her while they strolled around the room, stopping frequently so that he could introduce her to people he knew.

Waiters threaded through the crowded room carrying trays of canapés and drinks. Ava sipped champagne and felt the bubbles explode on her tongue. Her senses seemed sharper, and she was intensely aware of Giannis's hand resting on her waist and the brush of his thigh against hers. He was holding a flute of champagne but she noted that he never drank from it.

'Do you ever drink alcohol?' she asked him curiously. 'You didn't have any wine at the fundraising dinner, and I noticed that you are not drinking tonight.'

'How very perceptive of you, *glykiá mou*.' He spoke lightly, but Ava felt him stiffen. 'I avoid drinking alcohol because I like to keep a clear head.'

Something told her there was more to him being teetotal than he had admitted. But, before she could pursue the subject, he took her glass out of her fingers and gave it and his own glass to a passing waiter. Catching hold of her hand, he led her onto the dance floor and swept her into his arms.

Her head swam, not from the effects of the few sips of champagne she'd had, but from the intoxicating heat of Giannis's body pressed up against hers and the divine fragrance of his aftershave mixed with his own unique male scent. He was a good dancer and moved with a natural rhythm as he steered them around the dance floor, hip to hip, her breasts crushed against the hard wall of his chest. He slid one hand down to the base of her spine and spread his fingers over her bottom. Her breath caught in her throat when she felt the solid ridge of his arousal through their clothes.

Ava closed her eyes and reminded herself that Giannis's attentiveness was an act to promote the deception that they were engaged. But there was nothing pretend about the sexual chemistry that sizzled between them. She had never been more aware of a man, or of her own femininity, in her life. Her traitorous mind pictured the big bed in the hotel suite they were sharing. Of course she had no intention of also sharing the bed with him, she assured herself. She had agreed to be his fake fiancée in public only.

But, to keep up the pretence, when the disco music changed to a romantic ballad and Giannis pulled her closer, she slid her hands up to his shoulders. And when he bent his head and brushed his mouth over hers, she parted her lips and kissed him with a fervour that drew a low groan from him.

'We have to get out of here,' he said hoarsely.

Her legs felt unsteady when he abruptly dropped his arms away from her. 'Come,' he growled, clamping his arm around her waist and practically lifting her off her feet as he hurried them out of the museum. The car was waiting for them and, once he had bundled her onto the back seat and closed the privacy screen between them and the driver, he lifted her onto his lap, thrust one hand into her hair and dragged her mouth beneath his.

His kiss was hot and urgent, a ravishment of her senses, as passion exploded between them. Ava sensed a wildness in Giannis that made her shake with need. She remembered Diane Duberry, the fashion journalist at the show, had congratulated her for having tamed the tiger. But the truth was that Giannis would never allow any woman to control him.

Her head was spinning when he finally tore his mouth from hers to allow them to drag oxygen into their lungs. His chest heaved, and when she placed her hand over his heart she felt its thudding, erratic beat. The car sped smoothly through the dark Paris streets and Ava succumbed to the master sorcerer's magic. Giannis trailed his lips down her throat and over one naked shoulder. She did not realise he had unzipped her dress until he tugged the bodice down and cradled her breasts in his big hands.

Her sensible head reminded her that it was shockingly decadent to be half naked in the back of a car and her wanton behaviour was not what she expected of herself. But her thoughts scattered when Giannis bent his head and his warm breath teased one nipple before he closed his mouth around the rosy peak and sucked, hard. Ava could not repress a moan of pleasure, and when he transferred his attention to her other nipple she ran her fingers through his silky dark hair and prayed that he would never stop what he was doing to her.

'I have no intention of stopping, *glykiá mou*,' he said in an amused voice. Colour flared on her face as she realised that she had spoken her plea aloud. But when he returned his mouth to her breasts she tipped her head back and gasped as lightning bolts of sensation shot down to her molten core between her thighs.

Giannis yanked up her long flared skirt and skimmed his hand over one stocking-clad leg, but the dress was designed to fit tightly over her hips and he could not go any further. He swore. 'I hope the other clothes you bought are more accessible.'

Ava shared his frustration but while she was wondering if she could possibly wriggle out of her dress the car came to a halt and Giannis shifted her off his knees. 'We've arrived at the hotel,' he said coolly, straightening his tie and running a hand through his hair. 'You had better tidy yourself up.'

His words catapulted her back to reality and she frantically pulled the top of her dress into place. 'Will you zip me up?'

He refastened her dress seconds before the driver opened the rear door. Giannis stepped onto the pavement and offered Ava his hand. She blinked in the glare of camera flashes going off around them. Photographers were gathered outside the entrance to the hotel and she felt mortified as she imagined how dishevelled she must look as she emerged from the car.

'Here, have this.' Giannis slipped off his jacket and draped it around her shoulders. Glancing down, Ava saw that she had failed to pull the top of her dress up high enough, and her breasts were in danger of spilling out. Hot-faced, she huddled into his jacket as he escorted her into the hotel.

They entered the lift and Ava's reflection in the mirrored walls confirmed the worst. 'I look like a harlot,' she choked, running her finger over her swollen mouth. 'The photographers must have guessed we were making out on the back seat of the car. If the pictures they took just now appear in tomorrow's newspapers, everyone will think that we can't keep our hands off each other.'

Giannis was leaning against the lift wall, one ankle crossed over the other and his hands shoved into his trouser pockets. His bow tie was dangling loose and Ava flushed as she remembered how she had frenziedly torn off his tie and undone several of his shirt buttons. He looked calm and unruffled, the exact opposite of how she felt.

'The point of tonight was to advertise the news of our engagement to the press.' He dropped his gaze to where her breasts were partially exposed above the top of her dress. 'Thanks to your wardrobe malfunction we certainly got maximum exposure,' he drawled.

He sounded amused, and Ava felt sick as she realised what a fool she was. 'I suppose you knew that the paparazzi would be at our hotel,' she said stiffly. 'Is that why you made love to me in the car?'

'Actually I didn't know. But I should have guessed that they would find out which hotel we are staying at.' His eyes narrowed on her flushed face. 'I'm sorry if the photographers upset you.'

'I'm sorry that I ever agreed to be your fake fiancée.' The lift stopped at the top floor and she preceded Giannis along the corridor, despising herself for her fierce awareness of him even now, after he had humiliated her.

'But you are not sorry that your brother has avoided a prison sentence,' he said drily as he opened the door of their suite and ushered her inside. He caught hold of her arm and spun her round to face him. 'I kissed you because you have driven me insane all evening and I couldn't help myself. I have never wanted any woman as badly as I want you.'

With an effort Ava resisted the lure of his husky, accented voice that almost fooled her into believing he meant it. 'You can stop acting now that there is no audience to deceive. We're alone, in case you hadn't noticed.'

His dark eyes gleamed. 'I am very aware of that fact, *glykiá mou.*'

CHAPTER SIX

SOMETHING IN GIANNIS'S voice sent a shiver of apprehension—if she was honest it was *anticipation*—across Ava's skin. She did not fear him. It was her inability to resist his charisma that made her fearful, she admitted. She broke free from him and marched into the suite's only bedroom, intending to lock herself in. But he was right behind her and his soft laughter followed her as she fled into the en suite bathroom.

Splashing cold water onto her face cooled her heated skin, and she removed the silver clips that were hanging from her tangled hair. But she could not disguise her reddened mouth or the hectic glitter in her eyes. She felt undone, out of control, and it scared the hell out of her. If she was going to survive the next month pretending to be Giannis's fiancée, she would have to make it clear that she would not allow him to manipulate her.

Taking a deep breath, she returned to the bedroom but the sight of him in bed, leaning against the pillows, made her want to retreat back to the bathroom. His arms were folded behind his head and his chest was bare. Her heart lurched at the thought that he might be naked beneath the sheet that was draped dangerously low over his hips. She was fascinated by the fuzz of black hairs that arrowed over his flat stomach and disappeared beneath the sheet. Her eyes were drawn to the obvious bulge of his arousal beneath the fine cotton.

'Feel free to stare,' he drawled.

Blushing hotly, she jerked her eyes back to his face and his expression of arrogant amusement infuriated her. 'When you said we would discuss the sleeping arrangements, I assumed that *you* would spend the night on the sofa,' she snapped.

'The replica eighteenth-century chaise longue looks beautiful but it is extremely uncomfortable.' He picked up the big bolster cushions that he'd piled up behind his shoulders and laid them down the centre of the bed. 'It's a big bed and I won't encroach on your half—unless you invite me to.' He grinned at her outraged expression. 'I must say that I am encouraged by your choice of nightwear.'

It was only then that she noticed the confection of black silk and lace arranged on the pillow next to Giannis. She remembered the personal shopper had picked out several items of sexy lingerie, but Ava hadn't explained that her engagement to Giannis was fake and she would not need them. She guessed that the hotel chambermaid who had unpacked her clothes must have laid out the nightgown. Although gown was an exaggeration, she thought darkly as she snatched the tiny garment off the pillow and stalked into the dressing room.

The clothes she had brought with her from London were still in her suitcase. She found her grey flannel pyjamas and changed into them before she hung the velvet evening dress in the wardrobe. That was the last time she would dare to wear a strapless dress, she vowed, wincing as she remembered how her breasts had almost been exposed to the photographers until Giannis had covered her with his jacket.

She had been grateful for his protective gesture. And

he'd insisted that he had not expected the paparazzi to be outside the hotel. Ava bit her lip. Perhaps she was a fool but she believed him. After all, he had kept his side of their deal and halted the criminal case against her brother.

She grimaced as she looked at herself in the mirror. Her passion-killer pyjamas had been designed for comfort and when Giannis saw them she was sure he would have no trouble keeping to his side of the bed. Which was what she wanted—wasn't it?

She pictured him the previous night at the hotel in London, his sleek, honed body poised above her before he'd slowly lowered himself onto her as he'd entered her with one hard thrust. Why not enjoy what he was offering for the next month? whispered a voice of temptation. Sex without strings and no possibility of her getting hurt because—unlike in a normal relationship—she had no expectations that a brief affair with Giannis might lead to something more meaningful. Their engagement was a deception but he had been totally honest with her. Maybe it was time to be honest with herself and admit that she wanted him.

Before she could chicken out, she pulled off her pyjamas and slipped on the black negligee. It was practically see-through, dotted with a few strategically placed lace flowers, and it was the sexiest item of clothing she had ever worn. She walked into the bedroom and the feral sound Giannis made as he stared at her tugged deep in her pelvis.

'I hope you realise that the likelihood of me remaining on my side of the bolsters is zero. You look incredible, *omorfiá mou*.'

There was no doubt that his appreciation was genuine. His arousal was unmissable, jutting beneath the sheet, but more surprising was the flush of dark colour on his cheekbones. Ava's self-confidence rose with every step she took across the room towards him. The light from the bedside lamp sparked off the pink sapphire on her finger as she looked down at the engagement ring, watching its iridescent gleam.

'You can keep the ring after our engagement ends,' Giannis told her.

'No!' She shook her head. 'I am giving you a month of my life but you haven't bought me. I will wear your ring and pretend to be your fiancée in public. But when we are alone—' she pulled off the ring and put it down on the bedside table '—whatever I do, however I behave, is my choice.'

His eyes narrowed as she untied the ribbon at the front of her negligée so that the two sides fell open, exposing her firm breasts and betrayingly hard nipples. 'And what do you choose to do?' he said thickly.

'This.' She whipped the sheet away to reveal his naked, aroused body and climbed on top of him so that she was straddling his hips. 'And this,' she murmured as she leaned forwards and covered his mouth with hers.

For a heart-stopping second he did not respond and she wondered if she had misunderstood, that he didn't want her. But then his arms came around her like iron bands and held her so tightly that she could not escape. He opened his mouth to the fierce demands of her kiss and kissed her back with a barely leashed hunger that made her heart race.

'So you want to take charge, do you?' he murmured as she traced her lips over the prickly black stubble on his jaw. His indulgent tone set an alarm bell off in her head. Clearly, Giannis believed that he was the one in control, and he was simply allowing her to take the dominant role while it suited him.

'You had better believe it,' she told him sweetly. Still astride him, she sat upright and ran her hands over his chest. Her smile was pure innocence as she bent her head and closed her mouth around one male nipple, scraping her teeth over the hard nub.

'Theos...' His body jerked beneath her and he swore when she moved her mouth across to his other nipple and bit him, hard. 'You little vixen.' He tried to grab her hair but she shook it back over her shoulders and moved down his body, pressing hot kisses over his stomach and following the line of dark hairs down lower. Very lightly, she ran her fingertips up and down his shaft and he tensed.

'Not this time, angel,' he muttered. 'I want you too badly.'

She flicked her tongue along the swollen length of him and gave a husky laugh of feminine triumph when he groaned. 'I'm in charge and don't you forget it,' Ava told him. 'I'm not your puppet, so don't think you can control me.'

'You are so fierce.' He laughed but there was something in his voice that sounded like respect. And when he moved suddenly and rolled her beneath him he stared into her eyes for what seemed like eternity, as if he wanted to read her mind. 'You fascinate me. No other woman has done that before,' he admitted.

He slipped his hand between her legs and discovered that she was as turned-on as he was. Keeping his eyes locked with hers, he eased his fingers inside her until she moaned. 'Who is in charge now, angel?' he teased softly. But Ava no longer cared if she won or lost the power struggle. She reached down between their bodies and curled her hand around him, making him groan. Maybe they were both winners, she thought. 'You are ready for me, Ava *mou*.' He swiftly donned a condom before he moved over her and entered her with a slow, deep thrust that delighted her body and touched her soul. With a flash of insight that shook her, she acknowledged that she would always be ready for him. She guessed that Giannis had made a slip of his tongue when he'd called her *my* Ava.

They flew to Greece the next day, and in the evening attended a party held at reputedly Athens' most chic rooftop bar where the cosmopolitan clientele included several international celebrities. The paparazzi swarmed in the street outside the venue and there was a flurry of flashlights as Giannis Gekas and his English fiancée posed for the cameras.

From the rooftop bar the views of the sunset over the city were amazing. But Giannis only had eyes for Ava. She looked stunning in a scarlet cocktail dress that showed off her gorgeous curves, and he was impatient for the party to finish so that he could take her back to his penthouse apartment and reacquaint himself with her delectable body. Their sexual chemistry was hotter than anything he'd experienced with his previous mistresses.

He smiled to himself as he imagined Ava's reaction if he was ever foolish enough to refer to her as his mistress. No doubt she would reply with a scathing comment designed to put him in his place. He enjoyed her fiery nature, and never more so than when they had sex and she became a wildcat with sharp claws. He bore the marks from where she had raked her fingernails down his back when they'd reached a climax together last night. Afterwards, she had reminded him of a contented kitten, warm and soft as she snuggled up to him and flicked her tongue over her lips like a satisfied cat after drinking a bowl of cream.

Giannis had intended to ease his arm from beneath her and move her across to the other side of the bed. But he'd felt reluctant to disturb her and he must have fallen asleep because when he'd next opened his eyes his head had been pillowed on Ava's breasts, and he'd been so aroused that he ached. He had kissed her awake and ignored her protests that had quickly become moans of pleasure when he'd nudged her legs apart with his shoulders and pressed his mouth against her feminine core to feast on her sweetness.

With an effort Giannis dragged his mind from his erotic memories when he realised that he had not been listening to the conversation going on around him. The group of guests he was standing with were looking at him, clearly waiting for him to say something. He glanced at Ava for help.

'I was just explaining that we haven't set a date for our wedding yet,' she said drily. 'We are not in a rush.'

'On the contrary, *agápi mou*, I am impatient to make you my wife as soon as possible.' He slipped his arm around her waist and smiled with his customary effortless charm at the other guests. 'I hope you will forgive me for selfishly wanting to have my beautiful bride-to-be to myself,' he murmured before he led Ava away.

'Why did you say that we will get married soon?' she demanded while he escorted her out of the crowded bar. Once they were outside and walking to where he had parked the car, she pulled away from him. 'There was no need to overdo the devoted fiancé act. All that staring into my eyes as if I was the only woman in the world was unnecessary.'

He grinned at her uptight expression. 'I need to convince Stefanos Markou that our engagement is genuine and I am serious about settling down. The woman in the blue dress who we were talking to is a journalist with a popular gossip magazine. No doubt the next edition will include several pages devoted to discussing our imminent wedding.'

Ava bit her lip. 'More deception,' she muttered. 'One lie always leads to another. I realise it's just a game to you, but when our fake engagement ends I will face public humiliation as the woman who nearly married Giannis Gekas.'

'It will cost my company in the region of one hundred million pounds to buy Markou's fleet of ships. An investment of that size is hardly a game,' Giannis told her curtly. 'Once I've secured the deal with Stefanos I will give a press statement explaining that you broke off our engagement because you fell out of love with me.'

It wouldn't be the first time it had happened, he brooded. His jaw clenched as he thought of Caroline. At least he'd discovered before he'd made an utter fool of himself that Caroline had been more in love with his money than with him.

Giannis sensed that Ava sent him a few curious glances during the journey back to his apartment block. He parked in the underground car park and when they rode the lift up to the top floor he could not take his eyes off her. She was a temptress in her scarlet dress and vertiginous heels and he had been in a state of semi-arousal all evening as he'd imagined her slender legs wrapped around his back.

His desire for her showed no sign of lessening—yet. But he had no doubt that it would fade and he'd grow bored of her. His mistresses never held his interest for long. Perhaps if he sought some sort of counselling, a psychologist would suggest that his guilt over his father's death was the reason he avoided close relationships. But Giannis had no intention of allowing anyone access to his soul.

After ushering Ava into the penthouse, he crossed the huge open-plan living room and opened the doors leading to his private roof garden. 'Would you like a drink?' he asked her.

'Just fruit juice, please.'

He headed for the kitchen, and returned to find her out on the terrace, standing by the pool. The water appeared black beneath the night sky and reflected the silver stars. 'Is that how you keep in such great physical shape?' she murmured, indicating the pool.

His heart lurched at her compliment. *Theos*, she made him feel like a teenager with all the uncertainty and confusion brought on by surging hormones, he acknowledged with savage self-derision. 'I complete fifty lengths every morning. But I prefer to swim in the sea when I am at my house on Spetses.'

Ava sipped her fruit juice and glanced at the bottle of beer in his hand. 'You don't need to keep a clear head tonight?' She obviously remembered the reason he had given her for why he hadn't drunk champagne at the fashion show in Paris.

'It's non-alcoholic beer,' he admitted.

'Why are you afraid of not being in control?'

Rattled by her perception, his eyes narrowed. 'I'll ask you the same question.'

'Touché.' She smiled ruefully. 'I don't like surprises.'

'Not even nice ones?'

'I've never had a nice surprise.' She looked at the city skyline. 'The Acropolis looks wonderful lit up at night. Have you always lived in Athens?'

Giannis could not understand why he felt frustrated by her determination to turn the conversation away from herself. In his experience women were only too happy to talk about themselves, but Ava, he was beginning to realise, was not like any other woman.

He shrugged. 'I grew up just along the coast at Faliron and I am proud to call myself an Athenian.'

'Perhaps I could do some sightseeing while you are at work? I know you have arranged for us to attend various social functions in the evenings so that we are seen together, but you have a business to run during the day.'

'I'll show you around the city. One of the perks of owning my own company is that I can delegate.' As Giannis spoke he wondered what the hell had got into him. He'd never delegated in his life and his work schedule was by his own admittance brutal. Driven by his need to succeed, he regularly worked fourteen-hour days and he couldn't remember the last time he'd spent more than a couple of hours away from his computer or phone.

The more time he spent with Ava, the quicker his inexplicable fascination with her would lead to familiarity and, by definition, boredom, he assured himself. He put down his drink and walked towards her, noting with satisfaction how her eyes widened and her tongue flicked over her lips, issuing an unconscious invitation that he had every intention of accepting.

'There is an even better view of the Acropolis from the bedroom,' he said softly.

She hesitated for a few seconds and when she put her hand in his and let him lead her through the apartment to the master suite he was aware of the hard thud of his heart beneath his ribs. He stood behind her and turned her to face the floor-to-ceiling windows which overlooked Greece's most iconic citadel, situated atop a vast outcrop of rock. 'There.'

'It's so beautiful,' she said in an awed voice. 'What

an incredible view. You can just lie in bed and stare at a piece of ancient history.'

'Mmm…' He nuzzled her neck and slid his arms around her to test the weight of her breasts in his hands. 'I can think of rather more energetic things I'd like to do in bed, *agápi mou*.'

She pulled the pink sapphire ring from her finger and dropped it onto the bedside table. 'I'm not your love now that we are alone,' she reminded him.

'But you are my lover.' He unzipped her dress and when it fell to the floor she stepped out of it before she turned and wound her arms around his neck.

'Yes,' she whispered against his mouth. 'For one month I will be your lover.'

As he scooped her up and laid her down on the bed, Giannis knew he should be relieved that Ava understood the rules. But perversely he felt irritated. Perhaps it was because her words had sounded like a challenge that provoked him to murmur, 'You might want our affair to last longer than a month.'

'I won't.' She watched him undress and reached behind her shoulders to unclip her bra, letting it fall away from her breasts. 'But you might fall in love with me.'

'Impossible,' he promised her. 'I already told you I don't have a heart.' He pushed her back against the mattress and covered her body with his, watching her eyes widen when he pushed between her thighs.

'However, I do have this, *glykiá mou*,' he murmured before he possessed her with one fierce thrust followed by another and another, taking them higher until they arrived at the pinnacle and tumbled over the edge together.

Afterwards, he shifted across the bed and tucked his hands behind his head, determined to emphasise to Ava that sex was all he was prepared to offer. Too many people mistook lust for love, Giannis brooded. He'd made that mistake himself once, when he had fallen for Caroline. But he had learned his lesson and moved on.

After busy, bustling Athens, Ava discovered that life on the beautiful island of Spetses moved at a much slower pace. Thankfully.

She frowned as the thought slipped into her mind. She should be glad that she was halfway through her fake engagement to Giannis. So why did she wish that time would slow down?

She hadn't expected to *like* him, she thought ruefully. They had stayed at his apartment in the city for two weeks, ostensibly so that they could be seen together at high society events. The shock news that Greece's most eligible bachelor had chosen a bride had sparked fevered media interest, leading Ava to remark drily that Stefanos Markou could not have missed reports about their romance, unless he had been visiting remote indigenous tribes in the Amazon rainforest.

But for the most part they'd managed to evade the paparazzi when Giannis had kept his word and showed her Athens. Not just the tourist attractions, although of course they did visit the Acropolis and the nearby Acropolis Museum, as well as the Byzantine Museum.

They climbed the steep winding path to the top of Lycabettus Hill and sat at the top to watch the sunset over the city. He took her to the pretty neighbourhood of Plaka and they strolled hand in hand along the narrow streets lined with pastel-coloured houses where cerise-pink bougainvillea tumbled from window boxes. And he took her to dinner at little *tavernas* tucked away in side streets off the tourist track, where they ate authentic Greek food and Giannis entertained her with stories of the places he had visited around the world and the people he had met. He was an interesting and amusing companion and Ava found herself falling ever deeper under his spell.

Spetses was a twenty-minute helicopter flight from Athens, although most people did not have a helipad in their garden like Giannis, and visitors to the island made use of the red and white water taxis. The island was picturesque, with whitewashed houses and cobbled streets around the harbour. Cars were banned in the town centre and the sight of horse-drawn carriages rattling along gave the impression that Spetses belonged to a bygone era. That feeling was reflected in Villa Delphine, Giannis's stunning neo-classical mansion, with its exquisite arches and gracious colonnades. The exterior walls were painted pale yellow, and green shutters at the windows gave the house an elegant yet homely charm.

Ava was relieved that Villa Delphine looked nothing like the extravagant but tasteless house in Cyprus where she had lived for part of her childhood, until her father had been arrested and she had discovered the truth about him. Every happy memory from the first seventeen years of her life now seemed grubby, contaminated by her father's criminality. But at least Sam had been given another chance, and she was hopeful that he would keep out of trouble from now on.

She returned her phone to her bag and watched Giannis walk up the beach towards her. He had been swimming in the sea and water droplets glistened on his olive-gold skin and black chest hairs. His swim-shorts sat low on his hips and Ava's mouth ran dry as she studied his impressive six-pack. Heat flared inside her when he hunkered down in front of her and dropped a tantalisingly brief kiss on her mouth.

'Did you get hold of your brother?'

'I've just finished speaking to him. He is helping out on my aunt and uncle's farm in Cumbria and he says it hasn't stopped raining since he arrived. I didn't tell him that it's twenty-five degrees in Greece. I'm just relieved he's away from the East End and its association with—' She broke off abruptly.

'Association with what?'

'Oh…historically the area of London around Whitechapel was well-known for being a rough place,' she prevaricated. Desperate to avoid the questions that she sensed Giannis wanted to ask, she placed her hands on either side of his face and pulled his mouth down to hers. He allowed her to control the kiss and, as always, passion swiftly flared. But when Ava tried to tug him down beside her, he lifted his lips from hers with an ease that caused her heart to give a twinge.

'Unfortunately there is not time for you to distract me with sex,' he said in a dry tone that made her blush guiltily. 'My mother is joining us for lunch.'

She packed her sun cream and the novel she had been reading into her bag and stood up. 'I thought your mother was in New York?' Giannis had told her that his mother, Filia, and his younger sister, Irini, shared the house next door to Villa Delphine. Irini was an art historian, currently working at a museum in Florence.

'Mitera has flown back from the US early to meet you,' he said as he followed her along the path which led from the private beach up to the house.

Ava halted and swung round to look at him. 'You *have* explained to your mother that I am not really your fiancée—haven't you? We can't lie to her,' she muttered when he remained silent. 'It's not fair. She might be excited that you are going to get married and perhaps give her grandchildren.'

'My mother is an inveterate gossip,' he said curtly. 'If I told her the truth about us, she would be on the phone within minutes to tell a friend, who would tell another friend, and the story that you are my fake fiancée would be leaked to the press within hours.'

He lifted his hand and traced his finger over her lips. 'Don't pout, *glykiá mou,* or it will look as though we have had a lover's tiff,' he teased. His earlier curtness had been replaced by his potent charm and he pulled her into his arms and kissed her until she melted against him. But had his kiss been to distract her? Ava asked herself as she ran upstairs to shower and change out of her bikini before his mother arrived.

When she walked into the salon some half an hour later, wearing an elegant pale blue shift dress from a Paris design house, she heard voices from the terrace speaking in Greek. The woman dressed entirely in black was evidently Giannis's mother. Ava took a deep breath and was about to step outside and introduce herself, but she hesitated as Filia Gekas's voice drifted through the open French doors.

'Have you been honest with this woman who you have decided to marry, Giannis? Have you told Ava *everything* about you?'

CHAPTER SEVEN

SECRETS AND LIES. They lurked in every corner of the dining room, taunting Ava while she forced herself to eat her lunch and attempted to make conversation with Giannis's mother. It was an uphill task, for Filia was a discontented woman whose only pleasure in life, it seemed, was criticising her son.

Ava had no idea what the other woman had meant, or what Giannis was supposed to have told her. Perhaps it was something that would only be relevant if he truly intended to marry her—which, of course, he did not. She was trapped in a deception that would only end once he had secured his business deal with Stefanos Markou.

She glanced at him across the table and found he was watching her broodingly as if he was trying to fathom her out. Ava guiltily acknowledged that she had her own secrets. But why should she tell Giannis that her father was serving a prison sentence for armed robbery? In a few weeks' time there might be a brief media frenzy when it was announced that the engagement between Greece's golden boy and his English fiancée was over, but the paparazzi would quickly forget about her, as, no doubt, would Giannis.

She pulled her mind back to the conversation between Giannis and his mother. 'I don't know why you paid a fortune for a holiday to the Maldives,' Filia said sharply. 'You know I dislike long-haul flights.'

'It is hardly any longer than the flight time to New York,' Giannis pointed out mildly. 'I bid for the trip at a charity auction because I hoped you would enjoy a spa break in an exotic location.'

His mother sniffed and turned to Ava. 'I was surprised when Giannis told me that the two of you are engaged to be married. He has never mentioned you before.'

Ava felt heat spread over her cheeks. 'It was a whirl-wind courtship,' she murmured.

Filia gave her a speculative look. 'My son is a very wealthy man. Can I ask why you agreed to marry him?'

'Mitera!' Giannis frowned at his mother but she was unabashed.

'It is a reasonable question to ask.' She turned her sharp black eyes back to Ava. 'Well?'

Ava said the only thing she could say. 'I…love him.' Her voice sounded strangely husky and she did not dare look across the table at Giannis. One lie always led to another lie, she thought bleakly. But she must have sounded convincing because his mother gave her a searching look and then nodded.

'Good,' Filia said. 'Love and trust are vital to a successful marriage.'

Ava gave a quiet sigh of relief when Giannis came to her rescue and asked his mother about her trip to New York. Evidently it had been a disaster, for which she blamed him. The five-star hotel where he had arranged for her to stay had, according to Filia, been atrocious. 'Rude staff, and the bed had a lumpy mattress.'

'I am sorry you were disappointed,' he told his mother with commendable patience. Ava glanced at him, telling herself that if he looked amused by her lie about being in love with him she would empty the water jug over his head, and never mind what conclusion his mother might draw.

He met her gaze across the table and the gleam in his dark eyes made her tremble as a shocking realisation dawned on her. It couldn't be true, she assured herself frantically. But the erratic thud of her heart betrayed her. Had she managed to sound convincing to his mother because she was actually falling in love with Giannis?

The helicopter swooped low over the sea and Ava felt her stomach drop. She did not realise that her swift intake of breath had been audible, but Giannis looked up from his laptop. He was seated opposite her in the helicopter's luxurious cabin and leaned forwards to take her hand in his warm grasp.

'Don't worry,' he said reassuringly. 'Vasilis is a good pilot. We will be landing in a few minutes. Stefanos's private island, Gaia, is below us now.'

She nodded and turned her head to look out of the window at the pine tree covered island, edged by golden beaches and set in an azure sea. It was easier to let Giannis think she was nervous of flying in the helicopter. She certainly could not tell him of her terrifying suspicion, which might explain the nauseous feeling she'd experienced for the past few days.

She'd put her queasiness down to some prawns she'd eaten at a restaurant a few evenings before. But while she had packed her suitcase this morning she'd found the packet of tampons she had brought to Spetses with her in the expectation that she would need them.

Her period was only a couple of days late, Ava tried to reassure herself. But a doom-laden voice in her head reminded her that she was never late. Her mind argued that Giannis had used a condom every time they'd had sex. Even when he'd followed her into the shower cubicle and stood behind her so that she had felt his arousal press against her bottom, he had been prepared. She could not be pregnant. Probably her churning stomach and uncomfortably sensitive breasts were signs that her period was about to start.

She sighed. Her mood swings were another indication that she was worrying unnecessarily. When the helicopter had taken off from Spetses she had been thankful that her oversized sunglasses hid her tears. Ava knew she was unlikely to ever return to the island. Giannis had said that they would go to his apartment in Athens after meeting Stefanos Markou and he would arrange for his private jet to fly her back to London.

Apart from the awkward lunch with Giannis's mother, the past two weeks that they had spent at Villa Delphine had been like a wonderful dream where each perfect day rolled into the next, and every night Giannis had made love to her and their wildfire passion blazed out of control. But since Ava had woken early that morning, feeling horribly sick, and crept silently into the bathroom so as not to wake him, her insides had been knotted with dread.

The helicopter landed and Giannis climbed out and offered Ava his hand to assist her down the steps. 'You are still pale,' he said, frowning as he studied her.

'I'm nervous,' she admitted. 'Your hope of buying Markou Shipping is the reason we have spent the last month pretending to be engaged, but what if Stefanos guesses that I am your fake fiancée?'

'Why should he? People tend to believe what they see. That is why conmen are sometimes able to persuade elderly ladies to hand over their life savings.'

Her father had been the cleverest conman of all, Ava

thought bitterly. He had fooled his own wife and children with his affable charm. Suddenly she could not wait for the deception she was playing with Giannis to be over. But then her relationship with him would finish—unless her suspicion, and a pregnancy test when she had a chance to buy one, proved positive. The knot of dread in her stomach tightened.

As they walked across the lawn towards a sprawling villa, Giannis slid his arm around her waist and urged her forwards to meet the grey-haired man waiting for them on the terrace. Stefanos Markou shook Giannis's hand before he turned to Ava.

'I admit I was surprised when Giannis announced his decision to marry. But now that I have met you, Ava, I understand why he is in a hurry to make you his wife.' Stefanos smiled. 'My wife read in a magazine that you are planning a Christmas wedding.'

'Christmas is more than two months away and I don't think I can wait that long,' Giannis murmured. Ava's heart gave a familiar flip when he looked down at her with a tender expression in his eyes that her common sense told her was not real. He was a brilliant actor, she reminded herself, but her mouth curved of its own accord into an unconsciously wistful smile.

Stefanos laughed. 'The other bidders who want to buy Markou Shipping are already here. So, let us get down to business, Giannis, while Ava talks of wedding dresses with my wife and daughters.'

He led them into the villa and introduced Ava to his wife, Maria, and his three daughters, who between them had seven children of their own—all girls. Stefanos sighed. 'It seems that I am not destined to have a grandson to pass Markou Shipping on to. Unfortunately my only nephew is a hopeless businessman and so I made the decision to sell the company and retire.'

The small island of Gaia was a picturesque paradise. Stefanos's wife and daughters were friendly and welcoming, but Ava felt a fraud for having to pretend to be excited about her supposed forthcoming wedding. The little grandchildren were a delight, but when she held the youngest baby of just six weeks old she found herself imagining what it would be like to cradle her own baby in her arms. She tried to quell her sense of panic, and inexplicably she felt an ache in her heart as she pictured a baby with Giannis's dark hair and eyes.

Eventually she made the excuse of a headache and slipped away to walk on the beach. When she turned back towards the villa, she saw Giannis striding along the sand to meet her.

'Well?' she asked him anxiously.

A wide grin spread across his face and he looked heartbreakingly handsome. He put his hands on either side of her waist and swung her round in the air. 'It's done,' he told her in a triumphant voice. 'I persuaded Stefanos to sell his company to me. I had to increase my financial offer, but the main reason he agreed was because he is convinced that when you and I marry I will settle down to family life and embrace the values that Stefanos believes are important. Work can start immediately to refit and upgrade the Markou fleet of ships to turn them into luxury cruisers.'

'And I can go home,' Ava said quietly.

Giannis set her back on her feet, but he kept his arms around her and a faint frown creased between his brows. 'It will take a few days for the paperwork to be finalised and signed. Stefanos is giving a party tonight for all the Markou Shipping employees and he will announce that

I am buying the company. It will be an opportunity for me to reassure the workforce that they will continue to be employed by TGE. Stefanos has invited us to spend the night on Gaia and the helicopter will pick us up and take us to Athens in the morning.'

The breeze blew Ava's long hair across her face and Giannis caught the golden strands in his hand and tucked them behind her ear. His dark eyes gleamed with something indefinable that nevertheless made her heart beat too fast. 'I cannot see a reason why you should rush back to England, can you, *glykiá mou*?' he murmured.

She *should* remind him that they had made a deal, and now that she had kept her side of it there was no reason for her to stay in Greece with him. Was he saying that he did not want her to leave? What would he say if she *was* pregnant? Would he still want her and their child? Her thoughts swirled around inside her head. She caught her lower lip between her teeth, and the feral growl he made evoked a wild heat inside her so that when he claimed her mouth and kissed her as if he could never have enough of her she gave up fighting herself and simply melted in his fire.

That evening, the guests were ferried from the mainland to Gaia by boat. As the sun set, the usually peaceful island was packed with several hundred partygoers enjoying Stefanos's generous hospitality. A bar and barbecue had been set up on the beach and a famous DJ had flown in from New York to take charge of the music.

Ava had convinced herself that her niggling stomach ache was a sign that her period was about to start, and with Giannis in an upbeat mood she decided to have fun at the party and live for the moment. He was flatteringly attentive and hardly left her side all evening.

She told herself that he was continuing to act the role of adoring fiancé until his business deal with Stefanos had been signed. But the way he held her close while they danced and threaded his fingers through her hair was utterly beguiling.

'Don't go away,' he murmured midway through the evening. He claimed her mouth in a lingering kiss, as if he was reluctant to leave her, before he went to join Stefanos on the stage at one end of the ballroom. There was loud applause from Markou Shipping's employees when Giannis explained that everyone would keep their jobs and be offered training opportunities at TGE.

'Gullible idiots.' A voice close to Ava sounded cynical. She looked over at the man who had spoken and he caught her curious glance. 'You don't believe that Gekas will keep his word, do you? He has promised to retain Markou's workforce simply to persuade the old fool to sell the company to him. But Gekas isn't interested in saving Greek jobs. All he wants is the ships and in a few months he will sack the workers.'

The man laughed at Ava's startled expression. 'Giannis Gekas fools everyone with his charming manner, including you, it seems. You obviously haven't heard the rumours that Mr Nice Guy has a nasty side.'

It must have been the cool breeze drifting in through the window that made the hairs on the back of Ava's neck stand on end. 'What do you mean?'

'Rumours have circulated for some time that Gekas has links with an organised crime syndicate and that he uses TGE to hide his money-laundering activities.'

'If there was any substance to those rumours, surely the authorities would have investigated Giannis?' Ava said sharply. 'And Stefanos would not have sold Markou Shipping to someone he suspected of being a criminal.'

'It's like I said. Old Markou is a fool who has been taken in by Gekas's apparent saintliness. Setting up a charity to help young Greeks establish new businesses was a clever move.' The man shrugged. 'As for the police, it's likely that some of them are being bribed, or they are too scared of what will happen to them and their families if they start to investigate Gekas's business methods. The Greek mafia are not a bunch of Boy Scouts; they are ruthless mobsters.'

Ava's mouth was dry and she could feel her heart hammering beneath her ribs. 'Do you have any proof to back up your allegations, Mr...?' She paused, hoping the man would introduce himself.

'Of course nothing can be proved. Gekas is too clever for that. And I'm not telling you my name because I don't want to end up at the bottom of the sea with a bullet through my brain.'

Nothing the man had said could be true, Ava tried to reassure herself. But what did she *actually* know about Giannis? whispered a voice in her head. She stared at the man. 'You have no right to make such awful, unsubstantiated accusations against Giannis. Why should I believe you?'

'How do you think that Gekas became a billionaire by his mid-thirties? The luxury cruise market was badly hit by the economic meltdown in Greece and other parts of Europe, yet TGE makes huge profits.'

The man laughed unpleasantly. 'Racketeering is a more likely source of Gekas's fortune. Some years ago a journalist tried to investigate him but your fiancé has powerful friends in high places and I assume the journalist was bribed to keep his nose out of Gekas's private life.'

With another sneering laugh the man walked away and disappeared from Ava's view in the crowded ballroom. The dancing had started again and she saw Giannis walk down the steps at the side of the stage. None of what she had heard about him could be true. *Could it?* He had captivated her with his legendary charm but was she, along with all the other people at the party, including Stefanos Markou, a gullible fool who had been taken in by Giannis's charisma?

She had seen it happen before. Everyone who had met her father had fallen for his cockney good humour, but at his trial Terry McKay had been exposed as a ruthless gangland boss who had used bribery and intimidation to evade the law. She had no proof that the accusations made by a stranger against Giannis were true, Ava reminded herself.

A memory pushed into her mind, of the morning in the hotel in London after they had spent the night together. He had opened his briefcase and she'd been shocked to see that it contained piles of bank notes. At the time she had thought it odd that he carried so much cash around but she'd been focused on trying to persuade Giannis to drop the charges against her brother. However, the incident had reminded her of how her father had kept large quantities of bank notes hidden in odd places in the house in Cyprus.

Then there was what she had overheard Giannis's mother say. *'Have you told Ava everything about you?'* What had Filia meant? What secret about himself had Giannis kept from her? And why did his mother disapprove of her only son?

The throbbing music was pounding in Ava's ears and she felt hot and then cold, and horribly sick. The flashing disco ball hanging from the ceiling was spinning round and round, making her dizzy, and she was afraid she was going to faint.

'Ava.' Suddenly Giannis was standing in front of her, his chiselled features softening as he studied her. 'What's the matter, *glykiá mou*?'

His voice was husky with concern, and Ava despised herself for wishing that she could ignore the rumours she had heard about him. But why would the party guest have made up lies about Giannis?

'Migraine,' she muttered. 'I get them occasionally and the bright disco lights are making it worse. If you don't mind I'd like to go to bed and hopefully sleep it off.'

'I'll take you back to our room and stay with you,' he said instantly.

'No, you should remain at the party and celebrate winning your business deal.'

Giannis swore softly. 'The deal isn't important.'

'How can you say that, when it was the reason we have pretended to be engaged?'

His smile made Ava's heart skip a beat, despite everything she had heard about him. 'Our relationship may have started out as a pretence but I think we both realise that the spark between us shows no sign of fading,' he murmured. He frowned when she swayed on her feet. 'But we won't discuss it now. You need to take some painkillers.'

She needed to be alone with her chaotic thoughts, and she was relieved when she saw Stefanos beckon to Giannis from across the room. 'I think you are needed. I'll be fine,' she assured him, and hurried out of the ballroom before he could argue.

Later that night, when Giannis quietly entered the bedroom and slid into bed beside her, Ava squeezed her eyes shut and pretended to be asleep. And the next morning when she rushed to the bathroom to be sick he was sympathetic, believing that a migraine was the cause of her nausea. His tender concern during the helicopter flight back to Athens added to her confusion. It seemed impossible that he could be involved with the criminal underworld.

Her father had given the appearance of being a loving family man and she had adored him, Ava remembered bleakly. She had been devastated when details of Terry McKay's violent crimes were revealed during his trial. For seventeen years her father had hidden his secret life from her. In the one month that she and Giannis had pretended to be engaged she'd learned virtually nothing about him, except that he was a good actor.

A car was waiting to drive them from Athens airport to the city centre. On the way, she persuaded Giannis to drop her off at a pharmacy, making the excuse that she needed to buy some stronger painkillers for her headache.

'I wish I didn't need to go to the office but I have an important meeting.' He pressed his lips to her forehead. 'Take the migraine tablets and go to bed,' he bade her gently.

One lie always led to more lies, Ava thought miserably when she bought a pregnancy test and hurried back to the penthouse apartment. Her hands shook as she followed the instructions on the test. She still clung to the hope that her late period and bouts of sickness were symptoms of a stomach upset.

The minutes went by agonisingly slowly while she paced around the bathroom. Finally it was time to check the result. Taking a deep breath, she looked at the test and grabbed the edge of the vanity unit as her legs turned to jelly. Her disbelief as she stared at the positive result swiftly turned to terror.

She was expecting Giannis's baby. But who—and more importantly *what*—was Giannis Gekas? Was he the charismatic lover who she had begun to fall in love with? Or was he a criminal who hid his illegal activities behind the façade of a successful businessman and philanthropist?

Feeling numb from the two huge shocks she had received in the space of twenty-four hours, Ava placed a trembling hand on her stomach. It seemed incredible that a new life was developing inside her and she felt an overwhelming sense of protectiveness for her baby. She would have been worried about telling Giannis of her pregnancy *before* she had heard the rumours about him. This was the man, after all, who had insisted that he did not have a heart.

Now the prospect filled her with dread. Supposing he was a man like her father—a criminal and a liar? A cold hand squeezed her heart. What if her ex, Craig, was right and there *was* a criminal gene that her baby might inherit from *both* parents? Ava was the absolute opposite of her father, and she had spent her adult life subconsciously trying to atone for his crimes in her job supporting victims of crime. She would bring her child up to be honest and law-abiding, but would Giannis share her ideals?

She sank down onto the edge of the bath and covered her face with her hands. Even if she could bring herself to ask him outright if he was a criminal, he was bound to deny it. She did not know if she could trust him—and for that reason she dared not tell him that she was having his baby.

Giannis let himself into the apartment and walked noiselessly down the passageway towards the bedroom. He had a ton of work to do following his successful bid to buy Markou Shipping, but he'd been unable to concentrate during his meeting with TGE's board because he had been worried about Ava. She had looked pale and fragile when he'd left her at the pharmacy and he felt guilty that he had not taken care of her. His conscience pricked that he should have brought her home and stayed with her while he sent his housekeeper out to buy medication for Ava's migraine.

He did not understand what had happened to him over the past month. His plan that Ava should pose as his fake fiancée had seemed simple enough. But they had become lovers and, more surprisingly, friends. He had even taken her to Spetses, although he'd never invited any of his previous mistresses to Villa Delphine, which he regarded as his private sanctuary. He'd told himself that the trip to the island was to promote the pretence that they were engaged but, instead of staying for a weekend as he'd intended, they had spent two weeks there. He had even found himself resenting the few hours each day that he'd had to get on with some work because he'd wanted to spend time with Ava, at the pool or the beach or—his preferred option—in bed.

She was beautiful, intelligent, sometimes fierce, often funny and always sexy. It was little things, Giannis mused. Like the way she ate a fresh peach for breakfast every morning with evident enjoyment, licking the juice from her lips with her tongue. Or how she migrated over to his side of the bed in the middle of the night so that when he woke in the morning she was curled up against his chest, warm and soft and infinitely desirable.

Theos, he was behaving like a hormone-fuelled teenager, Giannis thought impatiently as he felt the aching hardness of his arousal. He opened the bedroom door quietly, not wanting to disturb Ava if she was asleep. But the bed was empty. He recognised the suitcase standing on the floor as the one she had brought with her from

London. A passport was lying on top of it. The wardrobe doors were open and he could see hanging inside were the dresses that the personal shopper in Paris had helped Ava choose.

Something was not right and he felt a sinking sensation in his stomach as Ava walked out of the bathroom and froze when she saw him. She carefully avoided his gaze and Giannis's eyes narrowed. He leaned nonchalantly against the door frame and kept his tone deliberately bland. 'Are you going somewhere, *glykiá mou*?'

'There is no need for you to refer to me as your sweetheart now that you have secured your deal with Stefanos.' She finally glanced at him and he wondered why she was nervous. 'I managed to book a seat on a flight to London leaving this afternoon.'

Icy fingers curled around his heart. 'You need to get back to the UK in a hurry? How is your headache, by the way?' he said drily.

A pink stain swept along her cheekbones. 'It's much better, thank you.' She caught her bottom lip between her teeth and Giannis fought the urge to walk over to her and cover her mouth with his. 'I thought that now you have persuaded Stefanos to sell his company to you, there is no point in me staying in Greece. I really want to go back and focus on my career.'

Anger flickered inside him and he wanted to tell her that there was every bloody point. They were good together—in bed and out of it. Not that he had any intention of admitting how much he enjoyed her company. This inconvenient attraction he felt for her—he refused to call it an obsession—*would* fade. He just could not say exactly when.

'I thought we decided at Stefanos's party that there was no reason for you to return to the UK immediately.'

'*You* decided. You didn't ask me what I wanted.' She glared at him. 'It sounds familiar, doesn't it?'

What the hell had happened to have brought about a dramatic change in Ava's attitude? Giannis searched his mind for clues that might explain why she was speaking to him in a cool voice that echoed the wintry expression in her grey eyes. Before they had gone to meet Stefanos she had responded to him with an eagerness that made his heart pound. But he noticed how she stiffened when he walked towards her.

She had acted oddly, almost secretively, when she'd shot out of the car and hurried into the pharmacy earlier, he remembered. Maybe her edginess was because it was a certain time in her monthly cycle. Relieved that he had found a likely explanation, he relaxed and murmured, 'I have a suggestion. You are not due to begin your new job in London for nearly another month. Why not stay in Greece until then? And when you return to England we could still meet up. I visit London fairly regularly for business, and I could rent an apartment for us.'

'Are you asking me to be your mistress?'

Giannis hid his irritation. Had she been hoping for more? For him to suggest that they make their fake engagement real, perhaps? Women were all the same, always wanting more than he was prepared to give. With a jolt of surprise he realised that he was not completely opposed to the idea of having a conventional relationship with Ava.

He shrugged. 'Mistress, lover—what does it matter?' He stretched out his hand to stroke her hair and his jaw hardened when she shrank from him. They could play games all day, he thought grimly. He had a sudden sense that he was standing on the edge of a precipice and his gut clenched with something like fear as he prepared to leap into the unknown. 'What matters is that I don't want this...us...to end—yet. I need to know what you want, Ava.'

He thought she hesitated, but maybe he imagined it. She picked up her suitcase and said in a fierce voice that stung Giannis as hard if she had slapped him, 'I want to go home.'

CHAPTER EIGHT

A BLAST OF bitingly cold January air followed Giannis through the door when he strode into TGE UK's plush office building in Bond Street. He disliked winter and London seemed particularly gloomy now that the party season was over. Even the festive lights along Oxford Street had lost some of their sparkle.

He had spent a miserable Christmas with his mother, swamped by guilt, as he was every year, because he knew he was the cause of her unhappiness. For New Year he had stayed at an exclusive ski resort in Aspen. But as the clock had struck midnight he'd made an excuse to the sultry brunette who had hung on his arm all evening and returned to his hotel room alone.

Maybe he was coming down with the flu virus that was going around, he brooded. He was rarely ill, but it might explain his loss of appetite, inability to sleep and a worrying indifference to work, friends and sex. Especially sex.

When Ava had handed him the pink sapphire heart ring before she'd walked out of his apartment in Athens without a backward glance, Giannis had assumed that he would have no trouble forgetting her. He'd thought he had been successful when he'd danced at the New Year's Eve party with the brunette whose name eluded him. But when Dana?—Donna?—had offered to perform a private striptease for him he had thought of Ava's long honey-blonde hair spilling over her breasts, her cool grey eyes and her fiery passion and he had finally admitted to himself that he missed her.

There were a few unopened letters on his desk and he frowned as he flicked through them. His secretary at the UK office had been rushed into hospital with appendicitis shortly before Christmas. The temp who had replaced Phyllis should have opened his private mail and forwarded anything of importance to him. It was obvious that some of the envelopes contained Christmas cards, but as it was now the second week in January he was tempted to throw them in the bin. Exhaling heavily, he opened a card, glanced at the picture of an improbably red-breasted robin and turned it over to read the note inside.

The handwriting was difficult to decipher and he was surprised to see the name 'Sam McKay' scrawled at the bottom of the card. Giannis remembered that Ava had said her brother had struggled at school because he was dyslexic.

Dear Mr Gekas
I wanted to say thanks for letting me off about the damage done to your boat. It was desent of you. Sorry about you and Ava not getting married. Its a shame it didnt work out and about the baby.
Happy christmas
Sam McKay

Baby! Giannis reread the note twice more and tried to make sense of it. Whose baby? He looked at the date stamp on the card's envelope and swore when he saw that Sam had posted it on the fifteenth of December—more than three weeks ago.

He could hear his heartbeat thudding in his ears as a shocking idea formed in his brain. Could Ava be pregnant with *his* baby? If so, then why hadn't she told him? The blood in his veins turned to ice. What the hell had Sam meant in his badly written note when he'd said that it was a shame about the baby? Had Ava suffered a miscarriage? Or had she…?

Giannis swallowed the bile that rose up in his throat. The memory of when Caroline had told him that she was no longer pregnant still haunted him. He had felt as if his heart had been ripped out, but Caroline had regarded her pregnancy as an inconvenience.

He stared at Sam's unsatisfactory note and sucked in a sharp breath when he thought back to the day three months ago at the apartment in Athens when Ava had acted so strangely. Had she known that she was pregnant but had decided that a baby would not fit in with her career?

Theos, he was terrified that history was repeating itself. First Caroline, and now Ava. Something cold and hard settled in the pit of his stomach. He had lost one child, but if Ava was expecting his baby he would move heaven and earth to have a second chance at fatherhood.

Giannis picked up the phone on the desk and noticed that his hand was shaking as he put a call through to his secretary's office. The temp answered immediately. 'Cancel all my meetings,' he told her brusquely. 'I'll be out for the rest of the day.'

There was a 'sold' sign outside the terraced house in East London where, four months ago, Giannis had taken Ava to collect her passport before they had flown to Paris. If she had already moved away he would find her, he vowed grimly as he walked up the front path and hammered his fist on the door. If she was pregnant and hoped to keep his child from him, she would discover that there was nowhere on earth she could hide.

The front door opened and Ava's eyes widened when she saw him. She quickly tried to close the door but Giannis put his foot out to prevent her.

'What do you want?' she demanded, but beneath her sharp tone he sensed her fear. Of him? He ignored the peculiar pang his heart gave and used his shoulder to push the door wider open so that he could step into the narrow hallway.

'I want the truth.' He handed her the Christmas card he'd received from her brother. Looking puzzled, she read the note inside the card and flushed.

'I haven't explained to Sam that I pretended to be your fiancée so you would drop the charges against him,' she said stiffly. 'I suppose he thinks I'm upset that our engagement is over—which I'm not, of course.'

'Only one part of your brother's note interests me,' Giannis told her coldly. 'Is the baby that Sam refers to *my* baby?' He watched the colour drain from Ava's face and felt dangerously out of control.

'I don't have to tell you anything. And you have no right to force your way into my house.' She backed up along the hallway as he walked towards her.

'Were you pregnant when you left Athens?'

Instead of replying, she spun round and ran into the sitting room. Giannis was right behind her and he found that he had to squeeze past numerous boxes. Evidently the contents of the house had been packed up ready to be loaded onto a removals van. He came out in a cold sweat, thinking that if he had not read Sam's note for another few days he would have been too late to confront Ava.

'Answer me, damn it,' he said harshly.

Ava was cornered in the cramped room and she grabbed a heavy-based frying pan from one of the packing boxes. 'Stay away from me,' she said fiercely, waving the frying pan in the air. 'I'll defend myself if I have to.'

Giannis forced himself to control his temper when he heard real fear in her voice. 'I'm not going to harm you,' he growled. 'All I want is your honesty. I have a right to know if you had conceived my child.'

After several tense seconds she slowly lowered her arm and dropped the frying pan back into the box. Her teeth gnawed on her bottom lip. 'All right...*yes*. I had just found out that I was pregnant when I flew back to London.'

Giannis stared at her slender figure in dark jeans and a loose white sweater. Her honey-gold hair was tied in a ponytail and her peaches-and-cream skin glowed with health. She looked even more beautiful than he remembered. But she did not look pregnant. Surely there would be some sign by now? When his PA in Greece had been expecting, her stomach had seemed to grow bigger daily.

He shoved his hands into his coat pockets and clenched his fingers so tightly that his nails bit into his palms. 'You said that you *were* pregnant,' he said stiltedly, fighting to hold back the volcanic mass of his emotions from spewing out. 'Does it mean that either by accident or design there is no longer a baby?'

Now she stared back at him and her eyes were as dark as storm clouds. 'Accident or design? I don't think I understand.'

'Your brother said in the Christmas card that it was a shame about the baby. And before you left Athens you told me you wanted to focus on your career. Did you terminate the pregnancy?'

She reeled backwards and knocked over a box of

Christmas decorations, sending gaudy baubles rolling across the carpet. '*No*, I did not.'

Giannis snatched a breath. He needed her to spell it out for him. 'So you are carrying my child?'

'Yes.' Her voice was a whisper of sound, as if she was reluctant to confirm the news that blew him away. 'Sam thought it was a shame that we had broken up when I am expecting your baby,' she muttered.

Euphoria swept through Giannis but it was swiftly replaced with anger. 'Why the hell did you try to keep it a secret from me? I had a right to know that I am to be a father.'

'Don't take that moral tone with me. You have no rights to this baby, Giannis.' Colour flared on Ava's pale cheeks and her eyes flashed with temper. 'I know what you are. I've heard the rumour that you are involved with the Greek mafia.'

'*What?*' Shock ricocheted through Giannis. He wondered if Ava was joking, even if the joke was in very poor taste. But as they faced each other across the room full of packing boxes and spilt shiny baubles he realised that she was serious.

'No doubt you will deny it. But I didn't tell you about my pregnancy because I won't take the risk of my baby having a criminal for a father.' She crossed her arms defensively in front of her and glared at him.

He kept his hands in his pockets in case he was tempted to shake some sense into her. Not that he would ever lay a finger on a woman in anger, and certainly not the mother of his child. Giannis's heart lurched as the astounding reality sank in that Ava was expecting his baby.

Five years ago he had lost his unborn child, but by a miracle he had been given another chance to be a father. A chance perhaps of redemption. He wanted to be a good father, as his own father had been, and he would love his child as deeply as his father had loved him. Emotions that he had buried for the last fifteen years threatened to overwhelm him. But he had to deal with Ava's shocking accusation and somehow defuse the volatile situation.

'Of course I deny that I belong to a criminal organisation because it's not true. Who told you the rumour about me?'

'I'm not prepared to say.'

'It must have been at Stefanos's party.' Giannis knew he had guessed correctly when Ava dropped her gaze. He remembered that her attitude towards him had changed when they had spent the night on Gaia. She had left the party early, saying she had a headache. When she had been sick the next morning she had blamed it on a migraine, but she must have known then that she was pregnant.

Fury swirled, black and bitter, inside him at the realisation that Ava had tried to hide his child from him because she had believed an unfounded rumour. A memory flashed into his mind.

'I saw you talking to Petros Spyriou at the party while I was with Stefanos. Did he tell you the ridiculous story that I am a criminal?'

'I don't know the name of the man who spoke to me.'

'So you believed the words of a stranger without question and without giving me a chance to refute his slanderous allegations?' When she bit her lip but said nothing, Giannis continued, 'We had been lovers for a month before we went to Gaia, yet what we shared clearly meant nothing to you.'

'What did we share, Giannis, other than sex and lies? You blackmailed me to be your fake fiancée so that you could trick Stefanos to sell his company to you.' Her voice faltered. 'When I heard a rumour that you use TGE as a cover for your criminal activities I didn't know what to believe.'

'So you ran away,' he said scathingly. The savage satisfaction he felt when colour flared on her face did not lessen his unexpected sense of betrayal, of hurt, *damn it*, that she had so little faith in him.

When they had stayed on Spetses he had spent more time with her than he'd done with any other woman. Even when he had dated Caroline for nearly a year, their relationship had amounted to meeting for dinner a couple of times a week and occasional weekends together when their work schedules had aligned.

'Petros Spyriou is Stefanos's nephew,' he told Ava. 'Petros believes that his uncle should have put him in charge of Markou Shipping instead of selling the company to me. He is jealous of me, which is why he made up disgusting lies about me.' Giannis gave a grim laugh. 'Petros succeeded in scaring you away but he'll find himself in court facing charges of slander and defamation of character.'

'He said that a few years ago a journalist tried to investigate you but was dissuaded from publishing information that he'd discovered about you.'

Inside his coat pockets, Giannis curled his hands into fists and wished that Stefanos's weasel of a nephew was standing in front of him. His criminal record had been expunged ten years after he'd served his prison sentence, which was standard procedure in Greek law. But somehow a journalist had found out about it and demanded money to keep quiet. Giannis had been loath to give in to blackmail, but coming soon after he'd broken up with Caroline, and the loss of his first child, his emotions had been raw and he'd been desperate to keep the details of his father's death out of the media spotlight.

He had no idea how Stefanos's nephew had found out about the journalist, and he guessed that Petros did not know what information the journalist had discovered. But the suggestion that there were secrets Giannis wanted to keep hidden must have been useful to Petros when he'd told Ava lies about him being involved with the Greek mafia. The story was so crazy it was laughable—yet Ava had believed Petros and as a result she had hidden her pregnancy, Giannis thought bitterly.

His jaw clenched as he remembered that while they had lived together at Villa Delphine he had been tempted to confess to Ava that he had been responsible for his father's untimely death. Thank God he had not bared his soul to her. He certainly would not tell her the truth now. He could imagine her horrified reaction and he dared not risk her disappearing again with his baby.

'Everything Petros told you was pure fabrication.' He shrugged. 'Believe me, or don't believe me. I don't give a damn. But you won't keep my child from me. If you attempt to, I will seek custody and I will win because I have money and power and you have neither.'

'No court ruling would allow a baby to be separated from its mother,' Ava snapped, but had paled.

Giannis flicked his eyes over her, his emotions once more under control. 'Are you willing to take the risk?'

His black gaze was so cold. Ava gave a shiver. It seemed impossible that Giannis's eyes had ever gleamed with warmth and laughter. Or that they had once been friends as well as lovers. But their wild passion had resulted in the baby that was growing bigger in her belly every day. Giannis's child. It was strange how emotive those two words were, and even stranger that when she had seen him standing on the doorstep her body had quivered in response to his potent masculinity.

She must be the weakest woman in the world, she thought bleakly. He had barged his way into her home and threatened to try to take her baby from her, yet her heart ached as she roamed her eyes over his silky hair and the sculpted perfection of his features. She had thought about him constantly for the last three months but, standing in the chaotic sitting room, he was taller than she remembered and his shoulders were so broad beneath the black wool coat he wore.

He was like a dark avenging angel, but was his anger justified? Had she been too ready to believe the rumour that he was a criminal because of her father's criminality? Ava wondered. Supposing Stefanos's jealous nephew *had* lied? If she hadn't had that devastating conversation with Petros, she would have told Giannis as soon as she'd done the test that she was pregnant, and perhaps he would not be looking down his nose at her as if she were something unpleasant that he had scraped off the bottom of his shoe.

A loud knock on the front door broke the tense silence in the sitting room. She glanced towards the window and saw a lorry parked outside the house. 'We'll have to continue this conversation another time,' she told Giannis. 'The removals firm are here to take my mother's furniture into storage now that she has sold the house.'

He frowned. 'I thought this house belonged to you, and you had sold it because you planned to move away so that I couldn't find you.'

'I lived here with my family before we moved to Cyprus. My father had registered the deeds of the house in my mother's name. After my dad...' she hesitated '...after my parents divorced, Mum, Sam and I came back to live here, although I went away to university. My mother and her new partner have bought a bed and breakfast business in the Peak District.'

'So where will you live? I assume you will need to stay in the East End to be near to your work. At least while you are able to continue working until the baby is born,' Giannis said, the groove between his brows deepening.

She looked away from him. 'I was made redundant from my job when the victim support charity I worked for couldn't continue to fund my role. I've arranged to rent a room in a friend's house, but I'm thinking of moving back to Scotland where property is cheaper and I will be nearer to Sam and Mum.'

She would need help from her family after she became a single mother, Ava thought as she hurried down the hallway to open the front door. The removals team trooped in and it quickly became clear that she and Giannis were in the way, when the men started to carry furniture and boxes out to the van.

'You had better go,' she told him. 'My friend Becky, who I am going to stay with, offered to come over later to collect my things as I don't have a car.'

'I'll put whatever you want to take with you in my car and drive you to her house.' Giannis's crisp tone brooked no argument. 'Which boxes are yours?'

She pointed to two packing boxes by the window and when his brows rose she said defensively, 'I don't like clutter, or see the point in having too many clothes.'

'Is that why you left the dresses that I'd bought for you during our engagement back at the apartment in Athens?'

'I left the clothes and the engagement ring behind because you did not buy me, Giannis.' The idea that he had paid for the designer dresses and the beautiful pink sapphire ring with money he might have made illegally was repugnant to Ava, and a painful reminder of her privileged childhood which she'd later discovered had been funded by her father's crimes.

Giannis's eyes narrowed but he said nothing as he picked up one of the boxes which contained her worldly possessions. But when Ava bent down to pick up the second box he said sharply, 'Put it down. You should not be lifting heavy things in your condition.'

'Who do you think packed all the boxes and lugged them down the stairs?' she said drily. 'Mum is busy getting her new house ready and I have spent weeks clearing this place, ready for the new owners to move in.'

'From now on you will not do any strenuous activity that could harm my baby,' Giannis growled. His accent was suddenly thicker and he sounded very Greek and *very* possessive. Ava supposed she should feel furious that he was being so bossy, but her stupid heart softened at his concern for his child. Since she'd left Athens she had debated endlessly with herself about whether she should tell him she was pregnant. One reason for not doing so was that she had assumed he would be angry at having fatherhood foisted on him. She was surprised by his determination to be involved with the baby.

She had already given the house keys to the estate agent and when she walked down the front path for the last time Ava realised that she was severing the final link with her father. Number fifty-one Arthur Close was where Terry McKay had plotted his armed robberies and controlled his turf. He had been a ruthless gangland boss, but to Ava he had been a fun person who had built her a treehouse in the garden. She had been utterly taken in by her father's charming manner but finding out the truth about him had left her deeply untrusting.

After the bitterly cold wind whipping down Arthur

Close, the interior of Giannis's car was a warm and luxurious haven. Ava sank deep into the leather upholstery and gave him the postcode of Becky's house.

'Put your seat belt on,' he reminded her. But, before she could reach for it, he leaned across her and she breathed in the spicy scent of his aftershave. He smelled divine, and for a moment his face was close to hers and she hated herself for wanting to press her lips to the dark stubble that shaded his jaw.

He secured her seat belt and she released a shaky breath when he moved away from her and put the car into gear. Did her body respond to Giannis because it instinctively recognised that he was the father of her child? How could she still desire him when she did not know if she could trust him? she wondered despairingly. The sight of his tanned hands on the steering wheel evoked memories of how he had pleasured her with his wickedly inventive fingers. *Stop it,* she told herself, and closed her eyes so that she was not tempted to look at him.

He switched the radio onto a station playing easy listening music, and the smooth motion of the car had a soporific effect on Ava. She'd been lucky that she'd had few pregnancy symptoms and the sickness she had experienced in the first weeks had gone. But the bone-deep tiredness she felt these days was quite normal, the midwife had told her at her check-up. It was nature's way of making her rest so that the baby could grow.

When she opened her eyes she wondered for a moment where she was, before she remembered that Giannis had offered to take her across town to Becky's house. So why were they driving along the motorway? The clock on the dashboard showed that she had been asleep for nearly an hour.

She jerked her gaze to Giannis. 'This isn't the way to

Fulham. Where are you taking me?' Panic flared and she unconsciously placed her hand on her stomach to protect the fragile new life inside her.

'We are going to my house in St Albans. We'll be there in about ten minutes.' He glanced at her. 'We need to talk.'

'I don't want to talk to you.' She reached for the door handle and Giannis swore.

'It's locked. Are you really crazy enough to want to throw yourself out of the car travelling at seventy miles an hour?'

His words brought her to her senses. 'I have nothing to say to you. You…threatened to take my baby from me.' Her voice shook and she sensed that he sent her another glance.

'I was angry,' he said roughly.

'That doesn't make it okay to speak to me the way you did.'

'I know.' He exhaled heavily. 'I don't want to fight with you, Ava. But I want what is best for the baby, and I do not believe that being brought up in a bedsit and being dumped in a nursery for hours every day while you go to work is anywhere near the best start in life that we can give to our child.' He paused for a heartbeat and said quietly, 'Do you?'

Unable to think of an answer, she turned her head to look out of the window so that he would not see the tears that had filled her eyes when he'd said *our child*. For the first time since she had stared in disbelief at the positive sign on the pregnancy test, she felt that she wasn't alone. It made her realise how scared she had been at the prospect of having a baby on her own, with no one to share the worry and responsibility with. Her mother was busy with her new life and partner, and her brother thankfully seemed to be sorting himself and enjoyed working on their aunt and uncle's farm. There was no one she could rely on apart from Giannis. But, despite his assurance that he wasn't a criminal, she did not know if she believed him.

They left the motorway and drove through a small village before Giannis turned the car through some wrought iron gates which bore a sign saying 'Milton Grange'. At the end of the winding driveway stood a charming Georgian house built on four storeys, with mullioned windows and ivy growing over the walls.

Snow had been falling lightly for the last half an hour and the bay trees in front of the house were dusted with white frosting. But, although the snow looked pretty, Ava was glad to step into the warm hallway where they were greeted by Giannis's housekeeper.

'The fire is lit in the drawing room and lunch will be in half an hour,' the woman, whom Giannis introduced as Joan, said when she had taken their coats.

'What a beautiful house,' Ava murmured as she looked around the comfortably furnished drawing room, decorated in soft neutral shades so that the effect was calming and homely.

'I bought it as an investment,' Giannis told her. 'But it's too big, especially as I do not live here permanently. I arranged for a charity which provides help to parents and families of disabled children to use the top two floors as a respite centre. Builders reconfigured the upper floors and in effect turned one large house into two separate properties.'

Ava sat down in an armchair close to the fire and furthest away from the sofa where Giannis took a seat. He gave her a sardonic look but said evenly, 'Would you like tea or coffee?' A tray on the low table in front of him held a cafetière and a teapot.

'Tea, please. I should only drink decaffeinated coffee,

but actually I've gone off coffee completely since I've been pregnant. Just the smell of it made me sick at first.'

He frowned. 'Do you suffer very badly with morning sickness? It can't be good for the baby if you are unable to keep food down. Are you eating well?'

'I'm fine now, and I'm eating too well.' She gave a rueful sigh. 'If I'm not careful I'll be the size of a house.'

'You look beautiful,' he said gruffly. Ava swallowed as her eyes met his and she felt a familiar tug deep in her pelvis. He was *so* handsome and she suddenly wished that the situation between them was different, and instead of offering her a cup of tea he would whisk her upstairs and make long, slow and very satisfying love to her.

'How far along is your pregnancy?'

'I'm eighteen weeks. At twenty weeks I am due to have another ultrasound scan to check the baby's development and I'll be able to find out the sex.' She bit her lip. 'It's possible that I conceived the first time we slept together in London.'

'As I recall, neither of us slept much that night,' he drawled in that arrogant way of his which Ava found infuriating.

'But now we must deal with the consequences of our actions,' she said flatly.

He took a sip of his coffee and said abruptly, 'I would like to come to your scan appointment. Do you want to find out the baby's sex?'

'I think I do. I suppose you hope it's a boy.' If the baby was a girl, perhaps Giannis would lose interest in his child. Her hand shook slightly as she placed the delicate bone china teacup and saucer down on the table.

'I will be equally happy to have a daughter or a son. All that matters is that the child is born safe and well.'

His words echoed Ava's own feelings and her emotions threatened to overwhelm her. She was too warm sitting by the fire, but she did not want to move nearer to Giannis. Instead she pulled off her jumper and only then remembered that the strap-top she was wearing beneath it was too small. The material was stretched over her breasts, which had grown two bra sizes bigger. She hoped he would assume that the flush she could feel spreading across her face was due to the warmth of the fire and not because she'd glimpsed a raw hunger in his eyes that evoked a molten heat inside her. She tensed when he stood up and strolled over to where she was sitting.

'You said that you are currently without a job, so how were you planning to manage financially?'

'My old job in Glasgow is still available. Working as a VCO is not a popular or well-paid career,' she said ruefully. 'I will be entitled to maternity pay for a few months after the baby is born, but then I'll have to go back to work to support both of us.'

'I want to be involved with my child,' Giannis told her in a determined voice. 'And of course I will provide financial support for you and the baby.'

'I don't want your money,' she said stubbornly. She could not bear for him to think that she had trapped him with her pregnancy because he was wealthy.

'What you want and what I want is not important. The only thing that matters is that we do the right thing for our child, who was unplanned but not unwanted—am I right that we at least agree on that?' he said softly.

His voice was like rough velvet and Ava nodded, not trusting herself to speak when she felt so vulnerable. 'What do you suggest then?' she asked helplessly.

He hesitated for a heartbeat. 'I think we should get married.'

CHAPTER NINE

FOR A FEW seconds Ava could not breathe, and there was an odd rushing sensation in her ears. Giannis had not said that he *wanted* to marry her, she noted. And why would he? All he wanted was the baby she carried, and she was simply a necessary part of the equation.

'You're crazy,' she said flatly. 'It wouldn't work.'

He pulled up a footstool and sat down in front of her, so close that it would be easy to stretch out her hand and touch the silken darkness of his hair—easy and yet impossible.

'What is the alternative?' he asked levelly. 'Even if we came to an amicable agreement about shared custody, a child needs stability, which I can provide in Greece at Villa Delphine. I could buy a house for you in England and we could send our child back and forth between us like a ping-pong ball—Christmas with you, first birthday with me, and so on. But that wouldn't make me happy, I don't think it would make you happy and I'm certain it would not be a happy childhood for our son or daughter.'

Ava couldn't argue with his logic. Everything Giannis said made sense. But her emotions weren't logical or sensible; they were all over the place. She tensed when he took hold of her hand and rubbed his thumb lightly over the pulse thudding in her wrist.

'Like it or not, you and the baby are my responsibility and I want to take care of both of you.' He met her gaze and the gleam in his dark eyes sent a quiver of reaction through her. 'Our relationship worked very well for the month that we pretended to be engaged,' he murmured.

It would be too easy to be seduced by his charisma and fall under his spell, but if she was going to survive him she had to be strong and in control. 'We did not have a relationship—we had sex,' she reminded him tartly.

The word hung in the air between them, taunting Ava with memories of their wild passion and Giannis's body claiming hers with powerful thrusts.

'Don't knock it, *glykiá mou*,' he drawled. 'You enjoyed it as much as I did.'

Hot-faced with embarrassment, she dropped her gaze from his amused expression and wondered what he was thinking. Her pregnancy was not really showing yet, but she was conscious of her thickening waistline which meant that she had to leave the button on her jeans undone. Before Giannis had met her, he had slept with some of the world's most beautiful women—and she doubted his bed had been empty for the past months that they had been apart.

'So, do you expect it to be a proper marriage?' she said stiffly.

His eyes narrowed. 'I do not expect anything, certainly not intimacy, unless you decide it is what you want.'

She should feel relieved by Giannis's assurance that he would not put pressure on her to consummate their marriage, but Ava felt even more confused. He was a red-blooded male and celibacy would not be a natural state for him. But perhaps he intended to find pleasure elsewhere. For her own protection she needed to ignore the chemistry between them while she was still unsure if she could believe his insistence that he was not a criminal.

Giannis stood up and offered her his hand to help her to her feet. 'What is your answer?'

She ignored his hand. 'I need time to consider my options.' Her tone was as cool as his. They could have been discussing a business deal instead of a decision which would affect the rest of their lives. But her pregnancy had already had a fundamental effect, and it occurred to her that, whether or not she accepted his proposal, they would be linked for ever by the child they had created between them.

'Do not consider them for too long,' he said as he ushered her out of the drawing room and across the hall to the dining room. 'I intend for us to be married well before the baby is born.' The implacable note in Giannis's voice warned Ava that the only option he would accept was her agreement to become his wife.

'The gel will feel cold, I'm afraid,' the sonographer said cheerfully before she squirted a dollop of thick, clear lubricant onto Ava's stomach.

Ava tried to suck her tummy in as the sonographer smeared the gel over her bump. She was intensely conscious of Giannis sitting beside the hospital bed where she was lying for the ultrasound scan. Her top was tucked up under her breasts and her trousers were pushed down low on her hips, leaving her stomach bare. From her angle, looking down her body, her stomach seemed huge, which was hardly surprising after she had spent the past couple of weeks enjoying Giannis's housekeeper's wonderful cooking, she thought ruefully.

'I understand you need to eat for two,' Joan had said cheerfully when Giannis announced that he and Ava would be getting married as soon as it could be arranged. The wedding could not take place until twenty-eight days after they had given notice at the local register office.

The bright lights in the scanning room made the pink sapphire ring on Ava's finger sparkle. This time her engagement was real, and her heart lurched at the thought that very soon she would be Giannis's wife.

She had accepted his proposal the day after he had asked her to marry him—following a sleepless night when she'd faced the stark choice of having to believe him or Stefanos Markou's nephew. On a practical level she knew that Giannis was determined to be a father to his baby and she concluded that she would be in a better position to safeguard herself and her child if she was married to him.

'You can choose a different ring if you would prefer not to wear this one,' he'd said when he had returned the pink sapphire heart to her.

Ava had slid the ring onto her finger and told herself that she hadn't missed it being there for the past few months. 'It seems fitting to keep the ring that you gave me while I was your fake fiancée, seeing as our marriage will be one of convenience,' she'd said stubbornly, determined he would not know how much she had missed him.

His eyes had gleamed dangerously but he'd said evenly, 'Whatever you wish, *glykiá mou.*'

What she had wished was for him to pull her into his arms and kiss her senseless so that she could pretend they were lovers back on Spetses—before rumours, doubts and her pregnancy had driven a wedge between them. But Giannis had walked out of the room and she'd felt too vulnerable to go after him and make the first move to try to break the stalemate in their relationship.

She pulled her mind back to the present as the sonographer moved the probe over her stomach. 'If you look on the screen, here is Baby's heart—you can see it beating. And this here is one of Baby's hands…and just here is the other hand…' The sonographer pointed to the grey image on the screen. 'You can make out Baby's face quite clearly.'

Ava caught her breath as she stared at her baby's tiny features. She felt Giannis squeeze her fingers. She'd already had a scan at twelve weeks, to accurately date her pregnancy, but this was his first experience of seeing his child and she wondered how he felt now that the baby was a tangible reality rather than something they had spoken about.

The sonographer spent several minutes studying the baby's vital organs and taking measurements. 'Everything looks absolutely as it should do,' she said at last. 'I understand that you have decided to find out the baby's sex.'

'Yes,' they both replied at the same time.

The sonographer smiled. 'You are going to have a little boy. Congratulations.'

Ava tore her eyes from the image of her son—*her son*! Blinking back tears of pride and joy, she glanced at Giannis. Her heart turned over when she saw a tear slide down his cheek as he stared intently at the screen. He dashed his hand over his face and when he turned to her he showed no sign of the fierce emotion she had witnessed although, when she looked closely, his eyes were suspiciously bright.

'Now we know what colour to paint the nursery,' he murmured.

She nodded, unable to speak past the lump that had formed in her throat. Whatever happened between them, she knew now, without doubt, that Giannis would love his son and would never be parted from him. Which meant that somehow they would have to make their unconventional marriage work.

Another thought slid insidiously into her mind as she remembered her ex's scathing comments when she had admitted to him that her father was the infamous East End gangster, Terry McKay. Craig had decided against marrying her for fear that their children might grow up to be criminals like their grandfather.

Of course there was not a 'criminal' gene, Ava tried to reassure herself. But she couldn't forget what Stefanos's nephew had told her about Giannis being involved in organised crime. If the rumour about him was true, and if there was such a thing as a 'criminal' gene, what would the future hold for the baby?

In the car on the way back to Milton Grange neither of them spoke much. Ava's thoughts were going round and round in her head and she did not have the energy to try to breach the emotional distance that existed between her and Giannis. His playboy reputation when she had first met him had made her believe that he was not capable of feeling strong emotions, but that was patently not true, she realised as she remembered the tears on his face when he had seen the scan images of his baby son.

When they arrived at the house he went straight to his study, citing an important business phone call that he needed to make. The cold, grey weather at the end of January did not encourage Ava to go out for a walk, and instead she made use of the heated swimming pool in the conservatory.

She hadn't got round to buying a maternity swimsuit, and the bikini that she'd bought from a boutique on Spetses barely fitted over her fuller breasts. But no one was going to see her, and the midwife had said that swimming was a good form of exercise during pregnancy. The water was warm and she swam several laps before she climbed out of the pool and wrung her dripping-wet hair between her hands. A sudden blast of cold air rushed into the conservatory as the door opened, and her heart gave a jolt when Giannis strode in wearing a towelling robe.

'You said you would be working all afternoon,' she muttered, feeling heat spread over her face as he stared at her ridiculously small bikini that revealed much more of her body than she was comfortable with. She was tempted to run across to the lounger where she had left her towel, but she couldn't risk slipping on the wet tiles.

'I was bored of working and decided to come and swim with you.' He shrugged off his robe and Ava roamed her gaze hungrily over his muscular chest covered in black hairs that arrowed down his taut abdomen and disappeared beneath the waistband of his swim-shorts.

'Well, I've got out of the pool now.' Her flush deepened when she realised the inanity of her statement.

'I can see that,' he mocked her softly. But as he walked towards her his smile faded and his dark eyes glittered with a feral hunger that confused her.

'Stop staring at me.' She tried to cover the gentle swell of her stomach with her hands but could do nothing to disguise the fact that her breasts were almost spilling out of her bikini top. She felt exposed, knowing she looked fat, and sure that Giannis must be comparing her to all the gorgeous women who had shared his bed in the past.

He halted in front of her and she noticed a nerve jump in his cheek. 'How can I take my eyes from you when you take my breath away?' he said thickly.

Ava bit her lip. 'I was slim the last time you saw me in a bikini.' She had nearly said naked, but memories of when they had lain together, skin on skin, their limbs entwined and their bodies joined would only add fuel to the fire burning inside her.

'You look incredible.' Dark colour winged along his cheekbones. 'Can you feel the baby move?'

'I've felt flutters rather than kicks at this stage but the midwife said that the baby's movements will become stronger as he grows bigger.'

Giannis was focused on her bump. 'May I touch you?'

She gave a hesitant nod. It was his baby too, and she could not deny him the chance to be involved in her pregnancy. But when he placed his hand on her stomach and stretched his fingers wide over its swell she trembled and hoped he had no idea of the molten heat that pooled between her thighs.

'There, did you feel that?' She caught hold of his hand and moved it slightly lower on her stomach just as a fluttering sensation inside her happened again.

He drew an audible breath. *'Theos,'* he said in an oddly gruff voice. 'Between us we have created a miracle, *glykiá mou.'*

Standing this close to him was creating havoc with her emotions. She needed to move away from him and break the spell that he always cast on her. But it was too late, and she watched helplessly as his dark head descended.

'Giannis,' she whispered, but it was a plea rather than a protest and the fierce gleam in his eyes told her that he knew it. His breath warmed her lips before he covered her mouth with his and kissed her the way she had longed for him to kiss her, the way she had dreamed about him kissing her every night since she had left Greece.

She couldn't resist him. It did not even occur to her to try. He was the father of her unborn child, the man she was going to marry, and she wanted him to make love to her. Even the knowledge that *love* played no part in their relationship did not matter at that moment, as desire swept like wildfire through her veins. She had been starved of him and she pressed her body up against his, closing her eyes as she sank into the sensual pleasure of his kiss.

His hand was still resting on her stomach, and she held her breath when he moved lower and ran his fingers over the strip of bare skin above the waistband of her bikini bottoms. She willed him to slip his fingers beneath the stretchy material and touch her where she ached to be touched. She wanted him to push his fingers inside her, and incredibly she felt the first ripples of an orgasm start to build deep in her pelvis before he had even caressed her intimately.

Tension of a different kind ran through her as she faced up to where this was leading. How could she give herself to Giannis when she had doubts about him? In many ways, it had been easier to have sex with him while she had pretended to be his fiancée because she'd assumed that their relationship would end at the same time as their fake engagement. But now she was going to be Giannis's wife—if not for ever then certainly until their child was old enough to be able to cope with them separating. If she made love with Giannis she would reveal her vulnerability that she was desperate to hide from him.

But then suddenly it was over as he wrenched his mouth from hers. She swayed on her feet when he abruptly snatched his arm from around her waist. He swore as he swung away from her and dived into the water.

Ava watched him swim to the far end of the pool and wondered if he had somehow been aware of her doubts. A more likely explanation for his rejection was that he found her pregnant shape a turn-off. Giannis had been attentive because she was carrying his child, but he'd made it clear that he did not want her.

At least she knew where she stood with him, Ava told herself as she dragged her towel around her unsatisfied body to hide the shaming hard peaks of her nipples. He was marrying her to claim his baby. And she had agreed to be his wife because she feared that he would seek custody of their son—not immediately perhaps, but she couldn't bear to live with the threat hanging over her.

Why the hell had he come on to Ava like a clumsy adolescent on a first date? Giannis asked himself furiously as he powered through the water. He heard the conservatory door bang, signalling her departure, but he kept on swimming lap after lap, punishing himself for his loss of control.

Since he had seen the grainy scan images of his child he'd felt as if he were on an emotional rollercoaster. Ava's pregnancy had seemed unreal until the moment the sonographer had pointed out on the screen the baby's tiny heart beating strongly. In that instant he'd realised that nothing—not money or possessions or power—were important compared to his son.

Back at the house he'd paced restlessly around his study, unable to concentrate on a financial report he was supposed to be reading. Work had always been his favourite mistress, the area of his life where he knew he excelled, but—just as when he had taken Ava to Spetses—he had wanted to be with her instead of sitting at his desk.

Walking into the pool house and seeing her in a tiny bikini had blown him away. Pregnancy had turned her into a goddess and he had been transfixed by her generous curves—her breasts like ripe peaches and the lush swell of her belly where his child lay. He'd wanted to touch her and feel a connection with his baby, and when he'd felt the faint movements of a fragile new life a sense of awed wonder had brought a lump to his throat. Something utterly primal had stirred in his chest. His child. His woman. He would die to protect both of them, he acknowledged.

Had he kissed Ava to stake his claim? With savage self-derision he admitted that he'd felt a basic need to pull her down onto a lounger and possess her in the most fundamental way. Desire had drummed an insistent beat in his blood and in his loins. He had forgotten that she did not trust him—although he should not be surprised by her wariness after he had threatened to take her child, he thought grimly.

He had kissed her for the simple reason that he could not resist her, but when he'd felt her stiffen in rejection he knew he had no one to blame but himself. When he'd persuaded her—or pressurised her, his conscience pricked—to marry him, he had promised himself that he would be patient and wait for her to come to him. Instead he'd behaved like a jerk, and in truth he was shocked that she had got under his skin to the degree that she dominated his thoughts and disturbed his dreams.

It would not happen again, Giannis vowed as he climbed out of the pool. He would control his desire for Ava because too much was at stake. He had discovered that he wanted more from her than sex. He wanted everything—her soft smile and infectious laughter, her cool, incisive intelligence and her fiery passion. And he wanted his child. Even if he failed to win all that he hoped for, he *would* have his son.

By the middle of February a thaw had turned the winter wonderland of snow and ice to grey slush, just in time for the wedding which was to take place in the private chapel in the grounds of Milton Grange. Not that Ava cared about the weather when her marriage to Giannis would be as fake as their engagement five months earlier had been.

Since the incident by the pool they had maintained an emotional and physical distance from each other. The closest contact they'd had was when their hands had accidentally brushed as they'd passed each other on the landing, on the way to their separate bedrooms.

She was thankful that the wedding would be a small affair. It had been arranged at short notice, and both her mother and Giannis's mother were on holiday in the warmer climes of the southern hemisphere and could not attend. Her best friend Becky was coming, and Sam had promised to be there. Ava was looking forward to seeing him—although if her brother had not been partly responsible for damaging Giannis's boat she would not now be pregnant and about to marry a man who had become so remote that sometimes she wondered if the close bond she had felt between them on Spetses had been in her imagination.

But the problem was not only Giannis, she acknowledged. Her trust issues meant that she found it difficult to lower her guard. And now her father was once more in the forefront of her mind.

It had started with an email she'd received from an author who was writing a book about East End gangs and had discovered that Ava was Terry McKay's daughter. The author wanted to ask her about her childhood growing up with her notorious gangster father.

She sent a message back saying that she never discussed her father. But Ava knew she could not stop the book being published. People were fascinated by crime, and even though she had changed her name to Sheridan there was always a chance that she would be revealed as Terry McKay's daughter.

It would be unfair for Giannis to find out about her father in a newspaper article or book review, her conscience nagged. She ought to tell him the truth about her background before she married him. Especially as she had come to believe that Stefanos's nephew had lied about Giannis having links to a criminal organisation.

But she could not forget Craig's suggestion that her children might take after her criminal father, and she was fearful of Giannis's reaction. Would he reject her and his son? Maybe she should just keep quiet and hope that he never discovered her real identity. Tormented by indecision, she withdrew into herself—which did not go unnoticed by Giannis.

'You're very pale, and you have barely spoken a word all day,' he commented during dinner on the evening before their wedding. He frowned. 'Do you feel unwell? The baby...'

'I feel fine, and I've felt the baby kicking and I'm sure he is fine too,' she was quick to reassure him. She knew that Giannis's obsessive concern about her health was because he cared about his child. But how would he feel if he was to learn that his son's genes came from a very murky pool? She pushed her food around her plate, her appetite non-existent. 'It's just pre-wedding nerves.'

He gave her a brooding look from across the table. 'There is no reason for you to feel nervous. I have told you that I will not make demands on you,' he said tersely.

If only he would! Ava wished he would whip off the tablecloth, plates and all, and make hot, urgent love to her on the polished mahogany dining table. Sex would at least be some sort of communication between them, rather than the current state of simmering tension and words unspoken.

There had been times over the past weeks when she had caught Giannis looking at her with a hungry gleam in his dark eyes that made her think he still desired her. But then she remembered how he had wrenched his mouth from hers that day by the pool, and her pride would not risk another humiliating rejection if she made the first move.

She went to bed early, giving the excuse that she was tired, and ignored his sardonic expression as he glanced at the clock which showed that it was eight o'clock. Surprisingly she fell asleep, but woke with a start from a dream where she was standing in the church with Giannis and someone in the congregation halted the wedding and denounced her as a gangster's daughter. The look of disgust on Giannis's face stayed in her mind after she had opened her eyes and her stomach gave a sickening lurch as she jumped out of bed and, without stopping to pull on her robe, ran down the hall to his room.

'Ava.' Giannis was sitting up in bed, leaning against the pillows. The black-rimmed reading glasses he wore only added to his rampant sex appeal and in the soft light from the bedside lamp his bare chest gleamed like bronze, covered with whorls of dark hairs. He dropped the documents that he had been studying onto the sheet and sat bolt upright, concern stamped on his handsome face. 'What's wrong?'

'I can't marry you,' she blurted out.

CHAPTER TEN

GIANNIS'S BREATH WHISTLED between his teeth. It was not the first time that Ava had made him feel as if he had been punched in his gut. Her accusation that he was involved in criminal activities had made him furious and her lack of faith in him had hurt more than he cared to admit. Did she still believe Petros's lies, or was there another problem? He racked his brain for something he might have done which had caused her to want to call off the wedding.

'I have done my best to reassure you I do not expect anything from our marriage that you are not willing to give,' he said curtly.

The way she bit her lower lip had a predictable effect on his body and he was grateful that the sheet concealed his uncomfortably hard arousal. She looked mouth-wateringly sexy in a peach-coloured silk negligee that showed off the creamy upper slopes of her breasts—so round and firm, separated by the deep vee of her cleavage where he longed to press his face. He forced himself to concentrate when she spoke.

'I am well aware that you find me sexually unattractive,' she snapped, but her voice shook a little and Giannis had the crazy idea that she sounded hurt. 'That isn't the issue.'

'What is the issue?' He was too tempted to pull her down onto the bed and clear up the misunderstanding about his sexual feelings for her to give a damn about an 'issue'. But Ava was clearly distraught and he resolved to be patient. 'Come, *glykiá mou*,' he murmured. 'Tell me what is troubling you.'

She stopped pacing up and down the room and swung round to face him. 'I haven't been honest with you.'

For one heart-stopping second Giannis wondered if the child she carried was his. She had told him it was likely that she'd conceived the first time they'd had sex, but could she have already been pregnant when he'd met her? If that was so, why would she have hidden her pregnancy from him after she'd left Greece? his mind pointed out.

'When you asked if I wanted to invite my father to the wedding, I told you that I am not in contact with him,' Ava said in a low tone. 'What I failed to say is that my father is serving a fifteen-year prison sentence for armed robbery.'

Giannis released his breath slowly as the tension seeped from him. He felt guilty that he had doubted her. Of course the baby was his. But it occurred to him that there would be no harm in following his lawyer's advice and arranging for a paternity test when the baby was born.

'Do you mean you do not want to get married without your father being present?' It was the only reason he could think of that might explain why she was so upset.

'I mean that I am the daughter of Terry McKay, who once had the dubious honour of being Britain's most wanted criminal.' She buried her face in her hands and gave a sob. 'I'm so ashamed. My father carried out a string of jewellery raids in Hatton Garden and he was involved in drug smuggling and extortion. We—my mum,

Sam and I—knew nothing about his secret life as a criminal until he was arrested and sent to prison.'

Giannis slid out from beneath the sheet and quickly donned a pair of sweatpants before he walked over to Ava and gently pulled her hands down from her face. The sight of tears on her cheeks tugged on his heart. 'Why do you feel ashamed? You were not responsible for your father's behaviour,' he said softly.

'I loved my dad and trusted him. I had no idea that he was a ruthless gangland boss.' She gave another sob. 'The man I thought I knew had fooled me all my life. I find it hard to trust people,' she admitted. 'I was desperate to prevent my brother from turning to a life of crime.'

'I can understand why you were so anxious to save Sam from being sent to a young offenders' institution. And why you believed Petros's lies about me,' Giannis said slowly. He drew Ava into his arms and his heart gave a jolt when she did not resist and sank against him while he lifted his hand and smoothed her hair back from her face. Oddly, he felt as though a weight had been lifted from him now that he knew why she had listened to Stefanos's nephew.

'I'm sorry,' she said huskily. 'I should have known that you are a million times a better man than Petros tried to convince me when he said you were involved in criminal activities.'

A better man? Giannis rested his chin on the top of her head so that he did not have to look into her eyes. What would Ava say if he told her that he had killed his father? Not deliberately—but his stupidity and arrogance when he was nineteen had led to him making a terrible mistake that he would regret for the rest of his life. His conscience insisted that he *should* tell her what he had done. But then she might refuse to marry him or allow him to see his child. His jaw hardened. It was a risk he was not prepared to take.

'I was afraid to tell you about my dad because of how it might make you feel for the baby.'

Puzzled by her words, he eased away from her a fraction and stared at her unhappy face.

'My ex-boyfriend decided not to marry me in case our children inherited a criminality gene. What if our child—?' She broke off, choked by tears.

'Your ex was clearly an idiot.' Giannis drew her close once more. 'Children learn from their environment and our son will have the security of being loved and nurtured by his parents. The things we teach him when he is a child will shape the man he'll grow up to be.'

'I suppose you're right,' she said shakily. Giannis felt her body relax against him as he stroked his hand down the length of her silky golden hair. Hearing that her father was a criminal explained a lot of things and he admired her determination to protect her brother.

He could not pinpoint the exact moment that his desire to comfort her turned to desire of a very different kind. Perhaps she picked up the subtle signals his body sent out—the uneven rise and fall of his chest as his breathing quickened and the hard thud of his heart.

He looked into her eyes and saw her pupils dilate. She licked her tongue over her lips in an unconscious invitation and the ache in his gut became unbearable.

'I know you want me,' he said thickly, and watched a flush of heat spread down from her face to her throat and across her breasts. 'Why did you reject me when we were in the pool house?'

'It was *you* who rejected me. You dived into the swimming pool because you couldn't bear to be near me.'

'You froze when I put my hands on you, and I assumed that you did not like me touching you.'

Ava's blush deepened. 'I liked it too much. But I wasn't sure if I could trust you.' She hesitated and said huskily, 'I'm sorry I listened to Petros.'

'So, do you like it when I touch you here?' Giannis murmured as he slid his hand over the swell of her stomach. He felt a fierce pride knowing that his baby was nestled inside her. He moved his hand lower and heard her give a soft gasp when he lifted up the hem of her negligee and stroked his fingers lightly over the silky panel of her panties between her legs.

'Don't tease me,' she whispered. 'My body has changed from when we first met. I don't want pity sex.'

He made a sound somewhere between a laugh and a groan as he pulled off his sweatpants and pressed the hard length of his arousal against her stomach. 'Does this feel like pity sex, *glykiá mou*?'

His hands shook when he tugged her nightgown over her head and cupped her bounteous breasts in his palms. 'It's true that your body has changed with pregnancy and you are even more beautiful. Have you any idea how gorgeous you are with your erotic curves that I want to explore with my hands and lips? Do you know how it makes me feel when I look at your body, so ripe and full with my child? I feel like I am the king of the world,' he told her rawly. 'And I want to make love to you more than I have ever wanted anything in my life.'

'Then stop talking and make love to me,' she demanded, her fierce voice making him smile before he claimed her mouth and kissed her as if the world was about to end and this was the last time he would taste her sweet lips. He was so hungry. Never in his life had he felt such an overwhelming need for a woman. But

Ava was not any other woman—she was *his*, insisted a primal beast inside him, and the possessiveness he felt was shockingly new.

Despite their mutual impatience, Giannis was determined to take the time to savour every delicious dip and curve of Ava's body. Her breasts, he discovered, were incredibly sensitive, so that when he stroked his hands over the creamy globes and flicked his tongue across one dusky pink nipple and then the other she gave a thin cry that evoked an answering growl deep in his throat.

He lifted her and laid her on the bed, but when she tried to pull him down on top of her he evaded her hands and moved down her body, hooking her legs over his shoulders before he lowered his mouth to her slick feminine heat.

The taste of her almost sent him over the edge, but he ruthlessly controlled his own desire and devoted himself to his self-appointed task of pleasuring her. And he was rewarded when she arched her hips and dug her fingers into his shoulders. Her honey-gold hair was spread across the pillows and Giannis had never seen a more beautiful sight than Ava's rose-flushed face in the throes of her climax.

Only then, when she was still shuddering, did he spread her legs wide and position himself above her, entering her with exquisite care until he was buried deep within her velvet softness.

'I won't break,' she whispered in his ear, as if she guessed that he was afraid to let go of his iron self-control. She moved with him, matching his rhythm as they climbed to the peak together, and when he shattered, she shattered around him. And beneath his ribs the ice surrounding Giannis's heart cracked a little.

* * *

The following day, pale sunshine burst through the clouds and danced over the carpet of snowdrops in the church-yard when Ava posed on the chapel steps with Giannis for the wedding photographer. On her finger was the simple gold band he had put there, and next to it the pink sapphire heart ring that had been his unexpected choice when she'd been his fake fiancée, a lifetime ago, it seemed.

And in a way it was a lifetime. Her name was no longer Sheridan, or McKay. She was Ava Gekas, Giannis's wife, and in a scarily few months she would be a mother.

'Your bump barely shows,' Becky—whom Ava had chosen to be her maid of honour—whispered when the two of them had entered the private chapel where the other guests were assembled and Giannis was waiting for her at the altar. The ivory silk coat-dress Ava had chosen instead of a full-length bridal gown was cleverly cut to disguise her pregnancy, and her bouquet of palest pink roses, white baby's breath and trailing ivy made a pretty focal point.

Giannis was devastatingly handsome in a charcoal-grey suit that emphasised his lean, honed physique. Ava found she was trembling when she stood beside him, ready for the ceremony to begin.

'Are you cold, *glykiá mou*?' he murmured as he took her unsteady hand in his firm grasp. 'I'll warm you later.' The wicked glint in his eyes brought soft colour to her pale cheeks. He might not love her, but their wild passion the previous night was proof that he desired her and gave her hope that they could make something of their marriage. For their child's sake they would have to, Ava mused, and decided that the burst of winter sunshine was a good omen.

The wedding reception was held at a hotel in the village, and afterwards a car drove them to the airfield where Giannis's private jet was waiting to fly them to Greece.

'We will come back after the baby is born,' he said when the plane took off and Ava gave a wistful sigh. 'If you would prefer to live at Milton Grange, I can move my work base to England.'

She stared at him in surprise. 'Would you really do that? I thought you wanted our son to grow up in Greece.'

'We'll make a safe and secure home for him wherever we live, but I want you to be happy, *glykiá mou*.'

Hope unfurled like a fragile bud inside Ava. She had been worried that Giannis might want everything his way, but it sounded as if he was willing to make compromises. She smiled at him. 'I'll be happy living at Villa Delphine. Spetses is a beautiful place to bring up a child, and thankfully it's warmer than England,' she said ruefully. 'I'm looking forward to swimming in the sea.'

He laughed. 'You won't be able to do that for another few months. The sea temperature doesn't warm up until about June.'

'When the baby is due.' She felt butterflies in her stomach at the prospect of giving birth. 'It will be good to take the baby swimming when he is a few months old.'

'And I'll teach him how to sail when he is old enough. I was five when my father first took me sailing, and I loved the excitement of skimming over the waves in Patera's yacht.'

Giannis rarely mentioned his father. Ava looked at him curiously. 'Did your interest in boating have anything to do with your decision to run a cruise line company?'

He nodded. 'My father ran a business giving chartered cruises around the Greek islands. The *Nerissa* was his first motor yacht. There was a lot of competition from other charter operators but, instead of getting into a price war, Patera's idea was to offer a high standard of luxury on the boats, aimed at attracting wealthy clients.' A shadow crossed his face. 'After my father died, I continued to offer exclusivity rather than cheap cruises. The Gekas Experience was my father's brainchild and I was determined to make it successful in his honour.'

'You must miss him,' she said softly.

'I think about him every day. He was a wonderful man and a kind and patient father, as I hope I will be to our son.' Giannis hesitated and Ava sensed that he was about to say something else, but he turned his head and looked out of the window and she felt his barriers go up.

The idea that he was hiding something from her was not an auspicious start to their marriage. But when they arrived on Spetses just as the sun was setting, Giannis insisted on carrying her over the threshold of Villa Delphine as if she were a proper bride and their marriage a true romance, as his staff who were waiting in the entrance hall to greet them clearly believed.

'I have a surprise for you,' he said as he took her hand and led her upstairs. He opened the door on the landing next to the master bedroom. 'What do you think?'

Ava looked around the room that had been turned into a nursery, with pale blue walls and a frieze of farmyard animals. There was a white-painted cot that at the moment was filled with a collection of soft toys, but soon it was where their baby would sleep.

'We can change anything that you don't like,' Giannis said when she remained silent.

She swallowed the lump in her throat. 'It's beautiful and I don't want to change a thing.'

'I asked the builders to create a connecting door into our room,' he explained.

'Our room' had a nice sound, Ava thought as she followed him through the new doorway into the bedroom and went unresistingly into his arms when he drew her towards him.

'I love the nursery.' *I love you.* She kept the words in her heart. Giannis did not love her and that made her feel vulnerable. She felt guilty that she had not trusted him at the beginning of her pregnancy, and it was understandable that it might take him a while to forgive her. But last night had proved that he desired her, and it was a start. She wound her arms around his neck, smiling at his impatient curse when he discovered the dozens of tiny buttons that fastened her dress.

'Patience is a virtue,' she reminded him sweetly, and he punished her by ravishing her mouth with his before he trailed his lips down her throat and tormented her nipples with his tongue until she pleaded for mercy. 'I want you,' she told him when they were both naked and he pulled her down onto the bed.

He grinned as he lounged back against the pillows like an indolent Sultan and beckoned her by crooking his finger. 'Then take me,' he invited. And she did, with a fierce passion that made him groan when she took him deep inside her and made love to him with her body, her heart and her soul.

Afterwards, when he held her in his arms and stroked her hair, Ava pressed her lips against his shoulder and silently whispered the secret in her heart. Give it time, she told herself when he kissed the tip of her nose and settled her against him.

'Go to sleep, *glykiá mou.* You've had a tiring day,' he murmured. They were not the words she longed for him to say, but she thought that he cared for her a little. For the first time since she had learned the truth about her father when she was seventeen, Ava finally relaxed her guard and allowed hope and happiness to fill her heart.

Springtime in Greece arrived earlier than in the UK and the countryside on Spetses was a riot of colourful red poppies and white rock roses with their bright orange centres. Pink daisies bobbed their heads in the breeze and the scents of chamomile and thyme filled the air.

Ava loved the island and quickly grew to think of it as her home. It helped that she spoke Greek, and she chatted with the locals in the market and the little cafés where she stopped for coffee when she went shopping in the pretty town around the old harbour. Some days Giannis travelled to his office in Athens by helicopter, but more often he worked in his study and joined her for lunch on the terrace.

He introduced her to his friends who lived on the island and Ava was surprised that some of them were married couples with children. She had been worried that he would miss his playboy lifestyle and she was heartened that he seemed comfortable and relaxed when they met up with other families.

The weeks slipped by and it seemed that every day the sun shone in the azure sky. The only black cloud to darken Ava's sunny mood was Giannis's mother. Filia had been away, staying with relatives in Rhodes, but when she returned to Spetses Giannis invited her to dinner at Villa Delphine.

Her sharp gaze flew to Ava's baby bump. 'I wondered why the wedding was arranged so quickly,' she said with a sniff. 'Giannis did not do me the courtesy of telling me that I am to be a grandmother.'

Ava shot him a startled glance. It was strange that he hadn't announced her pregnancy to his mother. During dinner she was aware of an undercurrent of tension that her attempts at conversation could not disguise. 'Did you enjoy your trip?' she asked Filia in a desperate bid to break the strained silence between mother and son.

Filia shrugged. 'Loneliness travels with me wherever I go,' she said as her black eyes rested on Giannis. Ava was glad when the uncomfortable evening came to an end. Filia gathered up her shawl and purse. 'I hope you will act more responsibly when *you* are a father than you did with your own father,' she told Giannis.

'Do not doubt it. I will take the greatest care of my son,' he replied curtly.

Later, Ava found him standing outside on the terrace. The night was dark, the moon obscured by clouds, but it emerged briefly and cast a cold gleam over Giannis's hard profile. He looked remote and austere and she did not know how to reach him.

'Your mother is an unhappy woman,' she observed quietly.

He stiffened when she placed her hand over his on the balustrade. His reaction felt like a very definite rejection that stirred up her old feelings of vulnerability. 'I was the cause of her unhappiness,' he said in a clipped voice, but he did not offer any further explanation and Ava was too uncertain of their tenuous relationship to ask him what he meant.

'I'm going to bed,' she murmured. 'Are you coming too?' When they made love she felt closer to him, emotionally as well as physically, and maybe she would find out what was on his mind.

'I have some paperwork to read through and I'll be up in a while.' He brushed his lips over hers but lifted his head without giving her a chance to respond, leaving her longing for him to kiss her properly. 'Don't wait up for me.'

Giannis watched Ava walk back inside the house and swore beneath his breath as he pictured her hurt expression. He knew he should go after her, scoop her into his arms and carry her up to their bedroom, as he knew she had wanted him to do. Of course he wanted to make love to her. Sex wasn't the problem. She was in the third trimester of her pregnancy and he found her curvaceous figure intensely desirable. Their hunger for one another was as urgent as it had always been—although she did not have quite so much energy and often fell asleep in his arms before he'd even withdrawn from her body.

He felt an odd sensation as if his heart was being crushed in a vice when he thought of her curled up beside him, her face flushed from passion and her honey-gold hair spread across the pillows. He loved to stroke his hands over the swell of her stomach where his son was nestled inside her. Sometimes when the baby moved, Giannis could actually see the outline of a tiny hand or foot. It would not be long now before the baby was here, but his excitement was mixed with trepidation. What did he know about fatherhood and caring for a baby? What if he made a mistake and harmed his son, as he had made a tragic mistake years ago?

Tonight, his mother's reference to what he had done had reminded him of the fragility of life. As if he needed reminding, he thought grimly. He could never forget the consequences of his irresponsibility when he was nineteen, or forgive himself, as quite clearly his mother was unable to do. Now, as he awaited the birth of his baby, he missed his father more than ever. It tore at his heart to know that his son would not meet his grandfather, and would never know the affection and kindness that his *patera* had showered on Giannis. But he would love his own son as deeply as his father had loved him, he vowed.

He gripped the balustrade rail and stared across the beach at the black sea, dappled with silver moonlight. His father had loved the sea, and Giannis felt closest to him on Spetses. That was why he wanted his son to grow up on the island, and thankfully Ava seemed happy living at Villa Delphine. But would she be happy to live in Greece with him if he admitted that he had caused his father's death and been sent to prison for driving after he'd drunk alcohol, which the coroner had suggested had been a likely reason for the fatal car crash?

She might decide that he was not fit to be a father and take his son back to England. The memory of Caroline's reaction to his confession five years earlier haunted him. He could not risk losing his baby, and with a sudden flash of insight he realised that he did not want to lose Ava. He had married her so that he could claim his child, but over the past months since their wedding she had slipped beneath his guard.

His jaw clenched. If he wasn't careful he would find himself falling in love with Ava, which had never been part of his plan. He had been in love with Caroline—at least he'd be certain at the time that he loved her, and her rejection had hurt. But the loss of his first child had hurt him far more. A voice inside him whispered that what he had felt for Caroline had been insignificant compared to the riot of feeling that swept through him when he thought of his wife.

Theos, what a mess. Giannis strode across the terrace and entered the house. He hesitated at the foot of the stairs before he turned and walked resolutely into his study,

CHAPTER ELEVEN

Ava had no idea what time Giannis had come to bed the previous night. With only six weeks to go until her due date, she often felt a bone-deep tiredness and, despite her efforts to remain awake and talk to him, she had fallen asleep. In the morning she had seen an indent on the pillow next to her where his head had lain, and when she'd gone downstairs he was already working in his study.

But at least his black mood seemed to have lifted and he greeted her with a smile when she reminded him that she had a routine check-up with the midwife. In a couple more weeks they would move into the apartment in Athens so that she would be near to the private maternity hospital where the baby would be born.

'I'll come to your appointment with you,' he offered. 'But it's too far for you to walk into town. Thomas can take us in the horse and carriage.' His phone rang, and his smile faded and was replaced with a disturbingly harsh expression when he glanced at the screen. 'I'm sorry, *glykiá mou*, I need to take the call. What time is your appointment?'

'In half an hour, but I want to do some shopping first. Thomas will take me to the town, and I'll see you later.'

Cars were not allowed in Spetses Town, and Ava enjoyed the novelty of travelling in an open-topped carriage,

shaded from the hot sun by a parasol and listening to the
sound of the horse's hooves clipping along the road. She
gave a soft sigh of contentment. Her life at Villa Delphine was idyllic and Giannis's tenderness towards her
lately made her feel cherished in a way she had never
felt before. For some reason he had a difficult relationship with his mother, hence his tense mood last night.
But Ava was focused on becoming a mother herself and
pregnancy cocooned her from the real world.

At the clinic, the midwife listened to the baby's heartbeat and was satisfied that all was well. 'I'll give you your
medical notes so that you can take them to the maternity
hospital on the mainland when you go into labour,' the
midwife explained as she handed Ava a folder.

Out of idle curiosity Ava skimmed through her notes.
She spoke Greek fluently but she was not so good at reading the language, and she assumed she must have misunderstood the last sentence on the page.

'Does it say that a blood sample will be taken from
the baby when he is born?' Her confusion grew when the
midwife nodded. 'Is it standard procedure in Greece?'

'Only when a paternity test has been requested by the
parents,' the midwife told her.

Ava's heart juddered to a standstill. She certainly had
not requested a test to prove the baby's paternity. But
Giannis must have done so—which meant he must have
doubts that the child she was carrying was his.

Somehow she managed to walk calmly out of the
clinic and smiled at Thomas when he helped her into
the carriage. But she felt numb with shock. Since she'd
married Giannis, she had believed that all the misunder-
standings between them had been resolved and they did
not have secrets. But all this time he had suspected her

of trying to foist another man's child on him. She felt sick. So hurt that there was a physical pain in her chest.

When she arrived back at the villa and heard the helicopter's engine—an indication that Giannis was about to leave the island—anger surged like scalding lava through her veins. She almost collided with him in the entrance hall as she ran into the house, and he was on his way out.

He looked tense and distracted, and he frowned when she thrust the folder containing her medical notes at him. 'I need to talk to you.'

Concern flashed in his eyes. 'Is there a problem with the baby?'

'The baby is fine. The problem is *you*.' As she spoke, Ava asked herself why Giannis would be so anxious about the baby's welfare if he really believed it wasn't his child.

'Why did you ask for a paternity test to be carried out when our son is born?' she demanded. 'Don't try to deny it,' she said furiously when his eyes narrowed. 'The request for a blood test is written in my notes. Do you think that when I left you after we had been to Stefanos Markou's party, I immediately hooked up with some other guy?'

'No,' he said tersely. 'But at the time I asked for the paternity test I thought it was possible that you had already been pregnant before we slept together in London.'

She shook her head. 'How could you doubt my integrity like that?'

'Like you doubted me when you believed a jealous man's lies about me being a criminal?' he shot back. He raked his hand through his hair, and Ava noted that he avoided making eye contact with her. 'Look, something important has come up and I have to go to Athens.'

'You're *leaving*? Am I not important enough for you to want to stay and discuss a major issue with our relationship? Clearly I'm not,' she said dully when he picked up his briefcase and strode across the hall.

He paused in the doorway and turned to look at her. 'I realise that we need to talk, and we will as soon as I have dealt with a…problem at the office.' His voice sounded oddly strained. 'To tell you the truth I had forgotten about the paternity test. And it could not have been carried out without your consent.'

'The truth is that you don't care about me and I was stupid to hope that you would ever fall in love with me, as I…' She broke off and stared at his granite-hard features.

'As you…what?'

'It doesn't matter,' she said wearily. 'You're in too much of a hurry to talk to me, remember?'

Giannis looked as though he was about to speak, but he shook his head. 'Something arrived for you while you were out. Look in the bedroom,' he told her before he walked out of the villa.

A few minutes later, Ava heard the helicopter take off while she was climbing the stairs up to the second floor. She pushed open the door of the master bedroom and stopped dead, the tears that she had held back until then filling her eyes. On her dressing table was the biggest bouquet of red roses she had ever seen. At least three dozen perfect scarlet blooms arranged in a crystal vase and exuding a heavenly fragrance that filled the room. Propped up against the vase was a card and she recognised Giannis's bold handwriting.

For my beautiful wife. You are everything I could ever want or hope for. Giannis

There was no mention of love, but surely the roses were a statement that he felt something for her? Ava's fingers trembled as she touched the velvety rose petals. She sank down onto the edge of the bed and gave a shaky sigh. If the roses had been delivered before she had gone to her antenatal appointment and discovered that Giannis had asked for a paternity test on their baby she would have taken his romantic gesture as a sign that he loved her and she would have told him how she felt about him.

Now that she had calmed down, she could understand why he had requested the test. They had been strangers when they had slept together for the first time. Not only had she believed Stefanos's nephew's lies about Giannis, but she had kept it secret that her father was a criminal. They had both hidden things from each other, but if their marriage was going to work—and the roses were an indication that Giannis wanted her to be his wife—then they must be honest about their feelings.

He had promised that they would talk when he returned home. But the prospect of waiting for him at the villa did not appeal to Ava, and she picked up the phone and asked Thomas to take her to Athens on the speedboat that Giannis kept moored at Villa Delphine's private jetty.

By the time she reached TGE's offices in the city it was lunchtime and most of the staff were away from their desks. Giannis's PA, Sofia, greeted Ava with a smile. 'He's still in a meeting. I'm just off to lunch but I'll let him know that you are here.'

'No, don't disturb him,' Ava said quickly. 'I'll wait until he has finished.' It would give her a chance to prepare what she wanted to say to him. How hard could it be to say the three little words *I love you*?

But as the minutes ticked by while she waited in his secretary's office, she felt increasingly nervous. Maybe he had given her the red roses simply because he knew that she liked flowers, and wishful thinking had made her read more into his gift?

From inside Giannis's office, Ava could hear voices. She stiffened when one voice suddenly became louder and distinctly aggressive. 'I'm warning you, Gekas. Give me one million pounds or I'll go public with the story that you spent a year in prison for killing your father when you were drunk. I can't imagine that TGE's shareholders will be so keen to support Greece's golden boy when they hear that you are an ex-convict,' the voice sneered.

'And I'm warning you that I will not tolerate your blackmail attempt,' Giannis snarled. His eyes narrowed on the lowlife journalist who had called him that morning and demanded to see him. Demetrios Kofidis was the reason he'd had to leave Ava and come to Athens, and he was impatient to deal with the scumbag so that he could hurry back to Spetses and reassure his wife that he trusted her implicitly.

He cursed himself for ever thinking of having a paternity test when he knew in his heart that the baby was his. It was a pity he had not listened to his heart, he thought grimly. He could only hope that he hadn't left it too late to tell Ava in words what he had tried to say with the roses.

'You paid me to keep quiet about your past five years ago,' the journalist said. 'Pay up again, Gekas, or I'll sell the story to every tabloid in Europe and beyond.'

Giannis pushed back his chair and stood up. 'You think you're clever, Kofidis, but I recorded our conversation and before you arrived I alerted the police about you. If you publish anything about me you will be arrested for attempted blackmail quicker than you can blink. Now get out of my sight.'

He kept his gaze fixed on the journalist when he heard

the faint click of the office door opening. 'I told you that I don't want to be disturbed, Sofia.'

'Giannis.' Ava's voice was a whisper, but it sliced through Giannis's heart like a knife as he jerked his eyes across the room and saw her standing in the doorway. One hand rested protectively on the burgeoning swell of her stomach. Her honey-blonde hair was loose, tumbling around her shoulders, and she was so beautiful that his breath became trapped in his throat.

'What are you doing here, *glykiá mou*?' he began, trying to sound normal, trying to hide the fear that churned in his gut as he wondered how much she had heard of his conversation with the journalist. 'Sweetheart…'

'You went to prison, and you didn't tell me.'

'I can explain. It was an accident… I drove my father home from a restaurant and…'

'You didn't tell me,' she repeated slowly. 'I thought there were no more secrets between us, but all this time you held something back from me—because you don't trust me.'

'I *do* trust you.' Giannis crashed his hip bone against the corner of the desk in his hurry to reach Ava, but as he strode across the room she stepped back into the outer office.

'There have been too many secrets and lies between us—and that is the biggest lie of all,' she choked, before she spun round and ran over to the door.

'Ava, wait.' Giannis cursed as he followed her into the lobby. His offices were on the ground floor and the lobby was bustling with staff returning from their lunch break. He apologised when he knocked into someone. Ahead of him Ava had reached the front entrance. The glass doors slid open and she walked out. Moments later he followed her outside.

'*Ava.*'

She was hurrying down the flight of concrete steps in front of the building and glanced over her shoulder at him. In that instant she stumbled, and Giannis watched in horror as she lost her footing and fell down the remaining steps. It seemed to happen in slow motion and, just as when he had taken a bend in the road too fast sixteen years earlier, he felt shock, disbelief and a sense of terror that made him gag.

He was still at the top of the steps and there was nothing he could do to save Ava. She gave a startled cry and landed on the pavement with a sickening thud. And then she was silent. Motionless.

Giannis heard a rushing noise in his ears and a voice shouting, '*No! No!*' Much later he realised that it had been his voice shouting, pleading. *No!* He couldn't lose Ava and his baby.

He raced down the steps and dropped onto his knees beside her, carefully rolling her onto her back. Her eyes were closed and her face was deathly pale. A purple bruise was already darkening on her brow.

'Ava *mou*, wake up.' He felt for her pulse and detected a faint beat. Glancing up, he saw a crowd of people had gathered. 'Call an ambulance,' he shouted. 'Quickly.'

Someone must have already done so, and he heard the wail of a siren. But Ava did not open her eyes, and when Giannis looked down her body he saw blood seeping through her dress.

His heart stopped. *Theos*, if she lost the baby she would never forgive him and he would never forgive himself. If he lost both of them... A constriction in his throat prevented him from swallowing. He brushed his hand over his wet eyes. He could not contemplate his life without Ava. It would be a joyless, pointless existence, and nothing more than he deserved, he thought bleakly.

From then on everything became a blur when the ambulance arrived and the paramedics took charge and carefully lifted Ava onto a stretcher. As the ambulance raced to the hospital her eyelids fluttered on her cheeks, but she slipped in and out of consciousness and her dress was soaked with blood.

'My wife *will* be all right, won't she?' Giannis asked hoarsely.

'We will soon be at the hospital,' the paramedic replied evasively. 'The doctors will do everything they can to save her life and the child's.'

The last time Giannis had cried had been at his father's funeral, but his throat burned and his eyes ached with tears as he lifted Ava's cold, limp hand to his lips. 'Don't leave me, *agápi mou*,' he begged. 'I should have told you about my father, and I wish I had told you that I love you, my angel. I'm sorry that I didn't, and I promise I will tell you how much you mean to me every day for the rest of our lives, if only you will stay with me.'

He thought he might have imagined that he felt her fingers move in his hand. And he needed every ounce of hope when they arrived at the hospital and Ava was rushed into Theatre. 'A condition called placental abruption occurred as a result of your wife's fall,' the doctor explained to Giannis. 'It means that the placenta has become detached from the wall of the uterus and she has lost a lot of blood. The baby must be delivered as soon as possible to save the lives of both the child and the mother.'

For the second time in his life he had maybe left it too late to say what was in his heart, Giannis thought when a nurse showed him into a waiting room. Pain ripped through him as he remembered how he had stood at his father's graveside and wished he had told his *patera* how much he loved and respected him, and how one day he hoped to be as good a father to his own child.

Now his baby's and Ava's lives were in the balance. They were both so precious to him but he was unable to help them. All he could do was pace up and down the waiting room and pray.

Ava opened her eyes, and for the first time in three days her head did not feel as if a pneumatic drill was driving into her skull. In fact the concussion she'd suffered after falling down the steps had been unimportant compared to nearly losing her baby. Of course she had no memory of the emergency Caesarean section she'd undergone or, sadly, of the moment her son had been born.

When she'd come round from the anaesthetic Giannis had told her that, despite the baby's abrupt entry into the world six weeks early, he weighed a healthy five pounds. They had settled on the name Andreas during her pregnancy and, although she had still felt woozy when she had been taken in a wheelchair to the special care baby unit, she had been able to hold her tiny dark haired son in her arms and she'd wept tears of joy and relief that he was safe and well.

Now, seventy-two hours after the shocking events that had preceded the baby's early arrival, she looked across the room and her heart skipped a beat when she saw Giannis sitting in a chair, cradling Andreas against his shoulder. The tender look on his face as he held the baby was something Ava would never forget, and the unguarded expression in Giannis's eyes as he looked over at her filled her with hope and longing.

'You're still here,' she murmured. 'I thought you might

go back to the apartment for a few hours. The nurses will look after Andreas in the nursery now that he has been moved from the special care ward.'

'I'm not going anywhere until the two of you are ready to be discharged from hospital.' His gentle smile stole Ava's breath. 'How are you feeling?'

'Much better.' She'd had a blood transfusion, stitches and she was pumped full of drugs to fight infection and relieve pain, but her son was worth everything she'd been through. She sat up carefully and held out her arms to take the baby. 'He's so perfect,' she said softly. Her heart ached with love as she studied Andreas's silky-soft black hair and his eyes that were as dark as his daddy's eyes.

'He is a miracle. You both are.' Giannis's voice thickened. '*Theos*, when I saw you fall down those steps and I feared I had lost both of you...' His jaw clenched. 'I didn't know what I would do without you,' he said rawly.

It was the first time that either of them had mentioned what had happened, and the deep grooves on either side of Giannis's mouth were an indication of what he must have felt, believing he might lose the baby he had been so desperate for. Ava handed Andreas to him. 'He's fallen asleep. Will you put him in the crib?'

She rested her head against the pillows and thought how gorgeous Giannis looked in faded jeans and a casual cream cotton shirt. She was glad that a nurse had helped her into the shower earlier and she had managed to wash her hair.

He came back and sat down on the chair next to her bed. Suddenly she felt stupidly shy and afraid, and a whole host of other emotions that made her pleat the sheet between her fingers rather than meet his gaze. 'What happened to your father?' she asked in a low tone.

Giannis exhaled slowly. 'I was nineteen and had just

set up TGE with my father. We'd gone to a restaurant for dinner and during the meal I drank a glass of wine. I certainly did not feel drunk, but even a small amount of alcohol can impair your judgement. Driving home, I took a steep bend in the road too fast and the car overturned. I escaped with a few cuts and bruises, but my father sustained serious injuries.'

His eyes darkened with pain. 'I held him in my arms while we waited for the ambulance, and he made it to the hospital but died soon afterwards. I have never touched alcohol since that night, even though I've often wished that I could numb my grief and guilt.'

'Why didn't you tell me?' Ava could not disguise her hurt. 'It wasn't overhearing what you had done that upset me, but realising that you had kept such a huge secret from me. I trusted you when I told you about my father being a criminal, but you only ever shut me out, Giannis.'

'I was afraid to admit what I had done,' he said heavily. 'A few years ago I fell in love.'

Jealousy stabbed Ava through her heart. 'What happened?'

'Caroline fell pregnant. Her father was an American senator who was campaigning in the Presidential elections, and when I admitted that I had served a prison sentence Caroline refused to marry me because—in her words— having an ex-convict as a son-in-law might have damaged her father's political ambitions. She told me she had suffered a miscarriage, but I'm fairly certain that she chose not to go ahead with the pregnancy. I overheard her on the phone telling a friend that she had dealt with the pregnancy problem,' he answered Ava's unspoken question.

'So when you found out that I had conceived your baby, you were worried that I might do the same as your ex-girlfriend?'

He grimaced. 'I was determined to have my child, and I treated you unforgivably when I forced you to marry me.'

She stared at his handsome face and her heart turned over when she saw that his eyelashes were wet. This was a different Giannis—a broken Giannis, she thought painfully. His vulnerability hurt her more than anything else. 'You didn't force me,' she said huskily. 'I chose to marry you, knowing that you had asked me to be your wife because you wanted your son.'

'No, Ava *mou*. That was not the reason I proposed marriage.'

She dared not believe the expression in his eyes, the softening of his hard features as he stared at her intently. 'I need to tell you something,' she said shakily. 'I heard the things you said in the ambulance. At least, I think I heard you, but maybe I dreamed it…' She broke off and bit her lip, aware of her heart thudding in her chest. 'Why did you ask me to marry you?'

'I love you.'

The three little words hovered in the air, but were they a tantalising dream? Ava wondered. Did she have the courage to give her absolute trust to Giannis?

'Don't!' Her voice shook and tears trembled on her eyelashes. 'Don't say it if you don't mean it.'

'But I do mean it, *agápi mou*,' he said gently. 'I love you with all my heart and soul.' Suddenly his restraint left him and he leapt to his feet, sending his chair clattering onto the floor. He sat on the edge of the bed and captured her hands in his.

'I adore you, Ava. I never knew I could feel like this, to love so utterly and completely that I cannot contemplate my life without you.' He stroked her hair back from her face with a trembling hand. 'When you left Athens I couldn't understand why I was so miserable until my head accepted what my heart had been telling me. I missed you, and I decided to ask you if we could start again. But then I read the Christmas card from your brother and discovered you were pregnant with my child.'

'And you were angry,' Ava said quietly.

'I was scared. I don't deserve you or our son.' He swallowed convulsively. 'I destroyed my family with my reckless behaviour, and I'm terrified that I might somehow hurt you and Andreas. *Theos...*' His face twisted in pain. 'It is my fault that you fell down those damned steps and you and the baby could have died. I should have been honest with you about what happened to my father. And of course I don't want a paternity test. I know Andreas is mine. But I've made so many mistakes and I have to let you and my son go. If you want to take Andreas to live in England I won't stop you. All I ask is that you allow me to be part of his life.'

Ava listened to the torrent of emotion that spilled from Giannis. It was as if a dam had burst and his feelings— his love for her—poured out, healing her hurt and filling her with joy.

'Oh, Giannis. Darling Giannis.' She wrapped her arms around his neck and clung to him. 'The only way you could ever hurt me is if you stop loving me. The only place I want to be is with you, because I love you so much.'

'Really?' The uncertainty in his voice tore Ava's heart. She put her hands on either side of his face. 'You have to learn to forgive yourself and believe me when I say that you deserve to be happy and loved by me and your son and the family that we will create together.'

'Ava,' he groaned as he pulled her into his heat and fire and held her so close that she felt the thunderous beat of his heart. '*S'agapó, kardiá mou.* I love you, my heart. My sweet love.'

He kissed her then—wondrously, as if she was everything he had ever wanted or would ever need. And she kissed him with all the love in her heart and her tears of happiness mingled with his as he threaded his fingers through her hair and gently eased her back against the pillows.

'We will never have secrets,' Giannis murmured between kisses.

Ava smiled. '*Did* I hear you say in the ambulance that you would tell me every day how much you love me, or did I dream it?'

'It was no dream, *kardiá mou.* It was a promise that I intend to keep for ever.'

EPILOGUE

THEY TOOK ANDREAS to Spetses when he was four weeks old. Despite his traumatic birth he was a strong and healthy baby with a good set of lungs, his father noted ruefully at two o'clock one morning. Ava recovered remarkably quickly and was delighted to be able to fit into her jeans two months after her son's birth. Her confidence in Giannis's love grew stronger with every day, and the first time they made love again was deeply emotional as they showed with their bodies their adoration for each other.

Life could not be better, Ava thought one afternoon as she pushed Andreas in his pram around the garden of Villa Delphine. Giannis had reluctantly gone to his office in Athens, but he'd called her a while ago to say that he was on his way home. 'Your *patera* will be here soon,' she said to Andreas and when he gave her a gummy smile she told him that both the Gekas males in her life had stolen her heart.

Her spirits dipped when she saw Giannis's mother walking across the lawn. Filia's waspish expression softened as she looked in the pram. 'My grandson grows bigger every time I see him,' she commented, and Ava felt guilty that she did not invite her mother-in-law to Villa Delphine as often as she should. The visits were always strained and she knew that Giannis found his mother difficult.

'Where is my son?' Filia demanded. 'Giannis promised weeks ago that he would arrange for his private jet to fly me to Italy so I can visit my daughter, but I still have not heard when the trip will be. I suppose he has forgotten about me.'

'Giannis has been busy at work lately, and he spends as much time as he can with Andreas, but I'm sure he hasn't forgotten about your trip,' Ava explained.

'No doubt he expects me to take a commercial flight. He is so wealthy, but he gives me nothing.'

Ava nearly choked. She knew that Giannis had bought his mother the beautiful house she lived in on Spetses, and he paid for her living expenses and her numerous holidays. 'I don't think you are being fair to him,' she murmured.

Filia snorted. 'It isn't fair that I have spent the last fifteen years a widow, thanks to Giannis.' She gave Ava a sharp look. 'I suppose he has told you that he was responsible for his father's death?'

Giannis froze with his hand on the gate which led into the garden. He knew that the tall hedge screened him from Ava and his mother, who were standing some way across the lawn. But he could see them and he could hear their voices.

'Giannis told me what happened sixteen years ago.' Ava's voice was as cool and clear as a mountain stream. 'I know that he loved his father very much, and his grief has been made worse by his feelings of guilt. It breaks my heart to know that he can't forgive himself,' she said softly.

Hidden behind the hedge, Giannis brushed a hand over his wet eyes.

'Why do you defend him?' he heard his mother ask.

'Because he made a terrible mistake that I know he has regretted every day since the accident. It was an accident with devastating consequences, but it was an *accident*. I know that the man I love is a good and honourable man.'

'So you do love him?' Filia said with a snort. 'You did not marry him because he is rich?'

'I married Giannis because I love him with all my heart, and I'd love him if he didn't have a penny to his name.' Ava's fierce voice carried across the garden. 'What happened in the past was tragic, but it is also a tragedy that you have not forgiven your own son.' She put her hands on her hips. 'Your constant criticism of Giannis has to stop, or I am afraid that you will no longer be welcome at Villa Delphine to visit Andreas.'

His wife was a warrior, Giannis thought, shaken to his core by Ava's defence of him. She was amazing. He opened the gate and strode across the garden. His footsteps were noiseless on the soft grass, but his mother was facing him and she immediately appealed to him.

'I hope you will not allow your wife to threaten to withhold my grandson from me? Say something to her, Giannis.'

'There are many things I want to say to Ava. But I will speak to her alone. Leave us, please,' he told his mother curtly. She opened her mouth to argue but, after looking at his expression, she clearly thought better of it and without another word she turned and walked out of the garden.

'I'm sorry if I upset your mother,' Ava said ruefully. 'But I meant what I said. I won't let her upset you. What are you doing?' she asked as Giannis pushed the pram across the garden and into the summer house.

'The bedroom is too far away for what I have in mind,' he murmured as he pulled her into his arms.

Her eyes widened when he pressed his aching arousal against her pelvis. 'Mmm—what exactly do you have in mind?'

'I want to make love to you, darling heart,' Giannis said thickly. 'But first I need to tell you how much I love you, and thank you for loving me and for giving me our gorgeous son.' He tugged the straps of her sundress down and roamed his hands over her body.

'You are so beautiful, so perfect. Mine, for eternity.' He threw the cushions from the garden furniture onto the floor and laid her down before covering her body with his. And there he made love to her with fierce passion and a tenderness that made Ava realise that dreams could come true.

'Eternity sounds perfect,' she agreed.

* * * * *

LET'S TALK

Romance

For exclusive extracts, competitions
and special offers, find us online:

facebook.com/millsandboon

@MillsandBoon

@MillsandBoonUK

Get in touch on 01413 063232

For all the latest titles coming soon, visit
millsandboon.co.uk/nextmonth

JOIN THE
MILLS & BOON
BOOKCLUB

* **FREE** delivery direct to your door

* **EXCLUSIVE** offers every month

* **EXCITING** rewards programme

50% OFF
YOUR FIRST
PARCEL

Join today at
Millsandboon.co.uk/Bookclub

MILLS & BOON

THE HEART OF ROMANCE

A ROMANCE FOR EVERY READER

MODERN

Prepare to be swept off your feet by sophisticated, sexy and seductive heroes, in some of the world's most glamourous and romantic locations, where power and passion collide.

HISTORICAL

Escape with historical heroes from time gone by. Whether your passion is for wicked Regency Rakes, muscled Vikings or rugged Highlanders, await the romance of the past.

MEDICAL

Set your pulse racing with dedicated, delectable doctors in the high-pressure world of medicine, where emotions run high and passion, comfort and love are the best medicine.

True Love

Celebrate true love with tender stories of heartfelt romance, from the rush of falling in love to the joy a new baby can bring, and a focus on the emotional heart of a relationship.

Desire

Indulge in secrets and scandal, intense drama and plenty of sizzling hot action with powerful and passionate heroes who have it all: wealth, status, good looks…everything but the right woman.

HEROES

Experience all the excitement of a gripping thriller, with an intense romance at its heart. Resourceful, true-to-life women and strong, fearless men face danger and desire - a killer combination!

MILLS & BOON

MODERN

Power and Passion

Prepare to be swept off your feet by sophisticated, sexy and seductive heroes, in some of the world's most glamourous and romantic locations, where power and passion collide.